Her face still held that same sweet innocence that had first attracted him to her. But now there was a maturity about her that was just as attractive.

Paige ran to him and wrapped her arms around his waist. He froze, the reaction of the teenage boy he used to be. But the man in him recognized all those old feelings that had bound him to her years ago.

When he didn't return the hug, she went back to the table and he eased onto the bench across from her. He took a moment to gather his thoughts. What should he say?

"You look good," she said. "You filled out. The teenage boy I used to date doesn't exist anymore."

"He grew up, and so have you. The young girl of long ago has matured into a beautiful woman."

"Thank you." She smiled at him and his heart raced like a wild mustang's. "You were always good for my ego."

He didn't shift or act nervous. He couldn't do that now. He had to be the man he was supposed to be. For Zane. And for himself.

HOME ON THE RANCH:
A REBEL IN TEXAS

⚓

LINDA WARREN

PATRICIA THAYER

**Previously published as *Texas Rebels: Jude*
and *Brady: The Rebel Rancher***

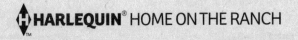

HARLEQUIN® HOME ON THE RANCH

Recycling programs
for this product may
not exist in your area.

ISBN-13: 978-1-335-00798-8

Home on the Ranch: A Rebel in Texas

Copyright © 2020 by Harlequin Books S.A.

Texas Rebels: Jude
First published in 2016. This edition published in 2020.
Copyright © 2016 by Linda Warren

Brady: The Rebel Rancher
First published in 2009. This edition published in 2020.
Copyright © 2009 by Patricia Wright

This edition published by arrangement with Harlequin Books S.A.

For questions and comments about the quality of this book, please contact us at CustomerService@Harlequin.com.

Printed in U.S.A.

CONTENTS

Two-time RITA® Award–nominated author **Linda Warren** has written over forty books for Harlequin. A native Texan, she's a member of Romance Writers of America and the RWA West Houston chapter. Drawing upon her years of growing up on a ranch, she writes about some of her favorite things: Western-style romance, cowboys and country life. She married her high school sweetheart and they live on a lake in central Texas. He fishes and she writes. Works perfect.

Books by Linda Warren

Harlequin Western Romance

Texas Rebels

Texas Rebels: Egan
Texas Rebels: Falcon
Texas Rebels: Quincy
Texas Rebels: Jude
Texas Rebels: Phoenix
Texas Rebels: Paxton

Harlequin American Romance

The Cowboy's Return
Once a Cowboy
Texas Heir
The Sheriff of Horseshoe, Texas
Her Christmas Hero
Tomas: Cowboy Homecoming
One Night in Texas
A Texas Holiday Miracle

Visit the Author Profile page at Harlequin.com for more titles.

TEXAS REBELS: JUDE

LINDA WARREN

Acknowledgments

A special thanks to Scott Conoly, MD, for graciously sharing his knowledge of medical school.

And thanks to Jenny Ferro Siegert for discussing courses and timeline for premed students.

Also, thanks to Crystal Breihan Siegert for taking time to answer questions about gifted children.

All errors are strictly mine.

Dedication

To my brother, Paul William, who generated laughter in all of us.

Prologue

My name is Kate Rebel. I married John Rebel when I was eighteen years old and then bore him seven sons. We worked the family ranch, which John later inherited. We put everything we had into buying more land so our sons would have a legacy. We didn't have much, but we had love.

The McCray Ranch borders Rebel Ranch on the east and the McCrays have forever been a thorn in my family's side. They've cut our fences, dammed up creeks to limit our water supply and shot one of our prize bulls. Ezra McCray threatened to shoot our sons if he caught them jumping his fences again. We tried to keep our boys away, but they are boys—young and wild.

One day Jude and Phoenix, two of our youngest, were out riding together. When John heard shots, he immediately went to find his boys. They lay on the ground, blood oozing from their heads. Ezra McCray was astride a horse twenty yards away with a rifle in his hand. John drew his gun and fired, killing Ezra instantly. Both boys survived with only minor wounds. Since my husband was protecting his children, he didn't spend even one night in jail. This escalated the feud that still goes on today.

The man I knew as my husband died that day. He couldn't live with what he'd done, and started to drink heavily. I had to take over the ranch and the raising of our boys. John died ten years later. We've all been affected by the tragedy, especially my sons.

They are grown men now and deal in different ways with the pain of losing their father. One day I pray my boys will be able to put this behind them and live healthy, normal lives with women who will love them the way I loved their father.

Chapter 1

Jude: the sixth son—the quiet one

A cowboy's broken heart.

They could say a lot of things about Jude Rebel, but they couldn't say he wasn't a good father.

He'd devoted his life to Zane.

But tonight for the first time in twelve years he was going out on a date. He swiped an electric razor lightly over his jawline, leaving a bit of scruff. Women liked an outdoorsy look, he'd been told. In reality he had no idea what women liked. Ever since the day Paige Wheeler had told him, "I'm pregnant," his fascination with the opposite sex had come to a screeching halt.

Paige. They'd discovered sex together and to him it was better than sneaking a beer with the guys or riding his horse or swimming in Yaupon Creek. It was better than anything he'd ever experienced in his life. Every spare moment, he'd spent with her, and they'd been inseparable. Until…

He shoved the memory back in place, tucked away in a dark corner of his mind. Never Never Land, he called it. A place he never wanted to visit again.

His phone lay on the bathroom vanity and he tapped it just to reread her message.

Tonight at seven. Can't wait.

Annabel Hurley—blonde, twenty-five and about the prettiest thing he'd seen in a long time—had asked him to dinner. She was one of Zane's teachers and they'd spent a lot of time together in the past year trying to figure out ways to keep Zane interested in school other than letting him play video games nonstop. His son was gifted and in the Pre-Advanced Placement program. He was still bored in class because he always completed his assignments before the other kids. Not wanting to move him up a grade for a second time, Jude searched for other answers. Annabel had been a godsend. She was so patient with Zane.

Going out with Annabel was his first step in putting Never Never Land behind him and not having to shove it to the back of his mind to keep from enduring the pain.

Jude had a day of work ahead of him and then he was going to get back in the game of living and experiencing life again. He walked into the bedroom and grabbed a T-shirt from a drawer and pulled it over his head. Shoving his arms into a Western shirt, he thought about Annabel. He liked her and enjoyed her company. He'd have to be dead from the waist down not to.

As he sat on the bed to put on his boots, his eye caught the photo on his nightstand. He picked it up. It was a photo of him holding Zane on the day after he was born. Jude looked so young and scared cradling the tiny baby wrapped in a blue blanket. All the fear of that day showed in the sad darkness of his eyes. Memories floated across his mind like gray thunderclouds about to dump a lot more tears on him.

What are we going to do, Jude? We don't know anything about babies.

Jude hadn't had an answer. He'd been shell-shocked and was trying to grasp what this meant for their future. So they'd done what naive, scared teenagers do: they ignored the problem in hopes it would go away. It didn't.

Paige started to show, but she'd never been slim and wore big bulky blouses so no one could tell she was pregnant. But he knew. They would sit in his truck while Paige talked about what they needed to do. Jude listened. But he never said anything.

I've been talking to the school counselor and I told her about the baby. She knows about my premed scholarship to Berkeley and how I dreamed of this for years. She said I had choices and I should consider them.

Choices? To him there were no choices. Just one—the baby was theirs and they had to raise it. But he never said so.

Of course, abortion is out of the question. The counselor said adoption might be an option for us. She knows a couple who wants a baby. They're educated and have a nice home and they would love and care for our baby, something that we can't do.

Why not? They were young, but his brother had raised

his daughter on his own, so why couldn't Jude? But he never said so.

We have to make a decision, Jude. We have to do something. The baby's due in August and we graduate in May. What do you think?

He'd shrugged.

You always do that. You never say anything and that makes me so mad. This is your baby, too. What should we do?

They were sitting in his truck at the high school and he stared out to the vacant parking lot. He knew what he would do, but so many things kept him silent. Paige had had an awful childhood and her dream was to get out of Horseshoe and live a better life. Her mother was an alcoholic and spent most of her time down at Rowdy's Beer Joint drinking and picking up strange men.

Many a night Paige would call Jude and he would go pick her up because she was scared of the men her mother brought home. One night a man had come into her room and she'd run outside and slept in the yard. Ever since then she'd been afraid when her mom had a man friend over. No one should have to live like that. Especially someone as sweet and gentle as Paige.

"Can you give up our child?" was the only thing he could say.

"I don't know." She started to cry and he took her in his arms and told her that whatever she wanted to do, he would be okay with it. He never said what he really thought.

Paige took care of everything and the adoption was set up. Jude hated the whole thing and he tried not to think about it. As August drew near, Paige gained a lot of weight all over and no one, not even her mother or sister, suspected she was pregnant. And everyone in Horseshoe knew Paige ate when her mom was on one of her drinking binges.

A week before the due date Jude told his mother he was taking a few days off to get away with his friends. Instead he picked up Paige and they drove to a clinic in Austin, one the adoptive parents had chosen, to have the baby. They would induce labor so Paige could have the baby early and continue on with her plans to go to California.

Not a lot was said on the drive. Paige had made up her mind and Jude wanted her to have her dream. She deserved better than the life she had and he didn't want to take that away from her.

They went into an office and signed papers. They would sign the adoption papers after the birth. The adoptive parents' lawyer had set everything up. Jude and Paige would never meet them, nor would they see their child. Jude's hand shook as he wrote his name and he fought tears that stung the backs of his eyes. But he was a Rebel and he wouldn't cry.

They hugged tightly and Paige was taken to an operating room. He waited. And waited. He wanted to talk to his brother Quincy to tell him what was going on, but Quincy was in the army and stationed in Afghanistan. And he couldn't heap another burden on his mother. He had to endure this alone.

It was hours later when the nurse came out and told him the baby had been born and he could see Paige. They had been asked if they wanted to see the baby and the counselor had advised against it. And against knowing the sex. It was best to make a clean break, she'd said. They would never know if they had a boy or a girl. Paige had listened to everything the woman had said and Jude had felt powerless.

Paige lay in a bed, pale and crying. That shook him. He sat by her bed, holding her hand as she continued to cry. They didn't say anything. Words now were useless. That night he slept in his truck and the next day, after they signed the adoption papers, he drove Paige back to Horseshoe.

She had her things packed and they loaded them into his truck and drove away. Paige had already said goodbye to her sister, so she didn't look back. There was nothing left for her in the small town where she'd grown up. Not even Jude.

Paige cried all the way to the airport. Being young and scared himself, he had no idea how to comfort her. They'd made a decision and now they had to live with it. As he stopped at the terminal, she leaned over and hugged him and whispered, "I'm sorry." Then she grabbed her bags from the backseat and ran into the airport. He never heard from her or saw her again.

Placing the photo back on his nightstand, he drew a heavy breath. On the way to the ranch Jude kept thinking, *I gave my child away.* The closer he got to home, the more those words hurt and the more he thought about his father, who had told him in the girls/sex speech to always take responsibility. *Be a man. Be a Rebel. A Rebel never shirks his responsibility and I expect my boys to never let me down in that respect.*

He'd let his father down. He'd given away his child.

By the time he crossed the cattle guard to Rebel Ranch, he knew he couldn't live with that decision. He'd thought he could, but he soon found that blood was thicker than any commitment he'd made to Paige.

He drove to the barn looking for Falcon in hopes that he could help him decide what to do. But Falcon and four of his other brothers were working on the ranch. His mom's truck was at the house and he quickly drove there. He had to tell her, even though he'd rather take a beating than see the look of disappointment on her face.

She was in the kitchen fixing supper and he would always remember the smell of chicken-fried steak wafting to him as he talked and told her where he'd been and what he'd done.

Her response was unusual. "Have you been drinking, Jude? If this was Phoenix, I would know it was a joke. But you…"

He was known for his quietness and his responsible behavior, so it was a shock to his mom.

"No, Mom. I need your help. I can't let them keep my child."

She removed her apron and slammed it onto the counter. "I'll get my purse." And then they were on their way back to Austin. His mom called her brother, Gabe, who was interning in a law firm, and he met them there.

They asked to speak with the administrator of the hospital and he told them that the adoptive parents were already with the baby. He suggested that Jude think about his decision a little more. His child would have a mother and a father, something he couldn't give it.

Jude stood on shaky legs and looked the man square in the eye. "I want my kid." This time he said it out loud.

It was a private adoption, so the administrator called the attorney handling the case. Once he arrived, Gabe asked to see the contract Jude had signed. It clearly stated that the parents, Jude Rebel and Paige Wheeler, had ten days to change their minds. The man then said they would need Paige's consent. Gabe pointed out the contract didn't say that, and he warned that if the baby wasn't brought to them soon, he would call the authorities.

The attorney and Gabe continued to argue about Jude's rights. Jude was sick to his stomach and had to go to the bathroom to throw up. His nerves were about to get the best of him. As he came out of the bathroom, he saw Mrs. Nancy Carstairs, the counselor who had advised Paige, standing at the end of the hall. That threw him. He didn't understand what she was doing at the hospital.

He went back to Gabe and mentioned it to him. Gabe flipped through some papers he'd gotten from the adoption attorney and gave him the answer: Tom and Nancy Carstairs were the adoptive parents.

Rage filled Jude. Mrs. Carstairs had given Paige advice that would make it easier to adopt their baby. She'd continued to feed her bad information to make sure Paige gave away their child. He stomped down the hall to Mrs. Carstairs and he lost his cool for the first time in his life. Gabe had to pull him away and his mom had to calm him down. He wanted to strangle the woman for what she'd done to their lives.

Gabe told the attorney and the administrator if the baby wasn't brought to them immediately, he would file charges against Nancy Carstairs for coercing Paige Wheeler into giving away her child. And he would notify the school board in Horseshoe of her deceit. And he would also bring charges against the hospital.

The Carstairs caved and walked out of the facility. The nurse in charge of the newborns said she would bring the baby, but not until Jude had a proper car seat and items to care for his child.

His mother went shopping while he and Gabe waited.

It was the longest wait of his life. His mother had come back by the time the doors opened and the nurse came out carrying a baby wrapped in a blue blanket. *He had a son.* His breath caught and it took a moment before he could breathe again. He had a son.

The days that followed weren't easy. He learned to change diapers, prepare bottles and wake at the smallest of cries. He followed his brother Falcon's example and raised his kid—because that was what fathers did. And no one was ever going to take his child again. Because he'd said so.

"Dad." Zane ran through the bathroom they shared into Jude's room. "The entry form for the race is supposed to be in today's paper. If Uncle Falcon doesn't bring it in, can I take your truck and go get it at the mailbox?"

His son loved horses and he was planning to enter the Horseshoe Founder's Day Horse Race at the end of April. That was all that was on his mind.

Jude got to his feet and stuffed his shirt into his jeans. "I'll get it." He looked at his son standing there in nothing but his boxer shorts. His dark hair fell into his eyes and he brushed it aside, as he often did. All arms and legs, he was going to be a gangly teenager just like Jude. His dark eyes and facial features were all Jude, too. But his sweet nature, which endeared him to everyone, he got from his mother. "Get dressed. It's time for breakfast."

"Okay, Dad." Zane dashed toward the bathroom. "Don't forget about the form."

As if Jude could forget. Zane had talked about the race nonstop since before Christmas and he'd been practicing with his paint horse, Running Bear, almost every day. Jude felt sure there wasn't a horse in the county that could beat him.

He made his way down the stairs to the kitchen, where his mom was cooking breakfast. The smell of bacon frying whet his appetite. He didn't know how he would've raised Zane if it hadn't been for his mom. She didn't criticize or judge him. She just pitched in and helped him and showed him how to be a father. The only drawback was he was thirty-one years old and still living with his mother. That, he could handle. Not having his son with him was something he couldn't.

"Mornin', Mom," he said, snatching a piece of bacon before pouring a cup of coffee.

She turned from the stove. "Mornin', son. Is Zane up?"

"Yes, and I didn't even have to wake him. He's so excited about this race that it's all he thinks about, even in his sleep." He took a couple of sips of coffee and placed his cup on the counter. "I'm going to the mailbox to get the paper so he can have the form to fill out or he's going to drive us all crazy."

Before he could get to the door, Falcon and Quincy, two of his brothers, came in. Quincy had the paper in his hand. He held it up. "I brought something for Zane. Is he up?"

Jude picked up his cup. "Yes, and he's ready for that form. He's saved up the entry fee and he's counting the days. Actually, he has a calendar in his room and he's marking them off."

"Who wants breakfast?" his mom asked.

"I had breakfast with Leah," Falcon replied. "Our children were asleep and it was nice."

"How about you, Quincy?"

"Elias had a late night, so I fixed breakfast for Grandpa." Quincy filled a cup with coffee and sat at the table.

"Your grandpa can come over here and eat if he wants breakfast," their mom snapped in a tone they knew well. "You have a wife and you need to be home with her and not pampering that old man." His mom and grandfather had a strained relationship that was difficult for the whole family.

Quincy stretched his shoulders. "Mom, my wife was up at 5:00 a.m. to be at work at six. We had coffee and went our separate ways. But we took time for ourselves, if you know what I mean."

"Quincy," his mother scolded. But Quincy only smiled. It was good to see his brother happy.

Jude filled his plate with bacon, eggs and biscuits and sat at the table.

Falcon flipped through the hometown paper, which usually had nothing in it but tidbits of gossip. Nothing ever happened in Horseshoe, Texas. But Falcon slid the paper over to Jude, pointing to a page.

Jude took a swallow of coffee, pushed his plate away and picked up the paper. The headline hit him between the eyes like a two-by-four.

Hometown Girl Made Good Returns.

Jude quickly scanned the rest of the story. Paige's mother had died and she was coming home for the funeral. Oh, man. He'd never expected this. Darlene Wheeler had fallen and broken her hip not long after Paige had left for California. Her daughter Staci had put her in a rehab center in Austin and from there she'd been moved to a nursing facility. That was the gossip Jude had heard.

A knot the size of a baseball formed in his stomach.

Never Never Land leaped to the forefront of his mind. The Wheelers still owned a house in Horseshoe and Staci paid the taxes on it. Jude wasn't sure why they'd never sold it. Twelve years had come full circle and it was time to tell Paige what he'd done.

That was his first thought.

The second was there was no way in hell. Zane was his and he had to think about his son now. About what this would do to him. Jude had always told him the truth. Zane was about five when he'd first asked about his mother. He wanted to know why he didn't have one. He almost thought that was normal since his cousin Eden hadn't had one, either. But Zane was smart and he soon realized that most of his friends had mothers.

At that time Jude had glossed over most of the story and said Zane's mother had wanted to further her education and had left for college.

As he grew older, Zane asked more questions and Jude decided then not to lie to him, because he knew his father would never have lied to him. Again, he told him how young they'd been and how they hadn't known anything about babies and they had decided to give him up for adoption so he could have a good life. Jude tried to sound matter-of-fact about what had happened, but Zane knew his mother had given him away.

He glanced at the paper one more time. Paige was returning to Horseshoe. How did he tell her what he'd done?

Or did he need to?

She'd made her choice and he'd made his.

But... That *but* carried a whole lot of guilt that was gnawing away at his insides.

Paige Wheeler, Zane's mother, would be back in Horseshoe.

Soon.

The knot tightened.

Chapter 2

Nausea churned in Paige's stomach as the plane touched down in Austin, Texas. She took several deep breaths to calm herself. She'd never expected going home would make her sick.

"Are you all right, dear?" the elderly woman next to her asked.

Paige took another deep breath. "Yes, I guess I'm just a little nervous."

"I was like that the first time I flew, but you get used to it."

Paige smiled patiently at the woman, not wanting to explain her nervous stomach had nothing to do with flying. It had to do with facing her past and all the mistakes she'd made. Actually, just one mistake. The big one that haunted her days and nights.

Passengers began to stand and Paige reached for her

carryall to join the queue leaving the plane. She navigated the airport and quickly made it to the baggage carousel to retrieve her luggage. Holding her suitcase, she looked around for her sister and saw her across the room, waving.

Time stood still for a moment as she gazed at the sister who had been a lifeline. Staci was two years older and had taken care of Paige, especially when their mother was on one of her rampages. And that had been quite often when she'd been drinking. Their mother had blamed them for her lousy life and she'd taken it out on them whenever she could.

She'd never hit them. That would have left bruises. She'd used words that left scars buried deep inside, scars that would never heal. Their brother, Luke, had joined the army right out of high school and that had left Staci and Paige to fend for themselves.

There'd always been men in their mother's life. The three of them all had different fathers, whose identities were a mystery to them and surely to their mother, too. Paige used to search the faces of men in town trying to find a resemblance, but she'd soon given up, knowing it wouldn't make any difference. But she would always wonder. That was just human nature.

A lousy childhood had not prepared her for the real world. Her dream was to leave Horseshoe and to get as far away from her mother as she could. That was why she'd studied constantly and gotten good grades—to win a scholarship so she could get out of a home life where she was criticized and demeaned.

Her ticket out had come with a price. One she'd thought she could pay, but she'd been wrong. The price was too high. A naive, troubled girl didn't realize it at the time. And she would pay that price for the rest of her life.

She walked toward her sister, carrying her luggage. Staci looked much the same, only older. They'd once had the same mousy-brown hair, as her mother had called it. When Paige was little, she thought she had mice in her hair. She hadn't quite understood the description. When she was older, she knew it was just one more criticism her mother had heaped upon her.

Other than that, they didn't resemble each other. And their looks had changed some over the years. With the help of a good stylist, Staci's hair was now a darker brown, which looked great with her blue eyes. Paige had trimmed and highlighted her thick tresses so she was now more of a blonde with dark green eyes. Their brother had brown eyes. They were an eclectic mix or a hodgepodge of their mother's love life.

Paige dropped her suitcase and hugged her sister tightly. She'd missed her. But not as much as she'd missed… She couldn't think his name. She just couldn't. Or the nausea would come back.

Staci drew back and looked at her sister. "My, look at you. Don't you look sophisticated in heels and a nice dress. I love your hair! California has changed you, or has being a doctor made this transformation?"

"Me?" Paige quickly steered the conversation in another direction. "Look at you! How much weight have you lost?" Both sisters had a tendency to gain weight. They had that in common.

"About thirty pounds." Staci swung around in her summer dress and did a bow. "I feel great. I have a fabulous job and great friends and I feel good about myself for the first time in my life."

"It shows." Staci had a job at a hotel in Austin. She'd started working at a hotel in Temple right out of high school and was soon offered a better job with more benefits in Austin. She was in charge of parties and banquets and she loved it.

Nothing else was said as they made their way to Staci's car and it gave Paige a chance to regroup and calm her shaky nerves. She'd talked to her sister many times over the years, but she never shared her deep dark secrets with anyone, not even her sister. The embarrassment and shame she couldn't share. It went deep into her soul where no one was allowed. She'd been a private person all her life and the only one she'd let get close was...

"Have you heard from Luke?" Paige asked to change her train of thought.

"Yes. He'll be at the funeral tomorrow. He's stationed at Fort Polk and he'll be leaving at the end of the month for another deployment."

"I know. We spoke last week." They reached the car and Paige put her suitcase in the backseat and got in the vehicle. "I'm so proud of him and what he's accomplished with his career in the army."

Staci backed out of the parking spot and headed for the exit sign. "I'm proud of all of us. After a traumatic childhood, we turned out pretty good."

Paige smoothed the fabric of her dress and then watched as the parking terminal flashed by. "Do you think any of us will ever be happy, though?"

"I'm happy," Staci insisted. "I meet so many wonderful people and they're kind and gracious and treat me with respect. That's all a person needs."

"And love," Paige murmured under her breath.

"Well—" Staci turned out of the terminal "—we're

kind of gun-shy in that department, but you know what love is. And one time you were madly in love with—"

"Don't say his name." Paige stopped her with panic in her voice.

Staci gave her a sharp glance as she negotiated the traffic. "Why not? It was a long time ago and you've both moved on. He has a little boy now. I haven't been back to Horseshoe all that much, so I don't know the details about his marriage."

He'd married someone else. He had a child. While she...

"Could we not talk about it, please?"

"Okay." They drove in silence for a long time before Staci said, "What's going on with you? You're tense and sad and it's not about Mom's death."

Paige swallowed the lump in her throat. "It's very upsetting to go back and relive all that heartache and pain."

"Yeah, I know, kiddo. I lived through it with you. But as I told you on the phone a couple years ago, the doctors at the mental hospital said Mom's problems started with the wreck that killed her parents. She suffered severe head trauma and back injuries, and she wasn't the same afterward. Even Uncle Harry said that. As the years passed, it just got worse because she refused any treatment and couldn't stay off the liquor."

Paige had always known there had to be a reason for her mother's behavior, but it still didn't wipe away a child's pain. Her mother was gone now and she had to learn to forgive. She knew all too well how circumstances could change a person's life.

"How often did you visit her?"

Staci heaved a sigh. "Whenever I could force myself to go—holidays, her birthday and Mother's Day. I al-

ways took her flowers and chocolates. At the end, she
was very sad, Paige."

She closed her eyes tightly, not wanting to hear any
good things about her mother. In her emotional state, she
couldn't handle it. The bitterness and the resentment held
her together like Elmer's glue, and if they were gone,
she would crumble into nothing. Her sins would rise to
the surface and she would have to admit that she was
worse than her mother. At least her mother had never
given away one of her children.

"Enough with the maudlin stuff. I have a two-
bedroom apartment and you and Luke are staying with
me. I thought it would be nice if we were together. He's
coming in tonight and we'll have dinner. I'm cooking.
And it's not peanut butter and jelly or corn dogs. How
did we survive on that?"

"Don't forget milk and cereal."

"Mmm. But, you know, the past is the past and what
we do now with our lives is up to us. Adversity has made
us stronger and we can handle anything."

Paige wasn't so sure about that. She didn't know if
she could handle going back to Horseshoe, Texas, and
reliving that terrible time.

Jude rode into the barn followed by his brother Phoenix. He was home from the rodeo circuit for a few days
and helping on the ranch. He and Phoenix had been born
in the same year, January and December, and they were
close growing up, almost like twins. But Phoenix had
always had an interest in the rodeo, while Jude had just
wanted to cowboy for real.

As they were unsaddling, Quincy and Elias rode in
from their day's work on the ranch. "I'll finish up for

you, Jude," Quincy said. "You got a date tonight and it's getting late."

Jude threw his saddle over a rail. "I canceled."

His brothers stopped what they were doing and stared at him. Quincy placed his hands on his hips. "Why?"

"I can't go out and have a good time with this Paige thing hanging over my head. I have to figure out what I'm going to do. I have to think about Zane and what's best for him."

Elias pulled off his hat, slapped it against his leg, making the dust fly. "The way I see it, Paige is here for a funeral, and as soon as it's over, she'll be gone again. She probably has a big practice out in California. I don't know what you're worried about."

"I usually never agree with Elias, but he could be right." Quincy hung his saddle on a rail and stared at Jude. "Go out and have a good time tonight and you'll be relaxed and able to see things more clearly."

"You wouldn't do that, Quincy. You wouldn't put your pleasure before someone you loved."

Quincy pulled off his gloves and stuffed them into his saddlebags. "Yeah, you're probably right."

"Paige is Zane's mother and I have to tell her what I did or I'll never be able to live with myself. Doesn't matter if she's married and has other kids. Zane has a right to know his mother and maybe get the chance to meet her."

All day, thoughts of Zane and Paige had gone round and round in his mind. It all came down to the same thing: what was best for Zane. Jude had lived his whole life with that in mind and he wasn't changing now, even if it was going to take a piece of his heart to face her.

Falcon walked into the barn. "Everybody through for the day?"

"Yeah," Quincy replied. "We have twenty-five heifers ready to go first thing in the morning to Mr. Hensley in Longview, Texas. Actually, we have twenty-six." He glanced at Elias. "Someone can't count."

"Math wasn't my strong suit." Elias smirked.

Falcon pointed a finger at Elias. "First thing in the morning before anyone goes to work, you'll get that heifer back to the herd."

"You're a hard-ass, Falcon. Why don't you just ask Mr. Hensley if he would like twenty-six? Maybe give them a discounted rate."

"I'm not discounting those heifers. They're prime stock and it's how we make our living. Have you forgotten that?"

Jericho, who worked on the ranch and was a friend of their brother Egan, came into the barn from the corral. "Don't worry about the extra heifer. I let one of the smaller ones out into the alley that connects most of the pastures and she took off running. I followed her on my horse all the way to the north pasture. She's now back with the herd."

Elias thumbed his nose at Falcon. "And that's how it's done, big brother."

Falcon shook his head and caught sight of Jude. "What are you still doing here? I thought you had a date tonight."

Phoenix held up his hands. "Okay, everybody, leave Jude alone. This is his decision, his kid, not yours."

Jude and Phoenix had shared a special connection ever since the shooting of Ezra McCray. Jude and Phoenix had been riding bareback while their father was fixing fences. Jude was in front and Phoenix sat behind him with his arms wrapped around Jude's waist. Almost as if it were yesterday, Jude could hear his brother.

Jump the fence, Jude. This horse can do it.

We'll get in trouble.

Dad's way over there and we'll be back before he misses us. Jump the fence, Jude.

Hold on, he said and kneed the horse.

The horse shot forward, galloping faster and faster as it neared the fence and they sailed right over it, but Jude couldn't stop the horse fast enough. Before he could turn back toward the fence, shots rang out and the next thing he knew, he was in a hospital bed with his mother crying and his dad looking as if the world had come to an end. His sun-browned face was a mask of pain, misery and suffering. At six years of age, Jude thought maybe Phoenix was dead and he started to cry, too. But he soon found out Phoenix was fine and that Ezra McCray had shot at them. And his father had killed the man. It was a lot for a six-year-old to understand. It was a lot for a six-year-old to go through.

From that day forward, Jude never spoke much. He was quiet and stayed close to his father, but even at that early age, he could see his dad was troubled by what had happened. Jude blamed himself and tried to make his father feel better. All his life he seemed to be fighting to make someone feel better and he had grown weary of the task.

"Why didn't Paxton come home with you?" Falcon asked Phoenix, his voice piercing Jude's troubled thoughts.

"He went on to another rodeo with Cole Bryant. He's focused and determined to stay on the top of his game so he can make the national finals in Vegas. He'll be home in a few days."

Paxton had had a rough year. He'd dumped his high-school sweetheart, Jenny, for someone he'd met at a rodeo and it had turned out to be a nightmare for him. It had almost done him in, especially since Jenny had fallen in love with Quincy and they were now married. The brothers had worked everything out, and Paxton wasn't letting anything or anyone interfere with his career again.

"Has anyone heard from Egan?" Falcon was doing his usual thing, keeping tabs on the brothers.

"No," Jericho said. "They're supposed to find out the sex of the baby today, but Egan wants to wait until the birth. If I was a betting man, and I gave that up a long time ago, I'd bet they're going to wait."

Jericho was one of a kind. He'd grown up on the streets of Houston, wrapped up with gangs and drugs. Egan had met him in prison, when he'd been unjustly sent there by an overzealous judge. Jericho had saved his life and Egan was forever indebted to him. When the family got Egan out, their mother promised Jericho a job for his bravery.

The man stood about six feet four inches tall. He had dark features with a scar slashed across the side of his face. His long dark hair was tied into a ponytail at his neck. No one knew his lineage, but Egan had said he was part white, black, Mexican and Indian. A scary figure to some, but to the Rebel family he was loved and trusted.

"Leah and I waited," Falcon said. "Of course, ours was a completely different situation, but I agree with Jericho. Egan will win this round because Rachel will do what he wants."

"You guys are pathetic." Elias laughed. "Why doesn't he just say no?"

"If you ever find anyone to marry you, we'll remind you of that," Falcon told him, and looked around. "Where's Grandpa?"

"He was right behind me." Elias walked to the barn door and looked out. "Can you believe this? His horse is tied to the chain-link fence at his house. Who does he think is going to unsaddle that horse and take care of it?"

Elias's cell phone buzzed before anyone could answer.

"That's probably him about to tell you," Phoenix said.

Elias fished his cell out of his pocket and frowned. "It's Grandpa. Thank you, Quincy, for buying him a phone." Elias clicked it on. "Yeah, Grandpa. I'll do it. What did you say?" Elias pushed Speakerphone and held the cell up. "You're my favorite grandson," echoed through the barn and everyone tried hard not to laugh. It was Grandpa's favorite saying, and he'd said it to every one of the brothers at some point.

Elias slipped the phone back into his pocket. "The favorite grandson is going to go help his grandpa. Now don't y'all feel guilty?"

Quincy's cell buzzed and he quickly grabbed it from his pocket. After a second, he said, "I got to go. That was Jenny. White Dove is in labor. Jenny has been watching that horse for days and I hope everything goes okay." He hurried toward the barn door and then turned back. "Jude, Zane wanted to be there. Do you want me to call him?"

"Go ahead." He threw a blanket over the saddle. "It would give him something to do while I'm out. I'm going into town to see Annabel. She deserves an explanation."

"Good for you." Quincy hurried away and Falcon and

Jericho soon followed. That left him and Phoenix to sort through the tangled mess of Jude's mind.

"You okay?" Phoenix asked.

Jude leaned against the railing. "Do you feel you will never be the same as you were when you were five years old?"

"Come on, Jude." Phoenix shoved his hands into the front pockets of his jeans as if that could keep the memories at bay. "This family will never be the same, but we have to learn to accept happiness and forgiveness into our lives. I'm doing that. Dad said it wasn't our fault and I believe him because I believed him all my life and I'm not going to change now. We were kids and kids do silly things. We're not to blame. Dad said so."

"It's just…"

"What is it with you and Quincy? You both seem to have a need to carry the weight of the world on your shoulders. Let it go. Please."

"Dad was gone two years when Paige got pregnant and I needed to talk to him so badly. Quincy was in the army and I couldn't talk to him, either. I made all the wrong decisions and I can't even say it was for the right reasons. I was just a scared kid and I didn't know what to do. I just wanted Paige to get out of a bad home life and the scholarship gave her that opportunity. I couldn't take that away from her."

"Jude, you did the right thing. You went back and got your son and he's an amazing kid. Pat yourself on the back for once. If you feel you have to tell Paige, then tell her. Zane is a different matter. But I'm sure you'll make the right decision for him, too. Stop agonizing over it." He grabbed the reins of Jude's horse. "Go spend some time with that pretty teacher and I'll take care of the horses. And, for heaven sakes, smile, Jude. You're freaking me out."

"I just don't want to hurt her."

The horses milled around, neighing, ready for feed.

"Well, I'm not judging her or anything, but I can almost guarantee you before this is over, someone is going to get hurt and I'm just hoping it's not you or Zane. Just saying."

Phoenix was right. He couldn't make any of this better for any of them. He just had to make sure his son wasn't hurt. While Paige was in town, he somehow had to explain what had happened all those years ago. She deserved that. He knew that with all his heart and nothing anyone said would change his mind. Sometimes in life he had to make the rough decisions because he was a father. He could only pray this decision was the right one for his son.

And Paige.

Chapter 3

"Dad, Dad…"

Jude sat up in bed and squinted at the clock. Five in the morning. "What are you doing up so early?"

Zane jerked on his jeans. "I want to go check on the new foal. It was amazing, Dad. White Dove was nervous and Uncle Quincy just talked to her and rubbed her head and her stomach and she calmed down. Her contractions were strong and Uncle Quincy kept her calm, you know, Dad, like you do. No one can do that but you and Uncle Quincy with cows and horses. You got the touch. And…"

"Take a breath." Jude sat up and watched the excitement on his son's face. Zane had been in bed when Jude had come in last night. He'd stayed longer than he'd expected at Annabel's. He'd wanted her to know the truth and found it easy to talk to her. She understood he wanted to wait until the situation with Paige was over. She didn't want to get involved, either, if his heart was somewhere else. Jude didn't know where his heart was. But then, he did. It was with this little boy whose eyes were sparkling like firecrackers on the Fourth of July.

"It was amazing, Dad, I tell you. Uncle Quincy taped her tail because she was swishing it and then Jenny washed White Dove's udder, teats and vulva with water and soap. And—"

"Vulva?"

"Yeah, it's—"

"I know what it is." He was surprised his son did, but that was Zane. He'd probably read about birthing and knew every detail. Once he learned something, he never forgot it. His memory was uncanny.

"Well, the foal's feet were like this." Zane stuck out his arms as far as he could and placed his head between them. "That's the way she came out, in a white amniotic sac. Jenny said it was a perfect birth and Uncle Quincy agreed. Once the front feet and head and shoulders appeared, it was like swoosh and the rest of it followed into a yucky mess. Jenny's already calling her Little Dove because she's white and black like her mama. It took four attempts before Little Dove could stand on wobbly legs and she's the cutest thing. You should've seen it, Dad. Do you think her legs are long like Bear's 'cause they're related?"

Jude swung his feet to the floor. "Yep, Red Hawk is their father." Zane had seen births before on the ranch, but he was extra excited because he spent a lot of time with Quincy and his paint horses.

"I think I want to be a vet."

Jude stared at his precious son with his hair in his

eyes. "How about a scientist or a chemist who discovers a cure for cancer?"

"Cool, Dad. I can do that, too." Zane grinned as he slipped a T-shirt over his head. "After everything was over, Quincy said I better go to the house or Grandma would be worried. He was right. She was sitting up, waiting on me. She said she can't go to sleep unless I'm safely in bed. I'm lucky to have a grandma like that."

"Yes, you are." Jude felt a pang of guilt for staying out so late. He didn't want his mother to stay up and wait for Zane. That was Jude's job. Once in twelve years wasn't bad, though.

"You were out with Ms. Hurley. Did you talk about me?"

"Our favorite topic of conversation."

"Cool, Dad. I'm going to check on Little Dove and then come back and get ready for school so I can find a cure for cancer." His cheeky son had the audacity to wink.

Zane darted out the door and Jude stood and stretched and then made his way to the shower. Today was the day. He would meet Paige for the first time in almost thirteen years. He wondered if she'd changed. Everyone changed in that amount of time. He certainly had. He wasn't that scared teenage boy anymore. Raising a child had toughened him up quickly. He had to stay on his toes to make good choices and cowboy up when things got rough.

That scared boy had become a man ready to take on the world for Zane. He'd never for one minute regretted going back to get his son. But today he would have to explain that decision to Paige. He was prepared now. The scared boy had surfaced for a moment because he was afraid of losing the one thing that mattered the most to him in this world: his son. That bond was rock-solid and Jude knew that better than anyone.

Since he was going to a funeral, Jude put on starched jeans and a white shirt. With his hair combed, his hat in his hand, he headed for the door, only to be stopped by Zane coming through it.

"That was quick." His son had a strange look on his face, one Jude knew well. Something was wrong and he knew not to push or Zane would clam up. "The foal okay?"

"Yeah. She was sucking, so I guess everything's okay."

"Didn't you talk to Uncle Quincy?"

Zane shook his head. "He and Aunt Jenny were curled up in the hay under a blanket asleep, so I didn't wake them."

"You could have. It would have been okay."

With his small shoulders hunched, Zane replied, "I don't know, Dad. It's different now."

"How is it different?"

"Uncle Quincy doesn't have much time for me anymore."

Jude sat on the bed and patted the spot beside him. Quincy had spoiled Zane, just as he'd spoiled Grandpa and everyone else by lavishing his attention on them. He was that type of person.

"Uncle Quincy still loves you and you're still his partner. But life is about changes. Nothing stays the same."

Zane looked up at him. "I think that's a line from a song, Dad."

Jude ruffled Zane's hair. "It's true. Having fun with Uncle Quincy will change, too. You'll want to spend more and more time with your friends and away from the ranch."

Zane's eyes narrowed. "I'm never leaving the ranch."

Jude didn't push it, because they'd had this conversation many times about college and it always upset Zane. "Trust me. You won't always think that way. You'll change. As much as you say you won't, you will. And if you don't, the ranch will always be here. It will always be home."

"And you'll always be here?"

"You bet." There was no place on earth Jude would rather be. Zane got that from him. By Zane's somber expression, Jude knew something else was bothering his son. "What is it, son?"

"Uh… Uncle Quincy and Aunt Jenny were curled up together. Uncle Quincy had his arms around her and they were like one person."

They'd already had the sex talk, so it couldn't be about that. Jude was sweating bullets thinking about how to answer his son.

Zane saved him. "Uncle Quincy really loves Aunt Jenny."

"And she loves him."

"Yeah. That's nice, huh?"

"Yes. You have one more person who loves you."

"Aunt Jenny gives big hugs and she smells good."

"So you see it's a good thing Uncle Quincy found someone."

"Yeah." There was still a slight hesitation in Zane's voice.

"If you want to talk to Uncle Quincy, just go over to his barn and talk to him. He won't disappoint you. I promise."

There was silence for a moment and Jude struggled to find words to soothe his son's bruised heart. Before Jude could find the right words, Zane looked up at him again and asked, "Did you love my mama like Uncle Quincy loves Aunt Jenny?"

Jude's throat closed up and every word he knew dissipated like smoke into thin air. He tried not to show any reaction but knew that wouldn't work. He'd always been honest with Zane, but now he struggled with the truth. He wasn't sure why. It was just difficult to talk about his feelings for Paige, especially with his son.

He swallowed hard. "Yes, I loved your mother more than I can ever tell you. We were inseparable in high school and…"

Zane wrapped his arms around Jude's waist and buried his face against him. "You don't have to talk about her, Dad."

He held his son close. "It's okay. You were conceived in love. That's why you're such a happy kid."

Zane drew back to gaze up at Jude. "I hope she doesn't come back like Eden's mom did. I don't think I would like her. It's just me and you, right, Dad? You and me against the world. We're Rebels and we're rowdy."

"You bet. Now you better get ready for school. Aunt Rachel will be here any minute."

"Okay." Zane stared at Jude. "Why are you all dressed up?"

Jude took a moment. "I'm going to a funeral this morning."

"Oh. I'm sorry someone died."

Jude hugged his son. Zane had this innate softness inside him, making him genuinely considerate and sincere. He was truly sorry someone had died. That was just the way he was. He got that from Paige.

Ruffling his son's hair, Jude said, "We need to get your hair cut again."

Zane pulled back, smiling. He was happy again. "I want to get it cut before the race because I don't want any hair in my eyes when Bear and I zoom past everybody. We're going to win, Dad! Uncle Quincy said so. I filled out the form and put it and my money in an envelope. When are you going to take it in to the paper?"

"I'll take it before I go to the funeral."

"Cool." Zane dashed into his room and came back with the envelope. "It's all there. You just have to give it to Miss Maureen and get my number. I hope it's a nine. Nine is my lucky number. Oh, yeah." Zane danced off to his room.

When had nine become his lucky number? That was news to Jude, but he had a feeling that as Zane grew, a lot of things were going to be news to him. Little boys tended to keep secrets. He knew that for a fact 'cause he'd kept many from his parents. Not biggies, but secrets.

In the kitchen, Falcon, Quincy and Egan were having coffee with their mother.

"So you're waiting till the birth to find out the sex of the baby?" his mother asked Egan.

"Yeah. I just would rather do that and Rachel agreed with me. Although she was very tempted to find out."

Jericho was right. Jude poured a cup and joined them at the table.

"I guess you're going to the funeral." His mother looked at him.

"Yes. I have to see her to test the waters, so to speak. At this point, I'm not sure how much I'll tell her. It depends on how much she wants to hear. I'll play it by ear and hope I make the right decision."

"You will, son," his mother assured him.

Egan twisted his cup. "I stopped by to tell you Rachel's going to the funeral."

Jude started at that news. "Why? I don't remember them being all that close in high school."

"Jude, it's a small school and we all know each other."

"I guess."

"Besides, Angie Hollister is Horseshoe's one-woman welcoming-and-funeral committee. And Rachel's her best friend. They thought it would be nice if someone from the town showed up. And don't worry—Rachel's not going to say anything. She's rather fond of Zane and, trust me, she's going to make sure no one hurts him."

Jude got to his feet. "Is Rachel still picking up Zane for school?" Rachel taught art and she and Egan lived down the road in a house they'd fixed up, so it was ideal for Rachel to give Zane a ride.

"She'll be here any minute," Egan said. "She notified the principal last night she was taking an hour off."

"I better go, then. Zane wants me to drop off the entry form and fee for the race."

"You haven't had breakfast," his mother reminded him.

"I couldn't eat a thing, Mom. I'll catch y'all later."

As he drove into town, Zane's words kept running through his mind. *Did you love my mama like Uncle Quincy loves Aunt Jenny?* Oh, yes, he'd loved Paige with all his heart. They'd been two teenagers who'd desperately needed someone to love. Someone to listen. Someone to care.

Paige's mother had been an awful person. He couldn't believe any mother could be so vile. She'd told Paige repeatedly that she was ugly and worthless and would never amount to anything. Every chance the woman got, she'd driven home that point to make Paige feel as low as she could. She'd shredded Paige's confidence until Paige was a walking case of nerves. Sometimes she'd break out in hives just from the stress.

Looking back, he realized there'd been so many options open to them other than listening to Mrs. Carstairs, but at the time they hadn't seen them. Jude could've gone to his mother and she would've been happy to help them. But talking was not Jude's strong suit. He almost would have rather died than tell his mother how he'd screwed up. He was to blame for everything that had happened and he fully carried that blame on his shoulders. If he had spoken up, things would've been different. But he hadn't known how Paige would've reacted if he'd asked her to marry him and give up her dream. He couldn't do that, pressure her to stay in a town that held so many bad memories. She deserved to fulfill her dream more than anyone he'd ever known. He'd made sure she did. Whatever had happened in the intervening years, he hoped with all his heart she was happy and had a full life.

He drove toward the Horseshoe cemetery, ready to face his past.

The April wind howled through the tall cedars of Horseshoe's country cemetery. Paige shivered and reached for Staci's hand. The ominous sound was a fitting lullaby for a woman who had been troubled most of her life. The noise would carry on into the hereafter.

They didn't shed tears. There were too many teardrops on their souls to pretend any grief now. Sadness, yes. Paige was sure it showed on their solemn faces as they said goodbye to a mother they'd never understood.

Out of the corner of her eye, she saw a silver SUV pull into the cemetery driveway. Angie Wiznowski and Rachel Hollister got out. They were older, but Paige recognized them, girls she had gone to high school with. Rachel was as beautiful as ever with her blond hair and blue eyes. She was pregnant. A pain shot through Paige but she quickly disguised it. Angie had changed the most. She'd always been sweet and nice but she was positively glowing. What were they doing here?

More cars turned into the cemetery. Angie's mom and Angie's sisters and brother had come. The sheriff and his wife arrived, as did Hardy Hollister, the DA, and Judge Hollister. Mrs. Peabody and the older ladies of the town came. Some of Paige's teachers also came. Some of Staci's and Luke's friends showed up. The people of Horseshoe offered their condolences and Paige was overwhelmed with a nostalgic feeling for a town she'd left behind.

As everyone stood around the grave site, the man from the funeral home read some verses from the Bible and the casket was lowered into the ground. A turbulent life was over.

Angie hugged her. "We're so sorry for your loss."

"Thank you," she managed.

Rachel hugged her, too. "It's so good to see you and you look absolutely wonderful. I guess the California good life agrees with you."

Paige didn't know how to answer. If they only knew. But they never would, because Paige would never open up with all the heartache and pain she'd suffered in the past years.

After everyone had left, Angie and Rachel lingered and they talked about Horseshoe and things that had happened while Paige had been gone. Angie was married to Hardy Hollister, Rachel's brother, which Paige had guessed by the way Hardy had hugged Angie. They had two children. Rachel had married Egan, Jude's older brother. That caught Paige's attention. She'd never known Rachel liked the Rebel boys. She seemed happy, as did Angie. Paige would never have that kind of happiness. She had destroyed her one chance at love.

"We have company," Rachel said as a pickup pulled up behind the SUV.

Angie hugged her one more time. "Come by the bakery before you leave and we can catch up on old times and hear about your amazing career." Angie's family owned the local bakery, a favorite hangout and the busiest place in town.

Paige didn't say anything, because she didn't plan on taking Angie up on her offer. She wouldn't talk about her life to anyone. She'd opened up last night to Staci and Luke because she had to tell them. She couldn't keep lying and holding everything inside. As family members who had been through hell with her, they understood. But the people of Horseshoe wouldn't, even friends like Angie and Rachel.

They walked away and Paige stared at the man getting out of the truck. Her breath caught and her body trembled as she stared at the boy who was now a man. The boy she'd loved more than anyone in her life.

He walked toward them with long strides. He'd changed, was her first thought. The skinny boy had filled out and his shoulders were wide and muscled. But his beautiful face, carved with the touch of an angel, was the same: dark eyes flanked by incredible eyelashes and lean structured facial bones that bespoke pure masculinity. He'd been a cowboy then and she was delighted to see he was still in boots, a Stetson and snug Wranglers. From out of nowhere a memory flashed through her mind of a lazy afternoon and her unzipping them. She was suddenly warm all over.

Luke met him and they shook hands. Paige couldn't hear what they were saying, but soon Jude walked toward her.

She said the first thing that came into her head. "Hey, Jude." It was the title of an old Beatles song that had been their favorite back then. They'd played it over and over just to sing "Hey, Jude."

He didn't smile, and a foreboding feeling came over her. "I'm sorry about your mom."

"Th-thank y-you." She stumbled over the words like a teenager. "I was going to call before I left town."

"Could we go somewhere and talk?" He looked around at the tombstones and graves nestled among stately cedars. "Someplace besides here?"

"Sure. I can use Staci's car. Where would you like to meet?"

"They redid the park that's two blocks from your old house. It's nice and we could meet there."

"Okay. I'll see you in about thirty minutes."

He nodded and strolled back toward his truck.

They were cordial and polite like strangers, but they had been so much more.

"What did he want?" Staci asked.

"Just to talk."

"You don't have to do that if you don't want to," Luke told her. "It might be best to let it go."

"I can't. I have to know if he thinks about our child all the time...like...I do."

"Oh, Paige." She didn't even know she was shaking until Staci put her arms around her.

"I didn't think it would be this hard to see him." She brushed away an errant tear. "He didn't even smile when I said, 'Hey, Jude.' It was our favorite song."

"Do you still love him?"

She didn't know, but she knew what the nausea was about. Jude. Seeing him again. And having to talk about that time and what they'd done. They had to drag out all the dirty laundry to see if it could be cleansed or if the stains of life's mistakes would haunt her forever.

Chapter 4

Jude parked at the curb of the new Horseshoe Park and made his way to where he saw Paige sitting at a picnic table. The brightly colored swings and slides and the new water park faded from his mind as he focused on the woman waiting for him.

The first thing he'd noticed at the cemetery was that she'd lost a lot of weight. Away from her criticizing mother, she must've stopped the binge junk-eating. She was now slim and her hair was more blond than brown. It suited her. Her face still held that same sweet innocence that had first attracted him to her. But now there was a maturity about her that was just as attractive.

Never Never Land never looked so good.

She got up and ran to him, then wrapped her arms around his waist and hugged him. The scent of lilac soap wafted to him. He froze, which was more the reaction of the teenage boy he used to be. But the man in him recognized all those old feelings that had bound him to her years ago. Maybe some things just never changed.

When he didn't return the hug, she went back to the table and he eased onto the bench across from her, removing his hat. The wind rustled through the tall oaks and he took a moment to gather his thoughts. It was like gathering bits and pieces from his past to guide him. What should he say? What should he do?

"You look good," she said. "You filled out. The teenage boy I used to date doesn't seem to exist anymore."

"He grew up, and so have you. I hardly recognized you at the cemetery. The young girl of long ago has matured into a beautiful woman."

"Thank you." She tilted her head slightly to smile at him and his heart raced like a wild mustang's at the look he remembered well. "You were always good for my ego."

He didn't shift or act nervous. He couldn't do that now. He had to be the man he was supposed to be. For Zane. And for himself.

"I'm sorry about your mom."

She shrugged. "Thanks. She's at peace now."

"So you've forgiven her for all the crappy stuff?"

"It's hard to hold on to all that bitterness. After Staci put her in the mental hospital, we found out her erratic behavior was because of the injuries to her head and spine in the accident that killed my grandparents. Alcohol only made it worse."

"I knew there had to be a reason for the way she acted." They were getting bogged down in ordinary conversation when he wanted to talk about something else entirely. "How's California?"

"Great. I'm busy, so I don't get to see a lot of it. But I've enjoyed my stay there."

"I'm glad you had the chance to make your dream come true." He really meant that with all his heart. But a small part of him wanted her to love him enough to have stayed and raised their son together.

"Do you still work on the ranch?" she asked quickly, as if she wanted to change the subject.

"Yes. I'll always be a cowboy."

She fiddled with her hands in her lap. "I heard you have a son." Her eyes caught his and all the guilt hit him, blindsiding him.

"Yes." *Our son. The one you gave away.*

She looked off to the tall oaks and the branches swaying in the breeze. "Do…do…you ever think about our child?"

His stomach roiled with a familiar ache. "Every day." He didn't try to avoid the subject, because he knew they'd have to discuss it thoroughly.

"I think about the baby all the time. I can't seem to shake all those guilty feelings and…and I think we made a mistake."

His gut tensed. "Why do you say that? We talked about it a lot and you said you could handle the feelings. You said the fact that our child would have a good home would be enough for you. What made you change your mind?"

She placed a hand over her heart. "I just have this need to know if I have a son or a daughter. We should have asked. We should have held our child. As a young girl, I was arrogantly boastful that I could handle all those emotions and all those feelings. I was wrong. It almost destroyed me."

"What do you mean?"

"I cried all the way to California and I cried for days afterward. I couldn't get over it. But that's in the past." She waved a hand to dismiss it. "I wanted to talk to you because I was hoping you felt the same and would want to know if we had a son or a daughter. Would you be willing to go with me to talk to Mrs. Carstairs? Maybe she would tell us if we both went."

"Paige…"

"I know you have a different life now and I don't want to interfere with that. But I have to know. Do you understand that?"

He didn't understand anything and he certainly hadn't expected this from her at this late date. He hadn't expected any guilty feelings from the woman whose career meant everything to her and who'd been positive she could handle the emotions. He searched for words to tell her the truth but they stuck in his throat like a wad of cotton.

"If both of us went, she might tell us if the baby was a boy or girl. We're not asking for our child back, just information. I'd really like to know if our child is happy. Don't you want to know these things?"

We have a son and he's with me. I've had him since the day after he was born. Simple words. Painful words. All he had to do was say them and it would ease her mind. He took a deep breath and tried to force the words out. Before he could, his cell buzzed. He reached into his pocket and pulled it out and saw it was Zane's school. He clicked the call on immediately.

"Excuse me," he said to Paige and got to his feet.

"Mr. Rebel, this is Sharon Thompson, Principal Bowers's secretary."

"Is there a problem?"

"We had an incident at school this morning and the principal would like for you to come in as soon as you can."

"Is my son okay?"

"Yes."

"I'll be there in ten minutes."

He shoved his phone back into his pocket and then picked up his hat. "I'm sorry—I have to go. Can we meet later?"

"I'm staying for two weeks. We're going to clean out our old house and put it on the market. You can catch me over there. Here's my cell number."

"Good. I'll see you then." He marched off without a backward glance, worried about his son. What had happened? Zane was never in trouble.

Jude made it to the school in record time. The school was shaped like a horseshoe. The administration office was in the center, with grades one through six on the left and grades seven through twelve on the right. The gym and cafeteria were in the back. The Horseshoe school system had always been in one spot, but the school was bursting at the seams because the town's population was growing. Soon they would have to have portable buildings to house some of the students.

He went through the double doors into the school. The principal's office was straight ahead and he hurried there. The halls were empty and the big clock on the wall said it was only five after ten.

"Jude."

He turned to see Annabel coming toward him in a spring dress and heels. She was beautiful, patient and loving. Everything he wanted in a woman. He wasn't sure why he held back on taking their relationship further.

"Where's Zane?"

She nodded at a door. "He's in there with Rachel. She's taking care of him."

"Taking care of him? What happened?" Fear edged its way up his spine and his nerves tightened.

Annabel touched his arm. "Calm down. Zane is fine."

Her touch had a calming effect. He took a long breath. "What happened?"

"After first class, the kids went to their lockers to get ready for second period. Dudley McCray was bragging about how fast his horse was and how he was going to win the Founder's Day Horse Race. Zane told him he had a fast horse, too, and he just might win. Dudley got mad and said no egghead Rebel was beating him. He then pushed Zane and Zane fell backward onto the floor, his books going everywhere. The kids rushed to help him, but he got to his feet, saying Dudley was upset because he was afraid Zane was going to beat him. Dudley told him he wasn't afraid of any egghead Rebel. Zane replied that only idiots weren't afraid. That really got Dudley angry and he went after Zane, but the hall monitor was there and several teachers kept him from hitting Zane again."

"Zane's not hurt?"

"No, he was very calm. I have to get back to class. I'll talk to you later." She gave him a smile and walked off down the hall. He watched her for a moment, thinking she could be his future, but he was tied to the past with a boulder around his neck pulling him down. Why he kept holding on, he wasn't quite sure. But the days ahead would provide closure or more heartache.

He opened the classroom door and went inside. Zane was sitting in a class chair and a very pregnant Rachel was stroking his hair as if to soothe him, and his son was eating it up.

"Hey, Dad." Zane jumped to his feet when he saw Jude.

Rachel kissed the top of Zane's head and said, "Your dad's here and I have to get back to class."

"Did they tell you what happened?"

"Yeah. Are you okay?" He looked Zane over to see if he had bruises or scratches on his face or arms.

"Yes. You told me to never fight unless it was necessary and it wasn't. I can hurt Dudley with words. He's an idiot. He thinks he's going to win the race, but he's not. You and Uncle Quincy said I have the fastest horse."

Jude squeezed his son's shoulder. "Son, we believe that Bear is fast, but a lot of things can happen in a race and I want you to be prepared for that."

"Okay, Dad. But Bear can win."

Jude squatted in front of his son. "I will be there supporting you all the way. I want you to do something for me, though."

"What?"

"I want you to stop bragging about Bear at school. At home, that's different. We'll let Bear do all the talking on race day."

Zane winked. "Gotcha, Dad."

Sharon opened the door. "The principal will see you now."

Jude stood. "Are you ready?"

"I've never been to the principal's office before." For the first time a note of anxiety entered Zane's voice.

Jude patted his son's back. "It won't be so bad."

As they walked toward the principal's office, Zane asked, "Did you ever have to go to the principal's office?"

"Yep. Your uncle Phoenix got me into a lot of trouble

with his antics." And Paige. They'd been caught kissing in his truck after the bell had rung and had been sent to the principal's office. He wouldn't share that, though.

"Did you get punished?"

"Not as much as we got punished at home. We couldn't go anywhere on Saturday or Sunday. We had to work."

"Are you going to punish me?"

"No, son. The principal will take care of all that."

The meeting was short. Zane was sent back to class and told all talk of the race was off-limits in school. Dudley was sent to a classroom by himself to read alone and think about what he'd done.

Jude sat outside in his truck for a while reflecting on those days of long ago. He and Paige had been too young to get involved so seriously. But no one could have told them that at the time. Even so, Jude would never regret having Zane. He wasn't going to apologize to Paige for going back to get him, either. That was his decision and he would stand by it to the day he died.

He started the engine. Now he had to tell Zane's mother about her son. It would be one of the hardest things he would ever have to do.

Paige changed out of her suit into jeans, a T-shirt and sneakers. They were cleaning out the house and it was dirty work. Dust and cobwebs were everywhere, emphasizing all the pain and sorrow that had happened within the walls.

"Hey, the refrigerator still works. How about that?" Staci diligently wiped it out with bleach and water. Staci had had the electricity turned on days ago so they could work. They had two weeks and they planned to repaint inside and out to make it attractive to a buyer.

The house was a nice three-bedroom two-bath brick home their mother had bought with the insurance money from her parents' death. Or more to the point, Uncle Harry, Darlene's guardian, had bought it for them. Uncle Harry and Aunt Nora had lived next door and they had been a godsend when they were growing up. Uncle Harry had died when Paige was fifteen. And Nora had followed six months later. For the first time the three Wheeler children were alone in the world. But Luke had already joined the army and that left just Staci and Paige and their mother.

Uncle Harry's house had been willed to the three children, but Darlene had sold it and made them sign the papers. With the money, she'd bought a new car and a used one for Staci. She'd blown the rest on frivolous stuff. They didn't live that far from the school and after Staci graduated and went to work, Paige walked to school. But after she fell in love with Jude, he always picked her up.

Jude.

He'd gotten her through high school. He'd gotten her through so much of her horrendous life. And then…

"How did your talk go with Jude?" Staci asked, frowning at the pan of dirty water from cleaning the fridge. "We can keep our cold drinks in here while we're working and that's probably it. The owners will probably dump it."

"We didn't get to talk much. He got a call from the school about his son and he left quickly."

"Did he say anything about his son or his wife or girlfriend?"

"No, and I really don't want to know. I just want him to go with me to talk to Mrs. Carstairs."

Staci stopped what she was doing to look at Paige,

who was throwing items from the cabinets into a big trash can. "Kiddo, do you think that's the best decision? It's been a long time and it might be best for you, for everyone, to let it go."

"I can't, Staci. I need answers to go on." Paige leaned against the cabinet. "I've made so many bad decisions and I know I can't go back and change that. But to go forward I have to feel good inside about what happened. I don't know if that's ever going to happen, but I know I have to have some answers."

"Did Jude say he would go with you?"

"He didn't say much of anything, but that's Jude. He doesn't talk much. He said he would come by here when he got through at school and I'm going to ask him again."

Staci closed the refrigerator and wiped her hands on her jeans. "I don't mean to hurt you, but how is knowing you had a son or daughter going to help you feel any better? The baby is still gone. I think it's time you face that. That's the only thing that's going to give you closure. Just be grateful you gave the child a life and probably a very good one with a nice family who's spoiling the devil out of it."

"But I'll never know." A sob clogged her throat and she took a moment to get her emotions under control. "It was so important to me to leave Horseshoe and Darlene behind that I couldn't see I was also leaving the most important part of me behind. Looking back, I get so mad at Jude for not speaking up and saying that we couldn't give the baby away. But he never said anything and now…"

"What difference would that have made?"

"What?"

"You were all set to go to Berkeley. What would you have done with the baby?"

"I don't know!" Paige wailed. "I just…"

"Oh, honey." Staci stepped over the junk on the floor and hugged Paige. "You've got to sort all this out and let go or you're never going to have any peace."

Paige wiped away a tear. "I should've talked to you. I should've talked to someone other than the counselor."

"Why didn't you? I know I was working a lot, but I've always been here for you. I never dreamed you were pregnant. You never shared that."

"Darlene… She said I would never amount to anything. I would wind up pregnant and living off welfare. I just couldn't let that happen. I couldn't…"

"Honey, you need to see a therapist or something. That's the only way you're going to be able to deal with this. Jude can't help you. He's moved on and has a life of his own now. I'll look for someone in Austin. Someone who you can trust and confide in and who has answers that can help you."

"I'm leaving in two weeks. I have to get back to my job. To my life. I'll be fine. It's just hard coming back here and facing the biggest mistake of my life."

Luke came in from the back door, interrupting them. "I have the truck loaded down with junk from the backyard. I'm taking it to the dump. I can take a few more things."

"There are several bags of trash," Staci said. "I'll help you load it."

Paige continued to wipe down the cabinets, her thoughts tumbling around like clothes in a dryer, round and round. She stopped as one thought became clear. There was no way to make her feel better. No counselor could do it. Jude couldn't do it. It was something Paige had to deal with on her own. Keeping a secret locked up inside for so long hadn't helped her. Her brother and sister were shocked at her actions. Paige was, too. There was a mixed-up young girl somewhere deep inside Paige whom she had to forgive. That was her magic. She had to forgive herself. And she had to let go of her child and let it have the life that she had given it. There was no way to go back.

And she had to stop blaming Jude.

She drew a jagged breath as the truth of that ran through her system. She had to forgive herself. That was her saving grace.

Staci came in. "Luke said when he gets back, he's going to mow the yard and start scraping the trim on the outside of the house. And you and I can start on the inside. But first we have to go into Temple to buy some paint."

"Do you mind if I stay here? I don't want to miss Jude." She wanted to apologize for her crazy actions earlier. There was no way Mrs. Carstairs would give her any information and she now understood that. She wanted her child protected at all costs. That was the only thing she could give it now.

"Paige…"

"I'm okay. We just need to talk. To say goodbye for good and I'll wish him well. We have a connection that will never be broken."

Staci eyed her. "You seem better."

"I've come to my senses. I can't go back." She shrugged. "I guess I was trying to rewrite the past. Wouldn't it be wonderful if we could do that?"

"Mmm." Staci grabbed her purse. "I'll see you later."

After Staci left, Paige started wiping baseboards and windowsills, basically ridding the house of all the dirt collected over the years. The bathrooms were a nightmare, but they were sparkling clean when Paige finished. Suddenly, the sound of a truck hummed from outside.

Jude.

Chapter 5

As he stared at the brick house, the past swelled around Jude once again. He'd lost track of the number of times he'd sat out here in his truck waiting for Paige. Most of the time she would come running out the door with her mother screaming behind her. The woman would be yelling vile things like "You're nothing but a slut sleeping around with that boy" or "If you get pregnant, you're on your own. I'm not taking care of any more brats."

Paige would get in his truck crying and he'd drive somewhere private so he could hold her until she felt better. Their whole relationship had been about making each other feel better. Jude had been dealing with a lot of emotion from his dad's death and being with Paige had eased his turmoil. It had to have been the saddest relationship on record. For once Jude wanted to feel some happiness and not wake up every morning with a giant knot in his stomach. Today he would start that process, because he was tired of feeling guilty and tired of all the stress. He wanted a life—for him and his son.

He got out and walked through the weeds to the front door. The dirty tan trim paint was peeling and he could see a lot of work needed to be done on the house. But homes were always in demand in Horseshoe and they shouldn't have a problem selling the place. Before he could knock, Paige opened the door and he stood completely still as the sight of her blindsided him once again.

Her hair was up in a ponytail, her green eyes vivid, and she wore jeans and a T-shirt, just like that girl of long ago. Dust lingered on her hair, her face and her clothes, and she'd never looked more beautiful. He grew weak from the sight, for he'd felt sure he was over Paige. They just had to talk about Zane. That was it. Wasn't it?

"Come in," she said, opening the door wider.

He followed her into a bright green kitchen with faded green gingham curtains. He'd been in the house only a couple of times. The wood table and chairs were still in the middle of the kitchen and she sat down, as did he, placing his hat on the table.

"Is everything okay with your son?" she asked as if she knew his son well.

"Yes. Everything's fine." But everything wasn't. He struggled once again with words.

"I'd offer you something to drink, but we don't have anything yet. Staci will probably bring something later."

"Thanks, I'm fine." He looked around the bare room. "Luke and Staci not here?"

"No, Luke's taken a load of trash to the dump ground and Staci's gone into Temple to get paint and supplies."

Privacy. Exactly what they needed.

"Luke has really filled out and Staci looks different, just like you."

"Yeah, we survived." Her mouth turned up at the corners.

"Life was a little crazy back then."

"Yeah." Paige brushed dust from her jeans. "How's your family?"

"Great. Leah came back and now she and Falcon have a year-old son."

Paige's eyes lit up. "That's wonderful. Everyone was so worried about her."

"It's a long story, but Falcon, Leah and the kids are all happy now."

"A happy ending," she murmured with a sad undertone.

"Quincy's married, too," he said to change the subject. "He married Jenny Walker."

She lifted her eyes to his. "Jenny? She dated Paxton, but I don't think he was as serious about her as Jenny was about him."

"She finally figured that out and fell in love with Quincy. And, of course, Egan married Rachel and they're expecting their first child."

"That was a surprise."

"To everyone." Jude relaxed, as he always did when talking to Paige. It was something they did really well.

"And your mom and grandpa?"

"Mom is fine, running the ranch, and Grandpa is Grandpa. Grouchy some days and loving the next. He's getting a little senile and we keep close tabs on him. Elias lives with him and has taken up most of the responsibility."

"Elias?" A bubble of laughter left her throat and he

was captivated. "He's the most irresponsible brother, as I remember. Always eager to fight."

"Now, don't bad-mouth Elias. He's changed a lot. He works hard and he plays hard, but he's there if you need someone."

"I think that's a Rebel tradition."

"Yeah." He stared into her warm eyes and couldn't look away. Where was his willpower?

"Where are Paxton and Phoenix?"

"They're on the rodeo circuit, winning and making money and enjoying life."

"That sounds like them. They'll probably never settle down."

"Probably not. They have wanderlust in their blood."

"Unlike you." She held his gaze and he was getting bogged down in an attraction he desperately wanted to deny.

"I'll never leave the ranch. That's just me." For some reason, he felt a need to say that. It wasn't clear in his mind why, but the words were important to him.

"Does everyone live on the ranch?"

"Yep. As I said, Elias lives with Grandpa in Grandpa's house, and Falcon and Leah and their kids live in the old family house. Paxton, Phoenix and Jericho, a friend of Egan's, live in the bunkhouse, Quincy and Jenny are building a new house, and Egan and Rachel live in a house they've renovated."

"Where do you live?"

All the warm feelings disappeared and a cold ball of reality slammed into his stomach. He had the urge to shift nervously, but he'd outgrown that behavior. But the inclination lingered.

"My son and I live with Mom in the big house." The

words tasted like dust on his tongue and he hated that reaction. He had nothing to be ashamed of. He had to remain strong.

Her green eyes were puzzled and he could almost see the questions gathering in her mind. "How about you? Are you in private practice or do you work for a hospital?"

Her head was bent as she stared down at something on her jeans and for a moment he thought she wasn't going to answer. "I was going to lie, but I'm tired of lying and I'm tired of secrets. I'm still in my medical residency. I have about three months before taking the Medical Licensing Exam."

"What? But it's been—"

"I know how long it's been, Jude." She got up and walked to the kitchen window and looked out into the backyard. "As I told you earlier, I cried all the way to California and I cried for days after. Actually, I couldn't stop crying for two months. I couldn't go to class. I couldn't eat. I couldn't do anything but sink into a well of depression."

Jude hadn't been expecting this and it took a few seconds for him to understand what she was saying. As per his old nature, he didn't say anything, because he had a feeling she had a lot more to get off her chest.

"I lost my scholarship and got kicked out of the dorm. I had nowhere to go and—"

"Why didn't you come home?" The words burst out, as he could no longer stay quiet.

"To what? To my mother saying she was right? The criticism and the shame was just something else I couldn't handle."

He clamped his jaw tight to keep the words in. He had to give her time to say everything she needed to.

"I had to go to a homeless shelter and they had toys there for children. I latched on to a teddy bear with a plaid ribbon around its neck. I clung to it day and night and I prayed it was my child. I think I had a nervous breakdown, but I was never diagnosed. I just lay in bed holding that teddy bear. Holding on to it was the only thing that kept me anchored."

"Paige…"

"The counselor came in two to three times a week to talk to people to try to inspire them to get jobs and to take control of their lives. She took an interest in me and I will forever be grateful for that. She listened to all my pain and she cried with me and she gave me hope. I told her my dreams and she said I could still have my dreams, but I told her my dream was not worth anything without my baby." Her voice wavered on the last word and Jude's stomach constricted so tight he couldn't breathe.

He cleared his throat. "You had ten days to change your mind. Did you forget that?"

She turned from the window and wiped away tears. "By the time I could tell her everything, ten days were long past and I had to accept that what I'd done was final, just like it was the day I left."

"You could have called me. You could—"

"Jude, please, let me finish."

He leaned back in the chair, his body tense and his heart desperately close to exploding with so much anger at what had happened to two naive teenagers.

"About eight months later, I showed her the contract that I had still stuffed into my suitcase and she said she didn't know Texas law all that well but she was positive that the adoption for my child was complete. It took about a month for me to accept that."

Jude curled his hands into fists and he wanted to pound on the table until something made sense. All it would've taken was a phone call and Paige could have seen her baby son and rectified a horrible mistake. How was he going to tell her now? The words rushed to his throat and he yearned to let them spill out, but he listened as she continued.

"Her name was Althea Wexton and she got me a job in a hospital answering phones and she encouraged me to get my life back on track. She helped me to file an appeal to get my scholarship reinstated. It took a while, but I finally got some of it back. She also found me a home with an older friend of hers who rents rooms. Ms. Whitman was a sweetheart. She let me live there until I started making some money and was able to pay my rent. Between my job and going to school, I was busy, but at night I still held that teddy bear."

She took a breath and it was an effort for Jude to remain quiet. For a man who didn't speak much, he wanted to start shouting, but he waited as patiently as he could.

"I went to school during the day and worked at night. I had very little sleep, but I didn't need much. Thea and Ms. Whitman were my cheerleaders. There truly are nice people in this world and I couldn't have gotten through the past twelve years without them. Perfect strangers and they feel like my family. I have three job offers when I finish my residency and my dream is finally going to come true. But it feels like a hollow victory."

"Did you call Staci during that time? Did you tell her about the baby?"

"No. I couldn't tell anyone."

"Why didn't you just come home? I would've sent plane tickets or come and got you. All you had to do was call."

She brushed a stray curl behind her ear. "Home to what? To listen to my mother say 'I told you so.' Home to the shame and humiliation. There was nothing for me here."

"Not even me?"

Their eyes collided in a wave of remembered love, of all the good times and all of the regrets.

"I didn't think there was any way for us to go back and be those two young people so much in love. We'd done the unforgivable and would always blame each other." She swiped a tear from her cheek. "I got a little emotional this morning asking about our baby. I realize we can't go searching for answers. That's out of the question. It's just coming back to Horseshoe has made me regret so many things."

"I'll never regret loving you."

Her eyes filled with more tears. "How did we make such a bad decision?"

"We were too young to see other options, and there were other options."

"Like what?"

"We could have gotten married and raised the baby like Falcon and Leah did, but I knew your heart was set on leaving and I never asked. That was my fault. I should've been more assertive and taken more responsibility for the child you carried."

"Oh, Jude, don't say any more." She turned back toward the window. "This is just too hard. Could you please leave?"

"Do you still sleep with the teddy bear?"

She swung around, confusion on her face. "Why?"

"I'm just curious."

"I could lie, but what's the use? Yes, the teddy bear is at Staci's apartment. I take it everywhere I go. It's my security blanket. I'm a medical professional and I cling to a teddy bear just to get me through the night."

Jude got to his feet, feeling stronger than he had in a very long time. "I know where our child is."

Paige's eyes opened wide and she took a step backward and reached for the counter for support. "How... how do you know that? Did Mrs. Carstairs tell you? Is the baby here in Texas? Oh!" She covered her mouth with shaky hands.

He took a couple steps toward her. "On the drive back to the ranch I kept thinking about my dad and what he told us about taking responsibility if we ever got a girl in trouble. How we should stand up and do the right thing and be a Rebel. A Rebel takes care of his own. I just felt I had let my father down and I had let my child down. I couldn't live with that. I went home and I told my mother what we'd done."

"You told your mother?"

He swallowed hard. "Yes, and it will forever be imprinted upon my brain. Something I thought would be extremely difficult was rather easy. She called her brother, Gabe, a lawyer, and we went back to the hospital."

"What?"

Speaking became difficult and he had to take several deep breaths. "I told the administrator of the hospital I wanted my baby. I was so afraid the adoptive parents had already left with it, but the baby had a cough and the doctor was checking it out."

"What?" Paige's face turned a pasty white.

"Since it was a private adoption, the administrator called the adoptive parents' attorney. I stuck to my guns. I wanted my kid. Gabe looked at the contract and it was my option to change my mind and I did. The attorney was ready to fight, saying I needed your consent to take the baby, but everything fell into place once we learned who the adoptive parents were."

"Who?"

"Mrs. Carstairs and her husband."

"What? No!" What little color was left on Paige's face drained away.

"She wanted your baby. That's why she gave you information that fed on your weaknesses and your fears. Once Gabe learned this, he threatened to file charges against her and her husband and to inform the Horseshoe school board of her actions concerning young girls in the school. They folded quickly. They brought the baby out and my mom and I took it home. Our baby has been with me ever since the day after the birth."

Chapter 6

"*What?*"

"Our child is with me, safe, loved and cared for. You don't have to wonder anymore."

The room swayed with an inky darkness and Paige reached out to grab the counter to keep from crumpling to the floor. Her body trembled.

She grappled with what Jude was saying and was vaguely aware that he had taken her shoulders and guided her to a chair.

"You...you went back. You went back. You went back." She couldn't stop saying the words, over and over, as if by doing so, they would be completely true and she could hold her child in her arms. She could see its face. She could...

Jude gently shook her. "Paige, stop it!"

She was on the brink of sinking into a hole so deep

she could never find her way out. But then she heard his voice. The voice that had always soothed and comforted her. She looked into his concerned eyes. "You have our child?"

He pulled a chair closer and sat facing her, within touching distance. "Yes."

So many questions rumbled around in her head like thunder, piercing and jarring, but one thing she had to know was at the forefront of her mind. "Your son is our…"

"Yes. His name is Zane."

"Zane." She said the word lovingly, rolling it around on her tongue, testing it, loving it. It was a strong name. A Rebel name. *Her* son. She began to tremble again and Jude reached out and clasped her hands.

"He's a bright, funny and happy kid. He's easygoing and it takes a lot to get him down. He gets frustrated with school because his IQ is the highest ever recorded in the school system, right above his mother's."

Tears slipped from her eyes and she didn't bother to brush them away. They were happy tears. Tears that warmed all the emotions churning through her like waves of glory.

"He loves horses, outer space, technology. He created the ranch's website and keeps it up-to-date. He has all kinds of videos on there and things that go over everyone else's heads. Once he learns something, he's learned it forever. His memory is phenomenal and sometimes it's frightening, the knowledge that he picks up. But inside, he's still a little boy."

"How…how did you manage with a baby?"

"It wasn't easy, but I figured if Falcon could do it, so could I. Of course, I couldn't have done it without my mother's help. She showed me how to change diapers, how to make formula, how to soothe him when he cried. After I got the hang of it, everything else became natural. Luckily, he didn't cry like Eden had. He was a happy baby and started sleeping through the night when he was two months old. I had his crib in my room and sometimes at night I'd touch him just to make sure he was still there and to make sure he was breathing."

"Oh." Without her even realizing it, a moan escaped her throat. She closed her eyes tight and then opened them quickly to see if she was dreaming. She had to be. This couldn't be true. Jude had their son. A son. She had a son.

"When he was a baby, Mom kept him in the office while I worked. We took turns working and looking after Zane. He was about four months old when I bought one of those carriers that strapped around my body and I started taking him with me on the ranch. I changed diapers under shade trees and he took naps on a blanket while we ate lunch. If he grew fussy or something, Grandpa would entertain him. He's the only person in the family who loves Grandpa's stories. He grew up on the rhythm of a horse. I guess that's why he loves horses so much."

"That must have been difficult, though."

"Yes, but my family helped and that's what made it easier. If it was really hot or really cold, one of us would stay behind with Zane at the house or the office. Quincy was a big help, too. He's Zane's second father and Zane confides a lot of stuff to Quincy that he won't tell me. I'm glad my brother is there for him."

"Sounds like he didn't even need a mother."

"But he missed having one."

Through all the wonderful things Jude was saying,

one thing kept piercing her happiness. She drew a quivery breath. "What have you told him about his mother?"

Jude pulled back and she missed the warmth of his hands on hers. She desperately needed it and wanted to snatch his hands back, but she remained still.

"The truth."

"The truth?" The trembling became intense and she struggled to catch her breath. "You told him we gave him away?"

"Yes."

"And that you went back to get him?"

"Yes."

"So…so he knows…he knows I gave him away." Each word struck her heart like a hammer and she fought to control her emotions, but she was losing the battle.

"He was about five when he started asking about his mother. He almost thought it was normal since Eden didn't have a mother, either, but he noticed kids in school had mothers, so he wanted to know where his was. I told him that you went away to school to become a doctor and I raised him."

"That's all you told him?"

"Until he was about nine. Then he wanted to know more and I told him the truth because I didn't want him to grow up and learn that I had lied to him. I was always honest and tried to answer his questions honestly."

She sank her teeth into her lower lip to keep from crying out. "He knows. He knows his mother gave him away. He knows…" Hard sobs shook her body. Uncontrollable sobs. After a moment, she gave up and just cried for everything that she had lost. Everything that she could never get back. Her son. Those precious years that she'd been holding a teddy bear, she should have been holding her son. It wasn't Mrs. Carstairs's fault. It was Paige's for being so gullible. No one was to blame but herself. Yet a part of her wanted to blame Jude. A part of her needed to blame Jude.

"Paige, come on. Stop this."

She lifted her head, choking back sobs. "How could you do that to me? How could you tell our son I gave him away? He'll never forgive me and I'll never forgive myself. How could you do that?"

"Paige…"

She jumped up and ran to the bathroom and slammed the door. She had to get away to sort out all the tumultuous emotions chugging through her. Outside the door she heard Staci's voice and knew she was back. Then she heard Luke's and Jude's and Jude was telling them about Zane. Her son.

Sitting on the edge of the bathtub, she cried as if there were no tomorrow. And for her, there wasn't. At least not one where she could live with herself and the mistakes that she'd made. She'd heard it said that life was about making mistakes and learning from them and moving on, but how would she get from point A to point B without having her heart ripped out once again?

Totally spent, she got up and rinsed her face with cool water. There were no towels, so she pulled up the bottom of her T-shirt and wiped her face. As she did, she took in the drab yellow bathroom that had once been bright yellow. The Southwestern yellow-and-orange-colored tile was atrocious and the years hadn't improved it.

When Paige was pregnant, she would sit in the bathtub and read stories to her baby. She'd had books in her backpack, and no one, not even Jude, had ever known that she read to their son every day. That should have given her a clue about her unstable emotions. Instead she'd told the baby how much she loved it and how she was going to give it a better life than she'd had. What a crock! How could a smart girl have been so dumb?

Taking a long steadying breath, she knew she had to face her past and do something she hadn't been able to do before. She had to face her son.

There was a tap at the door and she considered ignoring it, but that was no way to start the next phase of her life. She unlocked it and Jude came in. His handsome face was lined with worry, much as it had been when she'd told him she was pregnant.

"Are you okay?"

She pushed her hands up her face and drew a cool breath. "No. I'm never going to be okay."

"Paige…"

She stuck out her hand. "I don't want to hear any more. I want to meet my son."

"That's going to take time."

She narrowed her eyes. "What do you mean?"

"I have to prepare Zane and I need time for that."

That sounded reasonable. "Okay. Tomorrow will be fine."

Jude shook his head. "No. Zane is entered in a horse race on Saturday and I'm not going to tell him until after that. This race is important to him and if I tell him now, I don't know what he'll do or say. This is my call and you have to accept it."

"So you're only honest when it suits you."

His tanned skin paled. "As I said, this is my call. I'm doing what's best for my kid."

"He's my kid, too."

"I have full custody of Zane. You signed away your parental rights."

The statement was a blow to her chest. "How dare you say that to me."

The strong, stern lines of his face didn't flinch. "I'll let you know when I tell him. It's his decision whether to see you or not."

"How can you do this?"

"I'm doing what's best for my kid, as I have for the past twelve years. I put my life on hold for him and I'd do it over again in a heartbeat. That boy is my life and I will protect him with every breath I have. I'm not saying this to hurt you, only to protect Zane. This is going to be a blow and he needs time to adjust."

"I would never hurt him."

"Just seeing you is going to hurt him."

"So, what, Jude? You want me to go away?"

"I don't know." He swiped a hand through his hair in frustration. "You say you have two weeks before you have to go back to California. I'm just trying to figure out how Zane fits into your schedule."

She leaned back against the sink as reality intruded upon the wonderful news of her son. Once again she was faced with a monumental choice, but this time she was more mature and more able to handle it. This time she would not leave her son and Jude was not going to lay any kind of a guilt trip on her. Even though she might have deserved one.

She pushed away from the sink. "I'm not leaving until I see my son. Not until I can talk to him and beg his forgiveness. And not until I have some sort of peace of mind that he is happy. That's what's most important to me."

Jude sighed, as if he'd reached the end of his patience.

"Zane is focused on the race right now. That's all he thinks about and it's all he talks about. If I tell him now, it will shatter all his plans and I'm not doing that to him. After Saturday, I will tell him you want to see him and, as I said, it's his decision, not yours."

She looked into his dark eyes, the ones that used to be warm and encouraging and loving. Today they were not. They were cold and unforgiving and layered with something she'd never seen in them before. Anger.

"You blame me, don't you?"

"We can't go back and—"

"How many times did I ask you what we should do? What was your response, Jude? Every time?"

He looked down at his boots.

"You never said a word, Jude. You never said we had options or anything else. *You never said a word.*"

His gaze crashed into hers. "You had your whole life planned, and how was I supposed to shatter that? You wouldn't have listened to anything I had to say anyway. You listened to that stupid counselor more than you ever listened to me. So, yes, maybe I am laying some of the blame at your feet, but I also know a lot of it was my fault, too. I'm quiet by nature, but believe me, I've learned to speak up and I've learned to protect my son and I will do just that now."

"You…you…you…" She made a dive for him, and with her fists, she pummeled his chest, over and over. "How could you? How could you? I hate you. I hate you!"

He stood there taking the blows, not saying a word, and that made her even angrier.

Staci squeezed past Jude into the small bathroom and grabbed Paige's arms and pulled her away. "Stop it!" She looked at Jude. "You better go. This is getting out of control."

Jude walked out and she heard the front door slam. Staci gathered her into her arms. "Come on, kiddo. You're stronger than this."

"He won't…he won't…" she blubbered.

Staci took Paige's arm and led her to the kitchen and pushed her into a chair. "Take a deep breath." Staci rummaged in a bag on the table and pulled out bottled water. "Drink this."

Paige placed her shaky hands around the bottle and took a big gulp. It was cold, cooling the heated emotions inside her. She was so angry. That was so unlike her. After living for months in a homeless shelter, she'd vowed she would never lose control again. She'd just broken that vow.

Luke hovered near the door, looking at her as if she'd grown another head. Staci had the same expression on her face. What had she done?

Staci pulled a chair close to Paige. "Are you okay?"

Paige gripped the bottle and shook her head. "No."

"Just give Jude some time. This has been a shock to everyone, but you know where your child is now. He's with his father. That's good news."

"But Jude is never going to let me see him."

"Sure he will, but you have to decide what you're going to do. You have to go back to California to finish your residency. It's just like before."

Paige ran her thumb down the cold bottle and thought her life was like a never-ending circle of decisions. Bad decisions. Decisions that hurt. This was the ultimate one and she had already made it and she didn't understand why everyone kept pointing it out. Her son came first, this time. All the anger in her eased at the thought. Jude would not keep her away from Zane. Nothing would.

"His name is Zane," she said for some reason, maybe just to hear it.

"I know, kiddo."

"He's going to hate me." She had to say that, too. Maybe to hear someone else say it wasn't so. She got the answer she wanted.

"No. Kids forgive easily. Just stay positive."

"I just want to see his face. Touch him. Just to see that he's real."

Staci reached over and hugged her. "You will. You just have to be patient."

Something Jude had said triggered a thought. "Where's my phone?"

Staci pointed to the counter and Paige got up and brought it back to the table, touching the keypad on the screen.

"What are you doing?"

"Jude said Zane does the website for the ranch. I'm hoping there might be a picture of him on there. Here it is. Rebel Ranch. Hereford cattle." There were pictures of red cattle with white faces. Heifers for sale. Bulls for sale. Hay for sale. A link reading Rebel Family caught her eye and she clicked it. A picture of all the brothers with Miss Kate and Grandpa Abe in the center came up. No kids. Her heart sank. But then she saw another tab. Family Photos. Grandchildren. She clicked it and her heart almost pounded out of her chest when she saw Eden, a very grown-up Eden, sitting in a comfy chair holding a baby, and a boy was sitting on the chair's arm. Paige tapped the photo until she'd zoomed in on the boy in jeans, boots and a white shirt. He was smiling. Happy. He favored Jude. Her son.

She swallowed the lump in her throat and couldn't take her eyes from the screen. She'd wondered so many times what her child would look like and the photo eclipsed every thought, every picture, in her head. He was perfect. Just like his father.

She tapped, edited, clipped and refocused.

"What are you doing?" Staci asked.

"Making it my screen saver. I want to go into Temple to get some copies made." She got to her feet and headed for the door. Luke caught her before she could open it.

"Sis, take a moment and think about this. Just take a deep breath. You're turning back into that scared, frightened young girl and I know you're not her. You're stronger now. Act like it. You don't need copies of pictures. You need to get your second wind and regroup and wait for Jude. He will not let you down."

A tear leaked from her eye again and another followed. She held on to Luke as the walls that she had built around her heart began to crumble. "I'm falling apart, Luke. Please hold me. Don't let that happen."

Staci ran and wrapped her arms around them. "We're here for you."

"Don't let go!" she cried, and the Wheeler kids stood strong against the waves of despair that rolled over Paige. She had something that she'd never had before. She had strength. She had family. Nothing was going to break her again.

She would wait forever to hold her son. And she would wait for his father, too. Before her healing could even begin, Jude had to forgive her.

And she had to forgive herself.

Chapter 7

As Jude drove over the cattle guard, rain pelted his truck. He'd been so engrossed in his thoughts that he hadn't even noticed the dark clouds rolling in. By the time he reached the house, the storm vented its full fury with sheets of rain punctuated by lightning and earsplitting thunder.

He jumped out of his truck and ran into the house. In the utility room, he removed his hat, shook water from it and laid it on the counter to dry. Opening cabinet doors, he found a towel and wiped his face and dabbed at his wet shirt. Since it was raining, his brothers would be in soon. They couldn't work in the rain, so there was no need for him to saddle up and join them. Glancing at the wrought-iron clock on the wall, he saw it was after two. It had been a stressful morning and the time had flown.

He walked through the house to the den, not bothering to turn on a light. He didn't need one. He was still dealing with all the turmoil inside him. Sinking onto the sofa, he took a deep breath, hardly believing that he'd lost his temper with Paige. He'd said things he regretted, but he was fighting for his son. So many emotions warred inside him and he was desperately trying to make sense of it all.

The back door opened. Boots stomped. It wasn't his mother, so it had to be one of his brothers. Phoenix came into the room, dry as could be. Evidently, he'd had his slicker with him.

"Is the electricity off?" Phoenix asked, sliding into a leather chair across from Jude.

"No. I just don't need a light. Is everybody quitting for the day?"

"I'm sure with all this rain, but I had to go with the feed-store fertilizer truck to show the guy where to fertilize the coastal hay in the far west pasture. It's not doing as well as the other fields and Falcon thought it needed a boost. We got it on the ground before the rain. Now as long as it doesn't wash away…"

Jude stared down at his hands, seeing Paige's face, her tears, and his stomach cramped.

"Elias said he's going to kick my ass because I get all the easy jobs. He says I'm Mom's favorite. But, you know, I might just kick his ass for saying that."

"Have you seen Elias's muscles lately?"

"Yeah, how is that possible? He never works out and after work he spends all his time down at Rowdy's. You can't get those kinds of muscles lifting a beer can."

"He does the work of two men. Have you seen him drive a nail into a post?"

"Bam." Phoenix drove a fist into his palm. "One

whack and it's done. Takes me two to three tries before the nail goes in."

"Me, too." A small tug at the corners of his mouth, and he found that odd since mirth was the last emotion in his body.

"Hey, hey, look at that." Phoenix pointed. "I made you smile."

The back door opened again and his brothers filed into the living room, followed by Grandpa. Jude didn't want to deal with all of them right now and he had the urge to run as far away as he could. From himself. From all the heartache that was to come.

His brothers sat on the large leather sectional sofa and Grandpa made Phoenix get up so he could take the comfortable chair.

"It went that bad, huh?" Quincy was the first to speak.

Jude stared down at his clasped hands between his knees. "I lost my temper."

"Come on, Jude. You never lose your temper."

"I did this morning with Paige. I said things I regret, but I had to say them."

"What happened?"

His throat felt as if he'd swallowed a pinecone. "I told her about Zane and she wants to meet him."

"And you don't want her to?"

Jude unclenched his hands and told his brothers what Paige had told him. "She's had it rough and I didn't want to hurt her, but Zane comes first with me. He's so excited about the race and if I tell him now, it's going to take all the excitement away. I don't want to hurt him, either."

"That's a tough decision," Falcon said. "It took Eden a long time to warm up to Leah, but once the ice was broken, it's been a lovefest ever since."

"This is different, though. She has three months left on her residency and she goes back to California in two weeks. What kind of relationship can they build in two weeks?"

"You know," Falcon continued, "it took me a long time to forgive Leah and I sense you're feeling similar emotions. I never could understand why she couldn't come home until I got to know what her life was like in Houston without me and Eden."

Jude jumped to his feet as Falcon pointed out the reason for his anger. "All she had to do was call and I would have flown out to get her or sent money for her to come home. All she had to do was pick up the damn phone, but instead she spent months in a homeless shelter, depressed and lonely. All it would've taken was a phone call. Man, that just gets me."

"Get a grip, boy," Grandpa said. "I always preached to you boys about finding wives, but all this drama is a little hard on my heart. You just make it plain to her that Zane stays here."

"You've always been honest with Zane," Egan spoke up. "If he finds out from someone else in Horseshoe that his mother is here, he's going to wonder why you didn't tell him first."

"He's never asked her name, so he doesn't know it."

"Don't kid yourself, Jude," Egan told him. "Zane's birth certificate is on file at the courthouse, digital now, and with Zane's computer skills, I'll bet every penny I have he's already looked it up. He hasn't asked, because he already knows."

Jude ran a hand through his hair. "Oh, man, I hadn't thought of that."

"Every kid is curious about their parents, and in my

humble opinion, I think every kid has a right to meet them at least once in their lifetime."

Everyone stared at Elias. It wasn't like him to offer advice.

"What?" Elias lifted an eyebrow. "I have opinions and some of them are pretty damn good."

Paxton slapped him on the back. "And you're stone-cold sober?"

"Thanks, everybody," Jude said. "But I have to make this decision on my own and it's not easy."

Falcon got to his feet. "We're all here if you need anything, but it's your decision. None of us are going to interfere with that." He turned toward the door. "Now, it would be nice if we got all the tractors and trucks and trailers greased and oiled while the weather is bad."

Elias grabbed Phoenix around the neck. "I know someone who's going to get a little axle grease on his hands and Mama's not here to protect him."

"Come on, Elias. We all know you can pulverize me, but why go to all that trouble. I'm really a nice guy and I fetch really well."

"Good, you can fetch me a beer while we're changing the oil in the trucks and tractors."

His brothers trooped out of the room, but Quincy and Grandpa lingered. "What time does Zane get home from school?" Quincy asked.

"Rachel's bringing him home about four. I got called to the school this morning because there was an incident with Dudley McCray. They got into a thing over the race and Dudley ended up knocking Zane down."

"Did he get hurt?"

"No. Didn't even hurt his pride. He's so hyped up on

this race I'm not even sure he's going to hear me if I talk about his mother."

Quincy eyed him. "You don't want to tell him, do you?"

Jude heaved a sigh. "It's not that, but once I tell him, our lives will change. Everything will change. All the joy and happiness that's in his eyes right now will be gone. He won't be a little boy anymore. He'll be a twelve-year-old dealing with some serious issues. I want to protect him from that, but I know I can't. This is what life is about. And it's tearing me apart that Zane is going to feel the pain of Paige's and my decision of long ago."

"But he'll also feel the joy of his dad doing the right thing," Grandpa pointed out.

"Thanks, Grandpa."

Grandpa patted Jude's back. "You've always been a good kid, just like Zane, but don't you let that woman get her claws into him. That's my last word."

Quincy took Grandpa's arm. "Let's let Jude figure this out for himself." As they walked toward the kitchen, Quincy glanced back with a worried look in his eyes. No one was a better brother than Quincy. But now Jude had to step away from the support of his family and determine what to do based on what was right for his son. In the process, he would lose a piece of his heart. But he was a man now and he would handle it better than he had before Zane was born. Because along the way, he'd learned to speak up. And tonight he would say things he'd thought he never would. That was what fathers did.

That night after supper Zane talked and talked about Bear and the race and Dudley McCray. Jude's mom listened with avid interest, but Jude was thinking ahead to when he and Zane were alone.

"You have homework?" Jude asked his son.

"Nah, Dad. I just had to read a book and I already read it. We'll discuss it in class tomorrow."

"Finish putting dishes in the dishwasher and then go up and take a shower. I want to talk to you for a minute."

Zane's shoulders slumped. "Aw, Dad, I'm okay. We don't have to talk about Dudley anymore. It's over. He didn't hurt me or anything. He just thinks he's a big deal. That's all. I want to ride Bear one more time before bed."

"No. It's dark and you've already ridden Bear for the day."

"Uh-oh, Grandma. I think a blue norther just blew in."

"Go upstairs, Zane."

"Okay, Dad. I'm gone." He darted out of the room.

His mother gave him a dark look. "You're not hiding your feelings very well."

Jude carried his plate to the sink. "I know. I'm nervous and finding this difficult."

"Just calm down and everything will go fine."

"I just hate to shatter his world, but I have to tell him before someone else does."

His mother leaned against the counter, wiping her hands on a dish towel. "I've always known she'd regret her decision, but I never guessed she'd regret it as soon as she got to California. To give a baby away is a traumatic thing and I can sympathize with her feelings because I know Darlene Wheeler was a terrible mother. She inflicted so much mental pain on Paige and that's unforgivable. But it's time for all the hurting to stop, son, and for you and Paige to be as honest as possible with Zane. That's the only way you're going to salvage anything from this. And the only way any of you can go forward."

"I know, Mom. I'm going up to talk to him now." Jude

took his time going up the stairs, rehearsing words in his head. But none of them were right. Somehow he had to find a way to tell his son about his mother.

He went through his bedroom and bath into Zane's room. His son sat in the middle of his bed in his underwear and a T-shirt, clicking away on his laptop.

"Want to play a game?" Zane asked.

"Did you take a shower?"

"Yeah, Dad. I'm fast." Jude remembered those days when Zane was little and his bath took about one minute. His face would still be dirty and his fingernails filthy. Jude would have to make him take another bath and scrub clean. Zane hated taking the time. He wanted to be active, doing something else.

"Do I need to look behind your ears?"

"Come on, Dad. I've outgrown that." Zane's eyes went back to the laptop. "Let's play a game."

"No, I need to talk to you first."

"Ah, Dad. I'm okay. Dudley's just a lot of hot air. You don't have to worry about me."

Jude sat on the bed, facing his son. "It's not about Dudley or the McCrays. This is something else."

"Oh." Zane's eyes were big and round, and Jude could almost see the thoughts running through his head. "Does it have something to do with the funeral you went to this morning?"

"Yes." His son had just made it a little easier.

"Do I know this person?"

"No."

"But it made you sad?"

Jude took a moment, not wanting to be cruel. "I hadn't seen this person in a long time so, no, it didn't make me sad."

"Who was it?"

The room became so quiet Jude could hear himself breathing. He swallowed and forced the words out. "Your grandmother."

"Nah. My grandma's downstairs, probably getting ready to watch television. You…" Zane stopped as he figured it out quickly. "You mean my mother's mother?"

"Yes."

"Was *she* there?"

"Yes, your mother was there."

The light in Zane's eyes went out almost as if he'd flipped a switch. "Did you talk to her?"

"Yes. She's going to be here about two weeks and she would like to meet you."

"No!" Zane threw the laptop on the bed, jumped up and ran into the bathroom. Jude heard him lock the door.

He took a long breath and went to the bathroom door. "Zane, open the door. We need to talk."

Silence. Complete unnerving silence.

"Zane, I'm not going to make you do anything you don't want to. Open the door."

Jude ran out the bedroom door, into his bedroom and to the bathroom. It was empty. Zane was gone. He rushed downstairs. His mother was flipping through the channels on the television.

"Did Zane come through here?"

His mother frowned. "No. I haven't seen him. Why?"

"I told him his mother was in town and wanted to see him and he ran. He has to be somewhere in the house."

"I'll help you look."

He and his mother searched every room and closet but Zane was nowhere to be found. Fear lay in Jude's belly like sour milk and he fought the sick feeling. He had to find his son.

"I'm going to check the barns. Stay here just in case he comes out when I leave. He might talk to you."

"I will. Don't worry, son. He has to be here somewhere."

Jude thought the same thing as he hurried to the big barn, but Zane wasn't there. Then he dashed over to Quincy's barn. Quincy and Jenny were coming out of the small trailer they lived in while they were working on the new house. Quincy had on shorts and a T-shirt and Jenny wore only a T-shirt. Her brown hair was tousled, as was Quincy's. It was clear they were in their own private world.

"Sorry to bother you, but have you seen Zane?"

"No," Quincy replied. "He went to the house a long time ago. What happened?"

"I told him his mother was in town and he ran away. I can't find him. I'm going to check your barn."

"Go ahead."

"We'll help," Jenny offered.

They begin searching the horse stalls and Jude's heart stopped as he saw a small figure crouched in a corner of Bear's stall. He walked to where Quincy was searching.

"I've found him. He's in Bear's stall. Could you give me some time with him, please?"

"Do you want me to—?"

"No," Jude stopped him. "I have to talk to him and no one else."

"Sure. We'll be in the trailer if you need anything."

"Thanks. Would you call Mom and let her know I found him?"

Quincy nodded and they left the barn. Jude took a long breath and went back to the stall. Quietly, he opened the half door and went inside. Bear neighed and moved around in agitation. Jude stroked his face to calm him and then made his way to the corner where his son sat crouched, almost as if he wanted to disappear.

He eased to the hay beside him, not saying a word. Zane sat with his knees drawn up, his forehead resting on his knees, and his hands were folded on the top of his head, blocking his ears as if he didn't want to hear anything anyone had to say. Jude searched for words to ease his son's pain. He went with the truth, as he always did.

"I love you and I will never force you to do anything you don't want to. I hope you understand that."

Silence followed. Zane didn't even move, huddled in the corner in nothing but his underwear and T-shirt. The sight of his young son hurting tore at Jude's heart.

"When you turn eighteen, people say you're an adult, but that's not quite true. You're somewhere between a kid and an adult and it's a precarious place to be because nothing in life makes any sense. You try to make good decisions and hope for the best. Your mother and I were still kids who were faced with grown-up decisions. I've told you some of what happened back then, but now I'm going to tell you the whole truth. It's not pretty and your mother and I are both to blame for what happened."

The barn was dark now and the only light Quincy had on provided little illumination. That was just as well. What Jude had to say he'd rather say in the dark so he could get it all out without breaking down.

Zane kept sitting in the same position, giving the impression that he was trying to pretend Jude wasn't there.

"Your mother and I had a special relationship. I had just lost my dad and she had a mother who was verbally abusive. She would tell her that she was ugly and she would never amount to anything. Every day she heaped criticism after criticism upon her. Some days she'd break out in a rash and scratch until she drew blood. It was very stressful for me to watch and I vowed I would help her any way I could to get out of that house. Your mother worked very hard in school and she got the grades she needed to get a good scholarship for premed. She was happy and I was happy for her. She would get out of Horseshoe and have a life away from a woman who denigrated her every day of her life."

Bear neighed again as if he were annoyed that someone was in his stall. Jude ignored him as he tried to tell Zane what had happened back then.

"Then your mother found out she was pregnant and we didn't know what to do. I wanted her to have her dream and to get away from her mother. I wanted her to have a better life. One of the counselors in school spoke to her about adoption and I never said a word. When she asked me time and time again about what to do, I never spoke up. That was my fault. I should've said I didn't want to give away my kid. But I was caught between my feelings for her and the feelings for my unborn child. It was a rough time because we kept the pregnancy a secret. We both were struggling with our feelings as we continued to try to figure out the best thing to do for our child. You know the rest. But I don't think you know how your mother really felt at that time. I didn't know what she was really going through, because I was too wrapped up in my own feelings. I should've talked more. I should've done a lot of things that I didn't do. I blame myself and…"

Zane threw himself at Jude, sobbing into his chest. "Why didn't she want me?"

That heartbroken question took the breath from Jude's lungs. It burned all the way to his soul and he would remember this moment forever when he would have to account for his decision during that time. And when he would have to account for staying quiet when he should've spoken up. He wrapped his arms around his son and held on with all his strength, trying to convey to him how much he loved him and how much he would always regret that day.

But Jude didn't know if he had enough strength to endure breaking his little boy's heart.

Chapter 8

"Why didn't she want me?"

Zane wailed into Jude's chest and his heart splintered into jagged sharp pieces that could never be repaired. He held his son, trying to soothe him.

"Shh. Shh," Jude cooed, as if his son were three years old. When his sobs lessened, Jude said, "She did want you. She was just confused about so many things and the counselor gave her some really bad advice. But above everything, she wanted you to have a better life than she ever had. She regretted that decision later."

"She...did?" Zane hiccupped into Jude's chest.

"Yes." He told his son everything Paige had told him. He wanted Zane to know what had happened. "She couldn't get on with her life, because she was grieving for her baby she'd left in Texas."

"You...you came back. Why didn't she?"

"It wasn't that easy for her. She was so far away, struggling to survive when she lost her scholarship and her dorm. It wasn't easy for her to live in a homeless shelter."

Among the horses and the scent of manure and hay, a meaningful silence intruded. Zane sat up and wiped away tears with the backs of his hands. "I don't want to talk about it anymore. I'm sorry for what she went through, but I don't want to see her."

"That's your decision, but I want to point out this might be your only chance to meet your mother."

Zane shook his head. "No. I don't want to."

It wasn't like his son to be so stubborn, but Jude wasn't going to push him. He needed time to adjust to the fact that his mother was nearby.

"Do you know your mother's name?"

"Yes. I looked it up on the computer a long time ago."

"You didn't say anything. I would've told you if you had asked."

"I didn't want you to think I wanted to see her, because I don't. I was just curious."

It was just as Egan had said. Every little boy wanted to know who his mother was and Zane was no exception.

Jude stood. "We better go to the house. Your grandmother is worried."

Zane got up, too, and Jude was reminded that his son wore only his underwear and a T-shirt. He squatted. "Hop on my back. You don't have any shoes on and it's dark."

His son did as instructed and Jude placed his arms under Zane's legs and walked out of the barn. Zane buried his face in Jude's neck and Jude knew his son was still upset. He hadn't done that in years.

To keep Quincy and Jenny from fretting, Jude

knocked on their trailer door and then strolled toward the house. He didn't want to talk, because he knew Zane wasn't ready. He did the same thing at the house, going up the stairs without talking to his mother. She could see that Zane was okay and that was enough. Once Zane was in bed, he'd tell her how he'd reacted.

Zane slid off his back in the bedroom and asked, "Dad, did you get my number for the race?"

Zane seemed to wipe the events of the night from his mind, almost as if they hadn't occurred. He was in denial and Jude would let him get away with that, for now. But he had to face the fact that he had a mother and she wasn't going to go away.

"Yeah. It's in my truck."

"What's my number?" Zane looked at him with big inquisitive eyes and Jude wondered how he could shove all those emotions down inside him. Then he knew. His son was just like him.

"It's twenty-nine."

Zane raised his fist in the air. "I knew it. That's a lucky number for me. Oh, yeah. The race is looking better."

Where was the sobbing boy of a few minutes ago? Jude's head was spinning, but he would leave things alone…for the moment.

"Wash your feet before you get into bed."

"Okay, Dad. Can I go get my number out of your truck?"

"You can get it in the morning. It's time for bed. You have school tomorrow."

A few minutes later Zane was under the covers and Jude stood by his bedside, wondering if he should say something or do something. He wanted to help his son, but he didn't know how. He just didn't want him to be hurt any more than he was. Feeling helpless, he walked toward the door.

"Dad."

He turned back.

"I'm okay."

But Jude knew he wasn't. It was a whole lot of heartache for his little boy and it was going to explode into more heartache than Zane could handle. That was what worried Jude.

"'Night, son."

Jude stood outside Zane's door and knew the heartache extended to him. He now had to tell Paige that her son didn't want to see her.

Paige got through the night with the help of her sister and her brother. She didn't understand why she was leaning on them now when she couldn't before. Back then she'd put up so many barriers and no one could get through but Jude. He'd been her whole life, but the Jude of long ago was no more. He was a man now and looked at her in an entirely different way. There was no love, hope or desire in his eyes. Just a resignation that they shared the connection of a little boy they had created.

The next morning she woke up feeling much better and stronger. She called Ms. Whitman to tell her about Zane.

"That's lovely, dear. I'm so happy for you." Ms. Whitman was in her sixties and loving and caring to a fault. She had taken in so many people over the years. Paige had been one of them.

"Thank you. I'm so excited and worried at the same time but hopeful that I'll get to meet my son, my baby."

"I will keep you in my prayers."

"Thank you. Will you do me a favor, please?"

"Anything, dear."

"There's a box in the bottom drawer of my dresser. Would you mind shipping it to me?"

"Sure."

Paige gave her Staci's address and asked that she send it overnight. As she laid her phone on the bed, she missed the warmth and comfort of Ms. Whitman's home. It had saved her from drowning in her own misery.

She then called Dr. Spencer to let her know she would be away longer than two weeks. Dr. Spencer was a well-known doctor in obstetrics and Paige was lucky to get a residency in her medical clinic. She was very understanding, but Paige knew she had to get back to her residency and soon.

After that, she called her friend Thea and told her the good news. Thea advised her to go slow and not to expect too much. Paige thought about that as she dressed and went into the kitchen to join her sister and brother.

Luke and Staci were drinking coffee at the kitchen table. They both looked at her with worried eyes.

She put a French vanilla K-Cup in the Keurig and turned to face them. "I'm fine. Really. I just lost it yesterday, but last night I realized what a gift I've been given. Soon I will see my son. I just have to be patient."

"We've been talking," Luke said as Paige sat at the table. "With everything that has happened, maybe it would be best if we hired someone to paint the house."

"I need something to do while I wait for Jude and I like to paint."

Luke and Staci exchanged glances.

"Don't do that. I'm fine, and a little work will be good for me." She took a sip of her coffee. "Maybe it will exorcise some of those bad memories."

"Let it go, kiddo. I have and I know Luke has. It was

bad, but we all got through it and we're all stronger.
Now we need to smile and be happy and just enjoy life."

"I'm trying," Paige murmured. But she wondered
if the memories would always be there in her dreams.
Memories of her mother screaming at her. Memories of
scratching her skin until she drew blood. Memories of
the nausea churning in her stomach until she threw up.
Would they always be there just beyond the realm of
happiness, pulling her back?

On the way to Horseshoe, Paige kept her phone in
her lap and occasionally touched the screen to see her
son's face. It was a small thing, but it would get her
through the day.

By midmorning they were busy working. Luke was
scraping the trim on the outside of the house and she and
Staci were taping the baseboards so they could paint.
Staci had chosen a wheat color for the whole house. It
would give it a fresh look. Staci had Miranda Lambert
on the iPhone singing away as they wielded the paint
rollers over the walls.

Even through the music, Paige heard the knock at
the door. She carefully laid her roller in the pan with a
trembling hand. "That has to be Jude."

Staci followed suit. "I'll go help Luke scrape to give
you some privacy."

Paige took a deep breath and went to the front door.
Jude stood there tall and handsome and her heart did
a happy dance across her ribs. That wonderful feeling
when she saw him hadn't changed. It had been that way
since she was seventeen.

"Come in," she said, and walked into the kitchen,
queasy from anticipating what Jude was going to say.
She turned to face him. "Did you tell him?"

Jude looked down at the hat in his hand. "Yes."

"And…"

He raised his dark eyes to hers and from that one glance her heart fell to the pit of her stomach. "I'm sorry, but he doesn't want to see you."

"No, Jude, please." She'd promised herself she wouldn't cry or lose it again, but the words created another crack in her already shaky emotional facade. Tears trickled from her eyes and she was powerless to stop them or the tremors that ran through her body. She had to get a grip.

"It's his decision and I'm not going to push him."

Tears continued to roll down her face.

"Paige, don't do this. He's twelve years old and dealing with a lot. The fact is he's a lot like me. When he's faced with a difficult situation, he shuts down, but give him time."

"I… I don't blame him, but I was hoping, that's all. I gave him away and I can't expect him to get over that because I'm in town."

"I'm sorry I lost my temper yesterday," Jude said unexpectedly.

She wiped away a tear. "Me, too. Our emotions got the best of us."

"They always did."

"Yeah." She remembered hot kisses and passionate embraces that took them away to a special place with just the two of them. The outside world hadn't mattered. All they'd needed was each other. Feeling weak, she sank into a chair. "Tell me about our son."

Jude took a seat next to her and placed his hat on the table. "As I told you, he's normally a happy kid. One day he's doing all this technical stuff on the computer and the next day he's playing trucks with baby John. He's just a little boy who's dealing with a lot of pain right now. I'll give him a couple of days and then I'll talk to him again. But you have to understand, it's his decision."

She gripped her hands in her lap. "I know. I would just love to see him. I'm going to stay longer than two weeks and I'm hoping during that time he might change his mind."

"You're staying longer?" There was doubt in Jude's voice.

"Yes. I still can't get over the fact that you've had our son for years."

He shifted nervously. "I'm not going to apologize for that."

"I don't want you to. You did the right thing. Our son is not with the Carstairs but with a big loving family. His real family." How she wished she could be a part of it.

Jude looked around the drab kitchen. "So you're going to do the painting?"

"Yes. I need something to do while I wait for Zane."

"Paige…"

"You don't have to say anything. It's something I have to do for my own peace of mind. I realize he may never forgive me and—" she stared into his eyes "—you might not, either."

"As two confused teenagers, we did the best we could and I think we both need to move forward now. Your life is in California and mine is here. We're worlds apart, but we have a little boy who needs our utmost attention and patience."

"You really have grown up."

"I had to."

"I believe a lot of the old Jude is still there." She reached out and touched his chest. "Your big heart will never change."

He caught her hand and held it, his calluses rubbing against her soft skin. She remembered that, too. His touch was always so tender and gentle and invited more and more.

"I loved you so much back then." The words were hoarse and seemed to come from deep within him.

"Me, too." She squeezed his hand. "All those emotions sidetracked us into making bad choices. Or should I say, it sidetracked me into making a bad choice. I can't believe I trusted Mrs. Carstairs."

"No matter what Mrs. Carstairs said, we should have gotten it right, Paige. I should've asked you to marry me and we should have raised Zane together no matter what kind of future was in store for you. That was our obligation as parents and we failed him."

She licked her suddenly dry lips. "Why did you never ask me?"

"I should have. I'm not sure why I never did. But I think I didn't want you to feel trapped like you were with your mother. I wanted you to be free and I thought I could give our son to a loving family and walk away. I couldn't."

"My honorable Jude." She slipped onto his lap and wrapped her arms around his neck and held on for dear life. "I'm sorry I screwed up."

He kissed her cheek and the world stood still as she felt his skin against hers once again. "We have to stop placing blame. It's over, Paige, and we'll never get those feelings back again."

A pain shot through her as she realized everything she'd lost. Her throat clogged with words and she just kept holding him as if somehow she could instill his warmth into her cold body. But, as he said, their time was over. The sadness of it all still lingered, though.

She slid off his lap with as much dignity as she could manage. "Could you please let me know if Zane changes his mind?"

Jude reached for his hat and got to his feet. "Right now his mind is on the race on Saturday. After that, I'll talk to him again. I'm not promising anything, though."

"I know this is asking a lot, but do you have any pictures that I could look at just to see him as he was growing up?"

He put his hat on his head with a familiar gesture she remembered well, with swagger and bold masculinity. "Yeah, I've taken a bunch over the years. I'll drop them by for you."

"Thank you."

He nodded and walked toward the door and soon she heard him drive away. Polite strangers, that was who they were now. That was more than she'd hoped for.

"Paige."

She swung around to see Staci standing behind her. "How did it go?"

She swallowed the constriction in her throat. "Zane doesn't want to see me."

"Oh, kiddo, I'm sorry." Staci hugged her and it was a comfort she needed. How could she have stayed away from her sister and brother for so long?

"It's okay. I'm going to keep waiting until I see his face." It was really all she could do now.

"Was…uh…Jude still angry?"

Paige tucked her hair behind her ear. "No. We actually had a nice conversation. Just seeing him brings back so many wonderful times and so many bad ones. It's like I'm balancing on a seesaw. One minute I'm up and the next I'm down. But if I've learned anything in the past thirteen years, it's that we are shaped by the decisions we make. They either make us stronger or we sink into a deep hole of despair. I've been there and I'm not going back. I'm going to fight to see my son and I'm going to continue fighting until Jude forgives me."

"He was there, too, Paige. You're shouldering all the blame and that's not fair."

She slung an arm across Staci's shoulder. "Let's go slick some paint on the wall and turn up the music so we can block out the world." *And my thoughts.* That was what Paige wanted—to not think anymore, to just work until she was tired. Maybe tomorrow or the next day or the next, Jude would come to say that their son wanted to see her. That was what she waited for now. The day her decision would come full circle and she would have to explain to a little boy what an eighteen-year-old girl was thinking at that time. And she prayed she could do it without breaking down.

Chapter 9

Jude perched on the pipe fence and watched Zane race Bear to the cattle guard, around his mom's house and then all the way to Grandpa's and back to Quincy's barn. As he was watching, he thought of Paige. Over the years he'd managed to push her to the never-never part of his brain, but now she was in present-time reality. And he couldn't deny some of those old feelings were still there. They'd shared a lot and he didn't expect those emotions to just disappear.

Tomorrow he'd try to get some pictures to her. Maybe they would ease her pain. But he would go slow and make sure his heart wasn't involved this time. Once was enough for him.

Zane stopped Bear in front of him. "What do you think, Dad?" His voice was breathless with excitement and his eyes sparkled.

Jude jumped off the fence and rubbed Bear's face. "Very good. How's the saddle working?" Jude had made him a lighter saddle to get rid of some weight.

"Great. I can lean forward on Bear's neck and cut through the wind—" Zane demonstrated, angling his body close to Bear's neck "—like a jockey."

"Bear is sweaty. It's time to rub him down and feed him."

Zane slid from the saddle. "Okay. And, Dad, the protein feed you bought is really working. Bear has a lot more stamina."

Quincy and Jenny were working on the house, so they had the barn to themselves. Zane took care of his horse like an adult. He'd learned to do that early. When he was about three, he'd stand on a bale of hay to brush his horse Venus, otherwise known as Venie. As he grew, he'd wanted a faster horse. His boy loved fast horses.

After removing the saddle, Zane used a hose to cool down Bear. Then he rubbed him with a sponge and a brush. His son was not afraid of work. He'd learned that from Jude. Once the horse was fed and safely in his stall, they headed for the house and supper. Not once did Zane mention his mother. He'd give him another couple of days before bringing Paige up again.

The next morning over breakfast Zane was his usual happy self, talking about the race to his grandmother, Falcon and Quincy. Grandpa and Elias came in and Zane started all over again. Nowhere in his bubbly son was there a sign of sadness, but Jude knew it lurked just below the surface.

A car honked and Zane grabbed his backpack. "Gotta go. Aunt Rachel's here." He usually ran out the door hollering, "Bye, Dad." But today he ran to Jude and hugged him before dashing out. At twelve, Zane had stopped doing the hugging thing except at bedtime. He was a boy and it was embarrassing, Zane had said when he was about eleven.

Jude's brothers and his mom looked at him, but he had nothing to say. He wasn't asking for advice, either. Zane was his son and he would handle the problem. He took his plate and cup to the sink and headed for the back door.

On his way to the office, so many thoughts fought for dominance in his mind. The fact that Zane had hugged him showed that his son was feeling insecure and needed to be close to Jude. And Jude would be there for him every step of the way. Even if it meant standing between him and his mother.

At the office, Falcon talked about what needed to be done that day. After the rain, they had to wait to get a cutting on the coastal in the south pasture. They had hundreds of acres of coastal that would feed their cattle during the winter months. They sold hay, too. Hay baling would continue during the summer and into September. It was dirty, sweaty work, but their hay was always in high demand.

The brothers saddled up for the day to check the cattle. Jude and Elias went south, while Egan and Quincy rode north. Phoenix and Paxton took the east pastures. Falcon and Jericho went west. The ranch had hundreds of heads of cattle that needed attention on a daily basis.

Jude noted a lot of new baby calves on the ground. Springtime was a time of birth and during roundup they spent days tagging and branding the new ones. A heifer darted out of the bushes and two coyotes were fast on her heels.

Jude turned his horse in that direction and rode at a quick pace to distract the coyotes. Once the coyotes saw Jude, they sprinted away into the woods. The heifer kept running, frightened. Jude finally saw the cause of the coyotes' interest. A water sac was bulging out of the rear of the heifer. Then he saw two feet. She was having a problem giving birth.

"Elias," he hollered, and drew his rope looped across the saddle horn. He kept pace with the heifer and threw his rope when he was close enough. It landed perfectly over her head and Jude yanked the rope as his horse backed up, holding her tight. Jude dismounted and eased toward the heifer.

"Calm down. No one's going to hurt you. Calm down. That's it." The heifer was breathing heavily and didn't have much strength left. He reached her and stroked her head, talking soothingly. That was when he noticed the heifer's stomach cramping. He'd thought the calf was dead and they would have to pull it. But she was still in labor. The coyotes had interrupted her.

"Easy. Easy." He removed the rope, knowing the heifer didn't have any energy left for flight.

Elias rode up. "We'll have to pull it."

"No. She's still in labor. Coyotes thought she was an easy defenseless target. I have to get her to lie down."

Elias dismounted. "Good luck with that."

But Mother Nature gave him a hand. The heavy cramps brought the heifer to her knees and she sank to the grass. Jude knelt by her, continuing to speak in soothing tones.

Elias inspected the calf. "This is a done deal. That calf is dead and we have to pull it."

"Just give her a few minutes to calm down. She's still cramping."

"Jude, we have other things to do besides watch this heifer all morning."

Jude raised his head and looked at his impatient brother. "This calf is alive, I'm telling you. Are you gonna help me or are you gonna complain?"

Elias knelt in the grass. "You and Quincy got a double dose of sensitivity."

"Shut up. Your loud voice is disturbing her."

"Well, pardon me."

Jude gave him another look and Elias fell silent.

He could see the calf's feet, still in the same position. All the while, he kept rubbing the heifer and talking softly. "Easy. Easy. Just stay calm. Come on, a couple more pushes." But there was no movement.

"The calf is dead," Elias said again.

"She might need a little help." Jude got to his feet. "Come over here and rub along her back."

"You've got to be kidding. I only rub two-legged females."

"You're an ass." Jude bent down, his boots firmly planted on the ground, reached for the calf's front feet and gently tugged. A nose appeared.

In the meantime, Elias changed his mind and was rubbing the cow, trying to be supportive, which was almost comical. "Okay, this is it. Push."

Almost on cue, the heifer pushed and the calf came out in a big swoosh of water, mucus and blood. Most of it on Jude's boots. He stepped back and watched the wet matted form and waited for it to move. *Please move.*

Elias looked over. "It's dead. I told you."

Jude crouched down and used his gloved fingers to

clean mucus out of the calf's nose. After a moment, the calf let out a soft gurgle and Jude glanced at his brother. "Told you."

"Hot damn. That calf is alive."

Jude moved away from the calf and heifer, as did Elias, and let Mother Nature do her thing. The heifer stumbled to her feet and turned around and started to sniff and lick her baby. After a few minutes, the calf raised its wobbly head and staggered to its feet. Immediately, he started to look for nourishment, nudging his mother's stomach over and over until he found the teats.

Jude and Elias mounted their horses. "After she passes the afterbirth, we have to get them back to the herd," Jude said. "They're too vulnerable out here alone."

"Anything you say," Elias replied with a mock grin.

Jude ignored him, which was the best way to deal with Elias.

Late that afternoon, when he rode back to the barn, he thought about birth and how important it was for the baby to get that first nourishment from his mother and to make a special connection. It cut Jude deeply that his son had missed making immediate contact with the two people who had created him and would continue to love and support him. Every day Jude tried to make up for that.

Luke finished painting the outside of the house in record time and was ready to head back to Louisiana. Paige hugged him goodbye and held on tight because she knew it would be a long time before she would see her brother again.

"I'll call every time I get a chance," he said. "I hope everything works out for you, sis."

Paige didn't know how anything was going to go, but she knew she was going to miss her brother. "Take care of yourself and stay safe."

He kissed his sisters and walked out the door. They stood for a moment trying not to consider that it might be the last time they would see him. There were no guarantees in war.

She and Staci painted away with the music blaring, both trying not to think. Staci's cell rang and she grabbed it.

"I have to go into work tomorrow. We have a big wedding reception over the weekend and two people have called in sick, so I have to go play catch-up."

"That's okay." Paige put down her brush. "I really need to stay here. Do you think you could drop me in Temple so I can rent a car? That way you don't have to worry about picking me up."

Staci nodded. "I figured you're going to roost here until you see him."

Paige picked up a rag to clean her hands. "That's about it." She wasn't leaving Horseshoe until that moment happened.

An hour later she had a nice little car to drive. On a whim, she stopped at a paint store and bought more paint. Staci had bought enough for only the living room and Paige really wasn't liking the wheat color. She wanted fresh, inviting colors. If she was going to paint the house, she wanted it to look nice, instead of drab and plain.

She picked out a soft yellow for the kitchen, a silky green for her mother's bedroom and a nutmeg for Luke's. She was still undecided about her and Staci's room, but then she found a fresh peach color. It was late when she returned to the house to unload all her purchases. The doorbell rang as she finished carrying everything inside.

Stumbling over paint cans, she sprinted to the door. Jude stood there with a box in his arms and she took a breath to still her racing heart.

"Did Zane change his mind?"

He held up the box. "No, but I brought some photos for you."

She grabbed the box and carried it inside to the living room and sat on the floor. Her fingers trembled as she removed the lid. Jude slid down beside her and she thought nothing could be more perfect than looking at the photos with him.

There were two albums, plus loose photos.

"I put some in albums but got very lazy about that since a lot of photos are on my phone." Jude reached in and pulled out an album and opened it.

Her breath caught as she saw Jude holding a small baby wrapped in a blue blanket. "When did you know we had a boy?" She just had to ask.

"The moment they brought him to me in that blanket."

There were so many beautiful photos of a little boy growing up without a mother that it tore at Paige's heart, but she kept looking, as if by osmosis she could soak up some of that love she should have shared.

"He looks so much like you," she said, touching a photo. "His hair even curls a little."

"Yeah. He inherited a lot of things from me, but there's a lot of you in him, too."

"Like what?"

"Like his intelligence, his curiosity and his need to know more and more about things and the way everything works. Science and the universe intrigue him and he spends hours reading about the planets and stars and everything that makes up this universe. He knows more about the earth than I ever did. He completely blows my mind. That, he gets from you. He's never made a B and he plans to never break that record. I know someone else who used to be like that."

Paige sat cross-legged with the photos in her lap, remembering how important it had been to make all As. Without a 4.0 grade point average, she wouldn't get the scholarship she wanted. That had been the most important thing in the world to her. But looking back, she missed what was really important—all these photos in her lap of a little boy who needed her. Photos without her in them.

Jude scooted back and leaned against the wall, his long legs outstretched in front of him. "This morning I had to help a heifer have a calf and I thought about Zane's birth. As soon as the calf was on the ground, the heifer stood and sniffed and licked her baby, to let it know she was there to love and to protect it. We weren't there for Zane. We failed him."

A sob rose in her throat and she tried to suppress it but it escaped of its own volition. "You didn't. I…did." Suddenly the photos felt heavy and accusing in her lap.

"I never had the chance to ask, but was it an easy birth?"

Paige pushed down all the guilty feelings, wanting to answer his question. "After they gave me the medication to induce labor, it wasn't long before the cramps started, but they gave me an epidural and it eased considerably. I heard the baby cry and I put my hands over my ears. I didn't understand then why I did that. It was a defense mechanism. I was trying to protect myself.

But I've heard that cry for over twelve years and it has haunted me and it has sustained me at times."

"You were so upset afterward I didn't know what to say to you."

"There was nothing you could say. No words, not even from you, could erase the pain that I endured that day." She swallowed a lump that felt like hard clay. "When you took me back to the house to get my things, my mother was in full vitriolic mode. She yelled and screamed as I grabbed my suitcases to leave. She said I would come back with my tail tucked between my legs because I wouldn't last two months in a big-city college. I was a dumb country girl and too stupid to know it. And she wasn't letting me back in the house when that happened. I'd have to find another place to live because she was done raising stupid, ignorant children. That was probably the main reason I never came back. Without my child, there was nothing here for me."

Jude tensed and raised his knees and rested his forearms on them. "How could two teenagers get love so wrong?"

She lifted her eyes to his. "You're the only reason I made it through high school. Luke was in the army and Staci was already living in Austin. After that, home life turned into a nightmare."

Awkwardness crept into the silence and Paige began to put the photos back into the box.

"Are you seeing someone in California?"

A distressed sound left her throat. "I've spent all my time working, going to school, studying and trying to survive. I haven't had time for anything else."

"That's not much of a life."

She carefully placed the lid on the box. "Are you involved with anyone?"

"I've been seeing one of Zane's teachers. She's very good with him and I like her a lot."

She bit her lip, trying to find words that would not make her look like a jealous fool. "Does Zane like her, too?"

He didn't answer her. Instead, he said, "Paige, I'm trying to figure out what's the best thing to do here for Zane. If he continues to refuse to see you, I'm not going to force him."

She wanted to say she understood, but she didn't and her rights as a mother had ended long ago. But she wasn't giving up. Nothing would make her do that now.

"What do you want me to do, Jude?"

His eyes met hers like a dark wall of solid steel that nothing could penetrate. "I want you to leave and never come back."

Chapter 10

Jude's cruel words pierced the protective barrier she'd built around her heart. All the pain, misery, loneliness and suffering she'd manage to overcome blindsided her, and a renewed pain burned deep inside her. She wanted to cry out from the agony. Her throat closed up and air left her lungs. She didn't need to breathe. She didn't need anything anymore.

Somewhere in that realm of self-pity, the courage that kept her going for so many years resurfaced, saving her.

A barely audible "I can't" came out.

"I know," was his equally quiet response. His dark eyes held hers captive and she was mesmerized by the heartache and something else she remembered well. "And then there's this." He reached out and ran his hand around her neck, caressing her sensitive nape, and gentle waves of comfort flowed through her. It had been so long.

He pulled her forward, his mouth opening over hers. She moaned and wrapped her arms around him, getting as close as possible to return his heated kiss. The box of photos tumbled to the floor and neither noticed.

He kissed her as if he was starving for her taste, her touch, the feel of her. She was the same, needing to renew every inch of his muscled, firm body. Their lips and tongues did the talking and they couldn't get enough of the delicious sensation of each other. Locked tight in his arms, his lips on hers, she thought if she died like this, she would be a happy woman. Soon they had to breathe and Jude drew back slightly, resting his forehead on hers, and she breathed in the scent of him: leather, fresh country air and desire so thick they both recognized it.

"I don't want to hurt Zane and I don't want to hurt you, either." His words were soothing, like a familiar touch in the dark.

"I can't leave." She kissed the spot under his chin and the heat of his skin was a tangible thing that ignited her senses all over again.

"He's already hurting and ignoring his true feelings and I don't know how to help him."

"Just be there for him, but please don't ask me not to see him. Don't punish me. I've paid enough."

Jude got to his feet so quickly she couldn't stop him. Without a backward glance he walked to the door and soon she heard his truck leaving the driveway.

Feeling stunned and overwhelmed, she took a moment to collect her thoughts, trying to figure out what had just happened. He'd kissed her like a man, not a callow youth, but all those emotions were as vibrant as ever and she felt them all the way to her soul. He had to have felt them, too.

The photos were strewn around her. He'd forgotten them. That meant he would have to come back one more time. She gathered the photos like bits and pieces of a giant puzzle, except there was one important piece missing—her.

She touched her aching lips, feeling all his energy once again. How had she survived all these years without him in her life?

Hey, Jude. I still love you.

Jude drove to the ranch, tired and lonely and looking for answers. He'd been cruel once again to Paige when he hadn't meant to be. Then he'd done what he had wanted to do since the first moment he saw her again at the cemetery—he'd kissed her as if there was no tomorrow. For them there might not be.

Going into the house, he shut off his mind. He was good at that, but today it seemed to hurt a little more than usual. His mom was in the den reading the latest livestock report. She was always up-to-date on the price of cattle.

"Is Zane in his room?"

"Yes. You told him to do his homework and I suppose that's what he's doing. He came down for ice cream about thirty minutes ago and went back up."

"Thanks, Mom." He took the stairs two at a time and found Zane in his room, looking at shirts.

"What do you think, Dad?" Zane held up a white shirt and a red one.

"For school?"

"No, Dad." His son had the nerve to sigh with irritation. "For the race."

"Either will be fine."

"I think the white one. You can see me better in white."

"Okay."

Zane handed it to him. "You have to take it to the
cleaners."

"Zane." This time Jude sighed in frustration. "This is
Thursday and the race is on Saturday. You should have
told me this earlier."

"Mr. Grumby does one-day service."

"But I have a lot of work to do and not a lot of time
to run into town and take one shirt and then pick it up."

"Oh. I can ask Aunt Rachel."

"No. I'll figure something out." Zane was his kid
and he always took care of his kid. "Have you finished
your homework?"

"Does a duck have feathers?"

"You've been talking to Grandpa?"

"Yeah. He knows a lot of stuff. He and Uncle Elias
were here earlier and Elias told us how you saved a
baby calf today. He said you have more patience than
an old maid."

Just what he needed, his son getting barroom quotes
from Elias. He stretched his shoulders, realizing how
tight his muscles were. He had to loosen up. His time
with Paige had him tied up in knots and he needed to
do something.

"Time for bed. You have school tomorrow."

"Aw, Dad."

Jude placed his hands on his hips. Zane knew that
was a sign his dad wasn't going to give in. He jumped
into his bed in his underwear and a T-shirt. That was all

he ever slept in. Jude had bought him pajamas because he'd wanted to make sure his kid had all the right things in life. One itty-bitty thing that didn't amount to a hill of beans, as his grandpa would say. Sometimes all a kid needed was love. That was the magic formula.

"Can I stay on my laptop for a few minutes?"

"No, because I know how that goes. Once you get on there, I can't get you off. No to YouTube. No to Instagram. Yes to sleep."

"I wanted to post some pictures of Bear, the fastest horse in the West."

A smile threatened Jude's lips. "You can do that tomorrow."

Zane snuggled beneath his Star Wars sheets. "Night, Dad."

He leaned over and kissed his son's forehead. "Night, son."

Suddenly, Zane's arms reached out and hugged Jude tightly around the neck. Jude's stomach cramped at the desperation in those little arms. "Love you, son. Don't ever forget that."

"Love you, too, Dad, and I never forget it."

There was a message in there about his mother, but tonight was not the time to bring it up. That time would be later, when both of them were stronger.

Jude made his way into his bedroom with years of regret pulling him down into that maze of discontent. He sat on his bed, not bothering to turn on the light. Lying back on the comforter, he closed his eyes and all he could feel was Paige's lips on his, her soft curves pressing into him. All he wanted was to love her the way he had long ago…but that had only brought them misery.

How did they undo all the mistakes? There was no

clear answer, just as it had been years ago. Paige's life didn't run parallel with his. She had a career now and he felt deep in his gut there was no room for him or Zane. That was what he couldn't shake.

He knew she regretted her decision about Zane, but where did they go from here?

The next morning Paige was up early and so was Staci. The box from Ms. Whitman had arrived and Paige took it with her to Horseshoe. She was there by eight o'clock. She left it in the car because she wanted it with her if she saw Zane. The box was for him.

With a red kerchief tied around her hair and in jeans and a T-shirt, she started painting the kitchen. The barely yellow color made the room so much fresher and she loved it. She was almost finished when she heard a truck outside. She wiped her hands and ran to the front door.

Jude stood on the doorstep in worn jeans and an equally worn chambray shirt. His hat and boots had also seen better days. He was dressed for work on the ranch. "I forgot the photos last night."

He looked nervous and tense and she was sure the same emotions showed on her face. "They're in the kitchen. I hope you don't mind, but I had some copies made."

"No," he replied as he followed her.

"This looks nice," he said, staring at the new paint.

"Yeah. Wouldn't it be great if we could just paint over all our problems so they would stay hidden for the rest of our lives?"

"Life doesn't work that way."

"I know." She handed him the box. "I wonder how my life would have been if my mother had baked cookies and attended PTO meetings and the only vice she had was putting a little Crown Royal in her Coke."

"That's daydreaming."

"Yeah." She ran her hands down her faded jeans and realized she was making a fool of herself. "Thanks for letting me see the photos. It meant a lot. Do you think Zane is ever going to agree to see me?"

"The race is tomorrow. That's his focus. The thought of you is there, but he's not facing it right now. He will, though. I know my son. He's loving, caring and full of life and he won't avoid the issue of his mother for long."

Jude's words gave her hope.

He carefully placed the box on the table. "I just have to wonder, though, how long you plan on staying in Horseshoe and how he will fit into your life in California."

The hope died with a whimper. "I haven't figured it all out yet. For now I just want to see and hold my son and then I will make decisions for the future. Just don't ask me to leave again."

They stared at each other and the years and the mistakes were clearly pinpointed in their eyes. There was no way to go back. No way to keep daydreaming. No way to go forward but to accept those mistakes as human and move on. And to make sure one little boy wasn't hurt any more than he already was.

As if the topic was getting tedious, Jude quickly changed the subject. "You never said what kind of doctor you are."

"OB-GYN and my specialty is maternal fetal medicine."

"That means you deliver babies?" His face crinkled into an I-can't-believe-this expression.

"Yes. I deliver babies and treat the mothers afterward.

It has been the most rewarding experience of my life. With each birth, I feel a renewal of my tattered spirit and when we lose one, I grieve just as I did the day I walked away from mine." She took a long breath. "I'm doing my residency with Dr. Gwyneth Spencer in her medical clinic and she's an amazing teacher and doctor and I have learned so much from her."

"Why did you pick obstetrics?" His face still held the same expression, but it had softened.

"I guess my own experience caused me to have a keen interest in the field and my professors said I had a knack for it. Dr. Spencer said the same thing. She also runs a clinic for pregnant teenage girls and I wished I had had something like that years ago."

"What do you mean?"

"The girls that come there are not judged and they get counseling to help make the right decisions for them and their families. Dr. Spencer has a rule, though. The mother has to hold her baby and say goodbye before she gives it away. She says it's a telling moment. If a young girl can do that without breaking down, then she knows the girl is making the right decision."

His expression softened even more. "Do you think if you had held Zane, you would've changed your mind?"

She eased into a kitchen chair, needing something to hold her up. "I'm almost positive. That's why Mrs. Carstairs didn't want me to see the baby. She knew." She bit her lip, trying to control her anger. "I just needed someone there to talk to and the girls at the clinic get that from Dr. Spencer and her staff."

"I was there. Why couldn't you talk to me?"

She looked into his eyes, loving the way they crinkled in the corners and loving that everything about Jude was solid and true. Except for one thing: his quietness. "Jude, I don't want to hurt your feelings, but, really, you were more closed up than I was. We didn't do a lot of talking or consoling. If I was upset or if we argued, you'd kiss me and then we'd have sex. That was our problem solver and our *big* problem."

He removed his hat and swiped his hand through his hair. "Yeah."

"Recently we had a fifteen-year-old who gave birth to a little girl. She had already agreed to give it up and her mother was there to support her. The father wasn't in the picture. A couple in their thirties who had been unable to conceive were waiting for the baby. I was with the girl in the room when she held the baby and kissed it goodbye. Some of the things she said to the baby resonated with me."

"Like what?"

"She said she wanted the baby to grow up with two parents who would love her and they would live in a nice house with a big backyard and she would have everything she wanted. She didn't want the baby to live on welfare like she had. She added the baby would grow up to be a princess because that's what she deserved."

Paige cleared her throat. "I wanted our baby to grow up with the best of everything, too, and I knew that best was not with me in my home environment. By being strong, I felt I was giving him the best. I was so wrong."

"Did you tell the girl that?"

"No. She'd made her decision and she was comfortable with it, but there were lingering doubts, as I'm sure there are with every mother who gives a baby away. When the nurse took the baby, the girl started to cry and she asked if I would hold her. I did. She said she was so cold she was frozen inside. When she said that, I realized I had the same emotions the day I gave birth to Zane. I was frozen inside and I am still. I will never feel any warmth until I'm able to hold my son."

Silence crept over them and Paige grew weary of talking so much about her feelings. Did Jude even understand?

He swallowed visibly. "I'll talk to Zane after the race."

That was more than she had ever hoped for.

Chapter 11

Paige painted until midafternoon. She finished the kitchen, the living room and her bedroom. Everything was so fresh and she loved the colors. Her stomach growled and she realized she hadn't eaten anything all day. The morning had been emotional, but music had blocked her thoughts, and physical activity was what she'd needed.

After washing the paint roller, she got in her car and drove to a Dairy Queen and ordered a hamburger, something she would tell her patients to never eat. A healthy diet was the best. But today she felt like being naughty. She ate in the car, not wanting to visit with anyone. Not that anyone would recognize her, but she still wanted privacy.

As she ate, she considered the long drive to Austin every day. Since the house was looking so much better, she thought she might stay there if she had a bed. Downtown had several antiques stores and she drove there. Looking around, she found an old iron bed that she loved. Mr. Jenkins still owned the store and at first he didn't recognize her. After she asked him several questions, his eyes narrowed on her face.

"You're Darlene Wheeler's daughter."

She pushed the strap of her purse farther up her shoulder in a nervous gesture and she hated she couldn't control that. "Yes. I'm Paige."

He bobbed his bald head. "It's nice you've come home. I guess you got a fancy education."

"Yes, sir. I did."

"That's really good." And Paige read the rest of that sentence as *considering who your mother was*. She didn't say anything, because she didn't need to. She knew how the town felt about her mother and there was no way to get around that.

After a few minutes of talking back and forth, she bought the bed and asked about mattresses. He said he had some in the back in case people needed them. To get there she had to go through a maze of tables, furniture, bric-a-brac and everything known to man, even a toilet. Who would buy a toilet in an antiques store?

In the far back he had two sets of mattresses wrapped in plastic. "A fella passed through here and wanted to know if I was interested in mattresses. I bought four and I still have two." He pointed. "Your choice."

She bought one to fit the iron bed and Mr. Jenkins said he could deliver it out in the late afternoon. After that, she drove to Temple and bought towels, sheets, a microwave and a coffeepot. She also bought a few groceries. Then she called Staci.

"You're not serious."

"I want to be in Horseshoe if Zane decides to see me. The house is looking really nice. The new colors made a world of difference."

"Kiddo, don't get your hopes up. I'm afraid you're going to get hurt again."

"I have to see this through, even if it takes forever."

There was silence on the other end for a moment. "When will I see you?"

"Tonight. I have to get my things. And don't be all sad sack. You work all the time and I would just be sitting in your apartment."

"Yeah, I'm sorry about that."

"When you get some spare time, you can come spend the night with me in the house. It will be like old times."

"Pleeeease. Old times I do not want to relive."

Paige laughed and it was great to find humor in their terrible childhood. "I'll see you tonight."

When she pulled into her driveway, Mr. Jenkins drove in behind her. A teenage boy helped him and within fifteen minutes they had the bed and mattress set up.

"Nice seeing you, Ms. Wheeler." He tipped his baseball cap to her.

"Thank you, Mr. Jenkins." Nothing else was said and Paige was grateful he didn't ask a lot of questions.

She put away all the stuff she'd brought and then made the bed, placing the old worn teddy bear in the center. Blinds were still on the windows, so she didn't have to worry about anyone peeping in. She glanced at her handiwork and even though it wasn't stylish, it would do. It was crisp and clean and would be all she needed as she waited for her son.

* * *

Saturday morning dawned bright and early. Too early for Jude. Zane woke him up at ten to five and Jude pulled him into the bed and pretended to smother him with a pillow. Zane laughed and squirmed and they rough-housed as they often had when he was little.

"Come on, Dad. You have to get up. It's Saturday." Zane wiggled out of his arms and off the bed and stood there smiling with his hair in his eyes. No one would know his little heart was breaking.

Jude swung his legs over the side of the bed and sat up. "The race isn't until two."

"But we're having lunch there and everything. The whole town will be there to celebrate Founder's Day. We have to get there early so I can walk Bear around and he can get used to everything. You know he's kind of fidgety and nervous. I want him to be relaxed."

Jude reached out and caught his son's arm and pulled him down beside him. "I'm glad you're so excited about this, but we need to have the talk about winning and losing."

"Aw, Dad, we've had that talk. Winning is great, but there's no shame in losing." Eyes as dark as Jude's glanced at him. "Do you think I'm going to lose?"

"No, son, but I'm proud of you whether you win or lose and so is everyone in the family. Sometimes, though, you have to be prepared for both."

"I am, Dad."

"I'm also proud of all the energy and effort you've put into making Bear a faster horse. That shows maturity and it shows me how important this is to you."

Zane frowned. "Don't get mushy."

Jude hugged his son. "That would be terrible."

"Yes." Zane jumped up and slid across the hardwood

floor in his socks and underwear and it reminded Jude of an old Tom Cruise movie. "We gonna have a par-ty," Zane sang.

Jude wished Paige could see her son like this, all happy and excited with no worries in the world. After talking to Paige yesterday, Jude couldn't get her and all the pain she'd suffered over the years out of his mind. He'd never dreamed her life had been like that. He would talk to Zane on Sunday about his mother and make him listen. He had to face the fact that he had a mother and they needed to meet. It wasn't going to be easy, but he had to do it. It was the right thing to do for all of them.

"Dad, you have to wear a white shirt today."

Zane brought him out of his thoughts. "Why?"

"Because we're all wearing white shirts."

"Who's all?"

"The Rebel family." Zane dragged the words out slowly, as if his father might have a hard time grasping the fact.

"And whose idea was this?"

Zane thumbed into his chest. "Mine. Everyone on Team Zane is wearing a white shirt. Erin and Jody are wearing white and some other kids."

Erin was the DA's daughter and Jody was the sheriff's daughter. They were older than Zane, but because Zane had been moved up a grade, they were now in the same classes and had become friends.

"Well, then, I better find a white shirt, because I'm definitely on Team Zane."

The morning turned into a circus with Zane buzzing around like a pesky mosquito, annoying everybody. He was just so excited he couldn't calm down. He insisted on washing Bear and brushing his tail and mane so he would look beautiful. Jude finally sat him down and made Zane take a couple of deep breaths.

Paige had been just like that in school over tests and school activities she was involved in. She'd get all excited and break out in a rash and she'd cry and get overemotional. Her son was just like her. He panicked easily, except he rarely cried.

Finally, they made their way to the fairgrounds with Bear in the horse trailer. Jude's mother and Phoenix rode with them to help calm Zane. The fairgrounds were three blocks off Main Street. The land had been donated by Delbert Miller, whose ancestors had been one of the town's founding families back in the 1800s. He'd willed twenty-five acres and a house to the town of Horseshoe. The house had been redone and it was now used for weddings, parties, reunions and things like that. The race started at the house and went around the property and back. It was for kids nine to eighteen and all the Rebel boys had raced over the years, as every kid in Horseshoe had.

Bubba Wisnowski and his friends always set up a barbecue stand at the event. Usually everyone brought food, but the barbecue was the big deal. There were games and fun activities for all the kids. The Rebel family gathered beneath a big live oak tree by the house and everyone wore white shirts. Zane was happy.

His mother had brought fried chicken and the others contributed potato salad and sweets. They settled on quilts and ate lunch. There were a few chairs, occupied mostly by the women and Grandpa. Being pregnant, Rachel took a chair. Egan teased her that he'd never be able to get her up off the ground. They laughed and savored a spring afternoon with family.

Zane talked incessantly and Jude had to make him stop. He was nervous—that was very evident. The Mc-Cray family gathered on the other side of the house and Jude watched as Malachi McCray unloaded Dudley's horse. She was a brown mare with a blaze on her face and long legs. Just by looking at the horse, Jude could tell she was fast. A grain of doubt lay on his conscience and he knew his son had his work cut out for him to beat that horse.

The mayor gave a speech, as did Judge Hollister. Then everyone visited and talked and enjoyed the day.

"Fifteen minutes to race time," Wyatt, the sheriff, announced over the loudspeakers.

"Don't forget to watch me," Zane shouted to the family, and ran to the trailer where Bear was waiting. Jude and Quincy followed more slowly.

"Tuck your shirt in," Jude said. Zane's shirt was hanging out of his pants and there was a stain on it, but he didn't point that out. Ever since he was a little boy, Zane couldn't keep a white shirt clean more than fifteen minutes. Jude should have remembered that when Zane had asked about the shirts.

"Now, remember, partner, stay calm and focused and Bear will do the rest." Quincy was talking to Zane.

Jude pinned Zane's number on the back of his shirt.

"My lucky number."

Jude wanted to hug his son, but he didn't, because he knew that would embarrass him. "You can do this. You've worked hard and you can ride that horse to victory."

"Thanks, Dad." Zane, for the first time today, seemed to calm down. He put his foot in the stirrup and swung into the saddle. He rode to the starting line without another word.

His son looked so much older atop the horse, sitting in the saddle like a pro. And Jude stood there staring after him, wishing Zane's mother could see him now.

Paige sat at the kitchen table eating a salad and wondered how the race was going. She picked at the salad and then threw it into the garbage. Her nerves were tied into knots and she had to get back to painting. It would take her mind off the race. But that didn't help. She wanted to see her son. Jude hadn't invited her and she didn't want to go and cause a scene. But she wanted to see him so badly.

Ten minutes later she was in her car and driving into town. Nothing looked to be open, because everyone was at the fairgrounds, but she was hoping Mr. Jenkins's antiques shop was. She'd seen some old hats in his place yesterday and one of those was just what she needed to disguise herself. Her luck held. Mr. Jenkins was in front sitting in a rocking chair, watching the town. Usually several merchants stayed behind to keep an eye on things because even in Horseshoe there were thieves.

She bought a big floppy hat that tied beneath her chin and made her way to the fairgrounds. Her car was small, so she was able to find a parking spot near the starting line. Riders on horses were milling around waiting for a signal. She could see clearly, so there was no need to get out.

Her eyes scanned the riders and then she saw him on a paint horse wearing a white shirt. No one had to point him out. Her son was a clone of his father. She stared, soaking up every little detail. He was thin, which he must've gotten from Jude, too, because Paige had never been thin until grief had killed her appetite.

He was so handsome she couldn't look away. He handled the horse expertly and guided him to the starting line. Most of Horseshoe was here today, but only one person held her attention. It might have been wrong for her to be there, but she was going to watch her son win this race.

Jude frowned as the boys lined up. Zane was on the right and Dudley on the left. The other racers were in between. Jude didn't like that positioning and he wished he'd talked to Zane about that, but it was too late. He felt Zane was going to get crowded out. Now Jude was nervous.

Wyatt spoke to the boys and told them the rules. Then he stepped back and everyone waited eagerly. The Rebel family stood together, their attention on the race. Even baby John stopped toddling around, as if he knew something important was about to happen.

Wyatt pulled his revolver from his holster and pointed it toward the sky. On the count of three, he fired. The thunder of hooves echoed and the race was on.

Just as Jude feared, Zane was pushed to the side, but he made up time quickly. The race went around the property and was more like an obstacle course as it went uphill and then down through Yaupon Creek. The riders were soon out of sight but Jude caught a glimpse every now and then through the mesquite and the oaks. But he had no idea who was leading the race.

Quincy slapped him on the back. "Stop worrying. Zane has this."

"He was just so excited about it and I don't want him to be disappointed."

"He's not." Phoenix joined the conversation. "He's the best rider out there."

They saw the dust billowing before they saw the riders. Zane and Dudley were out front, neck and neck, racing toward the finish line. But something was wrong. Zane wasn't straight in the saddle as Jude had taught him. He'd leaned slightly and that wasn't like his son at all.

"Here they come!" Grandpa shouted. "There's Zane right in front. Come on, boy!"

"Something's wrong," Jude muttered.

The Rebel brothers gathered around him. "Zane's leaning," Falcon said.

"I know." Jude moved toward the finish line and watched as his son suddenly leaned forward and Bear, with a burst of energy, shot away from Dudley. By the time Zane crossed the finish line, he was ahead by two links. But Bear kept running. Zane didn't pull him up and there had to be a reason for that.

Jude took off running for his son and looked on in horror as Zane slipped from the saddle to the ground, one boot caught in the stirrup. When that happened, Bear finally stopped and Zane was dragged only a few feet. Jude fell down by his limp son and stared at the blood on his face and shirt. Fear climbed inside him and held his heart in a vise.

Quincy grabbed Bear's reins and Phoenix gently removed Zane's foot from the stirrup. His other brothers had reached them by then and they knelt as Jude half lifted Zane into his arms, carefully cradling his head.

"What the hell happened?" Elias asked.

There was a cut on Zane's forehead and it was bleeding. The left sleeve of his shirt was shredded and it was caked with more blood.

"Zane," Jude called, and had to clear his throat as his

emotions twisted into a painful knot. "Zane, son, wake up." But Zane lay still, unmoving, and the bright sunshiny day full of hope turned into a nightmare.

"Get Jenny!" Jude shouted. She was a nurse and would know what to do. But someone else pushed in beside him and he didn't have to look to know who it was.

Paige.

Chapter 12

"Get some towels and water," Paige ordered.

Jenny crouched down beside her with the items. Paige took a towel and pressed it against the cut on Zane's forehead. "We have to stop the bleeding first. Hold it while I examine the other cuts."

Jude just watched as Paige dealt with their injured son. She undid the buttons on his shirt and removed it so she could see Zane's arm. "Another bleeder on his neck. We're lucky it missed the main artery." She applied another towel to his neck and held it.

"There's so much blood," Jude said.

"The are many blood vessels on the face and skull, and once the skin is broken, it tends to bleed excessively. Hopefully, we can stop it with pressure." She glanced at Jude then. "Remove his boots to see if his ankle is swelling from getting caught in the stirrup."

Her voice was firm, in control. This wasn't the anxious girl he'd known. This was a professional doctor.

He quickly stripped off Zane's boots and socks. "There's a slight bruise, but it's not swelling—yet."

"Good. He'll need an X-ray." She continued to look at Zane's arm. "Slashes have broken through the epidermis and the cuts look superficial, but I'm worried about his head hitting the ground. And it looks as if someone has beaten him with something."

Jude looked up and saw Dudley still on his horse holding a riding crop. Rage filled Jude. He got to his feet and marched to Dudley, who didn't have enough sense to ride away. Reaching up, he grabbed him by the collar and pulled him out of the saddle and onto the ground. Dudley tried to hit him with the crop, but Jude jerked it out of his hand and pressed his boot down on Dudley's throat.

"I'm going to show you what it feels like to be whipped!" He pushed his boot down harder and the boy gasped for breath.

"Jude," Quincy called. "Don't do this."

"Look at Zane and tell me not to do this. I'm going to teach this piece of crap a lesson." He leaned even harder on his foot and the boy started to turn blue.

"Jude, Zane's going to be okay. This isn't worth it." Quincy kept up his plea.

"Do something," Malachi said to Wyatt, who had finally made it to the scene.

"Let him up," the sheriff ordered. "I'll take care of this."

"Daddy." A little voice, Zane's voice, came out of nowhere and brought Jude to his senses. He was hurting a kid. He let up the pressure on Dudley's neck. "Tell me why you hurt Zane."

The boy coughed but didn't say anything. Jude pushed his boot down again and Dudley moaned, "O-kay."

"Why did you beat Zane with the crop?"

"Dad… Dad…said…if I didn't win…he'd beat me."

Jude looked at Malachi and all the years of the Rebels and McCrays fighting seemed to escalate in that moment. He threw the crop at Malachi and it bounced off his chest to the ground. Jude walked away to his son without another word.

Over his shoulder he saw Jericho pick up the crop and poke it into Malachi's chest. "You better watch your back."

"He's threatening me," Malachi told the sheriff.

Egan pulled Jericho away.

"You have a lot more to worry about than Jericho," the sheriff said. "I'm taking Dudley to the jail and you and your wife had better be in my office in thirty minutes."

Jude knelt once again by his son, who was now awake, and took a second to let the anger subside.

"Dad-dy, did… I win?" Zane asked.

"You bet you did."

"I want…my trophy."

"He needs to go to an emergency room," Paige said. "Keep something under his head and keep him awake. Make sure they do a CT scan of his head. And he needs a tetanus shot if he hasn't had one."

"Maybe you should come with us," Jude said.

Zane glared at Paige and cried, "No, Daddy." Zane never called him Daddy unless he was upset. "I want Aunt Jenny to come with us."

"I'm right here, sweetie." Jenny kissed the top of Zane's head.

Paige seemed undeterred by her son's outburst. A large purse was beside her and she pulled something out of it.

"The bleeding has stopped," Jenny said.

"Good." Paige poured some water over a towel and dabbed at the cut on Zane's forehead. "This is an alcohol wipe. I'm going to clean the cuts and apply some surgical strips. This might sting a little." She thoroughly cleaned the cut on his forehead and the one on his neck and applied the strips with the utmost care and concentration. Zane frowned and winced but didn't say another word.

"This will keep the cuts from opening again and maybe you won't have to have stitches or much of a scar." She sat back on her heels. "That should do it. Remember to keep his head supported at all times until you reach the ER."

"Daddy, what about Bear?"

"Don't worry about Bear," Paxton told him. "I'll take him back to the ranch."

"Is he hurt?"

"Nah. Bear's tough." They really hadn't looked at the horse yet and Jude was grateful that Paxton had gone with his gut on the answer.

The whole family had gathered around. Even Jude's mother and Rachel were kneeling on the ground beside Zane. Falcon had a close hold on Grandpa, who had a shattered look on his face.

Kate held Zane's hand and Jude could see tears in her eyes. Egan helped Rachel to her feet and she buried her face in his chest so Zane couldn't see her cry.

Quincy drove his truck up as close as possible and Jude lifted his son, with Jenny holding towels under his neck, and put him in the backseat.

"We'll meet you at the hospital," Egan called.

"No," Jude shouted back. "That's not necessary. Meet

us at the house and we're still going to have that party to celebrate like we planned."

In a few seconds they roared away with Phoenix in the passenger seat. Jude looked back to see Paige standing alone. People were walking away, even his family. He should have insisted that she come, but he couldn't. He was caught between his son and his son's mother.

Paige was frozen in place. She couldn't seem to move or do anything but feel the pain in her chest. Then her body started to tremble and she knew the reaction was starting. Wrapping her arms around her waist, she tried to control her emotions. She'd touched her son and braved the anger in his eyes. She hadn't expected anything less but, oh, it hurt. She felt as if someone had reached in and pulled out her heart. She gasped for air.

She'd been patiently waiting for the riders to make the turn and then she saw Zane and the other boy neck and neck, racing toward the finish line. She'd shouted out loud when Zane crossed the line first. But then Jude had started to run toward their son and she'd known something was wrong. To her horror, Zane fell from the saddle, and she quickly grabbed the small medical bag she always kept with her and dashed over to them. She hadn't even stopped to think that Zane would not want to see her. He was hurt and she would not let her pride or his anger keep her from helping him.

She was still reeling from the fact that the boy had whipped her son like an animal. The feud between the Rebels and McCrays was still as crazy as ever. So much hate. So much bitterness. Would it ever end?

"Paige."

She'd been so locked within herself she hadn't even

realized that Rachel had come back and now stood by her side.

"Are you okay?"

She tucked strands of hair behind her ear and felt a cool breeze on her face. The tightness in her lungs eased and she noticed that people were packing up for the day, loading horses and picking up trash. A sad ending to Founder's Day.

"No. I don't think I'll ever be okay again." And then she looked into Rachel's eyes. "You know, don't you?"

"Yes."

"How many other people know?"

"Just the Rebel family, I think. Egan told me and I would never betray his confidence. I haven't told a soul."

"Not even Angie?"

"Not even Angie."

Paige sucked air into her burning chest. "I made a huge mistake and I don't know how to make it better. I don't know how to explain it to my son. I don't even know how to explain it to myself."

Rachel put her arm around Paige and hugged her. "We all make mistakes, Paige."

"But not like the one I made."

"It may surprise you, but people can be very understanding."

"And very cruel. I remember that from high school."

"You had a horrid childhood and everyone in this town knows that. No one blames you." She squeezed Paige's shoulder. "Stop blaming yourself. You were amazing with Zane. You were always a cut above the rest of us in school and it showed today. You have an amazing talent and I'm glad you got the education you wanted.

Yes, it came with a price, but I'm betting Jude and Zane will feel the same way I do. Just give them time."

Paige choked back a sob and hugged her friend. She'd never expected anyone to be this generous and kind and it brought tears to her eyes.

They pulled apart and Rachel said, "You know, mistakes are like marks on a chalkboard. With a little effort and patience, they can be erased."

Paige smiled through her tears. "I don't know if I have an eraser that big."

"All it takes is love." Rachel touched her forehead. "My hormones are a little crazy right now, but I firmly believe you, Jude and Zane should be together."

"Honey," Egan called.

"Coming!" Rachel shouted back. "Call me if you need to talk."

"Thank you."

Rachel walked off toward Egan, and Paige made her way to her car. If not for Rachel's kind nature, Paige would probably have been crying her eyes out right now. That tiny spark of hope in her chest burned a little brighter.

She went back to her painting job, but she'd lost interest. She kept wondering how Zane was. Jude had her phone number and she was hoping he would call. By late afternoon the phone still hadn't rung and she knew Jude wasn't going to call. So that meant she had to make a big decision: whether to see her son or not.

Jenny called ahead to the emergency room and two orderlies were waiting with a stretcher when Quincy pulled in. Zane had a death grip on Jude's hand and wouldn't let go.

"It's okay, son. They have to get you out of the truck. It will only be for a few minutes. I'm not going anywhere."

Zane released his hand and the orderlies had him out in seconds and on the stretcher. Things happened fast after that. The ER doctor examined him and said he wouldn't disturb the surgical strips that someone had put on, because they had been done so expertly and the wound was already closing. Then they spent hours doing tests and Zane was nervous, but Jude never left his side. He was always near and Zane knew that.

By late afternoon they got the okay to go home. Zane was fine, just a little bruised. There was no swelling or bleeding of the brain.

Jude phoned the family to let them know they were on the way. The moment he opened the front door, everyone shouted, "Congratulations!" There were balloons, streamers and a banner that Eden and Leah had made. Cake and punch were on the dining room table and Zane was all smiles. The smile got even wider when he saw the trophy sitting next to the cake.

Falcon handed it to him. "Hardy brought this by and said to tell you congratulations."

"Wow! Look, Dad. It's so big."

He hugged his son. "I'm proud of you, but we have to get you upstairs to change your clothes." Zane's shirt was ruined and it had been left at the fairgrounds and Jude was sure someone had thrown it away. He had a hospital gown on and his jeans. That was it. They had wrapped his ankle to keep it from swelling and Jude had to keep a close eye on it. Zane limped slightly and the doctor had said for him to stay off that foot as much as possible for the next few days. That might be a problem.

Jude brought him down in his pajamas. He'd known

one day those things would come in handy. Zane sat on the sofa with the trophy in the crook of his arm. His grandmother brought him cake and punch and he was the center of attention, but Jude noticed the fear that was still in his son and probably would be for days to come.

There was a knock at the door and no one seemed to hear it, so he left his son in good hands and went to answer it. Paige stood there looking a little nervous.

"I'm sorry to intrude, but I have to know how he's doing."

Seeing the worry in her green eyes, Jude made a decision. It was time for Zane to talk to his mother. It might not be the best time, but Jude was going with his gut feeling.

He opened the door wider. "Come in. But be prepared for some attitude."

"I can handle it."

Jude felt that she could. She wasn't a shy, insecure teenager anymore.

The room fell silent as they walked in. Zane's eyes grew huge and he glanced down at the trophy in the crook of his arm, refusing to look at his mother.

His mom came forward and held out her hand. "Thanks for what you did for Zane today."

"You're welcome." The words came out low but they heard them.

Jude motioned behind Paige for everyone to go into the kitchen. His brothers and their families slowly got up and made an exit, followed by his mother and grandpa.

Zane looked nervously around. "No, come back."

Jude walked over and sat on the coffee table facing his son. "I want you to do something for me."

"What?" Zane spoke into his chest, not raising his head.
"Look at me."

Zane raised his head and Jude saw two black orbs of
anger staring back at him.

"I want you to talk to your mother and tell her everything you're feeling. Tell her all the anger and resentment
inside you. Let it all out, and then if you never want to
see her again, you don't have to. It's that simple, son. You
have to do this. I've never forced you to do anything,
but today I'm asking you to talk to your mother and let
her know exactly how you feel." He got up and went
into the kitchen to join the family, but he kept his ear to
the door. If his son needed him, he wanted to be there.
The rest of their lives depended on what Zane said now.

Paige gave Zane a few minutes and then she walked
over and perched on the coffee table where Jude had sat,
facing her very angry son. Confronting her mistakes was
harder than she'd ever imagined. The urge to leave was
strong, but she owed this little boy an explanation and
he was going to get it, even if it took a piece of her soul.

"Your color is much better. How do you feel?"

"Go away and leave me alone," Zane spat into his chest.

"I can't do that. I've waited for years to see what you
look like and this moment surpasses anything that I've
ever imagined. A day has not gone by that I haven't
thought of you. I hoped you were with a loving family who cared for you and gave you everything that I
couldn't."

"My daddy gave me everything I needed because
he loves me."

"He's a special kind of man and I've always known that."

There was silence for a moment, a silence that was pressing into her lungs, leaving her breathless.

"I love you, too."

His dark eyes finally lifted. Paige felt a chill like nothing she'd ever felt before.

"Then why did you give me away?"

"I was young and naive, dealing with a lot of emotional upset at home. My one goal was to leave Horseshoe and my mother and never come back. I could try to explain it and make myself look good, but the honest truth is I was just a scared teenager unsure about myself and the future and the child I was carrying. I so badly wanted you to have a better life than I ever had."

"That's just an excuse."

Paige reached into her big bag and pulled out the box she'd been saving all these years for him. She leaned over and placed the box beside him. "When I was about three months pregnant, I started reading to you. I had to do it in the bathtub, where my mother couldn't hear or see me. I read the books over and over to you and I wrote messages in each one for you. I meant to give them to the adoptive parents, but somehow in the emotional upheaval, I forgot. I saved them all these years. So if you want to know what I was feeling at that time, those books will tell you."

"I don't want them."

She swallowed hard, trying not to let his words derail her. "You can throw them away, then, but you'll never know how hard it was for me to give you away."

"Why did you come back? We don't want you here."

"My mother passed away and I came for the funeral and your father gave me this amazing gift. He had my baby, my precious baby, who I had been grieving for all these years."

"No, you weren't. You went on with your life, got an education and became a doctor. You didn't want a baby. That's why you got rid of me."

A sob blocked her breathing and it took a moment for her to gather her courage once again. "I don't know what else to say to you to ease your pain, but I love you and I can't tell you what a joy it was when your father told me he had you, and then to see your beautiful face for the first time was an incredible high."

"I wish you'd never seen me."

"Then I would've died a lonely and miserable woman."

"Good. I hope you leave and never come back."

Paige felt like a boxer in a ring, taking hit after hit and still having the stamina to keep fighting. But her strength was waning. She couldn't continue to do this to him or to her. It was too painful.

She got to her feet. "Maybe one day you'll open the box and maybe one day you'll open your heart and realize that life is full of decisions and sometimes we make the wrong ones. But we're blessed with an amazing ability to forgive. My hope for us is that we'll be able to do that in the future. Goodbye, my precious son."

Chapter 13

Jude wanted to go after Paige, but his son whimpering like a little puppy on the sofa stopped him in his tracks. The choices Jude and Paige had made years ago were tearing their son apart and Jude felt the weight of that like a mantle of solid steel on his shoulders.

After the emotional day, Zane wasn't ready to talk to his mother. Now Jude had to deal with the aftermath. He picked up his son as if he was three years old and carried him upstairs to his bed and tucked him in.

"Daddy." Zane hiccupped.

"What, son?"

"My head hurts."

He wanted to say so many things, but once again his son had retreated into himself, blocking out the pain, blocking out his mother. It was a trait he'd inherited from his father.

Jude glanced toward Quincy and Phoenix, who lingered in the doorway with worried expressions. "Would you get the prescription we picked up at the drugstore?"

Phoenix turned and went downstairs to do as asked, but Quincy came farther into the room. "Can I speak to him for a minute?"

"Quincy—" Jude could take care of his own son and he didn't want anyone interfering, not even Quincy. But then he realized that he was being a little touchy. Zane loved Quincy, so Jude stepped aside and motioned for his brother to come forward.

Quincy squatted by the bed. "Hey, partner. You did great today and I'm so proud of you."

Zane just lay with his head on the pillow, reminding Jude of a broken doll, unable to communicate.

"Don't worry about Bear. I checked him over and he's fine. He's fed and in his stall for the night."

"Thank you, Uncle Quincy."

Quincy brushed hair from Zane's forehead. "Get some rest and I'll see you tomorrow."

Phoenix came back with the medication and a glass of water. Jude gave Zane a pill. "This will ease the pain in your head and help you to rest."

Zane took it without a word and curled into a ball in the bed. The sight did a number on Jude's control. The last thing he wanted was for his son to get hurt.

Jude's mother came into the room and he knew he had to put a stop to all the family togetherness. He and Zane had to deal with this alone. But he would never be rude to his mother.

"I just want to say good-night," Kate said, kissing Zane's forehead. "Good night, my precious baby."

"Don't call me that," Zane snapped, and Jude moved

toward the bed. Zane had never been disrespectful to his grandmother and Jude wouldn't allow it, either.

"Zane."

"I'm sorry." Then he started to cry and Jude gestured for everyone to leave the room.

Jude sat on the bed and gave his son a minute. "I know you're hurting, but sometimes we have to feel the pain before we can feel the joy. I'm here to help you and I love you. So many people love you."

"I don't want to see her again."

Jude swallowed, knowing a line had been drawn and he had to honor what he'd told his son. He wouldn't force him to see or talk to Paige again. "Okay." He pulled the Star Wars sheets over Zane and kissed his cheek. "Good night."

"Dad-dy." The name was drawn out and Jude knew his son was drifting into sleep. Jude sat with him until he was sound asleep.

Slowly, Jude went into his room and stopped short when he saw Phoenix lying on the bed. He sat up when he noticed Jude.

"How's the kid?"

"Not good." He ran a hand through his hair. "I shouldn't have forced it. It was too soon, but I thought…"

"It's been a rough day. Don't beat yourself up. Tomorrow everything will be better."

"I don't know, Phoenix. I've never seen Zane this upset."

"I know absolutely nothing about kids, but I've been told that they're tough. And Zane's a tough little kid. Dudley tried to knock him out of the saddle, but Zane kept holding on, refusing to give up. I think that says something about his character. He's mad at his mother.

He made that abundantly clear. My guess is that will pass. You just have to give him time."

"She was so hurt by his words."

"Yeah, but she had to have known it wouldn't be a picnic."

"She said she was prepared, but how do you prepare for something like that?" Jude had been peeping around the door, just in case Zane needed him, and he'd seen the shattered look on Paige's face. She hadn't been prepared at all.

"Can you stay here for a little while?"

"Um… I guess. Why?"

"I have to make sure she's okay."

Phoenix groaned. "Jude, don't do this. You barely survived the first time and now you're jumping right back…"

"Zane should sleep for a while. I won't be gone long. Call me if he even stirs. Just don't leave him alone."

Phoenix lay back on the bed and reached for the remote control. "Okay, but you better get your butt back here in a hurry."

Jude was out of the house in five minutes. His mother was in her room, so he didn't have to explain anything. Everyone else had gone to their own homes. It was like living in a fishbowl.

It didn't take him long to make it to Paige's house. He was just hoping she hadn't driven back to Austin. A car was in the driveway and the house was dark. The car wasn't Staci's, so Paige must have rented one. That puzzled him. Was she staying in the house?

He wasn't sure what he was doing here. He thought she might need comforting after the talk with Zane, but clearly she had gone to bed or had left with Staci. He'd worried for nothing. Then it hit him. He was repeating an old pattern of comforting Paige. So many times he'd come here when her mother had been so vile to her. But Paige didn't need him anymore. It was about time he faced that. Even though he was still attracted to her, she had moved on to the life she'd wanted without him. But those old habits still died hard.

Paige didn't bother with the lights in the house. She went straight to her bedroom and cried as though her whole world was crashing down around her, and in a way, it had. Her son's anger destroyed all her confidence and made her weak because he had that much power. He had every right to say what he wanted. She just hadn't been prepared for the pain.

The sound of a door opening had her sitting up straight. She hadn't locked the door, but this was Horseshoe and she felt safe. She got out of bed and tiptoed to the doorway and down the hall. She could see a figure, a tall dark figure, standing near and her heart leaped into her throat.

"Paige."

She sagged against the wall at the sound of the voice that was dear to her. *Jude.*

"I'm in the bedroom." She went back and sat on the bed, waiting for him.

"Why are there no lights on?"

"Because I like the dark. In the light, I can see all my flaws and there are many."

His shadowy figure framed the doorway. "Well, it's hard to see. Are you living here now?"

"Yes. With the new paint and all, it looks so much better and I wanted to be near in case Zane…you know…"

"Yeah." He moved farther into the room.

"Why are you here and not with Zane?"

He sat on the bed beside her and it sagged, drawing them closer. "His head was hurting, so I gave him a pill the doctor prescribed and he's out for the night. I was worried about you."

"What if he wakes up?"

"Phoenix is with him. How are you?"

"I've cried until I can't cry anymore. Now I'm just numb. I knew it would be hard, but I never imagined it would hurt this bad. It hurts."

He put his arm around her and she rested her head on his shoulder, loving his strength and his softness at the same time. There was no one like Jude, with his big heart and his code of honor. That was why she never minded too much when he was quiet. She knew she could trust and depend on him no matter what.

"I'm sorry." He kissed her hair and his lips trailed to her cheek, to her jaw and then to the corner of her mouth. She touched his face and felt the stubble of his beard and breathed in the scent of him, which, oddly, smelled like birthday cake.

"You've been eating cake."

"Mmm. Mom baked a celebration cake for Zane."

"Jude." She buried her face into his chest and burrowed against him, trying to get as far away from herself as she could. If she could soak up one ounce of goodness from him, maybe she could breathe normally again.

His arms went around her and he held her, rocking her gently, and her feelings for him were as new and vibrant as they'd ever been. "We've made mistakes, Paige, and it's time to stop paying for them. It's time to start living."

"It just kills me that he's hurting."

"Shh." His lips touched hers and it was like striking

a match. Every sense ignited and all she wanted was him. Completely and forever. His mouth opened over hers, their tongues tasted and danced, and they took and gave until they were breathless with need. Time and place ceased to exist. It was just them, two teenagers or two adults. It didn't matter. It was all the same because it was Jude and Paige and it would always be that way.

Her hand went to his belt buckle. She knew what she wanted.

"Paige."

His voice was hoarse and she reveled in the husky undertone. "Don't think, Jude. Just feel."

"But…"

"No worries." She pulled his shirt out of his jeans and her hands splayed across his roughened masculine skin. After that, there was no turning back for either of them. She unsnapped his shirt with lightning speed and her T-shirt was gone in an instant. The rest of their clothes were thrown to the floor.

And they were skin on skin, renewing all those feelings that had been dormant for way too long. He lay back and she lay on top of him, enjoying his hardened muscles, which fit perfectly into hers. His hands touched all those sensitive places he knew so well and she in turn stroked and caressed every inch of him until they both were sweaty, panting and beyond rational thought.

He rolled her onto her back and they came together in perfect harmony, as they always had. The moment his body joined hers, a thought ran through her head: *Welcome home.* That was the way it felt. She was home in his arms.

She bit into his shoulder as pleasure rocketed through her body. The taste of salt and blood filled her senses and she wanted to remember this moment forever. Because she knew beyond any doubt that their love would never end.

Jude breathed deeply and tried to calm his racing heart but he was far from calm. He was charged. Fulfilled. Complete. In a way that only she could make him feel.

He softly kissed her nose, her mouth, then trailed down to her tender breast. Her skin was a satiny palette and he soaked up every sweet nuance that was Paige. His Paige. His beautiful, intelligent, incredibly naive Paige.

The hum of a passing car outside invaded his fantasy. His paradise. He winced at the reality. He drew away and pulled her with him. They lay together in the darkened room as the outside world went on. For a moment in time the world had stood still. Just for them. Now he had to face one more mistake.

Loving her didn't feel like a mistake.

He'd forgotten her. Gotten over her. Now everything was as real and new as ever.

But it still was a mistake.

Her life wasn't in Horseshoe. His would always be. He pushed it to the never-never part of his mind and held her because he couldn't let go just yet. He selfishly held on to these minutes that he needed just to survive.

She slept peacefully in his arms. Content. Her breath fanned his cheek and a pain shot through him as he pulled away and reached for his clothes. Silently, he dressed. She slept on and he was grateful for that. He had to go. His son was waiting. Their son.

Unable to resist, he kissed her one more time.

"Jude," she murmured.

He took a long breath and walked out of the room. As he did, he was very aware that he'd made everything that much worse. How many mistakes could one man make in a lifetime?

Paige woke up to a lethargic feeling. She rolled over and reached for Jude, and all her hand encountered was an empty spot. He'd gone. But then, she'd known that he would. Their son needed him. She was just happy that he'd come last night to help soothe her aching heart. She pulled the sheet over her naked body and went back to sleep.

Two hours later she was up and dressed and busy painting, but her thoughts were on Jude and Zane and she hoped her son was much better this morning. She kept waiting for a phone call from Jude to let her know how things were, but it never came. By midafternoon she knew it wouldn't. His quietness now would test her patience.

Zane slept until ten the next morning and at first it worried Jude. But his son had had a rough Saturday, so Jude let him sleep in, knowing he needed the rest. When he woke up, he was bubbly and chatty, as always. The ankle was a little more swollen and Zane said it didn't hurt that bad. Jude didn't give him any more medication, because he wanted to save it for when he really was in pain.

After a shower, Zane changed into shorts and a T-shirt. "Look at my trophy, Dad." He stood on one foot in front of the dresser where it was displayed, stroking it lovingly. He ignored the box his mother had given him, sitting next to it.

They were back to pretending Paige didn't exist. Zane

hobbled around on one foot and Jude helped him down the stairs to the living room. His grandmother made a fuss over him and Zane was all smiles. Jude just hated that once again they would have to tackle the subject of the elephant in the room: his mother. But not until later.

"I'm making a special dinner just for you," his grandmother told him. "Chicken-fried steak, mashed potatoes and gravy."

"Oh, boy."

"It's almost eleven. Would you like a glass of milk or something to hold you over?"

"Okay."

"Dad, could you bring my trophy downstairs, please?"

Jude did as his son requested and the morning passed quickly as the whole family turned out to cheer up Zane. He was the center of attention, except when baby John stole it every now and then wanting to kiss Zane's boo-boo.

Over lunch, Zane talked about the race and Dudley hitting him with the crop. Jude was glad he was talking about it, because he didn't want him suppressing that, too.

"The next time I see Dudley McCray, I'm going to beat the crap out of him," Elias said.

Zane's face crumpled. "No, Uncle Elias, don't do that."

"Hey, buddy, I was just joking," his brother hastened to reassure him.

"Good, because I don't want you to hurt him. It doesn't feel good to be hurt."

Elias did something unexpected. He got up and hugged Zane. "No one's going to hurt you again."

There was gut-wrenching silence around the table and then Phoenix slayed the emotion-stealing moment with, "Who wants to play poker this afternoon?"

"I do!" Zane shouted, and Jude stared at his son. His brothers played poker a lot and Zane had never shown any interest in it.

"You got any money?" Elias asked with a gleam in his eye.

"Yes. It's in my room." Zane looked at Jude. "Can you get it, Dad?"

"I don't know if I want you playing poker with…"

"Dad, please."

"The boy wants to learn, so let him," was Grandpa's response. "I'll make sure these yahoos don't mistreat him."

Jude had never feared for one moment that his brothers would mistreat Zane. He was just hoping that he and Zane could have some time alone this afternoon. But maybe fun time with his uncles would be best.

He gave his son five dollars out of his pocket and told him when he lost that, the game was over. But he knew his son. He learned things quickly and easily. If his brothers and Grandpa didn't watch out, he'd clean their clocks.

Jude left his son in his brothers' hands and went to his saddle-making workshop to be alone. He had to think. Paige filled his mind so completely that he had to get his thoughts straight. He'd wanted to call her this morning but had thought better of that. He had to talk to her soon, though. He just wasn't sure what to say. Being quiet solved a lot of problems. He didn't have to stress over words. That left a big wad of emotions that were never expressed. And it was the reason he'd found himself at a hospital signing away his rights to his son. He never wanted to go back to being that person.

The moment he opened the door, the scent of leather greeted him and he relaxed. His parents had worried about the fact that he was so quiet, and they'd wanted to get him involved in something that would help him. So he'd taken woodworking and leather craft in school just to get them off his back. To his surprise, he'd loved it and he'd loved the teacher, who had taught him so much. He'd diligently worked at his craft and improved. It was something he was proud of and something he could talk about. Now it was more than a hobby. Every saddle he sold went into Zane's college fund. But Zane would very likely be like his mother and receive a full scholarship. There would be extras, though, and Jude wanted to be prepared. He spent many evenings cutting and working with leather.

A black saddle with silver conchas took pride of place in front of his desk. He'd made the saddle for his father when he was fifteen and his father had used it until the day he died. One day Jude would give it to Zane, who had never met his grandfather. Jude wanted his son to have a part of the man who had shaped Jude's life.

He picked up a soft cloth and leather cream and rubbed it into the saddle. Every time he did this, he felt closer to his father. The leather was smooth and had a sheen to it. Jude leaned back on his desk and stared at the saddle. He could almost hear his father's words. *Do your best, son. That's all I'll ever ask of you.*

I'm trying, Dad, Jude replied silently. *I still love her, but I don't see a future for us.*

"Jude?"

Chapter 14

"Paige." Jude swung around with a startled look on his face.

"I don't mean to intrude, but a guy with long hair and a scar on his face told me you were in here. I wanted to know how Zane is today. I thought you would call."

"I've been busy." His words were testy and the new feelings of the morning began to fade. "He's pretending you don't exist and I'm giving him time before I force it again."

She drew a steadying breath and looked around the room, with its tables covered with leather pieces, a working stool, different machines, a big sink, leather-making tools covering one wall and a big desk. "You have your own shop now."

"Yeah, I built it about two years after Zane was born.

I needed to make extra money for him. I wanted him to have everything."

Her throat clogged at the accusing implication, and the man who'd made love to her last night was gone. A cold stranger was staring back at her. She walked over to the black saddle and touched it. "I remember when you made this in school. We weren't dating then, but everyone knew how excited you were to give it to your dad."

"Yeah. I never dreamed he would die that quickly."

"I'm so sorry about that. I know how much you loved him."

He stared at the rag in his hand. "I wish he could've seen Zane. He would have loved him." He moved to a table and placed the rag on it and then turned to her. "What are you doing here?"

"I wanted to check on Zane."

"I wished you'd called first."

"I did, but you didn't answer your phone."

He patted his shirt pockets and then his jeans. "I must've left it at the house."

"How's he feeling?"

"Sad, but my brothers are cheering him up."

"I see." She should have never come here, but with the newfound emotions of the night, she couldn't stay away. Clearly it was only one-sided. But she wasn't going to walk away without an explanation. "What's wrong? You're different this afternoon."

He swallowed visibly and remained silent, as he always did. That angered her. She had hoped he'd outgrown that.

"If you don't talk, we can't solve anything."

"You want me to talk? Okay." His words were sharp, as if he'd been honing them for years. "When you first came back, you said there was nothing here for you. And you said the same thing over twelve years ago. I'm here, Paige. Didn't that mean anything to you?"

"Of course it did."

"No, it didn't. You went on with your plans as if I didn't exist."

"That's not true. We talked about the baby and you never offered any solutions. I kept waiting, Jude, for you to make suggestions, but you never did. So don't lay a guilt trip on me."

He took a deep breath and stared at the ceiling. "When I took you to Austin to the airport, you kept crying, and I didn't know what to say to you. Words were just not there. When did we stop talking? That's what I'd like to know. When did we start forgetting the important stuff?"

"The moment I told you I was pregnant, things changed. You were different and more quiet than usual. That's why I listened to Mrs. Carstairs. But we both decided the baby would be better off with a loving couple."

"We were a loving couple!" he shouted, and for a moment a spasm of fear gripped her. "I just kept thinking we were doing the right thing, but in my heart I knew we weren't. I focused on you and your career and your dreams and I should've been focusing on the baby and his life and his dreams."

She wanted him to talk and now she had to listen and she had to bear each word, even though they cut right through her skin.

"I was going to join Phoenix and Paxton and rodeo that summer. I had to pack and I was going to meet them in Amarillo the next day. But every mile I drove toward Horseshoe, I wasn't thinking about the rodeo. I was thinking about that baby I left behind. He was mine. He had my blood and the closer I got to Horseshoe, the more the rodeo faded from my mind. I couldn't live with myself if I just walked away. Telling my mother was the hardest thing I've ever had to do, besides giving my son away. She supported me and I was able to get Zane back and I will always be grateful for that. I've protected him for over twelve years now. Everything I do is for Zane."

He ran both hands through his hair and seemed to stagger with all the words that had come out of him. Words he'd never said before. "I knew nothing about babies. I'd bounced Eden around and played with her, but I never fed her or changed her diapers. It was a rude awakening for an eighteen-year-old boy. I learned everything I had to do, and for someone who slept soundly, I learned to wake up at the slightest noise because Zane might need me. It wasn't easy by any means and I've made so many bad decisions. But if Zane doesn't want to see you again, I'm going to ask you to leave."

"No, Jude, please." The plea came from deep within her and she would beg if she had to. She might not deserve it, but she was willing to do anything to be a part of her son's life.

"How long do you plan to stay in Horseshoe?" he asked instead of answering.

The question flustered her. "I don't know. As long as it takes."

"But you have to go back?"

"Yes, I have to finish my residency."

"And what about Zane? You're going to walk away from him once again?"

"Why are you being so mean?"

"Because I'm a father and I have to look out for what's

best for my son. If he gets to know you and you leave, how do you think he's going to feel?"

She hung her head and stared at the concrete floor as twelve years came full circle and she now had to face the biggest decision of her life. This time she would get it right, even if it meant giving up everything she'd ever worked for. But Jude wasn't going to believe that.

"I'm not trying to be mean," he said before she could formulate a response. "I thought about it since last night. I'm falling back into that old pattern of trying to comfort you and then we have sex and that doesn't solve anything. It only makes everything much worse. We have to stop now and put Zane first."

She gathered the remnants of her shattered pride and raised her head to stare into his dark troubled eyes. "I know you want me to leave, but I'm not going to. Zane knows I'm here and I'm hoping eventually he'll open the box and want to see me. That's my last hope and until it's gone, I'm not going anywhere." On feet that felt as heavy as lead, she walked to the door.

"Paige."

She turned to look at him one more time. "You can stop talking now, Jude. Really."

Jude sat in his chair, leaned his head back and waited for the roof to cave in on him. That was the way he felt, as if his world had just been destroyed. But he'd done what was needed to protect Zane and to protect himself.

It was just as Phoenix had said: Jude had barely survived the first time and he couldn't do it again. As much as he loved her, there was no future for them. There hadn't been years ago and there wasn't now. God only knew why they were so attracted to each other.

With a sigh, he got up and went in search of his son. Zane was all that mattered to him. Laughter rode on the afternoon breeze and brightened the spring day. It was Zane. The death grip on his heart eased at the sound. His son was happy again.

He stopped as he saw Quincy, Jenny and Zane coming toward him. Quincy had Zane piggyback and was evidently taking him to the house.

"Hey, Dad," Zane shouted. "Uncle Quincy took me to see Bear and Little Dove."

"I see," he said as he reached them. "Is the poker game over?"

Zane slid to the ground and stood on one foot. "I made a bunch of money. Grandpa says he's not playing with me anymore. And Uncle Elias wants to know how I did it. I told him I just learned it."

Jude mussed his son's hair. "It's time for you to get some rest."

"Aw, Dad."

Jude squatted in front of the boy and Zane climbed onto his back. "Thanks for taking care of him," Jude said to Quincy and Jenny.

"No problem." Quincy waved as they walked away.

"Where did you go, Dad?" Zane asked.

To rip my heart out.

"I'm starting a new saddle and had to get some things done while you were busy."

"Oh."

"How's the foot?"

"Good. I haven't been walking on it."

As they made their way to the house, Zane laid his head against Jude's. That one little action showed Jude his son was still torn up inside. He wanted to be close to his father. Zane didn't have to worry. Jude was doing everything he could to protect him. But it came with a dose of regrets followed with a chaser of what-could-have-been.

Paige went home and painted and painted. If she kept busy, she couldn't think, and that was what she wanted. Just to be numb for a while to let the pain sink in so she could deal with it.

The green in her mother's bedroom didn't suit her, so she drove to Temple to buy more paint. She knew she wasn't acting rational, but that didn't matter, either. She was just going through the motions.

This time she bought candy-apple red and painted one wall. The rest she painted wheat. Even though she wasn't crazy about the color it accented the red. She stood back and looked at her handiwork. It was fiery, loud and bold. Just like her mother. It was perfect.

She had no idea what time it was. It was dark outside and her eyelids grew heavy. She curled up on the carpet to rest a bit. That was where Staci found her the next morning.

Staci sat on the floor beside her. "What's wrong? Are you high on all this paint? It smells in here."

"I have the windows opened."

"I've been calling and you're not answering your phone."

Paige stretched her shoulders. "I've been busy."

"Why are you sleeping on the floor?"

Paige brushed hair out of her eyes and realized her ponytail had come undone. A lot of things had come undone, and she pushed everything down inside her, not wanting to talk about it.

"Don't do that."

"What?"

"Pretend you're not upset. What happened?"

All kinds of lies ran through her head to tell her sister so she wouldn't worry, but she was too tired to voice any of them. What did it matter? Nothing seemed to matter anymore.

She got to her feet and went to the kitchen to make coffee. Staci followed. Sitting at the kitchen table, she bared her soul because she was too weak to do anything else.

"Zane was hurt yesterday and now Jude wants you to leave?"

She swallowed the sob in her throat. "Yes. Then we wouldn't have to face that we have a problem. Zane doesn't want to see me or have anything to do with me and Jude doesn't want to push him."

"Oh, honey, I'm sorry."

Staci got up and brought the coffee back to the table. "He just needs time, Paige. Don't let it get to you."

"I'm like a pincushion and I don't think one more stick is going to bother me, but it just might do me in, too. I deserve all of this and that's what makes me so sad. What kind of mother would allow someone to persuade her to give her child away?"

"I'm not even going to answer that, because you're feeling sorry for yourself and that's not the way to handle this. I firmly believe that everything you did was for that baby's welfare. Since I lived with our mother, I know exactly how you were feeling, so no one had better ever say that to me."

A hint of a smile threatened her lips. "It's nice to have someone in my corner."

"I'm there, kiddo. Always." Staci played with her

cup. "I'm not saying this to hurt you or anything, but you were always so sensitive about what Mom said to you. You always took it to heart. Whereas Luke and I let it wash right over us. We were good at running out the door to friends just to get away from her. But you always stayed so she wouldn't be alone. That was your first big mistake."

Paige stared at the new yellow paint on the wall, bright and sunny, and it reminded her of something. "When you graduated and packed your things to leave for your new job in Temple, I was sad because I felt more alone than ever. Mom went out and bought me a pretty yellow sundress and sandals to match. It was so beautiful. I went down to the bakery and hung out with Angie, Rachel and Jenny. I had nice clothes just like they did and I felt a part of the group. I came home later that evening and Mom was drunk in the front yard. She couldn't even make it to the door. I helped her get into the house and all my newfound confidence just evaporated. Funny how I remember that one little incident, and her kind gesture was then like a slap in the face, as so many other things were."

Staci clapped her hands loudly and Paige jumped. "I want you to stop this. Stop all the remembering. You don't see me doing that. I put it all behind me and so has Luke. Now you have to do the same."

Paige took a gulp of coffee. "Why can't I?"

Staci reached across the table and clasped Paige's hand. "Listen to me. Mom asked about you all the time and she told the people at the facility that her daughter was smart and becoming a doctor."

"She did?"

"Yes, one of the nurses even asked me if it was true and I told her it was. I think she treated you badly after Luke and I left because it was her way of forcing you to stay. If she criticized and demeaned you enough, you wouldn't have the confidence to do anything else but stay. She had a fear of being alone, so she did everything she could to keep you here. When you left, she fell apart. She stayed drunk all the time and I had so many calls to come do something with her and I finally did when she fell and broke her hip. I knew it was time. I think she just really missed you."

A tear slipped from Paige's eye and she remembered all the times she was there to help her mom and all the times she was so embarrassed and all the times she wished her mom was someone else. Life had a funny way of showing the past through a two-way mirror. Paige needed her mother and her mother needed Paige. But they'd never made the connection as mothers and daughters should. And that was the saddest thing of all.

She drew a deep breath and let it flow through her system and wash away all the inner turmoil that had been building in her. It was time to let it go. Her childhood had shaped her into an insecure, naive teenager. But she had grown stronger and she'd built a life of making decisions and choices that were better for her and now she had to embrace the present with all that confidence and go after what she wanted. She had to stop feeling sorry for herself. She had to stop blaming everyone else. She had to take full responsibility for her life.

No one was talking her into doing something she didn't want to do. Not ever again.

Not even Jude.

* * *

Jude was up early and showered. He slipped into jeans and quickly ran a razor over his face. He had to take Zane to the doctor, so looking presentable was required. Otherwise he wouldn't, because they would be baling hay today and it required no personal maintenance.

As he was snapping his shirt, he heard Zane moving around in his room and he went to see what his son was up to. The boy was stuffing books into his backpack.

"What are you doing? You're not going to school. You have to go to the doctor this morning."

Zane grabbed his jeans and sat on the bed to put them on. "I can go later. I have to go to school, Dad. I can't break my record. I haven't missed a day of school since second grade when I had the flu."

"The ER doctor said you had to rest for a couple of days. As soon as your doctor's office is open, I'm going to call and see if he can work you in. We'll take it from there."

"No." Zane zipped his jeans. "When Aunt Rachel comes, I'm getting in her car and going to school and you can't stop me."

Not one of those days, please.

Jude placed his hands on his hips. "You want to say that again?"

Zane shook his head. "It took all my courage to say it the first time."

Jude didn't smile at the admission. When Zane talked back, Jude had to apply all of his parenting skills. "This is how it's going, son. As I said, I'll call the doctor's office as soon as it's open and you're going to go in. If he says you can go to school, then I'll take you. But if he says no, you're coming home and spending the day with Leah and baby John."

"Aw, Dad."

"Do you need some help getting dressed?"

"No."

"I'll help you downstairs when you're ready."

"You treat me like a baby."

Jude stared at his son. This was so unlike him and Jude knew it was because of everything that happened over the weekend. But Jude had rules for his son and he didn't want him to be a spoiled brat.

"And you're treating me with disrespect."

Zane's eyes opened wide. "I just want to go to school."

"You will when the doctor says you can. This conversation is over, Zane, and you better get in a better frame of mind, because I'm losing my patience."

Jude headed to his room and finished dressing. When he went back into Zane's room, his son was dressed with the backpack in his hand. Jude noticed the trophy tucked inside, the top sticking out. He sighed, not wanting to get into another argument. He'd deal with the trophy later.

He piggybacked him downstairs to the kitchen. All the brothers were there and Zane perked up. As they ate breakfast, the doorbell rang. Jude pushed his plate back and went to see who it was.

The sheriff, Hardy Hollister, the DA, a woman who Jude thought was Malachi's wife and Dudley stood there. Now what?

Chapter 15

"Could we speak to you for a minute, Jude?" the sheriff asked.

Jude stepped aside and followed them into the den. After everyone was seated, Wyatt continued, "This is about what happened on Saturday."

Jude rested his forearms on his knees with his hands clasped together. "I figured as much. Dudley deliberately beat my son to win a race. I'm not happy about that."

"I'm not, either, Mr. Rebel," the woman said. "Actually, I'm quite horrified by the fact that my son would do this."

Jude looked at Wyatt, trying not to be swayed by the woman. "What do you want from me, Wyatt?"

"Mrs. McCray is asking for leniency, but I'm not inclined to be too lenient. If this had happened to my kid, I'd probably file charges."

"Then I don't understand what you're doing here. You're the law. Do what you have to."

"He'll be charged with assault and sent to juvie for time specified by the judge. He'll have a criminal record."

"I don't have a problem with that. Dudley has picked on Zane for years and it has to stop. That time is now."

"Please, Mr. Rebel," the woman pleaded. "I'm begging you. It's not Dudley's fault. He's influenced by his father, who routinely beats him. I'm finally standing up for my kids. From this day forward he'll never lay a hand on one of them again, nor will he lay a hand on me in anger. If you will give my child a second chance, I promise he'll never be mean to your son again. We'll pay all the hospital bills and whatever you want us to do."

Jude didn't let the desperation in the woman's voice get to him. "How can I be assured he won't hurt my kid again? Zane has scars that he will have for the rest of his life and showing mercy to a kid who did that is just not in my nature. And Malachi is an angry, bitter man. He will continue to do what he always does and I don't think your stand now is going to help."

"I already told Malachi that if he does anything to harm my children again, I will leave and take them with me and he'll never see them again. My family is a Christian family and I'd never been hit in my whole life until I married Malachi. I'm tired, Mr. Rebel, of this kind of lifestyle, but it was my choice and now I'm trying to make it work for my kids. But if it doesn't, I will be gone and you have my word on that."

"Ma'am—"

"My name is Cheryl," she interrupted.

He didn't want to know her name or anything else

about the McCray family. He clenched his jaw, refusing to make this personal. "Ma'am, Dudley hurt my kid badly and I just can't overlook that."

"Dad." Zane hopped into the room and held on to the sofa. Jude got to his feet. He didn't want Zane to hear this. "Don't do it."

"Zane, go back to the kitchen."

"I was the one who was hurt and I should have a say in Dudley's punishment."

Dudley sat with his head bowed and hadn't moved or spoken a word and Jude had to wonder if this was all his mother's doing. He looked at the boy. "What do you have to say, Dudley?"

"Send me to jail. I don't care."

His mother paled and put her arm around him. "Lose the attitude and tell these people how you really feel. Tell them how you cried at what you'd done and you asked me a dozen times to call and see how Zane was doing. You didn't mean to hurt him."

"I didn't," Dudley muttered. "But I was afraid I was going to get beaten again and I had to win and I didn't know what else to do." The boy raised his head and turned to look at Zane. "I'm sorry I hurt you. But you're so smart and you're always so perfect it makes me mad."

"Is that why you call me names?" Zane asked.

"I guess."

"Do you promise to never call me names again and to never be mean to me again?"

Dudley nodded with a glimmer of hope in his eyes. "Yes."

Zane looked at his father. "I don't want to press charges, Dad."

"I'm not just letting this drop, son."

"It's not going to be dropped, Jude," Hardy said, getting to his feet. "If you agree, I'll ask the judge for a probation period for three months. During that time if Dudley does one thing to harm Zane or anyone else, he'll serve some time in juvie."

"But he has to keep his nose clean and Malachi has to abide by the rules, too," Wyatt said. "I'll make sure he understands them. And Mrs. McCray will see to everything else. Is that okay with you?"

Hell, no!.

But he looked at his son and saw forgiveness as bright as the sun shining outside. Zane had a big heart and Jude had to wonder why that consideration wasn't extended to his mother.

"Yes, and my son will be well watched by everyone in this family."

"I understand." The sheriff nodded and the group walked toward the door.

"Thank you, Mr. Rebel." The woman offered her hand and he shook it.

"Considering the relationship between the Rebels and McCrays, I told Mrs. McCray this was a waste of time," Wyatt added, standing at the door. "Maybe the younger generation is getting it right. Thanks, Jude." They shook hands.

Jude returned to his son. "That was very understanding of you."

"Dudley comes to school a lot with bruises on his arms and face and that has to be rough, to be beaten all the time."

"But he hurt you."

"I know." Zane looked down at the sofa. "But I don't want to hurt him. I would like it if we could just live in peace."

He'd never been more proud of his son than he was at that moment. Jude was still leery about the McCrays, though. But he was willing to offer the olive branch in hopes that peace was a viable thing for everyone.

His brothers had a lot to say about the olive branch, but Jude ignored them and called the doctor for Zane. The nurse said they could work him in at 8:30 a.m. if Jude could get him there. They were on the road to Temple in five minutes.

The doctor said everything was healing nicely and didn't see any reason for Zane not to go to school, except for the ankle. He'd received the X-rays on his computer from the ER, and as the ER doctor had said, there were no broken bones or sprains. It was merely bruised and would need a few days to heal. He suggested crutches and Jude bought them at the pharmacy nearby. The pharmacist showed Zane how to use them and Jude had Zane back in Horseshoe and at school by ten o'clock.

Zane grabbed his backpack from the backseat and Jude noticed the trophy sticking out and once again he thought he should say something. But Zane broached the topic first.

"Dad, would it be bragging if I showed off my trophy?"

"Yes, I think so, especially around Dudley and the McCrays. Why don't you take a couple of pictures and you can show Erin and Jody and all your girl friends."

"Dad." Zane sighed in irritation. "I have guy friends, too."

"I didn't notice that many on Saturday."

Zane removed the trophy from the backpack, took several pictures and then laid it on the backseat. "I'm a chick magnet. Maybe I take after Uncle Elias or Uncle Paxton." Zane laughed as he slipped on his backpack. He then hobbled toward the entrance to the school.

Jude waited until his son was in class before he went to see the principal to let him know what had happened and that he wanted Zane watched by all the teachers. The principal said he would take care of it. On his way out, he met Annabel in the hall.

"Jude, how nice to see you. How is Zane?"

He told her everything that had happened and added, "I'd appreciate it if you'd look out for him."

"No problem." She looked squarely at him. "How's it going with Zane's mother? I saw her and she really was amazing, the way she took care of his injuries."

"Yeah, she's an accomplished doctor, but things aren't going all that well. Zane refuses to see her and we're kind of in a holding pattern right now."

"I'm sure it will all work out." Her tone was different than it had been before. Cool and professional. Not like the extra-friendly teacher she had been.

"Thank you."

She walked off down the hall and Jude knew whatever they'd had was over. No one affected him like Paige. He might as well admit that. Also, he wasn't sure anything would've happened with Annabel even if Paige hadn't come back. Something was always holding him back. Or someone.

As he drove away from the school, he wanted to tell Paige how her son was doing. He wasn't apologizing for yesterday. He had to take a stand, even if it hurt. But he so badly wanted her to know that Zane was okay and back in school.

At the stop sign, he pulled out his phone to text her. His thumbs paused over the keypad. He couldn't keep doing this. He had to maintain some distance and texting her wasn't going to help their situation. He slipped the phone back into his pocket.

After showering and changing clothes, Paige was in a better state of mind. Seeing and talking to Staci was what she'd needed to get her head straight. After Staci left, she drove to the antiques store and bought a nightstand, a lamp and a picture frame.

She put Zane's photo in the frame and placed it by her bed. Again, she was just going through the motions. She had no plans to live in the house, only to keep busy, and she wanted her son's photo beside her.

The house had so many memories, but they weren't dragging her down like before. With the new paint, everything was fresh and bright, which was the way she wanted to feel inside. She would get there. It would just take time. She went to her mother's room and sat on the carpet cross-legged, staring at the red wall. All the yelling, screaming, crying, drunken binges, different men trailing in and out of their house, and people talking behind their backs cumulated into a hard ball in her stomach.

She sucked air into her lungs and she saw her mother for who she was: a needy person, a person who desperately needed to feel loved. And she'd gotten that love the only way she'd known how. It had hurt her children, but her mother had never seen that. Paige sucked another breath into her chest and released it. She had to let go of all the bitterness and resentment. It was over and she couldn't keep reliving the moments that tainted her life, her future.

Drawing another breath, she whispered, "I forgive you." The ball in her stomach rose up, and instead of giving in to the nausea, she swallowed hard and let go. The ball dissipated and she felt relief for the first time in years. And just like the room, everything was fresh and new again.

She sensed she wasn't alone and she didn't need to turn to see who it was. His presence was undeniable. Jude.

Without taking her eyes off the wall, she said, "Did you get your second wind?"

"You asked me to talk and I did. I'm not apologizing for that. Zane is always my top priority."

She scooted to face him and then wished she hadn't. He leaned against the doorjamb in tight jeans and a blue shirt. His dark hair fell forward over his forehead as if he'd just removed his hat. Raw masculinity seemed to reach out and touch her and she desperately wanted to jump up and wrap her arms around him, to just feel his heart beating against hers. But she couldn't do that. As he'd said, Zane was now *their* top priority.

"What are you doing here?"

"I took Zane to the doctor this morning and he said everything was healing nicely. He just needs to rest his ankle for a few days. The doctor suggested crutches. I took him to school because he insisted and the doctor okayed it."

"I'm glad." She rubbed a paint spot on her jeans.

"Did he open the box?" She didn't want to ask, but she couldn't help herself.

"No, it's sitting on his dresser. I don't think he's even glanced at it."

She bit her lip to keep the revelation from getting to her.

"I thought you'd like to know that he doesn't want me to file charges against Dudley McCray."

"Why? He viciously beat Zane."

"The sheriff and the DA came out to the house to talk to us. Dudley has his own problems with his father, and Zane doesn't want him to get into any more trouble than he's already in. Dudley is on probation. If he screws up, he's going to juvenile hall."

"That was very understanding and compassionate of Zane."

"Yeah. That's how he is. He's upset now because you've come back, but give him time."

Her heart felt heavy from the warmth cradling it. The fact that Jude had come over here to tell her that made all the difference in the world. There was no one like Jude. And her son was just like him.

"Thank you."

He pushed away from the doorjamb and said, "It's red."

"What?" She had no idea what he was talking about.

He nodded toward the wall. "You were staring at it as if you didn't know what color it was. It's red. Bright red."

She smiled. An honest-to-God smile that reached inside her and would buffet her emotions for days to come. "Uh...yeah. It's red."

Before the pregnancy had rocked their world, Jude used to tease her all the time, trying to cheer her up. He had a dry wit that always brought her out of the dumps and she was reminded of that today.

Without another word, he walked out of the room and out of the house. That was okay. That was pure Jude and she understood him better than anyone.

She got to her feet, feeling more optimistic than she had in a long time. Whatever the future held, she was ready to face it. With a man like Jude waiting on the sidelines, there was nothing else she could do. Or wanted to do.

In the afternoon she decided to tackle the washer and dryer in the garage to see if they worked. She managed to pull the washer out and saw the hoses were cracked. A box of Luke's tools was in the garage. She removed the hoses and took them down to the hardware store to see if she could get new ones.

Bubba Wiznowski, Angie's brother, was in the store and he helped her to find what she needed and then came to the house and put them on. In no time, he had the washer working. And to her amazement, with a little cleaning, the dryer came on, too. Her first load of clothes was in the rinse cycle when she heard the doorbell.

She ran to the door in hopes it was Jude again. It wasn't. Rachel stood there.

"I don't mean to bother you."

"Come in. You're not bothering me."

"I don't have time. I'm on my way home. Since Zane is on crutches, Jude picked him up and I thought I'd stop by for a minute. Once a month we have a ladies' night out at Angie's office. We eat, drink, talk, laugh and have a good time. I was hoping you would join us. We'd love to have you come."

"Thank you, Rachel, for thinking of me, but under the circumstances, I don't think so."

Rachel rested her hand on the top of her stomach. "Just think about it. We get there around seven."

"Maybe next time. Thank you for being so nice."

"If you change your mind, we'll be there." Rachel turned away and Paige thought of something.

"Oh, Rachel. Does Mrs. Brimhall still teach at the school?"

"Yes, she's still teaching and a stickler for perfect English."

"Thank you. I might stop in to see her."

Paige waved to her friend as she drove away. It was nice of Rachel to ask, but she wasn't ready to face the people of Horseshoe. She had to see someone else first to exorcise the ghost from her past.

It was a little after four and she quickly drove to the school, feeling Mrs. Brimhall would still be there. Paige was in luck. A thin woman with salt-and-pepper hair sat behind a desk in Paige's old English classroom.

"Mrs. Brimhall."

The woman looked up and pushed her thick wire-rimmed glasses up the bridge of her nose. "Yes, dear. Can it wait until tomorrow? I was just closing up for the day."

"You don't recognize me, do you?" Paige walked farther into the room, and at the puzzled look on the woman's face, she added, "I'm Paige Wheeler."

"Oh, dear, how nice to see you. Should I call you Doctor now?"

"You can just call me Paige." She didn't want to go

into detail. She just wanted answers. "I was looking for Mrs. Carstairs. I would like to see her while I'm in town."

"She moved away years ago."

Paige already knew that. "Do you have any idea where she lives?" Mrs. Brimhall and Mrs. Carstairs were close friends back then and Paige was hoping she would know where the woman lived now.

"Poor Nancy. She's had a rough time."

"What do you mean?"

"She and her husband so desperately wanted a child and they had an adoption all set up, but it fell through. Nancy never talked much about it, so I don't know what really happened, but afterward she and her husband divorced and Nancy moved to Austin to be closer to her sister. We stayed in touch for a while, but then she met Fred and he is really controlling. I haven't heard from her in years."

"So she remarried?"

"Yes." Mrs. Brimhall's forehead crinkled. "His name was Fred Wilhelm. Like I said, a grouchy, controlling man. I didn't like him, but Nancy was pleased about the marriage. He had three kids and she was happy to be their mother."

"I was so hoping to get to see her."

"Sorry. She lives in Austin now."

"Thank you, Mrs. Brimhall." She looked around the room at the desks, a chalkboard and the computers. "Everything looks the same, except for the computers."

"Oh, yeah. The world is changing, and I must say, I'm so happy that Horseshoe has a success story."

Paige left while she could. She had the information

she wanted and now she would see Nancy Carstairs face-to-face. She couldn't even begin to heal until she saw the woman who had tried to steal her baby.

Chapter 16

Paige was in Austin by seven that evening. She would have made it sooner, but the traffic was heavy. A gas station was on the right, so she pulled off the freeway to fill up. Afterward she sat in her car and did some checking on her phone to locate Nancy. It didn't take her long to find the address of Fred Wilhelm.

The house was in a nice subdivision in south Austin. She parked at the curb and checked out the redbrick home with a manicured lawn. Blooming flowers decorated the flower beds and hanging baskets hung on the porch. The suburban lifestyle. The good life.

Nancy had certainly moved on and Paige took a moment to question what she was doing here. It wasn't going to change a thing, but something in her needed to see the woman who'd led her down a path to total devastation. Before she could go forward, she had to deal with all her feelings about Nancy Carstairs.

Getting out of the car, she took a deep breath and marched up the brick walk to the front door. She rang the doorbell and waited. The door opened and Nancy stood there looking much the same as she had almost thirteen years ago. Her blond hair was now streaked with gray and she'd gained some weight, but she still was the woman Paige had trusted with her life.

"Can I help…? Oh…Paige!"

Paige walked past her into the foyer before Nancy could shut the door in her face. "Yes, it's me. I bet you thought you would never see me again."

"Please leave." Nancy's voice was shaky. "I have nothing to say to you."

"That's too bad, because I have a lot to say to you. I trusted you and I trusted that you were giving me good advice, but instead you were devious and underhanded and did everything you could to make sure I gave my baby away."

"The baby was a burden to you and I offered you a good solution to go off to college and have your dream."

"As a naive teenage girl, I believed every word you said. I was conflicted and torn, but I wanted my baby to have the very best of everything. And you told me many times that my home environment was not a place to bring a baby into. You also told me that it would be detrimental for me to hold the baby or to even know the sex. All of that was bull. You see, I'm in obstetrics now and we stress to teenage girls that it is very important to hold their baby and to say goodbye. If they can do that, then they can deal with the aftermath of giving the child away."

"What do you want from me?"

"Nothing. My mother passed away and I came home from the funeral to learn that my son was being raised by his father. It was a shock at first, but now it's an incredible gift that I will always be grateful for. And I will forever be grateful that Jude chose that moment to stand up and speak up for our child."

Nancy twisted her hands nervously. "I would've given that baby a good home."

"He has a good home, the very best, with his biological family."

"Why did you come here? Yes, I deceived you, but it was for a good reason. Your baby would've been well taken care of and I would've loved it. I didn't feel I was doing anything wrong."

Paige stepped closer to her. "It's wrong to deceive a teenage girl so you can have her child. I'm sure it's illegal, too, but that's all over with. I just have this need to see your face so that I can put it all behind me."

"Nancy," a male voice called, and in a few seconds a man entered the room with three young children behind him. "We're waiting for dessert." The man looked at her with a deep frown. "Who is this?"

"It's a student from Horseshoe. She stopped by to say hi."

"It would have been nice if she had called. This is our dinnertime."

Paige faced the man with the accusing voice. "Yes, it would be nice if people were considerate." She turned and walked to the door and Nancy followed her. At the door, she said, "I was going to tell you that I hoped you rot in hell, but I think you're already there."

She drove away with a feeling of elation, as if she'd

slayed the dragon and victory was hers. But victory was short-lived. She had a long way to go to banish all the ghosts from her past.

When Jude drove up to the house with Zane, Phoenix was just rolling up on a Polaris Ranger. "Hey, Zane, this is what you can use to get around on until your ankle heals."

"Why didn't I think of that?" Zane hobbled to the ATV and climbed on. He revved it up. "I'm going to check on Bear." And off he went to the barn. Jude and Phoenix followed.

"How's he doing?" Phoenix asked.

"Trying to forget that his mother exists."

"That can't be good for him. He doesn't have to love her or anything, but in my opinion, it would be good for him to talk to her without all the anger. A lot of mistakes were made back then, but now's the time to make it right again."

"Yeah, but I'm going to give it time. I just don't know how long Paige is going to stay here, though. She never answered me."

Phoenix stopped walking and stared at Jude. "Then ask again. Speak up, for heaven sakes, Jude. Don't let her get away with evasive tactics. Zane is involved, too, now. You know you're never going to love anybody but Paige. Everybody knows that. No one in Horseshoe has ever asked about Zane's mother, because they know. They just don't know how it happened. And no one is brave enough to ask that to your face. It's time to bring all this out into the open and figure out your life with Paige or without her."

Jude stared off to the evening sun sinking in the west.

Phoenix was right. He had to figure out what was best for all of them. But first Zane had to understand why his mother had done what she'd done, and he didn't know how long that would take.

He'd told himself that morning that he wouldn't stop by and see Paige. But he'd found himself at the little house all the same. He'd known she was hurting and he was the cause of some of that hurt. That bothered him because he didn't like hurting people. And then she was staring at that damn wall and he couldn't figure out why. Of course, he hadn't asked. At that point, he'd rather not have known—he was sure it had something to do with her mother. Her whole life revolved around a mother who'd never loved her or cared about her and he sincerely hoped she was finding peace with that.

Later, Zane was tired. Walking on crutches took a lot of extra energy. After supper and a shower, Zane was out for the night. And the box was left unopened on the dresser.

The days fell into a pattern and Zane never mentioned his mother or the box. By Friday the swelling in his ankle had gone down and Zane said it didn't hurt to step on it. The crutches found a home in the closet. Since Zane was doing so well, Jude was wondering whether to force the issue once again. Paige had texted every day to ask about Zane and it was a real test of his patience not to go over and talk to her. She'd been back only a week and he realized how much he missed seeing her, talking to her, touching her. Oh, man, he was in so much trouble.

Paige spent her days working on the house and in the yard as she waited. She pulled weeds out of the flower beds and planted new flowers. She made a trip down to the antiques store and bought things for the house. That was a little insane since she wasn't planning on staying there, but it kept her busy. She walked around the town and spoke to people and renewed her love of the small town. But she grew doubtful that her son was ever going to acknowledge her.

Jude stayed away, and every time she heard a car, she'd run to the window to see if it was him. Sadly, it never was and she began to see just how much she needed him. How much she needed to simply hear his voice and be with him. They'd been apart too long. Was there still a chance for them?

On Saturday, Jude, Elias and Jericho worked on the hay baler. They usually hired a man to bale the hay, but since he'd raised his prices, Falcon had decided it would be cost effective if they took up the task themselves again.

After lunch on Sunday, Jude worked in his saddle shop and Zane played poker with Grandpa and the brothers. But Jude's mind was totally on Paige and how she was handling the wait. Tonight he might broach the subject with Zane. He was in a better mood and might listen. Jude had to make his son understand his world wasn't going to change if he spoke to his mother. It was just something he needed to do for his own peace of mind.

A thought kept running through his mind: Once Paige visited with her son, would she be gone from their lives again? That cut deep into Jude. Would she stay or would she go? And would he survive this time?

When he went back to the house, his mother was alone in the den. "Where's Zane?"

"He went upstairs a long time ago. I hope he's feeling okay."

"I'm sure he is. He's probably counting the money he won at poker."

"They had a lot of fun. It's good to see him happy again." His mom closed the farm and ranch magazine she was reading. "I try to stay out of my sons' childrearing decisions, but…"

"I'm on it, Mom. I'm just waiting for the right moment." He took the stairs two at a time to avoid a discussion on what he should or shouldn't do. He didn't need any advice, not even from his mother.

Jude went through his room into the bathroom, washed his hands and then continued into Zane's room. He stopped short in the doorway. Zane was in the middle of his bed with children's books all around him. Paige's box sat at the foot of the bed, opened.

Children's books? The box had been filled with children's books?

"Dad, listen."

Jude pushed the box aside to do just that.

Zane read from one of the books. "'My precious baby, today I felt you move for the first time and realized that a tiny human being is growing in me. Someone your dad and I created. A gift from God. That fills me with so much joy. I want to make all the right decisions for you because I want you to grow up to be a strong, healthy and secure person.'" He held the book out to Jude. "See, my mother wrote messages to me in all of the books. Want to hear another one?"

"Sure." Paige had never told him about the books, but then, they hadn't talked much about the baby, just what they needed to do. Avoidance was their mode of communication back then.

"'My precious baby, I'm sitting in the bathtub reading to you because you fill my every waking thought. My mother is yelling at me and I'm trying to shut out her voice. I feel resentment and bitterness toward her. I can't bring a precious baby into the house, because I feel she will poison you like she's poisoned me. I want the very best life for you and I'm afraid that means I will have to let you go. It will break my heart, but I want you to have everything that I never had. I want you to have love.'"

Jude swallowed hard as all those old emotions churned inside him. He tried to concentrate on Zane and his reaction. That was what was important. Zane's eyes were bright and shining as if he'd just discovered something beautiful that only he understood.

"Here's another, Dad." Zane picked up a book and began to read. "'My precious baby, today your father and I will travel to Austin to bring you into the world. And today we will let go and it will be the hardest thing we'll ever have to do. But I believe in my heart we're doing the right thing for you. You'll have two loving parents who will treasure you and love you and give you all the things that you'll need in this world. I will think of you always. I love you, my precious baby.'"

There was silence for a moment and Jude was glad because words clogged his throat in a way that prevented him from speaking. He'd been right there with her through all of it, but he'd never felt it so deeply as he did at that moment as he experienced her pain, her suffering in letting go.

"There's a lot more about the counselor she spoke to who gave her advice and how she encouraged her to do the right thing for her baby. I don't like those, but I'm glad they're there because I can read what she was feeling at the time."

"*Brown Bear, Brown Bear* is my favorite. It's where she wrote she felt me move for the first time."

Jude swallowed the sob in his throat. "Do you want to talk about your mother?"

"She's pretty, isn't she?"

"Yes. I always thought so."

"She wrote in one of the books she overate because she was nervous and people never knew she was pregnant."

"That's true. Her mother's cruel behavior was hard on Paige and the reason she made so many bad decisions."

"She's a doctor now."

"Yes, she is. She's has a few more months before she takes the Medical Licensing Exam and then she'll be working in obstetrics. Her favorite part is working with teenage girls who are undecided about adoption."

"Really?"

"Yes. She doesn't want another girl to go through what she did and she certainly doesn't want a girl listening to a counselor who does not have her best interest at heart."

There was silence again as Zane ran his fingers over the words inscribed inside a book, as if to soak up the message. "Dad, why did you never ask my mother to marry you?"

That was a tough question and he didn't want to lie to his son, but the explanation hung in his throat.

As if sensing Jude's difficulty, Zane said, "Were you afraid she'd say no?"

He looked into those dark eyes so much like his own and wondered if the kid was a mind reader. That was exactly how Jude had felt. If he had asked and she had said no, he would've been devastated. Fear was a powerful thing and he'd controlled his emotions until the moment he realized he'd lost his son. Losing Paige was something he still hadn't grown accustomed to.

"Yeah. Her life was set and if I had asked her to stay, she would have had to give it all up and I didn't have the courage to do that."

"You're the bravest person I know, Dad. How many teenage guys would go back and get their kid after he had been given up for adoption?" Zane flipped through the book without looking at Jude. "Do you ever regret doing that?"

"Not for a second." That answer was easy. That one action in his life would stand out until the day he died and probably beyond. It had taken every ounce of courage he had.

"I don't think I want to be a teenager. They're crazy. Even Eden was crazy. What happens to them?"

Jude smiled at his son. "You're a smart kid and I'm betting you can figure it out."

"Yeah. It's about girls and sex and all that stuff."

"Yes, and all that stuff."

Zane picked up a book and placed it back into the box. "Dad, do you think we can visit my mother?"

And just like that, the world had righted itself and his son was now ready to face the woman who'd given him life. Jude couldn't have been happier.

Staci called, and Paige went to Austin to spend some time with her. There was a big wedding reception at two and she wanted Paige to see all the decorations. She had never seen her sister's work, so she drove in to have lunch and see the spectacular wedding Staci was raving about.

Paige, who had never been one to flip through wedding magazines, was impressed with the gala affair. The ballroom was decorated in pink and white and silver. She'd never seen so many flowers adorning tables, and just about everywhere, huge arrangements stood. Silver candelabras sat on the bride and groom's table, as did fine china, silver and crystal. Every chair was covered in white with a big pink bow on the back. Small pink boxes tied with white ribbon waited at each place setting.

"What's in the boxes?" she asked her sister.

Staci winked. "Chocolates, my dear."

"Everything's gorgeous." Paige looked around the room at all the beautiful decorations and wondered if tonight a young woman's fantasy would come true. She would marry her Prince Charming. Ah, how unrealistic that sounded. But it was every little girl's dream. Paige had found her prince and she had a sinking feeling he was never going to forgive her. But she would keep hoping and dreaming and maybe she wouldn't need all these decorations, just a four-leaf clover. And a prayer.

Things began to get a little hectic as Staci had to deal with the kitchen crew, the waitstaff, the decorators and the wedding planner. Paige kissed her sister goodbye and headed back to Horseshoe. She didn't want to be gone too long. She made it home at about four and took off her dress and heels and wondered what she was going to do for the rest of the evening.

Slipping on her jeans and a T-shirt, she thought she might walk around the town square and try to enjoy the evening. She might even stop in at the bakery and buy something delicious. A buzz interrupted her thoughts and she realized it was her phone in her purse in the kitchen.

She ran and fished it out and saw that it was Jude. He was calling, not texting. Could that mean…?

"Are you busy?" he asked.

"No. I went to Austin to see Staci and I just got back. Is Zane okay?"

"Yes. He's fine and walking without his crutches, as I told you."

"Oh, good. I thought something had happened."

"Something has. Could we come over for a minute?"

We. "Jude, do you mean you and Zane?"

"Yes."

Her heart raced and she had trouble pushing words from her throat. "Yes, I'll be waiting. Thank you."

She clicked off and ran around the house like a madwoman. Maybe she should put her dress and heels back on. No. Maybe she should put on some makeup. No. She already had makeup on. She ran her hands up her arms and felt cold and hot all at the same time. Her son was coming. Her son was coming. Her precious baby. She sank to the floor and began to cry. Uncontrollable sobs shook her body. It seemed as though she'd waited forever for this moment and she was so nervous she wanted to scratch her skin until it bled. But she'd outgrown that habit. She'd outgrown a lot of things.

The sobs subsided and she wiped tears away with her back of her hand. Rising to her feet, she drew a calming breath and went to the bathroom to wash her face. She had to get control of herself and she didn't have much time. Looking in the mirror, she saw she'd smeared her mascara. Oh, crap. She scrubbed her face clean and then applied lipstick. That was the best she could do.

She took several more calming breaths and forced herself to walk to the kitchen. Her son was coming, but she had no idea what he wanted to say. She had to brace herself for that. She had to brace herself for the reality that this was not going to go as she wanted. But it was a start. And she hoped her son had at least lost some of his anger.

The doorbell rang and she jumped.

Her precious baby was here.

Chapter 17

With a shaky hand, Paige opened the door. Zane stood in front of his father with the box in his hands, his eyes bright but cautious. The resentment she'd witnessed last Saturday wasn't there anymore. A sense of relief washed over her.

"I read what you wrote in the books," Zane said. "Could you read them to me?"

"I'd like nothing better. Come in." She opened the door wider and they came into the house. Paige's knees were trembling and she had to calm down or she wasn't going to get through this. "There's not much furniture here, though we have a table and chairs in the kitchen."

Zane placed the box on the table and sat in a chair.

"Zane, I'm going over to ask Bubba some questions about the hay baler we're working on. I'll be back in half an hour."

"Okay, Dad."

Paige didn't want Jude to feel he had to leave—or maybe she just wanted someone else here as she faced her twelve-year-old son. Before she could voice her concerns, Jude was gone and she was left staring into the most beautiful eyes she'd ever seen, just like his father's.

"I read what you wrote in the books," Zane said again. "And it made me... I don't know...sad."

She pulled a chair close to him. "Why did it make you sad?"

"Because I thought you gave me away because you didn't want me."

Her breath caught at his admission.

"But as I read, I could see how much you wanted me and how much you suffered in making your decision. I really don't like the counselor or your mother, but I don't know them and I'm glad that I don't."

"It was a very difficult time, but I felt in my heart I was doing the right thing for you. But once I reached California, I knew I had made the wrong decision and there was just no way to turn back the clock."

"My dad said you lost your scholarship and had to live in a homeless shelter."

"Yes, but I found there are good people out there. People who helped me to find myself again. And once I was on my feet, I worked hard to accomplish a dream I'd had since I was a girl, even though it cost me my baby."

"But it didn't. My dad came and got me. My dad, he's special."

"Yes, your dad is very special."

"He can do all sorts of things with horses and cows and he makes saddles and repairs hay balers and tractors. He can do just about anything, but he doesn't talk

much. Grandma says he's been that way since Ezra Mc-
Cray shot him."

"Sometimes people with as much character as your
father don't need to say a word. People know how he
feels." As she said the words, she knew they were true.
Jude didn't need to talk to her. She knew how he felt.

After that, Zane had loads of questions and she answered each one as honestly as she could. Her son was
a talker, so unlike his father. His eyes lit up as if there
were candles burning behind them. It was a joy just to
watch this amazing child who was hers. And Jude's.

She didn't say she was sorry and she didn't ask for
forgiveness. She didn't need to. It was clear her son had
forgiven her. That was a miracle in itself.

All too soon Jude returned and she wanted to hold
on to the moment and to never let it go. And to never
let her son go again. But summoning the maturity she'd
learned over the years, she hugged her son with everything that was in her heart and he hugged her back. It
was a moment she would remember forever.

She saw her son every day after that. He continued
to ask questions and she continued to answer them. She
wanted him to know everything that had happened and
some of the answers made her look bad. But she didn't
care. She wanted to be honest with her son.

Jude was busy baling hay and he asked if she could
pick up Zane from school. She happily agreed. Zane
wanted her to meet his teachers. He had no qualms about
telling people she was his mother. Every teacher she
talked to told her how bright Zane was and how he was
a pleasure to teach.

They went to the bakery to get kolaches and a drink
and Zane told Angie's mom and everyone in the place

that Paige was his mother. No one seemed surprised, not even Angie. They walked around the town square and Zane talked constantly, telling her about Horseshoe and its businesses as if she'd never been there. She listened avidly. They met Wyatt and Hardy on the courthouse lawn and once again Zane introduced her as his mother. And again they didn't seem surprised.

One afternoon Staci came to meet her nephew and there was no awkwardness at all as Zane chattered as if he'd known Staci all his life. Of course, most of his conversation was about his dad and it was very clear how much he loved Jude.

Everything was perfect, better than she'd ever imagined, except Jude wasn't there. He stayed away and she didn't know if that was on purpose or if he was busy. Or maybe he was just giving her time with their son. In a way, it hurt. She wanted to see him and share this experience with him.

Jude was dog tired from a full day of hauling hay. One more day and they would be through with the hauling. Then they would start on another pasture. It was a never-ending cycle during the summer.

He showered and changed clothes. Zane still wasn't home and Jude decided to go to his shop to work on a saddle. He should have just sat in a chair and rested, but when he did that, thoughts attacked him from all sides and he hated how his mind was filled with questions he couldn't answer. Hard work solved that problem. If he kept working, he'd be too tired to even think.

His mom stopped him before he could get out the door. "Eat something before you go, and don't say no. You've been working all day and you need nourishment."

For the first time he realized he was hungry. He filled his plate with pot roast, vegetables and a hot roll and took it to the table to eat. His mother brought him a glass of tea.

"When is Zane coming home?"

"I told him he has to be home by seven. Although Paige helps him with his homework now, so I guess just any time will do, but he'll be home by seven."

"He hasn't eaten supper here all week and I miss him."

Me, too. But he didn't say that to his mom. He didn't want her to know he was concerned about the future.

"He's getting to know his mom and I want that to happen. I'm stepping back so it can."

His mom patted his shoulder. "You were always too nice for your own good."

Before Jude could find a response, Quincy came in. "I thought Zane would be here. I haven't seen my partner all week."

"He's with his mom," Jude said.

"Do you want something to eat?" his mom asked Quincy.

"No, Mom, thanks. Jenny will be home soon." He took a chair across from Jude. "How do you feel about all this?"

Jude took a big swallow of tea and pushed his plate away. "I just told Mom that I want Zane to get to know his mother. Now I'm going to work on a saddle for a while." He was out the door before they could say another word. He wasn't answering any more questions. It was his life and this time he wasn't asking anyone for advice. He was going solo.

He turned on the lights in the shop and sat in his chair,

the scent of leather filling his senses. He'd started the tree, which was the seat of the saddle, and also cut the leather for the saddle horn. All he had to do was shape it and glue it to the tree. But he had no desire to get started. His thoughts were on his son. And Paige.

The past week he had felt left out. Paige never asked him to come when he got off work. She never asked him to do anything with them. And he understood that. But he couldn't deny that feeling of loneliness that was taking root in his soul again. Soon they had to talk and he dreaded that. It was his least favorite thing.

The door opened and Zane burst in. "Hey, Dad."

"Hey." His whole world lit up at the sight of his son. "Did you have a good day?"

"Yeah. Why are you still working?" His son answered too quickly and he didn't look at Jude.

"Because I have a saddle to finish."

Zane looked at the tree and then at him. "But you haven't done anything. It was like that days ago."

Jude stretched his shoulders. "I guess I am a little tired." Now he was lying to his son.

Zane strolled over to the black saddle and touched it. "Did Grandpa really use this saddle?"

"Yes, he did."

"Are you going to keep it forever?"

Zane was always full of questions and tonight Jude was just too tired to answer. Zane continued to walk around the room touching things. Something was different. His son wasn't happy, as he usually was when he returned from seeing his mother.

"What's wrong?"

"Nothing," Zane replied quickly again, and picked up an overstitch spacer tool and studied it.

Jude watched him for a moment and then asked again, "What's wrong, son?"

Zane made his way to Jude's desk and sat on it, facing Jude. "It's nothing, really, but Mama is going back to California soon."

Fury slammed into his stomach unexpectedly. He'd been dreading this moment. Ever since Paige had returned, he'd been wondering when she'd leave. For he knew beyond a doubt that she would.

"How do you know this?"

"She got a phone call and she seemed upset and I asked her what was wrong. She said her time here was up and she would have to return to California soon."

"How did that make you feel?"

Zane shrugged. "I'm fine, Dad."

But he wasn't. Jude could see that. "When is she leaving?"

Zane shrugged again. "I don't know."

"You didn't ask?"

"No, Dad, I didn't ask. I'm cool with it. Really. She gave up so much to become a doctor and now she has to finish it. I understand that. I'll see her again."

Jude didn't get it. She should have told him before she told Zane. That was what made him angry. He got to his feet. "It's getting late. We better go to the house."

"But it's Saturday tomorrow and we can sleep late."

Jude ruffled his son's hair. "Since when? We still have hay to get off the ground tomorrow and I'll be up before the sun."

Zane jumped off the desk. "I can help. Uncle Elias said he was going to teach me to be tough."

"Oh, really." They went through the door and Jude closed it.

"Can I ride piggyback, Dad?"

That threw Jude. Zane was acting insecure, needing to be close to Jude. That meant he was upset and acting much younger than he was. He was always telling everyone how big he was, but tonight he needed his dad.

Jude squatted and Zane climbed on and they made their way to the house. "How is Elias going to make you tough?"

"He said if I could pick up a bale of hay, I would get big muscles."

"You want big muscles?"

"Well, at the time I thought if I got stronger, the McCrays wouldn't pick on me anymore. But lately they've left me alone."

"Has Dudley said anything to you?"

"No, except one day I met him as I was going into my English class and he saw I wasn't on crutches anymore. I told him I was all healed and he nodded and walked away. He didn't say a word. I mean, I was the one who was whupped like an old coon dog who won't hunt. He could have said something."

His son was listening too much to Grandpa. Then, Jude had, too, at that age, even though Grandpa's stories and sayings were 99 percent fiction and 1 percent truth. All the Rebel boys had grown up with those stories and Jude wouldn't change a thing about it.

"There are a lot of McCrays, Dad. And there's only one Rebel. That's me. We need more Rebels in school."

"Baby John will be in school by the time you graduate."

"Yeah, I guess it's just me for now."

A quarter moon hung high in the sky and the darkness of the night surrounded them as Jude made his way to the house. Crickets chirped a song he knew well and horses neighed in the pasture. All familiar sounds. Home. Jude never wanted to leave.

Zane rested his head next to Jude's and an all-powerful protective force filled Jude. He never wanted anyone to hurt his son again. He was still steaming that Paige had told Zane before she had told him. Surely she understood that Zane would be upset.

"Dad, I have a tiny scar on my forehead where you have a scar. In the exact same spot. And both wounds were inflicted by a McCray. Did it hurt when you were shot?"

"I don't remember, son. It was a long time ago." Jude was reeling too hard from his anger toward Paige to even think about that time. "Why are you asking about it?"

"I don't know. I don't understand why people can't live in peace."

Zane had said this several times and it genuinely bothered him when people fought. He was probably thinking about his parents fighting because there were going to be fireworks when he saw Paige. This time he wouldn't be silent.

Zane was quiet the rest of the way to the house, and once inside, his grandma had banana pudding waiting and he sat down and ate a bowlful. After that, Jude made him go to bed with a promise that he could help with the hay hauling tomorrow. After his son was sound asleep, he slipped downstairs and told his mom he was going out for a while in case Zane woke up. But he never did. He usually slept soundly.

Jude got in his truck and headed toward Paige's. Tonight he wouldn't accept any evasive answers. She was telling him exactly what she had planned and he would tell her if she could continue to see Zane or not. He hated that it had come to this. But she owed them more than a goodbye. A hell of a lot more.

Jude drove into the driveway and noticed that the garage door was down but lights were on in the house. He walked to the front door and knocked. And waited. Frustrated, he knocked again.

"Paige, it's Jude," he called through the door.

"Just a minute!" she shouted back.

In a second the door opened and she stood there in nothing but a towel. She was drying her hair with another towel. The sight of her clean, smooth skin knocked all his rage sideways. But he recovered quickly.

He brushed past her into the kitchen, where the light was on, and turned to face her. "I trusted you not to hurt him."

"What?" She stopped drying her hair. "What are you talking about?"

"I'm talking about Zane. He's upset."

"About what? He was fine when I dropped him off at the house."

"You don't get it, do you? You just can't do that to a child."

Her eyes clouded with concern. "You'll have to explain what you're talking about."

"You told him you're leaving."

"Yes, and we talked about it. He seemed fine. Are you saying he's upset because I'm leaving?"

"Yes. He says he's not, but I know my kid and he's pushing down all his feelings again. How could you do that to him? And how could you tell him before me? At least I could have been ready for the fallout."

She headed toward the hall. "I have to see him."

He caught her arm and wished he hadn't. Her smooth,

satiny skin defused everything inside him but his need for her. With strength he didn't know he possessed, he removed his hand.

"No. I will take care of Zane and you will explain to me your plans and how you could hurt him like this. I don't want any evasive answers. I want to know your plans for the future concerning Zane."

"Okay." She tensed, her green eyes stormy. "Dr. Spencer called while Zane was here and explained my allotted time was up and I needed to return. I told her I would be in California on Monday. Zane asked me what was wrong because I was a little upset when I got off the phone. I told him that I had to go back for a couple of days to pack my things and explain to Dr. Spencer and the staff that I would be leaving. I promised him I would be back as soon as I could. Hopefully, not more than two days."

"What?" Jude was completely thrown and at a loss for words. "You're quitting at this stage?"

"I'm not spending any more time away from my son. Time is too valuable and I've missed too much. My career doesn't mean anything without him."

"You can't just give it up after all the work and the heartache."

"I don't plan on giving it up. I can finish later or work something out. I have to talk to Dr. Spencer first to see what my future holds. But I know one thing for certain—my son comes first this time."

What about me? She always conveniently left him out.

"I either misunderstood Zane or…"

"Leaped to the wrong conclusion," she finished for him. "Do you think that badly of me?"

"I'm not thinking at all, it seems, just reacting."

She moved closer to him. "Jude, let's get it right this time. I think you know how I feel about you. After all these years, how do you feel about me?"

He looked into her green eyes and saw everything he'd ever wanted, but the doubts still lingered. But this time he had to speak up. He had to say what he was feeling and he had to say what he wanted. And he was adult enough now to handle her answer.

When he remained silent, she asked, "Are you still involved with the teacher?"

"No. That was nothing. Our interest was Zane and that was it. Even if you hadn't come back, it probably would have fizzled out."

"Why?"

Words crowded his throat and he had to say them. He'd never dreamed it would be this hard.

"Why, Jude?"

He cleared his throat. "Because there's only one girl for me. And always will be." He reached out and gently stroked her cheek with his thumb. "I love you."

"Oh, Jude. I've never stopped loving you, either. What are we going to do about it?"

He took her hand and held it, wanting to get it right. Years ago he'd gotten it so wrong, but now he wanted it to be perfect. "Will you marry me?"

Both hands covered her mouth and she started to cry. "Oh, oh…"

"Paige…"

She threw herself into his arms then and he held her so tight he could feel her heart beating against his. "Yes, yes, yes!"

His lips found hers and they got lost together in the magic of love, of finding each other again and enjoying all its rewards. When he could breathe again, he took her hand and led her to the bedroom.

He cradled her face in his hands. "I'm so glad that there's always this. Perfect. Harmony. Together." He punctuated each word with a kiss and then slowly removed the towel. They fell onto the bed, both laughing, both happy, both enjoying the maturity that the years had brought.

Jude pulled the teddy bear from beneath him. "You don't need this anymore."

"No. I now have the real thing."

A long time later Paige woke up in Jude's arms, and even though the sun wasn't out, it was shining bright in her heart. This time they connected on a level they both understood and she would never let this man down again. She would love him for the rest of her life.

He stirred and they shared a long kiss. "I don't like the thought of being away from you," he said. "Not even for a couple of days."

"Then come with me to California."

He stroked her tangled hair from her face. "I was thinking the same thing. I don't want you to stop the residency. I want you to finish it. I haven't had a vacation in years. I've taken Zane to NASA several times and to SeaWorld and Schlitterbahn. He has about two and a half weeks' more of school and I think if I talk to his teachers, they will just go ahead and pass him because his grades are so good."

"What are you saying?"

"Zane and I are going to California with you and stay until you finish your residency."

She buried her face in his neck, breathing in the scent

of him, the essence of everything that was Jude. Her heart was so full she could barely talk. "You said you would never leave Rebel Ranch."

"I'm not leaving it forever. I'm taking a long vacation to be with a woman I love because I can't stand to be away from her anymore."

She raised her head to look into his eyes. Even though she couldn't see them in the darkened room, she could feel them. She could feel everything about him. Laying her head on his chest, she sighed with contentment and listened to his heartbeat.

Forgiving herself had come slowly, like a gentle rain of tears on her broken soul, seeping into the crevices and gradually reaching her frozen heart, nourishing and bathing it with renewed warmth until all the guilt and heartache was gone. She could now accept life for what it was and for what it had been. All because this wonderful man had given her back her life.

"Hey, Jude, I love you."

Epilogue

Three months later...

When the plane touched down in Austin, Texas, there were three happy Rebels on it. Jude was happier than he'd ever been, and the smiles on his wife's and son's faces reflected that feeling. They'd had a private bonding time and they'd become a family.

They had gotten married quickly, three days after Jude had proposed. Staci had wanted to handle the wedding and they'd let her. They were married by a minister in the hotel and the reception was there, too. It was small and private ceremony with just the family. And then they flew away on an adventure of a lifetime.

At first, Jude felt like a fish out of water in the city atmosphere. But he soon adjusted as he and Zane explored Berkeley, San Francisco, Oakland, San Diego and small towns along the Pacific coast. They went sailing, snorkeling and swimming and enjoyed the beach. Jude wore flip-flops and shorts and his whole body was getting tanned, as was Zane's. He also loved the cooler temperatures, but he wasn't crazy about the fog. When Paige had a couple of days off, they took trips to Disneyland and Hollywood. It was a vacation every day. And every day was perfect because they were together.

They lived in Ms. Whitman's house because she wasn't expecting new tenants until September. They had the run of the place because the lady had gone to visit her son and his family in Seattle. Jude liked the woman and he also liked Thea. They both were very warm and loving women and Jude was grateful that they had been there for Paige.

Even though they enjoyed sightseeing and exploring new places, their favorite time was when they went to the hospital with Paige. Zane loved going with his mother on rounds and just being in the atmosphere. Jude felt there would probably be another doctor in the family one day.

But Jude missed home. He missed the wide-open spaces, dirt beneath his feet and being on a horse. As long as he could wake up with Paige beside him and go to sleep with his arms around her, everything evened out.

While they'd been gone, a new Rebel had been born into the family. Egan and Rachel's baby son was now a week old and they couldn't wait to see him. His name was Justin.

Today was Zane's birthday and they'd made it home just in time. Their thirteen-year-old son ran ahead of them through the airport to the luggage carousel. Quincy and Jenny were picking them up. Jenny was now pregnant and there would be another Rebel in the family come March. Zane spotted them first and ran and jumped into Quincy's arms as if he was five years old. He'd missed his uncle.

"Hey, partner, happy birthday," Quincy said, still hugging his nephew. "I think you've grown a foot."

"Yeah. I'm getting tall like Dad."

Everyone hugged and then they started the trip home. Zane talked nonstop all the way about California and his mom and her job. Jude thought he might have to put a gag in his mouth, but it was nice to see his son so happy.

When they turned onto Rebel Road, Jude felt a lightness in his chest, and when he saw the cattle guard and the ranch, that sensation gave way to joy. He reached for Paige's hand. He was home. They were home. And it had never felt so good.

They'd talked about where they would live, but to Zane there was only one place to live. With Grandma. That was home to him. Jude wasn't going to get past living with his mother, but one day he wanted them to have their own home.

Everyone was waiting, even Staci, when they reached the house, which was decorated with balloons, banners and streamers for Zane's birthday. After all the hugging and kissing and once they'd all held the new baby, everyone sang "Happy Birthday." The smile on Zane's face said it all.

Later, he and Paige strolled to the barn to watch their son ride Bear. They leaned on the fence and Zane raced off on the horse.

"We made it." Jude put an arm around his wife. "Tonight we'll move my bed into Falcon's old room. It's bigger and has a balcony and we'll have our own bath. Our son will have his own bath, too."

"Now real life begins."

Paige had several interviews with different medical practices in Austin and Temple. She still had to take the Medical Licensing Exam. That was all in front of them. And Jude had to kick it in high gear since he'd been away. His brothers were still finishing up hay season and he would now be working long days.

She looked up at him, her eyes shining as bright as Zane's. "But it's all worth it." She smoothed the fabric of his Western shirt. "I was thinking, and don't freak out, of having another baby."

He smiled. "That's not freaking me out. That's making my day. I'd love nothing more than to have another child with you. Together. To experience everything it's supposed to be. And this time we'll get it right."

She glanced toward their son in the distance. "I think we got it right the first time. Just in a different way." She wrapped her arms around his neck. "I love you. Don't ever let me go again."

He didn't plan to. Ever.

* * * * *

Patricia Thayer was born and raised in Muncie, Indiana. She attended Ball State University before heading west, where she has called Southern California home for many years.

When not working on a story, she might be found traveling the United States and Europe, taking in the scenery and doing story research while enjoying time with her husband, Steve. Together, they have three grown sons and four grandsons and one granddaughter, whom Patricia calls her own true-life heroes.

Books by Patricia Thayer

Harlequin Western Romance

Count on a Cowboy
Second Chance Rancher
Her Colorado Sheriff

Harlequin Romance

Tall, Dark, Texas Ranger
Once a Cowboy...
The Cowboy Comes Home
Single Dad's Holiday Wedding
Her Rocky Mountain Protector
The Cowboy She Couldn't Forget
Proposal at the Lazy S Ranch

Visit the Author Profile page at Harlequin.com for more titles.

BRADY: THE REBEL RANCHER

PATRICIA THAYER

To the newest addition to the family, Finley Steven. Hero material for sure. And to his mother, Daralynn. You never stop amazing me. Thank you for another fine grandson.

Chapter 1

He'd always been told he was too cocky for his own good.

On a sunny November morning, Brady Randell hobbled out to the porch with the aid of a crutch. His left leg was bandaged from his last surgery and covered in a removable cast strapped from his foot up over his knee to his thigh. It served to protect the damaged bone so it could heal properly. If it ever did. Three months since the accident, and he wasn't feeling so damn cocky anymore.

With a groan Brady dropped into the Adirondack chair. This was about as far as he traveled these days. He was tired of doing nothing but sleeping, eating and sitting around. Oh, yeah, he forgot about going to therapy twice a week. Or maybe he should call it torture.

After all his hard work, he hoped for a payoff, some good news when he saw the doctor next week. With a little luck he could get the cast off and finally be able to walk on his own again.

"Wouldn't that be a miracle," he murmured in frustration.

He sighed, recalling the vivid details of the accident that had caused him to drop right out of the sky. He'd barely had time to eject from the cockpit before the crash of his F-16.

Brady tensed. He could still feel the bone-bruising tremors; hear the death screams of the powerful aircraft disintegrating as it plowed into the desert floor. He'd gone over and over in his head what he could have done differently. What had gone so terribly wrong that day?

Was this possibly the end of Captain "Rebel" Randell's air force career?

Now instead of being in the cockpit of the Fighting Falcon, he was parked on a porch of the foreman's house outside San Angelo, Texas. His daddy's home, the Rocking R Ranch. After Sam Randell's death, it now belonged to him and his half brother, Luke, who, after thirty years, he'd finally met. Since the accident, Brady had needed a place to heal. He thought a remote, inherited ranch would be perfect for a loner like him.

Brady stared out toward the barn and corral area where his new sister-in-law, Tess Randell, was working one of her horses in the large arena. She rode like nobody's business. Watching her skill and grace was the treat of his day. That and being left alone.

Brady closed his eyes and leaned back. Not that he was going to get any peace and quiet staying here. He had family coming out of the woodwork. Up at the main ranch house Luke lived with his bride and readymade family—a young daughter, Livy, Tess's father, Ray, who had Alzheimer's and kept referring to Brady as Sam's boy. And Aunt Bernice, who spoke her mind and could cook up a storm.

They weren't so bad, but the six Randell cousins who lived in the neighboring ranches with all their wives and kids were a bit much. And there were lots of kids. Evidently, there wasn't much else to do on the ranch during those long nights.

With a groan he shifted in his chair, recalling the last time he'd spent the night with a willing woman. It had been too long.

"Excuse me, are you all right?"

At the sound of a female voice, Brady's eyes shot open. He blinked and focused on a pair of big, emerald-green eyes staring back at him from the edge of the porch. They belonged to a petite woman dressed in snug jeans, a white blouse and a denim jacket. Her hair was the rich color of cinnamon, cut just at her jawline, and wayward strands brushed against her full lips. A black cowboy hat sat firmly on her head.

He swallowed the sudden dryness in his throat. "I'm fine," he told her.

"I heard you groan and—" she glanced down at his injured leg "—wondered if you were in pain."

Damn right he was. "I'm fine," he repeated.

She gave him a half smile and his heart began to race. "Then I apologize for disturbing you."

This woman could disturb a man in a coma. She looked like every man's dream. That was if you were into fiery redheads. Oh, yeah. He sat up straighter. "Are you lost or something?"

She looked around. "I'm here to see Tess Randell."

Brady glanced at the oversize case she was toting.

Great, a solicitor out in the middle of nowhere. "If you're here to sell her something, she's busy."

The woman shook her head and raised an eyebrow. "Actually, I was invited. She called me."

"Right."

Her shoulders tensed. "If you'll just direct me to Tess Randell, I won't bother you any longer."

From the corner of his eye, Brady saw his sister-in-law hurrying toward them. "Looks like we'll both get our wish," he told the pretty intruder.

Tess rushed toward them. "Good, you found us," she said a little breathless. The statuesque blonde wore her long hair tired back in a ponytail. "Did you have much trouble with my directions?"

The redhead glanced at Brady. "Nothing I couldn't handle."

Smiling, Tess's gaze shifted to him. "Have you two met?"

Before Brady could speak, the woman said, "We haven't had a chance."

"Brady, this is Dr. Lindsey Stafford. She's the new veterinarian taking over Dr. Hillman's practice while he's recovering from his hip surgery. Be nice, or you'll have to answer to the Randell cousins, especially Travis. He went all the way to Dallas to find her." Tess turned to the redhead. "Lindsey, this is my brother-in-law, Brady Randell. He's a captain in the air force."

Lindsey fought her nervousness. Not because the man was drop-dead gorgeous, but every time she met another Randell she was afraid someone would figure out who she was.

"It was nice to meet you, Brady." She held out her hand.

He shook it. "Same here, Doc. You'll excuse me if I don't get up."

She nodded, not missing the sarcasm in his voice. "Hope you have a speedy recovery."

Those midnight eyes locked with hers. "Not nearly as much as I do."

"Well," Tess began, "I better take you down to the barn." She turned to Brady. "You need anything?"

"No, I can manage."

Tess nodded. "If you see Luke, tell him where I went. Come with me, Lindsey."

Lindsey quickly followed Tess along the path. She didn't want to have any more conversation with the man.

"Sorry about my brother-in-law," Tess began. "He's recovering from an accident and is a little antsy with his confinement. Of course, that doesn't excuse his rude behavior."

"You don't have to apologize for him. I'll just keep my distance next visit."

Tess Randell was beautiful to begin with, but when she smiled she was gorgeous. Tall, with long legs, her every movement was graceful. Everything Lindsey always wanted to be. But at twenty-nine she was resigned to the fact she'd stopped growing at five-foot-three, and her freckles across her nose would not suddenly vanish.

They arrived at the pristine white barn and walked inside. Lindsey looked around the well-kept area where new-looking stalls lined both walls. She followed Tess down the center aisle to a section that was designated as the grooming area. A stable boy was washing one of the horses.

They continued past three beautiful quarter horses that peered over their gates to see the visitors. "These are horses I board and train, and their owner has given me permission to call you if I feel the need."

"Good." Lindsey stopped to pet one of the equines. "I'd hate to think about something happening to one of these beautiful animals."

"That's the reason I'm so happy you came here to practice."

"I was lucky to get the chance." She walked alongside of Tess. "I don't have much experience yet, and this will definitely help build my résumé." And she never dreamed she would get the opportunity to meet the Randells. It was a chance she couldn't pass up.

"The vet you interned for in Ft. Worth gave you a glowing recommendation. That's good enough for us." They stopped at the stall of a young bay stallion. "This here is Smooth Whiskey Doc. He's my number-one concern. I hope to have him compete in the NCHA Futurity."

Lindsey was mesmerized by the beautiful golden bay horse. When she went to him, he showed no shyness and came to the gate to greet her. She set her case down and he immediately nudged her hand. When she rubbed his muzzle, he blew out a breath.

"I think I'm in love," Lindsey said with a big grin. But her thoughts suddenly turned to the brooding Brady Randell.

"Be careful," Tess warned. "He's fickle."

"I don't doubt that for a second," she said, remarking about both stallions.

Whiskey bobbed his head as if to agree and they both laughed. All the time, Lindsey was looking the animal over. He was about sixteen hands high, his eyes were clear, and his coat shiny. Well cared for.

"What seems to be your problem, big boy?"

Tess swung open the gate and walked in beside the horse. Her hand smoothed over his withers across his back and down his rump. "It's probably minor, but I didn't want to take a chance with this guy." She talked soothingly as she leaned down to reveal the gash just below the hock on his hind leg.

"I was working him in a cutting exercise and he got clipped by a steer."

Lindsey ran her hand along the horse's rump as she crooned to him. She didn't want to get kicked because the animal was nervous. Tess did her part, too, to keep Whiskey still.

Lindsey examined the open wound closely, then asked, "When did it happen?"

"About a week ago. I've been treating it with the normal antiseptic cream and clean bandages."

"You were right to call me. In a few more days, this could have really gotten infected. I believe a strong dose of antibiotics will clear it up, but I want you to stop training for a few days."

Lindsey went to her bag. "I've looked over Dr. Hillman's file on Whiskey. He was examined just a month ago, but I'll give him a quick check just so I can get familiar with him."

Tess looked relieved. "That's fine with me."

After the exam, Lindsey gave Whiskey a glowing report. They came out of the stall in time to see a man walking down the aisle. He was tall with a muscular build, coal-black hair and a cleft chin. Obviously another Randell.

"Luke," Tess called, love shining in her eyes. "You're finished with the meeting already."

"Not exactly." He leaned down and kissed his wife,

then looked at Lindsey. "Hello, you must be Dr. Stafford. I'm Luke Randell."

She nodded. So, another cousin to Jack's boys. "Lindsey, please. Nice to meet you." Oh, my, another charming Randell man. Suddenly Captain Brady Randell came into her head. Correction. Not all were charming. Some were just too damn good-looking.

Brady stood leaning against the porch post as he watched for the redheaded vet to come out of the barn. Hell, why not? How often did a pretty woman—who wasn't a Randell—come around? It was the most excitement he'd had in days. Besides, he had nothing better to do.

That wasn't exactly true.

He glanced toward the large house on the hill. There were several cars parked in the driveway, probably for another business meeting with Randell Corp. He'd been invited to attend, but he'd declined. He wasn't into numbers and budgets. That was his brother's show.

All Brady had to do was sit back and let everyone else handle things. Hadn't that been what he'd done since he arrived here? Just sit around and heal. Isn't that what he wanted? Silence and solitude so he could think?

He raked his fingers through his grown-out regulation military cut, then across the two-day beard along his jaw. He'd let himself go to hell. Suddenly he cared, because a woman showed up here.

The sound of laughter brought him back to reality. He looked toward the barn to see Luke and Tess, escorting the pretty vet down the path toward the house.

Great. Why hadn't he gone inside sooner. The last

thing he wanted was for them to find him here. But before he could make his escape, his brother spotted him.

"Hey, Brady." He waved and they started to the porch.

He froze. "Hey, Luke."

They arrived all smiles and Brady suddenly felt left out. "Have you met Lindsey Stafford?"

He nodded, trying to balance his weight using the post. "We've met already."

The redhead looked up at Luke and smiled. "Brady mistook me for a salesperson."

"Really." Luke stood there looking smug.

Brady refused to let his brother outmaneuver him. He could sweet-talk as well as the next guy. "Well, Doc, no one said our new vet would look like you. I guess you could say I was blindsided."

Lindsey could see through Brady's sudden charming attitude. Well, she wasn't going to let him have the upper hand. "Believe me, it won't happen again," she told him, unable to understand why he seemed to dislike her so. "I should get back, Mr. Randell," she said, then turned away to go with Tess and Luke.

Before she could make her departure, she heard a curse and a thud. She swung around to find Brady Randell lying on the porch floor.

"Brady!" Luke called. He was the first to reach him. Lindsey followed behind him.

She knelt down beside Brady, who was lying flat on his back. He tried to raise his head, his face strained in pain. "No, stay where you are," she ordered.

He grimaced again. "Who made you the boss?"

"Are you going to fight me for the title?" She was eyeing the leg in a cast. "Did you twist your leg?"

"No, I fell on my arm, trying to catch myself," he said, still fighting her to sit up.

Once again, she pushed him back down. "Lie still," she ordered, then reached for his arm.

"What the hell are you doing?" He tried to pull away.

"I just can't resist you, Mr. Randell. So lie there and enjoy the attention."

Brady's angry gaze went to his brother, but Luke just held up his hand in surrender. "I suggest you listen to her."

"Then make it quick. And if you're going to get familiar, you can drop the mister." With a groan, he did as he was told.

Lindsey checked his arms and good leg, happy to find nothing broken. But she soon discovered a lump on the back of his head. She had him open those piercing brown eyes. Although they weren't dilated, he could still have a concussion.

She turned to Luke. "Seems nothing is broken. Could you help me get him on his feet and inside?"

"I don't need help, Doc," Brady continued to argue.

"Come on, Brady," his brother urged. "You need to listen, or I'm going to take you to the emergency room."

Brady grumbled and finally sat up. Lindsey couldn't help but notice his hard, flat stomach that his dark T-shirt didn't hide when his bomber jacket fell open. His chest and arms weren't bad, either. With Luke and Lindsey gripping his arms, they managed to get him to his feet.

Lindsey immediately felt his strength, his power and his masculinity, too. The sudden feelings he evoked surprised her. He was definitely not her type of man. Too dangerous.

Tess handed Brady his crutch, and Luke helped his

brother inside the cottage. Tess and Lindsey followed behind them and into a small living room that was cluttered with newspapers and magazines but clean otherwise.

"You want to go to your room or stay out here?" Luke asked.

Brady pulled away from his brother, made his way to the sofa and sat down. "I'm fine right here. So you all can leave."

Tess and Luke looked at Lindsey for confirmation.

"He's got a small lump on his head," she told them. "But his pupils aren't dilated."

"No concussion," Brady said. "So go."

Luke looked at his wife. "If you stay for thirty minutes, I can finish up the meeting and be back here."

"But Livy's bus is due," she said, and glanced at her watch.

"All of you go," Brady demanded. "I'll be fine alone."

"I can stay until you get back," Lindsey offered.

"Oh, thank you, Lindsey," Tess said. "I promise I'll be back soon as I pick up Livy."

"I'll get back as soon as the meeting is over. And I'm still thinking you should get checked out," Luke said, then followed his wife out the door.

Suddenly Lindsey was alone with this overbearing man.

"Well, now you're stuck," Brady said as he lifted his cast-covered leg onto the coffee table.

"I'm not stuck," she denied. "But it would be nice if you tried to be civil."

"Why should I? I just want to be left alone."

"And I'm sure you will be when your family learns you're okay. When do you see your doctor again?"

Brady started to say it was none of her business, but

found he liked her being here, though not exactly under these circumstances. "In a few days."

"Let him know what happened today. In fact you should call him and tell him."

"Lady, that's not going to happen."

She gave him a stubborn look. "I'm not the enemy here, Brady. So you aren't going to run me off. Not until I want to leave. That will be when Tess comes back."

Brady studied her for a few minutes. Lindsey Stafford was different than most women who hung around the base. Those females were overeager to please the hot-shot pilots. This woman had a take-me-as-I-am-or-not-at-all attitude.

"Maybe I've been a little hard on you."

Those big eyes widened in surprise. "You think?"

"Okay, I plead guilty. Now please sit down. You're giving me neck strain from looking up at you."

She sank down in an overstuffed chair across from him. "That's a switch."

Brady felt his mouth twitch. "Get picked on for your size, huh?"

She glared. "Not since seventh grade."

"That's a lie," he said as his gaze combed over her petite body. "What do you weigh? A hundred pounds?"

"One hundred and ten. I work out to build muscle. The added strength helps in my profession."

He'd like to see those muscles. Dear Lord, he was pathetic. "Why aren't you working with dogs and cats? It would seem easier."

She shook her head. "I love horses. My mother and stepfather are horse breeders. I grew up around them."

"Where are you from?"

She hesitated for a second. "North of Fort Worth.

Denton. What about you? Have you always been in the military?"

He nodded. "All of my life, and we moved around a lot. Dad was career air force, so I went into the academy after high school. I always wanted to fly."

She motioned toward his leg. "Is that how you were injured?"

He hated to think about that day. "Yeah, I had to eject from my aircraft and my landing wasn't the best."

"Well, it looks like you're on the mend."

He stiffened. "It's taking too long. I want to get back in the air."

Lindsey had heard some of the history of the Randell family, but Brady was a surprise to her. There was actually a Randell who wasn't a rancher. "So you're going back?"

"Why shouldn't I? I'm one of the best."

"And so humble, too." She forced a smile. "I'm sure the doctors are doing everything possible. Are you?"

His eyes narrowed. "What does that mean? Of course I'm doing everything, and that includes a lot of rigorous physical therapy."

"That's good." *Just keep your mouth shut, Lindsey*, she told herself as she looked around. *Where is Tess?*

"You don't like me much," he said.

"I barely know you, Captain Randell." And she wasn't sure she wanted to.

"You should know that I'm very good at what I do. And I plan to continue flying for the air force for a long time." He set his injured leg on the floor. "Sitting around a ranch house isn't for me."

"You don't seem to have a choice right now. So maybe you should use this time to count your blessings that you survived your accident instead of taking your anger out on every unsuspecting person who happens to cross your path."

"How the hell do you know what I've gone through?"

Lindsey was going through her own personal pain, too. Her stepfather didn't have such a rosy future.

"You're right, I don't, but I know you're healthy, with a family who loves you, and all you're doing is complaining."

His stony look told her that she'd gone too far. "I should go," she said. "I'm sure someone will be here shortly."

She stood, but before she could get to the door it opened and a little girl came running in.

"Uncle Brady, Uncle Brady. Mommy said you fell down." The little blonde went running to the stoic man on the sofa. "Are you hurt?" she cried.

"No darlin', I'm fine. I just tripped over my big feet and bumped my head."

The girl's worried look didn't leave until her uncle showed her the damage. "See, it's just a little bump."

The child leaned down and kissed it. "There, that will make it better."

Then it happened. Brady Randell sat back and a big smile appeared across the handsome face. Lindsey's heart leaped and she tried hard to remember the man with the bad attitude.

The little girl turned to her and smiled. "Mommy said you're Whiskey's new vet. I'm Livy Meyers Randell. My new daddy married my mommy and 'dopted me."

Lindsey smiled. "Well, it's nice to meet you, Livy Meyers Randell. I'm Lindsey Stafford."

"Hi, Miss Lindsey." A smile beamed on her cute face. "Thank you for taking care of Whiskey, and Uncle Brady."

"You're very welcome."

The child put her arm around her uncle's neck. "Did you know I'm gonna marry Uncle Brady when I grow up?"

You can have him, Lindsey thought. "Isn't that nice."

Lindsey hadn't planned to be gone all day, but she also hadn't planned to babysit an injured fighter pilot, either. That was until she'd been pushed aside by a five-year-old girl. It didn't matter her age, that female had already staked her claim on the man. What had amazed Lindsey was how Brady Randell's whole demeanor had changed when the child walked into the room.

She smiled. So he wasn't the tough guy he pretended to be.

Tired, Lindsey walked into the cabin the Randells had given her to use during her three-month stay. The one-bedroom structure was located in the Mustang Valley Nature Retreat. This cabin had been designed as a romantic getaway.

A big, river-rock fireplace, plush rug and overstuffed love seat were the centerpieces of the main room. The bedroom consisted of a large four-poster bed with satin sheets and an abundance of candles. It connected to a bathroom with a whirlpool tub that easily held two.

Definitely for a couple.

It was off season, so she had the place to herself except for the herd of wild mustangs that roamed freely in this area.

The only drawback was she had to park her SUV at the top of the rise and walk or ride down in a golf cart. There were no vehicles allowed in this area.

Hank Barrett, the patriarch of the Randell family, was adamant about keeping his wild ponies protected. Lindsey felt the same way. So many people thought of them as nuisances, but the Randells had made sure this area was going to be left untouched.

No development in this valley. Ever.

Luke Randell was the project manager for a gated horse community being built on the land that edged the valley. But the project had many strict rules.

It was dusk, and Lindsey looked out the picture window at the scene below. Picking up the binoculars off the sill, she focused in on the grassy meadow. She sighed at seeing the half-dozen mustang ponies grazing peacefully.

Her chest constricted at the incredible sight. How could Jack Randell ever have left this place? More importantly, after all these years, how could she get him to come here? Back to his home…his boys.

Chapter 2

The following week Brady got some good news. At his doctor's visit the day before, he learned his fracture was healing well. Well enough that the bulkier cast had been replaced with a walking cast, so he could finally put weight on his leg. That meant he could get rid of the crutches and use a cane. And start more-intense therapy.

Finally it was time to get back in shape so he could get back into the cockpit.

Brady had also succumbed to Luke's badgering and gone along as he toured the construction site. He cursed as the golf cart bounced over the uneven ground. He grabbed the frame as he nearly flew out of his seat. "Hey, do you think you could have missed a few potholes back there?"

Luke grinned as he continued to maneuver the vehicle

along the ridge. "Just wanted to make sure you haven't fallen asleep."

"Not the way you drive." Brady zipped up his flight jacket to help ward off the morning chill. "Besides, I don't need any more injuries added to my list."

His brother gave him a sideways glance. "I might have to call on the pretty veterinarian to come by. Seems she's the only one who can handle you."

Brady tensed. Not one of his proudest moments. "I didn't need to be handled by anyone. I was fine then and I'm fine now." He hadn't seen the hot redhead since that day. Probably a good thing. If he let her, Lindsey Stafford could be a powerful distraction.

Luke stopped the cart, then he sat back with a sigh. "Now, is this a view or what?" He motioned with his hand. "What do you think?"

Brady looked through the grove of ancient oak trees that shaded part of the valley below. A creek flowed around the sturdy trunks and through high, golden meadow grass.

In the peaceful silence, Brady felt a calm come over him. "Not a bad view." His gaze went to the other side of the rise where a small cabin nestled on the hillside. Farther on was another log structure, and another nearly hidden from view. "Who lives up there?"

"That's the Mustang Valley Nature Retreat. It's part of our holdings, too. There are about a dozen cabins that are rented out through the summer months. Some of the construction staff is living there now. And also your Dr. Stafford."

Brady refused to take the bait. "Why? Can't she afford to rent her own place?"

"Since she's here temporarily, Hank offered her one of the cabins for her stay."

"How temporary?"

"Just until Doc Hillman is able to handle his practice again." Luke stole a glance at his brother. "Tess would love for Lindsey to stay on permanently. Maybe it's because she's a woman, but she likes how Lindsey seems to take extra time with Whiskey."

"I take it the stallion's leg is healed, since I saw Tess working him yesterday. Is he okay to compete?"

Luke nodded. "We're headed to Fort Worth this next weekend. Tess is entering Whiskey in the nonpro NCHA Futurity. But don't worry, Bernice will be here if you need anything."

Brady hated everyone hovering over him. "I've managed to take care of myself most of my life, and I can handle it now."

Luke glanced down at Brady's new cast. "Seems you can get around better, too. How is the leg? Giving you any trouble since you've been walking on it?"

Sometimes it hurt like hell. "No. Between Dr. Pahl and the therapist conferring, I haven't been allowed to do much. But I get to start real therapy next week." His therapist, Brenna, was Dylan's wife, another cousin. She hadn't been easy on him so far, but he liked that about her. She'd warned him about starting out slow. He wasn't good at slow. He needed to get back into shape again, and fast. Granted, the wide-open beauty of Mustang Valley was peaceful, but he needed the vast sky through the cockpit of his F-16 to feed his soul.

"Is everyone around here related to us?" Brady asked.

Luke leaned back. "Just about. It takes getting used to, having all this family."

If he and Brady had anything in common, it was that they were both only children. "Being in the military, we moved around a lot. I didn't have a chance to make friends, so most of the time it was just the three of us."

"You had plenty of family—Uncle Jack's family— our dad just chose not to come back here."

Brady knew that he and Luke would never agree about Sam Randell. He'd abandoned his oldest son, but in truth, he wasn't around much to be a father to his second boy, either.

"So Dad chose a military career over ranching. I bet that didn't make a lot of people happy," Brady said.

"And he chose your mother over mine."

And me over you, Brady thought as his anger started to build. In truth, Sam had chosen his career over everyone. "Look, Luke, I thought you and I were okay with this. Whatever happened between our parents didn't have anything to do with us."

Luke stared out into the valley. "I'm okay with you, and our partnership. It's still hard sometimes." He let go of a long breath. "But like Tess said, I'm back home now." He turned to Brady. "And I finally got to meet my brother."

Brady wasn't about to get all mushy over the reunion. "And about a million cousins. Man, is there something about this valley that causes all these kids?"

Luke arched an eyebrow. "You got something against kids?"

"I don't mind one or two, but a squadron is a bit much."

Luke laughed. "I thought the same thing when I first came here. But they're all great kids, and our cousins are good parents. I believe it's because of their foster parent, Hank Barrett, who was a big influence on them. A lot more so than Jack Randell."

Brady smiled. "Oh, yeah, our uncle, the famous cattle rustler."

They both remained silent, reflecting on the past, when they spotted two riders. Brady recognized Tess on Lady and beside her another woman. A redhead with a familiar black hat.

"Looks like we have company." Luke leaned forward. "My Tess and your favorite doctor."

Brady groaned, but he found his pulse racing as he watched the two approach. Luke got out of the cart and went to his wife as she jumped down from her horse. Tess smiled at her husband, but when Brady turned his attention to Lindsey, she didn't show him any kind of special feminine greeting.

Good. He wasn't going to be here long enough to get tangled up with a woman. She wasn't his type, anyway. But as the redhead started toward him in her form-fitting jeans, cream-colored sweater and black nylon vest, his body suddenly called him a liar.

"Good morning, Mr. Randell."

Okay, he liked her a little, especially her attitude. "Since you've had your hands all over my body, don't you think you could call me Brady?"

She stopped next to the golf cart. "And since you're not that familiar with mine, you may call me Dr. Stafford."

He arched an eyebrow, letting his gaze speak for him. "The day isn't over yet."

She finally smiled. "How about Lindsey?"

"Oh, I don't know, I'm kind of leaning toward sexy doc."

She frowned. "Only if you want me to hurt you."

He glanced toward his brother and sister-in-law to see

they were out of earshot. "When it comes to a beautiful woman, the last thing I'm thinking about is pain." He climbed out of the cart and stood in front of her. "I'm more a pleasure kind of guy."

Lindsey didn't like Brady Randell so close, but she refused to back away. "How about we stop the innuendos and try to have a normal conversation?"

He nodded. "Nice weather for a ride."

"Yes it is," she told him. "Tess invited me to go along to help thin the mustang herd and check for injuries. We're going to meet up with Hank Barrett and some of your cousins."

"So you're going to play doc?"

"I don't *play* doctor."

He raised a hand. "I only meant I wish I could go along and see you in action. But all I'm traveling in these days is this cart."

Lindsey knew the confinement had to be hard for Brady. She glanced down at the new, smaller cast. "It looks like you're making progress and will be back in the cockpit soon."

"That's what I'm shooting for."

She could see the cocky determination on his face. No doubt he looked even more handsome in his flight jumpsuit. She glanced down at his worn jeans, then upward to his straw Stetson. He wasn't a bad imitation of a cowboy, either.

"Maybe if your doctor approves, you could go out for a short ride. Nothing strenuous, of course. But I bet Tess has a gentle mount."

"I'd take anything at this point."

"Can you drive a car, yet?"

He nodded. "Since it's my left foot, yes, but only if

it's an automatic. My '67 Chevy Camaro back at the base is a stick shift."

She never doubted that for a second, or the fact that the vehicle was a hotrod. Brady Randell was definitely not her type. She was all about settling down, safety and animals. He was a death-defying jet jockey with no intention of letting grass grow under his boots. She looked up into his piercing eyes and her heart went crazy. Okay, speaking from a sensual aspect, this man was any woman's type.

She really needed to stay clear of him.

"I should get going. I have appointments this afternoon." She turned to find Tess lost in her husband's arms. They were exchanging kisses and whispered lover's secrets. The couple seemed unaware anyone else was around.

Brady came up behind her. "Those two are like that all the time. I hate to say it, but it makes me a little jealous."

Lindsey felt Brady's breath against her ear. The warmth of his large body shielded her from the cool morning. She closed her eyes momentarily. Yes, she longed to be part of a couple. To find the right man. Someday.

Right now she had other things to think about. Top on her list was the true reason she'd come to San Angelo, and her time was limited to find the answers she needed. Getting involved with a man would only complicate matters. She finally moved away from temptation.

"Tess," she called. "We need to get going if we're to meet up with Hank and the others." She glanced at Brady. "I'm glad you're doing well."

He leaned against his cane. "Like I said, I wish I was going with you, Doc."

"Maybe when your leg is healed," she promised as she backed away. Was she crazy?

"I'll look forward to it," he called. "I'll work to make sure it's soon."

Lindsey was still chiding herself when they reached the edge of the valley. There was high grass mixed in with thick native mesquite bushes. Ancient oak trees arched over the riding path like a canopy filtering the sunlight. The November day was brisk, causing her skin to tingle. She felt exhilarated.

Her thoughts returned to Brady. She hadn't expected to see him again so soon. He'd looked considerably better than the last time. He'd shaved and was dressed in jeans and a gray U.S. Air Force sweatshirt under his bomber jacket. In a cowboy hat, he looked cocky and sure of himself.

"How are you holding up?" Tess asked as she rode up beside her.

"I'm fine. In fact if I could schedule it, I'd ride every day."

Tess smiled. "I come out to check the ponies every week during the winter. I could saddle up Dusty and bring him by the cabin for you."

"If I'm not busy, I'd love it." She patted the seasoned buckskin gelding, remembering her childhood days at the ranch. She loved the freedom of riding. It had been her escape from a lot of problems, especially during her parents' abusive marriage. "You sure you don't mind me borrowing Dusty?"

"Anytime. Since Dad can't ride anymore, I appreciate anyone who exercises him."

Lindsey's heart softened. Tess's father was in the beginning stages of Alzheimer's. "Good. I'll let you know my schedule."

"And maybe you can help get Brady up and riding, too."

Lindsey glanced over to see Tess's smile. "Shouldn't he walk before he gets on a horse?"

Tess shrugged. "Maybe he can do both. We're willing to try anything to get him out of the house. Luke managed today, but not without a lot of prodding."

She couldn't imagine the captain doing anything he didn't want to do. "It's a start."

"Since the two had never met until a few months ago, both Luke and Brady are still getting to know each other. If their father, Sam Randell, hadn't left them both the ranch, I wonder if they would have ever met."

"Then it's good they have this opportunity."

"I feel the same way," Tess said. "Although they do have very different views of their father. Luke was deserted by Sam when his parents divorced. Brady had him around most of his life."

Lindsey rested her hands on the saddle horn, letting Dusty take the lead. "Sometimes there isn't a choice."

"There's always a choice," Tess murmured, then pointed up ahead. "There's Hank, Cade and Chance."

Lindsey knew Hank Barrett was the one who'd taken in the three Randell brothers, Chance, Cade and Travis, to raise after their father, Jack, had been sent to prison.

As they got closer to the men on horseback, Lindsey could see the strong family resemblance between the brothers. It seemed all Randell men were tall, with that rangy, muscular build. The square jaw and cleft in the chin was like a brand, telling the world who they belonged to.

She'd met Chance and Travis earlier, but Cade looked

even more like the man Lindsey had called Dad for the past fifteen years.

The difference was these men shared his blood. She didn't.

Jack Randell was only her stepfather.

Just as soon as Jack and her mother returned home from their vacation and discovered she'd gone against his wishes, he wouldn't be happy.

It wasn't as though she'd planned to come to San Angelo. It had been curiosity that had her go to the job interview. She told herself she only wanted to meet Travis, one of Jack's sons. Then she found herself accepting the position. After all, it was only temporary.

Hank Barrett sat back in the saddle and watched Tess approach with the new veterinarian. Ever since Travis returned from Dallas singing Dr. Lindsey Stafford's praises, Hank had been anxious to meet her.

He smiled as the redhead rode closer. She was easy on the eyes, and if there was one thing he appreciated, it was a pretty female, no matter what the age.

Hank greeted Tess. "Hello, Mrs. Randell."

"Good morning, Mr. Barrett," she answered. "Hi, Cade, Chance."

Chance touched the brim of his hat in greeting. "Tess." He glanced at the redhead. "Dr. Stafford, nice seeing you again. This is our other brother, Cade. And this is Hank Barrett, the one who started the mustang project."

Hank nodded at the petite woman who sat comfortably in the saddle. There was something about her name that was familiar. "Dr. Stafford, I'm glad you could join us.

"Please, everyone, call me Lindsey." Her horse shifted sideways. "And thank you for inviting me along today."

"Well, Lindsey," Hank began, "I hope you still feel that way if the ponies don't cooperate. They've been known to be stubborn."

The doctor rewarded him with a smile. "I hear old Dusty here is pretty good at cutting out his target."

Cade reined his roan back. "I guess we'll know soon enough if he likes to chase wild ponies as much as cows." He grinned and Lindsey tensed, once again seeing the resemblance to his father.

"I'd say we better get going," Chance said, pointing to the herd off in the distance.

Lindsey looked at Hank for direction as they started down the trail.

"We'll let Chance and Cade take the lead," he said. "Wyatt, Dylan and Jarred are at the other end of the canyon to drive the herd toward us."

"I'll just follow you," she said.

Hank nodded. "Okay, let's go and get us some ponies."

They rode off, and Lindsey felt she was taking a step back in time. To see the wild ponies in their natural setting. This had been another big draw for her to come here. She just didn't realize how much she would already love it.

Two hours later Brady sat with Luke in his truck, waiting at the temporary corral at Hank's ranch, the Circle B Ranch. He was still wondering why he'd come. Of course, it beat the alternative, sitting back at the cottage. That had been what he told Luke, anyway. Not that he wanted another chance to see Lindsey Stafford again.

"They're coming," Luke called as he climbed down off the railing.

His own excitement growing, Brady got out of the

truck and looked to where his brother pointed. He saw the riders on horseback, chasing after the ponies. An assorted mixture of paints, bays and buckskins. Over a dozen as far as he could see. But he couldn't find Lindsey.

"There's Tess," Luke called.

It was easy to catch his sister-in-law's long blond hair. Then he spotted Lindsey's black hat. She was riding drag, a bandana tied around the lower part of her face to help filter the dust.

"Come on, bro, help me with the gates." Brady was glad he could finally manage to do something useful. He followed his brother, took one side and swung open the metal gate. It had been a while since he'd been around horses, but he knew they could be unpredictable at best. The first two ponies arrived and went into the pen, but the third and fourth decided to turn off.

Hanging on to the gate, Brady yanked off his hat, waved it around and yelled to turn the horse back. Then Chance and Cade showed up to take over. Finally the last of the ponies were in the large pen and the gate shut.

His cousins climbed off their horses and everyone went to the corral to check out their finds. Brady's gaze was on Lindsey. She dismounted and walked toward the metal railing with the old guy, Hank.

Barrett looked the part of mentor, father and grandfather. He didn't have to demand respect, but he got it. He wasn't a Randell, but he'd earned the title of family patriarch.

He nodded at Brady. "Good to see you up and around."

"It's a start."

"Well, if you get the doctor's okay, you can go out with us the next time."

Brady nodded. Chances were, if he was strong enough to chase wild mustangs, he'd be hightailing it for the cockpit of his F-16. "Thank you, sir," Brady said. "I'd like that."

Hank turned back to Lindsey. "I think we got ourselves a good-looking bunch this time."

Lindsey avoided Brady's gaze and went up to the gate. "I'm worried about the paint. See how he favors the right front leg?"

Brady looked, too, but he had to watch closely to see the slight limp.

"It could be a pebble. I'm going to have to examine him, but I have appointments this afternoon."

Hank agreed as he checked his watch. "Tomorrow, then. We'll separate them so they all can be examined and inoculated. How's that with you, Doc?"

"I could come by tomorrow afternoon for a few hours."

"Good, it will give us time to see which ponies are worth the time to saddle break."

"Why are you saddle breaking them?" Brady asked.

"So we can sell them at auction. Since we have to thin the herd, we want to find good homes for them."

Brady had his eye on a gray stallion that didn't like being confined in the pen. He kept moving back and forth along the fence.

Hank waved the group on. "Everyone is welcome to come up to the house for lunch. Lindsey, I hope you can join us."

"I'd like that." She pulled out her phone. "I just need to check my messages." She hung back from the group.

Hank looked at Brady. "How about you, Captain? I wouldn't mind hearing a few F-16 stories."

"I might have one or two that are worth repeating."

Using his cane, Brady managed to fall into step beside Hank. Although his steps were awkward, he was happy to be able to get around. What he couldn't understand was why he was feeling drawn to this family. Not to mention one vet.

They made their way into the compound where a large ranch house stood. It was painted glossy white with dark green trim. The barn and other buildings were also white and well kept.

"Nice place, Hank," Brady said.

"Thanks. My boys run things now. In the summer months we open it as a dude ranch of sorts, but it's a working ranch." He grinned. "You'd be surprised what people will pay just to do chores like a ranch hand."

Cade joined the group. "Yeah, Chance, Travis and I had to do the work for nothing growing up."

"It built character," Hank told him.

Cade laughed. "Well, I sure got a lot of that, then."

Brady listened to the teasing between the brothers and Hank. Suddenly he thought back to how much his own father had been away during his life. All the baseball games he'd missed, the birthdays and holidays. As a typical kid he did a lot to get Sam's attention. Most of it didn't work, until he got into ROTC in high school, then into the academy.

"You boys turned out okay," Hank said. "You've settled down with pretty wives and have families."

Brady glanced over his shoulder and caught sight of Lindsey hurrying to catch up, so he hung back.

"Do you have to run off?"

"No, I can stay for lunch. But I have a two-o'clock appointment."

"Good, that will give me time," he said.

She frowned. "Time for what?"

"Time to convince you I'm not a total jerk."

"Really." She looked skeptical. "You think I should go easy on you?"

"No, but I'm hoping my Randell charm will win out."

She smiled. "So the average guy doesn't have a chance over a Randell?"

"That's right."

They took slow, easy steps toward the back porch.

"Well, I disagree on that theory," she said. "Jarred Trager, and Dylan and Wyatt Gentry do all right in the charm department."

Brady fought rising jealousy, recalling how his cousins had been flirting with her earlier. They had their own wives. "That just goes to show you a Randell wins out."

She stopped and looked confused. "But they're not Randells?"

He nodded. "Yes, they are. Seems Uncle Jack had three more sons."

Chapter 3

As hard as Lindsey tried, she couldn't hide her shock. "Really" was all she could come up with.

Brady gave a sharp nod. "Evidently Uncle Jack was quite the lady's man when he was out on the rodeo circuit."

"Have Jarred, Wyatt and Dylan always lived here?"

Brady shook his head. "About half a dozen years ago, Jarred Trager showed up. He had found an old letter from Jack to his mother that talked about their affair. He came here and met Dana Shayne and her son, Evan. They married a short time later." He shrugged. "That's the condensed version that Luke gave me."

Lindsey took easy breaths as they continued on toward the Barrett house. She walked slowly so Brady could keep up, and so she could try to absorb what he told her. Had Jack known about his other sons?

"You say Wyatt and Dylan are your cousins, too?" She should have seen the resemblance in the men.

He nodded. "After their mother finally told the twins who their father was, Wyatt came to San Angelo looking for Jack, too. Wyatt ended up buying Uncle Jack's half of the Rocking R and found Maura Wells and her two kids, Jeff and Holly, living in the rundown house. A few months later his twin, Dylan, arrived after he'd been injured bull riding. He ended up marrying his physical therapist, Brenna. Who, by the way, is putting me through torture these days."

They reached the porch and he turned to her. "You seem pretty curious about the Randell family."

She shrugged. "The Randells are a big part of this valley. As an only child it's interesting to hear about a large family."

"Yeah, aren't we just one, big happy family."

"I'd take them," Lindsey told him, trying to act lighthearted. It was difficult. From the beginning, Jack had warned her and her mother about his shady past. She also realized that her stepfather needed to know about his other sons. If only to make amends with them.

Suddenly the back door opened and Hank peered out. "There you are. I was wondering if you two had gotten lost."

Brady used the railing to climb the steps. "No, I'm a little slow these days."

Hank smiled. "I thought you were just hanging back to get some time with a pretty lady."

"Well, that, too."

Lindsey felt her heart accelerate, but she put on a smile. "Well, now that we're here, how about some lunch?"

Hank ushered them into a huge old fashioned kitchen.

Sunny yellow walls were lined with maple cupboards. The white-tiled counter gleamed, and a tall, older woman was busy setting the table.

She turned and smiled. "Hello, you must be the new vet, Dr. Stafford. I'm Hank's wife, Ella."

"And I'm Lindsey."

Her friendly brown eyes searched Lindsey's face. "It's nice to meet you. Hank said you were pretty, and he's right."

Cade walked by her. "Hank says all the women are pretty."

"That's because all the women around here *are* pretty." Hank hugged his wife to his side, kissing her cheek.

Ella acted as if she were pushing him away. "Be careful, Lindsey. Hank will be wanting to know if you're a good cook, too."

Hank tried to look indignant. "I hardly know this woman. But if she can cook up any special dishes, I wouldn't mind sampling them, say at our next family get-together. Thanksgiving is coming up."

Cade grinned as he took his seat at the table. "Watch what you say, Hank, or Ella will have you sleeping in the bunkhouse."

The group hooted with laughter, and Lindsey quickly realized she'd been had. "Well, sorry to disappoint you, Hank, but I spent all my free time studying the last few years. So my culinary skills are sorely lacking."

Hank sighed. "That's going to make it harder for you to get a man."

Lindsey was too stunned to speak, but Tess did it for her. "Hank Barrett, stop your teasing. We want Lindsey to stay, not run her off." She turned to Lindsey. "Please sit down, unless you want to clobber Hank first."

Lindsey walked around the table. "I think I'll wait until I have some big instruments in my hand."

The table broke into another round of laughter as she took a seat next to Tess and Luke. Brady managed to snag the seat next to hers.

He leaned toward her and murmured, "You sure know how to hold your own, Doc. I should call you when I'm being chewed out by my commanding officer."

"I can't imagine that ever happening, not with your sweet disposition."

Those dark bedroom eyes bore into hers. "I'm workin' on changing that." He grinned. "Give me a little time, and my charm will melt you."

Lindsey knew Brady was more dangerous than any of the Randells. Because he was the one who could get to her. And when he discovered who she was, he wouldn't be happy. None of the Randells would be, not when they learned that Jack had hung around to play the doting father to her.

Brady hated being cooped up. That was the reason three mornings later he headed down to the barn. He needed the exercise. He'd been lifting weights to keep in shape, but hanging around the cottage was driving him up a wall.

He told himself it wasn't the possibility of meeting up with Lindsey and Tess coming back from their ride. It was just to take a walk. He ran into the groomer washing Lady and ended up helping with some of the light chores. He found that working his muscles felt good. Just being able to complete a simple task helped his mood. By the time an hour was up, the temperature had warmed.

He'd shed his jacket and was mucking out a stall when Tess and Lindsey came into the barn.

Both women were laughing, their cheeks flushed from the cool weather as they led their horses. Lindsey spotted him, and her smile dropped.

Tess spoke first. "Brady, what are you doing out here?"

"Earning my keep," he told his sister-in-law. "It's about time I did something around here."

Tess glanced down at the cast on his foot. "Just so long as you don't do any damage."

"I've been careful, *Mom*," he teased.

Tess fought a smile and lost. "Well, you can go out and play." She turned to Lindsey. "I hate to run off, but I need to meet Livy's bus. Juan can handle the horses until I get back."

"Not a problem, I can stay and take care of my horse," Lindsey said as she took the reins from her. "It's the least I can do for you letting me ride. So go on, go get your daughter."

"Thanks." Tess smiled as she backed away.

"I can help, too," Brady said.

"There's no need," Lindsey said. "I would hate to take you away from your job."

Brady didn't back away. "Then after I help you, you can help me. There are two more stalls to clean. Unless it's too dirty a job for you."

She made an unladylike snort. "I've probably mucked out more stalls than you've seen. I grew up on a horse ranch."

He took Whiskey's reins from her. He loved to see her get riled. It made her eyes turn a deep emerald green. "You probably have. We didn't live very long on our ranch."

They walked slowly to the stallion's stall. Right next to it was Dusty's. "Where was your ranch?" she asked.

"We had a small place in Utah not far from the base. Dad bought it with his reenlistment bonus. With the help of a foreman, he ran a small yearling operation for about four years. I was ten when he was sent overseas and had to sell the place." He wasn't sure why he was telling her this. He tossed the stirrup over the seat and unfastened the cinch, then pulled the saddle off the horse and took it to the stand outside the stall. After Lindsey pulled off Dusty's, he took it. He liked moving around, being active. He found his balance was a lot better.

"Thanks." She went to work on the rest of the tack. "It's a shame you never got to live here."

"Dad never told me about the Rocking R until last year when he got sick."

"Had he been ill for long?"

Brady shrugged, remembering the hulk of a man who had slowly faded away after he retired from the air force. Even his wife, Georgia, hadn't been enough to keep him happy and at home. She'd died alone.

"Dad ignored the doctor's advice," he told her. "After he retired, I don't think he cared much if he lived or died." He gaze met hers. "They say I'm a lot like him. All I've known is the military."

Lindsey paused at her task, hearing the sadness in his voice, seeing it in his eyes. She suspected coming here and meeting the Randells had been overwhelming for him.

She suddenly thought of Jack. What was going to happen to him, when he was too stubborn to help himself? Well, she couldn't let that happen, not without doing everything possible, at the very least to get him to see his sons.

"Are you okay?"

Hearing Brady's voice, Lindsey pushed away the wayward thoughts. "I'm fine. Just thinking about how lucky you are to find your brother," she said. "And to be able to come here, and be with family."

He snorted. "Hell, I knew nothing about all these cousins. Dad never talked about them. Most of the time, it was just Mom and me." He shrugged. "We moved around a lot. But, hey, I got to see the world before I was in high school."

"Too bad you never got to come here."

He straightened. "My dad had to go where the air force sent him. That's the way it was then, and the way it is now. You go where you're assigned."

Lindsey nodded. "I bet your dad was proud of you."

He blinked, as if the question caught him off guard. "Hell, I guess so. Why so many questions?"

She had no doubt this man didn't share much about himself. "I'm just curious."

"Okay, here's the lowdown. I'm a fighter pilot in the U.S. Air Force. I'm qualified to fly F-15 and F-16 and at this time stationed out of Hill AFB in Utah." He moved closer. "Do you want my rank and serial number?" He reached inside his shirt and pulled out his dog tags. The chain dangled in his hand as if to taunt her.

"No, I think I have enough info."

She returned to her task of removing the gelding's bridle, a little embarrassed. She didn't have any business questioning this man or thinking about developing any feelings for him.

"Family is important, Brady. Get to know your brother and cousins before the chance slips away."

"I don't seem to have a choice, for now, anyway." He

looked down at his injured leg. "There's no guarantee that I can go back to flying."

"Even if you can't fly again, there are other careers in the air force."

"Not for me." A muscle tightened in his jaw. "It's who I am. It's the only thing I've ever wanted to do."

"Flying can't define you as a person, Brady. It's what you love, yes, but not who you are. You can do something else, or go wherever. Maybe even live here."

"I hardly see myself as a rancher. I need a little more excitement." He relaxed as his dark-eyed gaze settled on her face. "Of course, if you'll be around…"

She was caught off guard. "My job here is temporary."

A slow, lazy grin appeared. No doubt a sample of the Randell killer charm. "Yeah, but you could make it permanent. Everyone wants you to stay on." His gaze moved over her. "And I could make a point to come back here for an occasional visit."

Lindsey refused to react to Brady's arrogant comment. She had other worries. For one, would she be welcome after they learned her real reason for being here? "You'd be wasting your time, Captain."

His dark eyes narrowed. "Why? Is there a man back in Fort Worth?"

She looked at him. "Yes, there is someone back home."

Brady hated being caught off guard, and he was truly blindsided by Lindsey Stafford. The only good thing was that Tess walked into the barn before she could tell him about her man.

He grabbed his cane and headed out the door. He didn't like the game Lindsey Stafford was playing. With women in the past, he set the rules. No attachments and no commitments. Have some fun, then walk away. So far there hadn't been any fun, but he sure as hell was doing the walking.

He should have known she'd be trouble the second he first saw her. He climbed the porch steps, went into the cottage and didn't stop until he got to the kitchen and pulled a can of iced tea from the refrigerator. After a long drink, he worked on calming down. He was going to erase her from his head. But he doubted anything would do the job.

What surprised him was why this even bothered him. She was leaving in a few months. So what? He was going back to his base in Utah. And besides there were other women…a lot of women.

A knock sounded on the door, but he ignored it. When the knocking continued he figured it was probably Luke or Tess. They wouldn't give up. He finally went and pulled open the door.

Damned if Lindsey wasn't standing there on his porch.

"Did you forget to tell me something else?"

She didn't act sorry. "Yes. Before you took off, I was about to mention that the man in my life—"

"Believe me," he interrupted, "I'm not interested."

She didn't move. "The man is my stepfather."

His heart began to race. "Your stepfather?"

"Yes. He's been ill recently, and I don't want to make any long commitments away from home."

Brady watched the sadness play on her face, and the sudden tightness in his gut caught him off guard. He reached for her and pulled her inside the house. Closing the door, he pushed her back against the wall.

"Do you know you had me crazy, thinking all sorts of things?"

She blinked as her breathing grew rapid. "You didn't let me tell you anything else," she whispered.

Her slim body was pressed against his, reminding him how long he'd been without a woman. "All I want to know is if you have someone special in your life, a husband, a significant other, a friend with benefits." He raised an eyebrow, praying she'd give him the right answer.

"No, none of the above."

Brady's resolve disappeared as he cupped her face and lowered his head to hers. "Maybe we should work on that," he breathed just as his mouth closed over hers.

She tasted sweet and sexy at the same time. He hungered for her like no woman before. He couldn't get enough of her as his tongue dove into her mouth. Lindsey murmured something deep in her throat and her arms slipped around his neck.

Brady slid his hands inside her coat, under her sweatshirt to her bare back, and pulled her as close to him as possible. The imprint of her breasts against his chest nearly drove him over the edge.

He still needed more. His fingers traced across her warm, soft skin to her breasts. The material was thin enough to feel her pebbled nipples through the lace. This time he groaned.

With a gasp, he broke off the kiss and sucked air into his starved lungs. He tried to slow the drumming of his heart as his gaze searched hers to find the same need and raw desire.

"You shouldn't have done that," she breathed.

He shook his head. "Probably not, Doc. But my common sense doesn't seem to be working right now," he assured her as his head lowered to hers again.

* * *

Lindsey had called herself every kind of fool by the time she made her way back to the cabin. She'd managed to escape Brady Randell's arms, but just barely.

Once inside she leaned back against the door and shut her eyes only to relive the man's mind-blowing kisses. The feel of his hands on her skin as his mouth expertly caressed hers turning her into a whimpering teenager. What in the world had possessed her to go after him? To soothe his ego? To poke at the lion in his den?

She could still see those dark eyes, and that sexy grin spread across his face, looking as if he'd just conquered Mt. Everest. Lindsey groaned. She didn't need this kind of distraction to add to the already complicated situation.

She hadn't come here to get involved with a man, especially a cocky jet pilot with an ego that needed to be stroked. Well, she wasn't stroking anything of Brady Randell's. He wasn't her type. She never could handle a casual affair, no matter how good-looking and tempting the man was.

It would be wise to keep her distance. She needed to focus her attention on Brady's cousins. Jack's sons.

Lindsey's thoughts turned to her stepfather and the phone conversation she'd overheard during her last visit home in September.

Ever since Jack's first leukemia diagnosis four years ago, she and her mother had kept a close watch on his health. She'd recalled her stepfather's year of intense chemotherapy. How they'd almost lost him. He pulled through, and had been in remission for nearly three years. Until this last checkup.

Jack didn't want to tell her, but he finally admitted what the doctor reported, that any chemotherapy treatment wouldn't help him. He needed a bone marrow transplant to survive. That was when Lindsey begged Jack to contact his sons. He refused adamantly, saying he'd done enough damage in their lives, he couldn't ask anything from them.

Then Jack made Lindsey swear she wouldn't tell her mother. He didn't want to ruin the long Panama Canal cruise they'd planned for months. He promised to tell her before they got back.

Lindsey reluctantly agreed, hoping she could help convince him to contact his sons. Then she saw the ad for a temporary veterinarian position in San Angelo and the referral name of Travis Randell. She had to go. If only to meet one of Jack's sons. One of the boys he'd abandoned when he was sent off to prison.

Suddenly her cell phone rang and she dug into her purse to find it. "Hello."

"Well, I was wandering if you'd ever answer your phone." Jack Randell's voice came through loud and clear.

She tried to calm her panic. "Dad, you're back?"

"Not quite, your mother and I are spending another week away. We're in Los Angeles visiting friends."

She sighed in relief. "That's great, you two haven't had a vacation in so long."

"How about you, Lindy? How's the job hunting going?"

"Oh, I've had a few interviews, but I'm still looking for just the right position." She'd already found it, but knew that she'd never be able to stay here.

She changed the subject. "Have you had a chance to tell Mom?"

There was a long hesitation. "The right time hasn't come up, yet."

She closed her eyes. "Oh, Dad. I wish you'd think about what I suggested."

"Look, Lin, your mother wants to talk to you, so I'll say goodbye for now. I love you."

Tears filled her eyes. "I love you, too, Dad."

"Lindsey?" her mother said when she got on the phone. "How are you, honey?"

"Outside of missing you guys, pretty good. The job hunting is slow." She lied again and hated it. She and her mom had gone through a lot together before Jack came into their lives. She didn't like keeping this secret from her.

"I think you should hold out for what you want. And you know Jack and I would love to have you close to home."

That was her problem. Lindsey had already felt as if she'd come home, right here. "I've got my résumé out there, but I might just have to take something temporary until the good job comes around. I still have school loans to pay back."

"You know we want to help you."

"Thanks, Mom. I'm fine."

"My independent daughter." She heard her mother giggle, knowing Jack was probably distracting her. "Maybe you should take some time off. Go on a vacation and find yourself a man."

Lindsey's thoughts turned to Brady. She already had, but she couldn't compete with his lifestyle. Captain Randell was definitely off-limits. For more reasons than she could count.

The next morning Lindsey was awakened by pounding on her door. "Just a minute," she called as she threw on a robe over her pajamas, walked out of the bedroom and across the tiled floor through the main room.

Who could be here this early?

She tossed her mussed hair back as she opened the door to find Brady on her porch. He was in jeans and his flight jacket and the usual straw cowboy hat.

"Brady?"

"Morning, Doc." He walked inside with a sight limp.

"Uh, it's a little early to visit don't you think?" She glanced at the clock over the fireplace that read 6:30 a.m. and hugged her robe together.

He smiled. "This is the best part of the day. I loved those early-morning runs, the sun just coming up over the horizon." He released a breath. "Nothing like it, being all alone with the endless sky overhead and the desert floor below." Then he came out of his thoughts. "Or if I'm in a roll, the sky below and the ground above."

She watched the flicker of emotions play over his face and it tugged at her heart. "You miss it, don't you?"

He shrugged. "There's no rush like it." Then he straightened. "I'm sorry to bother you, but I was taking a ride in the golf cart this morning. That's when I saw the mustang. A mare. She's either lame or hurt."

Lindsey was on her way outside before Brady finished explaining. The cold weather had her hugging her robe together. "Where? Is she close by?"

Brady looked out. "She was. It's that little buckskin. Maybe she just picked up a rock."

"Or maybe worse. Hank told me he had some trouble a few months back when one of the mustangs was wounded. He said it looked like someone was shooting pellets."

"You think we should call Hank?" he asked.

"I'll have a look first."

"I'm going with you."

She didn't need to be anywhere around this man. But he could help her find the pony. She looked down at her pajamas. "Give me five minutes."

The golf cart wasn't easy to maneuver over the rough terrain, but it was all they had at the moment. A few hundred yards away Brady spotted the small herd of mustangs. Hanging back from the others was the mare.

So as not to disturb them, he drove the cart along the edge of the trees. "That's her," he said, his voice soft and even.

Stopping, he handed the binoculars to Lindsey. As she adjusted the focus to watch the herd, Brady couldn't help but watch her. She was pretty, though not in the traditional way. Her eyes were too large for her face, and very expressive. Her mouth was full, those lips… He swallowed, recalling her taste. She sure got his attention.

When she'd opened the door this morning, he'd lost all conscious thought as to why he was there. Her hair wild, her eyes with that sleepy quality, her mouth looking so kissable. Like yesterday, he found it hard to resist her and wanted nothing more than to carry her back to where she came from. Bed.

"Bingo," Lindsey said, still watching the mare. "I can spot a smear of blood high on her right forearm."

"How bad?" He took the binoculars from her and looked for himself.

"Bad enough that the wound should be treated." She got out of the cart and reached in the backseat for her bag. "I wonder if she'll let me get close to her."

"No need. I'll get her." Brady got out, went to the

back of the cart, pulled up the seat and took a rope from the compartment.

She came after him. "You can't. Let me help."

He glared at her. "If I need your help I'll holler."

Lindsey had no doubt Brady could do this with or without a bad leg, or he'd die trying. And she had to let him.

"Fine." She went back to her seat.

For a big man, he moved quietly and swiftly in his athletic shoes, even with his walking cast. Most men would look clumsy. But not Brady.

After tying the end of the rope to a tree, he walked carefully behind the herd. One of the stallions whinnied and danced away, putting more distance between them. The mare looked up and began to shy away.

"It's okay, princess," Brady said, keeping his voice quiet and even. "I'm not going to hurt you, girl. I just want to help make you feel better."

The mare bobbed her head, but didn't move away from the intruder. Unlike the rest of the herd that had wandered farther down the meadow. Brady continued his journey as he crooned to the trembling buckskin. Surprisingly, he handled the rope expertly making the large loop. Mesmerized by his husky voice, Lindsey barely noticed when he slipped the lasso around the mare's neck, then led her back to the cart.

The docile pony followed without much resistance. Lindsey knew from Tess that the mare had been around for a long time. And by the look of the blood on her forearm, she was wounded.

"I guess my persistence as a kid learning to rope a steer paid off," he remarked as he held the mare steady.

"Hello, girl," Lindsey said softly. She moved slowly so she wouldn't spook the horse.

Brady shortened the rope so the animal couldn't move. "Come on, princess, Doc only wants to help you."

Lindsey tried to get a look, but the mare wouldn't let her too close. There was no doubt that there was blood and she saw the fresh entry wound of a bullet.

Lindsey stood. "She's been shot."

"Damn." Brady looked around. "Guess I should call Hank." He pulled out his phone. "He isn't going to be happy to learn someone's invaded Mustang Valley."

Chapter 4

It took nearly thirty minutes for Lindsey and Brady to lead the mustang to the Circle B Ranch. They could have transported her to the clinic, but Lindsey didn't want to take the time or traumatize the mare any more than necessary.

Lindsey had to anesthetize the animal to remove the .22 bullet embedded in the fleshy part of her forearm. The surgery went well, thanks to the help of Hank and Brady.

She went into Hank's house to clean up, then she returned to the barn to check the patient. The pony would be groggy from the anesthesia, and Lindsey wanted to keep a close watch on her for the next few days before they released her back out to the range.

When she entered the cool interior of the barn she paused at the sight of Brady leaning over the pony's stall, his injured leg rested on the lowest rail. Her attention went to his worn jeans pulled taut over his nicely shaped butt. She couldn't help but take the time to admire the view.

"How's my girl doing?" Brady crooned. Not surprisingly the little mare reacted to his voice. He didn't attempt to touch her, but waited until she came to him. She did, but only so close.

"Don't be afraid, sweetheart. I'm not gonna hurt you."

Lindsey closed her eyes as his deep voice reverberated through her. She didn't doubt that Captain Randell had spoken those words many times. To how many women? She also knew she couldn't be added to that list, but it was getting harder and harder to convince herself. Not even when she knew if she gave in it would be disastrous.

Suddenly Brady glanced over his shoulder, those dark eyes alert as he examined her closely. "Hi."

"Hi." She nodded toward the horse. "Looks like you've made a friend."

"What can I say? Females can't resist me."

She couldn't help but laugh. "And modest, too."

He walked toward her. "Haven't you heard? Viper pilots are a cocky bunch."

"How does that combination work for you?"

He shrugged. "Not bad." He leaned his forearms against the railing, his gaze zoned in on hers. "What works on you, Doc?"

Her heart pounded in her chest as she tried to come up with a believable lie. "I'm not interested in a fling, Captain. I'm too busy for one thing, and smart enough not to start something with a man who will be leaving soon."

He frowned. "You must know more than I do."

"Come on, Brady, we both know our careers come first. You're going to work like crazy to get back to flying your F-16, and I'm going to work just as hard to get my practice off the ground."

He took off his hat and ran his fingers through his short hair. "That doesn't mean we can't enjoy time with each other."

That would be a bad idea, she thought. "In the biblical sense, of course."

He gave her the once-over. "We don't have to jump into anything, but that could be…interesting."

"And like I said, that's dangerous."

"I would go for incredible. I seem to remember a kiss yesterday that nearly blew my socks off."

Hers, too. "So we just go for instant gratification?"

He shrugged. "Would it be so bad?"

She glared at him.

"Okay, okay. Then, how about we go for friends? You're just about the only person around here who isn't a Randell or related to one."

She tensed. Okay, technically she wasn't a Randell. But when her identity was discovered, Brady's loyalty would go to his family. That was the best reason she needed to put a stop to this. And now.

From the doorway of the barn, Hank watched Brady and Lindsey. Anyone who had any horse sense could see there was something brewing between those two.

The brooding captain's whole demeanor had changed since the pretty vet had shown up in town. Now, if they could just find a way to get Lindsey to give him a chance, then maybe they'd both stick around. Old Doc Hillman wanted to retire, or at least bring in another vet as a partner in the practice, and Lindsey Stafford would be perfect.

Stafford. He wished he could remember why that name sounded familiar.

"Hank?"

He turned around to see Ella. A rush of feeling stirred in him as he smiled at his wife.

"Is there trouble with the mare?"

"No, she seems to be coming along fine. I was just enjoying the scene." He nodded at the couple. "Mark my word, there's sparks between those two."

"Of course there is. They're young, good-looking and their hormones are on a rampage."

Ella had been the best thing that had happened to him in a long time. He'd been a fool to have taken years to realize his love for her. He drew her close to his side. "You don't have to be young to have those feelings."

She actually blushed and pushed him away. "Hank Barrett, stop talking like that. Someone might hear."

"So what if they do? We're not dead, woman. So don't put me out to pasture just yet." He took her hand. "Now come on, let's go see how the mare is doing."

Hank and Ella reached the stall. "How she doin'?" he asked.

"She's coming along fine," Lindsey said. "But you should keep her a day or two longer. I'll give her another dose of antibiotics in the morning." She raised an eyebrow. "Did you report the shooting?"

Hank nodded. "Called the sheriff, but I'm sorry to say that it isn't a top priority. A lot of people don't care for the wild horses. That's the reason I wanted to make sure this land was a haven for them. I thought it would keep them safe." He turned to the pretty vet. "I appreciate all that you've done, Lindsey."

"I'm just glad Brady found the mare in time."

Brady shrugged. "I got lucky."

Hank grew serious. "Lucky or not, we appreciate it, Brady. Thank you, too. And you can bet I'm going to take the threat to heart. This has happened before and it's time I put a stop to it. I won't allow someone to trespass on my land and endanger my stock, or worse, my family."

Hank sighed. "And since the sheriff won't do much, I'm going to have to go out myself and find these good-for-nothin' cowards. Even if it's some crazy kids, we still have to stop them."

"I'd like to go along," Brady said.

Hank knew the captain had a lot to prove, mostly to himself. "And I welcome your help, son, but I don't want any heroics here."

Brady nodded. "You give the orders."

"I thought we'd do some investigating. Maybe the person or persons left behind some clues."

"I can help, too," Lindsey volunteered.

Hank wasn't sure about that. "I was thinking about sending the boys out on horseback. And we might not get back until after dark."

"I've ridden after dark," she added.

"Maybe it would be safer if you went by truck with Brady. You two seem to make a good team."

By late afternoon Lindsey was exhausted when she entered the cabin. After leaving the Circle B, she'd finished her scheduled appointments, and now only had twenty minutes before Brady was due to pick her up. Although she was eager to help, she had plenty of apprehension over being paired with the one man she'd been trying to avoid. But she cared enough about the mustangs to want to find the person or persons who were responsible for the shooting.

After a quick shower, Lindsey hurriedly dressed in clean jeans and a sweatshirt over a thermal T-shirt and slipped on her comfortable boots. She slapped together two ham sandwiches and was just finishing up when a knock sounded on the door. She opened it to find Brady. He, too, was dressed in a sweatshirt, jeans and his bomber jacket.

"Ready?"

"No, I'm running late." She handed him a sandwich and a bottle of water.

"Thanks."

"Are we going to meet at Hank's place?"

"No. He gave me a map of the area he wants us to cover. Chance and Hank are teamed together in a vehicle searching the other side of the ranch. Cade and Travis are on horseback, along with Jarred and Wyatt. You and I are teamed up to check this side of the property."

"Okay, let's go, Captain." She pulled on her all-weather nylon jacket, a scarf and stocking cap for warmth.

He held the door open for her, and she ducked under his arm. He suddenly looked big and intimidating, and deadly serious. She realized this situation could be the same, too. Whoever was shooting at defenseless animals was dangerous.

Outside, they made their way along the path that led up the rise. Even without his cane, Brady didn't seem to have any trouble making the climb up to the parking area. Next to her SUV was the Randell Guest Ranch four-by-four truck. He opened the door and slid into the driver's side. Why not? His right leg was fine.

She got in the passenger side as he bit into his sandwich. That's when his jacket opened and she saw a flash of metal. A gun was tucked into the waistband of his jeans.

"You brought a gun."

He stared the truck. "Yeah, Doc, I did." The floodlight overhead illuminated part of his face. "I hope I don't have to use it." He took another hearty bite and chewed. "But there's no way in hell I'm going out there unarmed." His voice took on a husky quality. "Let's just say it's a precaution."

Lindsey could see the determination in Brady's face and heard it in his voice. He made her feel safe. Besides, they needed to catch whoever was shooting at the mustangs.

She glanced out at the fading daylight. "Where are we supposed to go?"

He handed her the area map from the bench seat between them, then backed the truck out and headed for the highway. "Hank's marked the area he wants us to search."

She looked over the written directions. "Okay, at the highway turn left and go down about a half mile to a service road."

Brady nodded and followed her navigation, trying to concentrate on his job and not think about Lindsey seated so close to him. How was he supposed to do that with her fresh lemon scent filling the small cab? It seemed to wrap around him, trying to distract him, reminding him how long it had been since he'd been with a woman. A long, long time.

With a groan, he shifted in his seat.

Lindsey turned to him. "You okay? Is your leg hurting you?"

Like hell. "No. I'm just trying to get into a comfortable position. If you can't see the directions, there's a flashlight on the floor."

"I can read just fine. If you'd rather I can drive."

"I said I can handle it," he told her, then finished the last of his sandwich.

"Okay, I'm just trying to help."

"Then read the map," he told her. "And get us to where we need to be."

"Then get ready." She pointed toward the driver's side of the road. "The turn-off should be coming up soon. There it is."

Brady pulled the truck onto the gravel road. After about twenty yards they came to a sign that read, Private Property. No Trespassing. But they soon discovered the gate was already open. "Maybe Hank left it open."

He threw the gearshift in park, reached for the cell phone and punched the buttons.

"This is Hank." Hank's voice came through laced with static. "Have you made it to your location?"

"Not quite. We're at the service road just off the highway. The gate's open. We weren't sure if you'd been here or not."

"Haven't been there in over a week, and none of the ranch hands would leave it open, either."

"Then we'll check it out."

"Call us if you see anything," Hank said. "We'll hightail it over there." There was a pause. "I know you won't walk into anything blindly, but be careful."

"Will do." Brady put the truck in four-wheel drive and moved cautiously down the road. He felt a rush of excitement. Besides bringing in the mare, this was the first useful thing he'd done in months.

When he came to a fork at the large tree, he slowed, then veered off to the right on the more-traveled road. They went along the uneven dirt path, passing through thick mesquite bushes that were so close they brushed the sides of the truck.

"Do you think this is the right way?" Lindsey asked.

He'd noticed the scratches on the truck when he'd gotten in. "I'd say this is a normal route. Besides, I have no choice but to keep going, even if it's just to turn around." He gave her a quick sideways glance, then returned his attention to the road. He slowed as they came out of the bushes into a grassy clearing. Right away he saw evidence that someone had been there recently.

"Bingo." Brady shut off the engine and got out. Lindsey followed after him. Together, they walked into the remnants of what was once a fire ring, a circle of rocks and some burnt wood.

"Well, someone sure as hell has been here," he said as he walked to the log and found scattered fast-food wrappers and several beer cans along with an empty whiskey bottle. "I'd bet there've been a few parties here."

"I'll call Hank," Lindsey said.

"Good idea." Brady went to the truck and returned with flashlights. He handed her one. "We're losing daylight fast. I'll search the area."

She punched in Hank's number and when he answered, she said, "We found a makeshift campsite about a half mile in. Looks like some kids have been here, and they've been drinking."

"Darn it, I was afraid of that. Is there any sign of anything else?"

"Brady's still looking around."

"Okay, we can be there as soon as we change a flat tire."

Lindsey hung up to see Brady wander off through the high grass. She caught up to him. "Hank will be here as fast he can. Maybe it would be better if you wait for Hank, and don't go out there alone."

He cocked an eyebrow. "Why, Doc, you're worried about me."

"I suspect you can handle yourself okay."

"Thanks for the credit. I've been able to get out of enemy territory, I think I can go look for some simple tracks." He pointed the flashlight down. "And in about ten minutes there'll be no light at all."

"Then I'm coming with you."

She followed after him, letting him lead the way.

He stopped and crouched down, motioning for Lindsey to do the same. "See how the grass is bent?"

She knelt down beside him. His hand pressed against her back, making it hard for her to concentrate on what he was saying.

"I don't think it was done by cattle. Hank doesn't have a herd even close to here. Could be the mustangs, but my guess is they're humans."

"So the shooter was probably here?"

He shrugged as his gaze met hers. "Or it could lead to a place one of the boys took his girl for some privacy." He raised an eyebrow. "A little private make-out place."

She felt the stirring in her stomach and she stood up. "We better keep looking."

Brady stood, too. He concentrated on finding some clues, anything that would prove a shooter was here. They continued to walk through the brush, then came to another clearing and more beer cans.

He aimed his flashlight along the perimeter and caught sight of a shiny object. He knelt down and picked up a brass shell casing, then another. He found a total of three.

"Well, I'll be damned."

Lindsey arrived at his side and looked at his hand. "Shell casings." She looked up at him. "So the shooter was here."

"He was, if these will match the bullet you removed from the mare." He noticed that she was shivering. "Come on, you're cold. Besides, it's too dark to find anything else. We'll wait for Hank." He pocketed the casings and guided her back to the truck.

Once inside, he started the truck and turned on the heater. "Sorry, I didn't notice the drop in temperature."

"It's okay, I'm fine." She smiled, but she was still shivering. "It was worth it. We found this place."

"And we might find who's responsible," he told her. He liked the fact that Lindsey Stafford wasn't afraid to get her hands dirty. He'd watched her yesterday with the mare. Saw firsthand her dedication.

He turned in his seat and leaned back against the door, stretching out his injured leg on the floor. Lindsey was huddled deep in her coat, trying to keep warm. He couldn't stand to watch her shivering.

"Lindsey." He spoke her name and she turned to him. Silently he held out his hands.

"Not a good idea, Brady."

"It's only to keep warm." He reached out and drew her into his arms. Once he opened his coat, she burrowed into his chest seeking warmth. He bit back a groan when her breasts pressed against him. Her hands were splayed against his ribs. He didn't dare take a breath.

After a few minutes of heaven, he asked. "Have you gone to sleep on me?"

"No, but I could use some." She turned her head and shifted position slightly. "My beauty sleep was interrupted by someone pounding on my door at dawn."

He smiled, feeling her soft hair against his chin. "I'd say it was for a good reason. Besides, sleeping is highly overrated." He looked down at the woman in his arms. "I can think of more interesting ways to kill the time."

She didn't open her eyes. "Aren't you a little old to be trying to seduce a woman in the woods?"

It was her fault that he'd been thinking like a high school kid. "Hey, there was a time when I could do a lot with some moonlight, a little privacy and a bench seat."

She finally sat up and glared at him. "I bet."

"What can I say? Every teenage boy had one goal in mind."

"I wouldn't know. I didn't date much in school. I was focused on getting into college."

"I'm sure the boys in your school were disappointed."

The faint sound of a song on the radio filled the cab. Even in the darkness, he could feel her eyes on him.

"Hardly, they were more into blondes."

"They were fools." He leaned closer, but Lindsey put up her hand.

"Stop right there."

"Why, darlin', you seemed to like my kisses well enough the other day."

She breathed in a sharp breath. "Well, you didn't give me much of the chance to turn you down."

He studied her cute button nose and stubborn chin. Damn, she was pretty. "You're the one who showed up at my door. To me that said you were interested."

"To you, interested is if a woman breathes."

"I'm more selective than you think. Not just any woman, Doc." He leaned closer and gave in to temptation as he brushed a soft kiss against her lips.

She sucked in a breath, but didn't pull away. "Brady, don't start this. Neither one of us needs this kind of complication."

"You talk too much, Doc. It's cold outside and we need to generate some heat."

"Turn up the heater."

His hand cupped her face and turned her toward him. "How about this instead?" He captured her mouth just as a whimper escaped, but she didn't stop him. It took a few seconds to convince her but slowly her arms went around his neck and she allowed him to slide his tongue inside and taste her.

By the time he broke off the kiss, they both needed air. "Damn, woman, you're dangerous."

She started to pull away and he stopped her.

He leaned forward and nipped at her lower lip, drawing another moan from her. "And I'm a man who lives for danger."

She broke free and sat up. "Well, I don't. So back off fly boy."

He had to admit he wasn't used to this kind of resistance. He held up his hands. "Fine."

Irritated, Brady sat up. That's when he saw the headlights.

Still a little shaky from the kiss, Lindsey managed to get to the other side of the cab and pull herself together.

"Stay here," Brady told her. "It's cold out."

She could only nod when Brady grabbed his hat and

climbed out of the truck. She could see he, too, had been affected by the kiss. That wasn't good.

"Hank," Brady called as they got out of the truck.

"What'd you find, son?"

"Over here." They walked to the campsite and shone the flashlights around the area. He handed Hank the casings. "Looks like whoever comes here has been doing it for a while."

Hank didn't look happy. "Well, I'm about to put a stop to it."

"Why not hold off on that for now? Instead, set a trap for them. That way you can let the law handle it. And hopefully stop the problem for good."

Chance stepped in. "What are you thinking of when you say trap?"

"Electronic surveillance." He glanced back at the truck, wanting to get back to Lindsey. "I could come by the ranch and discuss it with you." He glanced back and forth between the men.

"Sounds good," Hank said, but held up his hand. "I just don't want anyone to get hurt. Not us, or those kids. Nothing is worth that." He sighed. "So stop by tomorrow and we'll see if we can agree on a way to handle this."

Brady nodded. "Sounds good."

"Now, go and take Lindsey home. And thanks for the help."

They said their goodbyes, and Hank waved to Lindsey in the truck, then drove off with Chance.

Brady climbed into the warm cab, shifted into gear and followed the other truck out. "Looks like you got your wish, Lindsey. I can take you home and get you in bed."

"My, Captain, aren't you taking a lot for granted?"

He grinned and winked at her. Her heart tripped in her chest and she couldn't find any more words to say.

She was in big trouble.

Lindsey didn't talk on the drive back to the cabin. It had been a mistake going with Brady tonight, and letting him kiss her again was even more stupid. It was time to end any involvement with the man. Not give him encouragement, because in the end he'd walk away when he learned her connection to Jack Randell. The real reason she'd come here.

When they pulled into the parking area, Lindsey tried to get out of the truck before Brady could follow her. She wanted no repeat of what happened earlier. No more kissing Brady Randell was her recited mantra.

But the stubborn captain refused to take no for an answer and walked her to the well-lit porch. She unlocked the door but didn't go inside. Instead she turned around to face Brady. "Okay, I'm safely home. You can go now."

He leaned an arm against the doorjamb. "Look, Doc, I know you're ticked off at me right now, but if the truth be told, you were into that kiss just as much as I was."

"I'm not talking about this to you. So you need to go." She didn't want to admit how much she was drawn to him. "All I want is some sleep. My day starts early tomorrow."

Brady shifted his stance. He didn't have to get up at all, if he didn't want to. Even though his leg was throbbing like crazy, he didn't want to go back to the cottage and sit there alone watching some meaningless late-night television.

He raised a hand to argue when her cell phone went

off. She pulled it from her coat pocket. "Dr. Stafford," she answered.

Brady watched her forehead wrinkle in a frown.

"I should be there in about twenty minutes," she said as she went inside and picked up a pen off the counter. "Give me the directions," she said, then began to jot down the instructions. "Yes, I know the road. Okay." She nodded. "I'm on my way." She flipped the phone closed.

"What's wrong?"

"The Carson's mare is having trouble birthing her foal. I've got to get out there." She hurried into the kitchen area, grabbed a bottle of water from the refrigerator and headed for the door.

"Need some help?" he called to her when he caught up with her on the driver's side of her SUV. "It's been a while, but I helped my dad a few times with calves."

She stopped. "It's a messy job and could take hours."

He smiled. "I'm your man, Doc."

That was what she was afraid of.

Chapter 5

This was getting to be a habit.

Brady was behind the wheel of her SUV, and Lindsey sat in the passenger seat, giving directions to the ranch. It took nearly twenty minutes to get to the Carson's place. A boy about ten stood by the road and flagged them down, then pointed toward the barn. That was where they found the boy's mother, Bonnie Carson, with her quarter horse.

In the oversize stall, the young mare was already down, her head cradled in her owner's lap, and visibly in distress. Lindsey knelt on the fresh straw floor.

"Mrs. Carson, I'm Dr. Stafford. This is Brady Randell."

"I can't tell you how glad I am to see you, Doctor, Mr. Randell."

Lindsey could hear the fatigue and fear in the woman's voice. "This here is Under the Mistletoe. We call her Missy."

Lindsey studied the laboring mare. "How long has Missy been down?"

"She's been up and down for the last few hours, but this time it's been about ten to fifteen minutes. My husband would have been here, but he's stranded at the Denver Airport." There was a tremor in her voice. "Of course Missy chose now to go into labor." She nodded to her son. "Buddy has helped his dad, so I thought we could handle it. Then when Missy didn't seem to be getting anywhere, I called you."

Lindsey felt a strong contraction, and the horse's head came up and she let out a whinny. She soothed the animal until she calmed again. "It's okay, girl. We'll figure out what's taking so long." She looked at Bonnie. "I'll know more after I examine her."

Lindsey stood and went to her large case, not wanting to say out loud her suspicions that the foal might be breech.

Brady stood next to her. "What can I do?"

His voice was reassuring, and she was suddenly glad he was here with her. "You can bring me those clean towels and keep them handy." Stripping off her jacket, she nodded to the stack on a trunk outside the stall. She opened her medical bag and hung her stethoscope around her neck, then worked a waterless disinfectant over her hands and arms, took out a pair of latex gloves and slipped them on.

"I'll need you to go help Mrs. Carson, make sure that Missy stays down while I examine her."

"Done." Brady grabbed the towels and stacked them close by, then took his position to help the owner.

Lindsey knelt down and checked the horse's heart rate. Definitely fast. All the while she continued to talk softly as she slipped her hand inside the womb. She grimaced when she discovered the answer to the mare's long labor.

She sat back on her heels. "There's good news and bad," she said to Bonnie Carson. "The foal isn't a standard breech, but the legs are back. I need to bring them forward."

She looked at Brady. "Hold her still again." Their gaze met and he nodded, feeling a knot tighten his chest. He'd do his damnedest for her.

After another contraction, Lindsey reached back inside as far as her arm would allow and managed to get hold of one of the foal's legs. She pulled it forward. "Got one."

She looked at Brady and he sent her an encouraging wink. A little shiver rippled through her.

"Come on, Doc, one more to go," he whispered. "You can do it."

She had to glance away. That was when she spotted the preteen boy and a little girl peering between the stall railings. She didn't have to wonder what this horse meant to them.

Everyone went silent as if their concentration could help her search for the missing limb. It seemed to take forever, then she finally located it. "There you are." She maneuvered the leg in position as tears filled her eyes.

Entranced, Brady watched the intense focus on her face as she worked to help the mare. He soon discovered she was stronger than he could imagine. Beads of sweat popped on her forehead as she did her job. He could see her determination. With the next contraction, her efforts paid off when the mucus-covered hooves appeared.

"Come on, Missy." Tears filled Bonnie's eyes as she coaxed the horse to continue the birthing. With Lindsey's assistance the foal slid out into the world. The kids cheered as Lindsey wiped the reddish-colored filly with a towel and nudged her to stand.

"Good job, Doc," Brady said. He was surprised to see Lindsey's blush, then her attention went back to her other patient.

"Missy did all the work." She patted the still-down mare. "Take a rest, girl, you deserve it."

Ten minutes later a mother's instinct took over and the horse stood to check out her baby.

"Thank you so much, Doctor," Bonnie said. "I was so afraid we were going to lose them both."

"I'm glad you called me." She turned to the kids. "Have you two come up with a name yet?"

They shrugged shyly, then the boy said, "Maybe we can call her Doc Lindsey."

Two hours later they finally got back in the truck, Lindsey didn't even bother fighting Brady for the keys. She closed her eyes and leaned back against the headrest, feeling exhausted and exhilarated at the same time.

"Was this your first?" Brady asked. "Your first breech, I mean."

"Did it show?"

"No. You did an incredible job."

"Until tonight, I've only assisted in breech deliveries. Not that I would have told Bonnie Carson that."

"Well, mama and baby are doing fine. That's all that counts," Brady said.

His compliment meant a lot to her. "Thanks. And thank you for your help, too."

"Why? You did all the work."

"Keeping a large horse calm is a big help, but especially with a first-time mother, it isn't easy."

He reached across the seat, took her hand and squeezed it. "Just glad I was there for you."

She found she liked his reassuring touch. She needed it right now; she needed him. How easy it would be to let go. Even though he had danger written all over him, she would eagerly welcome his attention, his strength… his heart-stopping kisses. She sighed deeply.

Who was she kidding? Brady Randell was already buried deep into her thoughts. A man any woman would desire, and she was no exception.

Even if she wasn't truly related to Jack Randell, it still wouldn't be safe to get involved with a man who would leave her when his time here was up.

He'd go back to his first love, flying.

Brady pulled into the parking lot. "Home, safe and sound." He looked at her from across the car, and she quickly climbed out to avoid temptation.

He came around the car and gave her the keys, then slipped his hands in the front pockets of his jeans. "It's been quite a night, Doc. Thanks for letting me tag along."

"I need to thank you again, Brady. You were a big help." Lindsey needed to get away from the man, before she made a big mistake. "You really don't have to walk me down to my door. I know your leg has to be hurting."

"It's not a problem."

Shaking her head, she started to back away, praying he wouldn't pursue her. "You can watch from here to see that I get inside safely."

He looked disappointed but nodded. "Well, Doc, it's been an interesting evening to say the least." He took a step closer, but Lindsey wasn't about to let him kiss her. Oh, no, she'd be a goner for sure.

"Good night." She turned and hurried down the slope, then tossed him a wave as she opened the cabin door. She sighed with relief when he saluted back and headed for Hank's truck.

Once inside, she shut the door with a final click. She was alone. Brady was gone. Maybe for good. Suddenly she felt the absolute loneliness rush over her.

In the past ten years, she'd concentrated on school and her career. There hadn't been time in her life for a man. Not that she missed it. She hadn't found anyone yet who made her heart race, made her breath catch. Until now.

Until Brady Randell.

He wasn't the answer, she told herself. He didn't want commitment, or a future with a woman. He was the love-'em-and-leave-'em type. He got his thrills from piloting a F-16 thousands of feet over the earth. He was just killing time, hanging around and flirting with her.

"So get any silly thoughts out of your head," she told herself as she headed to the bedroom, stripping off her dirty sweater. Removing her boots, she kicked free from her jeans and tossed them in the corner, deciding to deal with them in the morning. She looked longingly at the huge canopy bed with the thick satin comforter that was definitely made for two, as was the large sunken tub in the bathroom. She pushed aside any thoughts of sharing these amenities with a man.

Right now she needed sleep. Grabbing a pair of pajamas from the drawer, she slipped on the cotton bottoms and was tying the drawstring when she heard the knock on the door.

She glanced at the clock. It was after midnight. Far too late for anyone to come by. She slipped on her T-shirt and robe, then hurried to the door.

"Who is it?"

"Brady."

She closed her eyes. "Look, Brady, I'm tired."

"Believe me, I'd like to be home and in a warm bed, too. But the truck won't start."

She opened the door, and cool air hit her. Brady Randell was huddled in his coat. She could see his breath. "What's wrong with it?"

"As far as I can tell it's a dead battery. I think I left the dome light on."

Lindsey realized she'd been the one who turned it on in the first place. She stepped aside to let him in. "Come inside where it's warm."

"Look, I hate to bother you, but I can't call Hank this late. Could you loan me your car to get home, and I'll bring it back in the morning?"

"Could you get it back by six?" she asked. "I have an appointment at seven."

He groaned, then glanced at the sofa in front of the fireplace. "Then I'll guess I'll just bunk down here for the night, okay?"

She saw the fatigue and pain etching his face and didn't have the heart—or the energy—to turn him away. "I'll get you some blankets."

He was in trouble.

Brady gripped the throttle hard, but he still couldn't control the vibration. In his head, he ran through the

*aircraft's checklist, reminding himself over and over that
he was an experienced pilot. He'd been able to bring
in crippled planes before, but his instincts told him this
was different. For one, he wasn't over friendly territory.*

*Another warning light screamed. The jet was losing
altitude. Fast. His heart pounded hard in his chest, he
sucked in oxygen, fought the panic.*

He was going down.

*The only safety net he had was his communication
with ground control. He made his Mayday call.*

*He was left with no choice but to eject. There wasn't
any time left to think about it. He reached for the yel-
low-and-black-striped handle, said a quick prayer and
yanked hard. He gasped at the powerful force that shot
him upward. He cried out, and everything went black.*

"Brady! Brady! Wake up!"

He gasped for air and jerked up. Oh, God. He blinked
away sleep and saw Lindsey's face. He groaned.

"Are you okay?" she asked.

He worked to slow his breathing and lied with a nod.
"Sorry. I didn't mean to wake you." He tried to turn
away. "Please, go back to bed."

She touched his arm, causing his gaze to meet hers.
"Were you dreaming about the crash?"

"It's not a big deal." He lifted his shoulders. "It happens sometimes."

Brady watched her stand up. A part of him hoped she
would leave him alone. Another part ached to pull her
down and hold her.

She went into the dimly lit kitchen and returned with
a bottle of water. She handed it to him, then sat down on
the floor in front of the sofa.

He took a hearty drink, then blew out a breath. After

finishing off the water, he dropped his head back on the pillow. "Please, Lindsey, go back to bed."

"I want to make sure you're okay."

"I'm fine." He closed his eyes.

"If you tell me about it, I might be able to help."

He released another sigh. "The way I'm feeling right now, Doc, I want a hellava lot more than just your sympathy. So if you know what's good for you, you better leave. Now."

Lindsey had been warned, so why didn't she go? She examined his solid and well-developed chest. He had the kind of six-pack abs most men only dream about.

Not only was he every woman's fantasy, he looked more than capable of taking care of himself. But there was something in those dark, brooding eyes that wouldn't let her leave him. His body might be healing quickly from his accident, but what about his soul?

"Lindsey, I said go...."

"Since when do you give the orders?" she tried to joke. "Besides, I'm awake now. So I guess you're stuck with me. You told me the other day you loved early mornings. So do I. To see the sun come up when everything is so fresh and new." She reached out a hand and touched his bare arm, not surprised to feel the sheen of sweat on his warm skin, the subtle tremble. He wasn't totally naked. He still had on his jeans.

Not much of a barrier, she warned herself, and she let her hand drop away. "There are times when we need to know that we're not alone, Brady."

"And sometimes we need to be by ourselves to think things through."

"And sometimes we *over*think things," she countered.

"Easy for you to say. I have to go through a Medical

Review Board and let them decide if I'm fit to fly again. And nightmares don't help my cause."

She was surprised at his admission. "Brady, it's okay to be afraid sometimes." She'd been there so many times herself. "I used to have nightmares. I was scared all the time, but nighttime was the worst of all. I was so afraid to close my eyes."

Brady rolled on his side and propped his head in his hand. "Afraid monsters would get you?"

"Yeah. But this monster was very real. My father." She shivered, hating that she still held on to the memories. "He liked to drink. And when he drank, he got mean…and nasty."

This time Brady reached for her hand and he gently squeezed her fingers.

"He used to take it out on my mother mostly."

Brady cursed. "Tell me he didn't come after you."

She shrugged. "A few times he tried. My mom stopped him, then she paid a big price for it." She felt the tears in her voice.

He growled. "Man, that's rough, Doc."

She shook her head. "No, I didn't tell you so you'd feel sorry for me. Just to let you know that we all have nightmares, Brady. And it's always worse when we're alone." She wasn't sure if she was speaking for him or herself.

"I'm glad you're here." He tugged on her hand, bringing her closer as he leaned toward her. "What I'm going to do right now has nothing to do with my nightmare. I'm going to kiss you, Doc. So if you want me to stop, let me know right now."

She didn't say a word.

His mouth descended on hers before Lindsey could resist. Not that she wanted to, because kissing Brady

Randell was like nothing she'd ever experienced before. The feelings he created in her were unbelievable.

He groaned and coaxed her up to lie down beside him on the sofa. He pulled her closer and deepened the kiss, tasting her thoroughly. She knew this wasn't wise, but she wanted this man so much, she refused to listen to common sense.

Her body quaked as he pulled her under him. She whimpered, feeling the wonderful weight of him. She sensed a new tension in his body as his hands went to work pleasuring her. He caressed her skin beneath her T-shirt, causing her to arch up, offering him her breasts. When he finally touched her, she gasped, bracing herself for the sensation he caused as he lifted her shirt and his lips drew a nipple into his eager mouth.

She cried out.

"Lindsey... I can't seem to keep away from you." His mouth returned to hers, the kisses became more and more intense.

Lindsey's hand moved over Brady's back, then bravely she slipped her fingers inside his jeans, finding his taut bottom.

With a groan, he raised his head and tugged her against his chest, skin to skin. "I've got to feel you against me, Doc." His gaze met hers reflecting his heated desire. "I want you."

Her heart drummed in her chest. She wanted him, too. "Brady..."

"We've been dancing around these feelings since we met. You want this, too, Doc."

She opened her mouth to speak, but her cell phone began to ring. "I've got to answer that."

With a groan he raised his arm, letting her get up.

Lindsey scrambled off the sofa, pulling her clothes back together as she grabbed the phone from the table. "Hello."

"Well good morning, Lin." At the sound of Jack's voice, Lindsey fought her panic but lost. She looked at the bare-chested Brady lying on the sofa and mouthed, "I need to take this call."

She nearly changed her mind on seeing the desire in his eyes, but common sense took over. She turned away and walked into the bedroom and closed the door.

"Jack, is something wrong?" A dozen things raced through her head, none good.

"No, but we're wondering about you. Your mother and I haven't heard from you."

"That's because you're on the trip of a lifetime. Who wants their kid calling all the time to check up on them?"

There was a long pause. "C'mon, Lin, we love hearing from you. And since you weren't answering at your apartment, we were kind of concerned."

She blew out a breath as she paced the bedroom. "I went to visit Kelly Grant," she said, which wasn't exactly a lie. She had gone to stay with her college friend nearly a month ago. "And I've been checking out some job prospects."

"That's good. Find anything interesting?"

"I'm not sure." She tried to change the subject. "How was your trip?"

"It was great. We got back yesterday. And if you come home this weekend we'll fill you in on everything and bore you with pictures."

Lindsey could hear the fatigue in her stepfather's voice. Had he told Mom the truth yet?

"We'd really love to see you."

"I can't this weekend, Jack. I've got a few interviews coming up. But I'll be home for Thanksgiving."

There was a hesitation, then Jack said, "I told your mother…everything. We talked most of the night and she finally fell asleep."

Tears filled her eyes. "Oh, Jack. How did she take it?"

"As well as can be expected. I know it would do her good to see you."

"And she'll get to. I promise I'll be there for her." She held her emotions in check. "You know I'll do anything I can to help you both."

"I know, Lin." There was another pause. "But there might not be any options this time. And you and your mother have to accept that."

"There are still some alternatives out there, Jack."

"Not as far as I'm concerned."

"How do you know if you don't try?"

"Please, Lin, don't push this. This is the way it has to be."

She knew the man was stubborn, but so was she. "Okay, I'll let it go for now. Tell Mom I love her and I'll call her later. I love you, Jack." She wiped the tears from her face.

"Love you, too, Lin."

She hung up the phone. Dear Lord, how was she going to convince him to come here? She turned and found Brady standing in the doorway.

She gasped. "I'm sorry the call took so long."

"Not a problem. Are you okay?" He came to her, and brushed a tear off her face. "I take it that wasn't a business call."

She shook her head. "It was my stepfather. My parents just got back from a cruise."

Lindsey was rambling, but if she stopped she'd end up back in his arms. Bury herself in his strength, but it would be fleeting. There couldn't be a repeat of that. Brady would be gone soon.

Lindsey stepped back from the temptation. "I should get ready for work."

Brady glanced at the clock. "You still have two hours. Are you sure you're just not afraid of what nearly happened between us."

She stiffened. "I need to get you home."

"I can call Hank or Luke." His eyebrows drew together. "Is everything okay with your family?"

Lindsey swallowed. "Yes. I'm going home for Thanksgiving."

She didn't want Brady Randell to be nice to her. She didn't want to like the man who just moments ago had been doing a good job of seducing her. The most important thing she needed to remember was that her stepfather, Jack, was also Brady's uncle.

And when she finally came clean about her true reason for coming here, the entire Randell family might just band together and run her out of town. Brady was a Randell. His loyalty would lie with his family.

She nodded. "If you don't mind, I need to take a shower."

He studied her for a long moment, then turned and walked away.

Lindsey had to fight hard to keep from calling him back. Then she reminded herself that he was only around temporarily, just like she was. In the end, they'd both go back to their separate lives. She thought about the scene on the sofa. Of the hunger of Brady's kisses, the incredible touch of his hands on her body. She drew a breath and closed her eyes, vowing not to let things go any further.

She knew she couldn't keep that promise.

Thirty minutes later the sun was up, a pot of strong coffee was on. Brady probably should have called Hank and let him know about the truck, but he decided he wasn't ready to leave Lindsey Stafford. She presented herself as a tough, independent veterinarian, but he knew better. After she'd told him about her father's abuse, he had a feeling that her stepdad was the man who'd been there for her.

Damn. He shouldn't get involved in any one else's problems. Brady took another sip of coffee. He had enough to concentrate on with his career and adapting to a place in his new family. That was about all he could handle right now.

When the door to the bedroom opened, he turned to see Lindsey. She had on fresh jeans and a white blouse under a navy sweater. Her auburn hair was shiny and curled against her shoulders.

She glanced around the living room, then turned toward the kitchen. He smiled and held up a mug of coffee.

"You looking for this?"

She blinked in surprise. "I wouldn't mind a cup." She came toward him and took her mug. "I can't function without caffeine."

Brady agreed. "I need that extra kick in the morning, too. If you had more time I would have treated you to my famous cinnamon pancakes." He grinned. "Maybe next time."

She stopped her mug's journey to her mouth. "Sorry, Captain, there isn't going to be a next time."

He faced her. "Oh, Doc, that's the one thing I am sure about. Things aren't settled between us. So there's definitely going to be a next time."

Chapter 6

About an hour later, Lindsey pulled up at the foreman's cottage to drop off Brady. What she didn't expect to find was his brother, Luke, Tess and another woman Lindsey didn't recognize standing on the porch.

"Please, tell me you called your brother to let him know what happened with Hank's truck."

"It was too late last night, and I guess I forgot about it this morning."

"You better think about answering some questions, because to them it's going to look like we spent the night together."

He looked at her and grinned. "We did. Technically."

"This isn't a game, Brady." She shifted the SUV into park not far from the porch. "I'm trying to build a reputation here."

His smile died. "So let's not tarnish it by letting

people think you spent the night with a washed-up jet jockey." He pushed open the door.

Lindsey grabbed his arm. "Brady, you know that's not what I meant. I like to keep my private life private."

"Don't worry, Doc. I'll stay clear of you from now on." He slammed the door and started toward the porch.

With a frustrated sigh, Lindsey hit the steering wheel. She hadn't meant to hurt his feelings, but that's exactly what she'd done. At the very least she'd stepped on his ego. She climbed out of the car and leaned against the hood. "Oh, Brady," she called out. "Thank you for last night."

He stopped, but didn't turn around. She didn't miss the tension in his broad shoulders.

She poured it on. "I had a great time. Call me anytime." With a wave to Luke and Tess on the porch, she got back into the car and drove off, calling herself crazy. Why should she care what Brady Randell thought?

Darn it, she did.

Brady walked up the pathway to the porch, surprised to feel a heat climbing up his neck. Lindsey had just let people think there was something going on between them. He suddenly smiled. So he was getting to her.

"Good morning, Luke, Tess. Hi, Brenna." He arched an eyebrow. "Am I late for my session?"

The cute therapist smiled. "Not for an hour or so. I came by to visit with Tess."

"Good, I'd like a chance to shower and change."

"I'll be back, though." She nodded to his injured leg. "How's the leg doing since our last workout?"

"Okay."

"All right, see you later." She and Tess headed up to the main house.

Luke stayed back. "I don't want to track your every move, but it would nice if you answered your cell phone."

Brady pulled it out and saw that the battery was dead. "I guess I didn't think about it. We were too busy looking for the guys who shot the mustang. When I took Lindsey home, she had an emergency call and I went along to help deliver a foal. By the time we got back, the battery in Hank's truck had died. So I spent the night at the cabin."

His brother nodded. "So you're seeing Lindsey?"

"I spent yesterday with her, but that isn't exactly 'seeing.' Why? You have a problem with that?"

Luke shrugged. "It's not my business what you do. I was just trying to have a conversation with my brother. And I want to help see that you heal and get back to what you want to do, fly. Isn't that what you want, too?"

For the first time Brady hesitated. "That doesn't mean I can't enjoy a beautiful woman's company while I'm here."

"I just don't want to see anyone get hurt."

Brady headed for the door as his brother stepped off the porch. "Look, Lindsey was joking around when she said what she said. I spent the night on her sofa." Not that it was where he'd wanted to be. He recalled how good it had felt when she'd come to check on him. How good she felt to hold. "You don't have to worry about her."

His brother stared at him. "Who says Lindsey is the one I'm worried about?"

"Do five more…but take it slower, then hold it," Brenna said. "That's it."

Brady fought a groan. He lay on the workout table in one of the cottage bedrooms, after taking off his removable booted cast from his leg, he'd strapped weights to his ankle as he did leg lifts.

Luke had made sure that there was enough equipment to help his younger brother stay in shape. And Brady had taken full advantage by working out the frustration of being confined to the house.

Although Brenna Gentry looked small and unassuming, she was strong as the dickens, working him through the isometric exercises and some light weight lifting. He wanted more. He wanted to get back to normal. And fast.

"Slow down," she told him, and grabbed hold of his leg as he pumped the weight. "You overdo and you could lose ground." She rolled those pretty brown eyes. "What am I saying? I normally have to prod my patients to work harder. But you I can't hold back."

"I want to get this over and be normal again."

"You'll get there, Brady," she told him. "You've made great progress."

"Not fast enough." He sat up and took the towel she offered. "It's been months since my accident."

"It's been three months. And you're coming along as scheduled."

"It's just not *my* schedule," he said.

"Then talk to your doctor at the next visit. Maybe he can give you a better idea."

"I plan to." He studied the pretty woman. "Thanks for all your help, Brenna. I couldn't have gotten this far without you."

"Don't you know I'm a sucker for Randell men?"

Brady hadn't had much of a chance to get to know his cousins. He'd heard a little about Dylan Gentry having been a bull rider. His career had ended after a bad spill off one mean bull. "You better not let your husband hear you say that. I don't need him coming after me."

She smiled. "Oh, I wouldn't worry so much. He's long past those wild days. He's practically a stay-at-home dad now."

His cousins and his brother all seemed content with their lives, happily married and with children. Brady had never stayed in one place long enough to want that. Growing up, family had been him and his mother. His dad was away too much.

"Well, I hope he realizes what he's got."

Her smile grew mischievous. "Oh, he knows, all right. But hey, feel free to tell him yourself if you come to Thanksgiving."

He frowned. "I don't do holidays." He thought about Lindsey being gone.

"You will now, Captain. But relax, it's not the entire family. This is the off year. Most wives around are going to the in-laws. Since my family will be gone, Tess invited us here along with a few others. So you aren't meeting everyone, yet. That will come a little later." She leaned back against the treadmill. "So Thanksgiving will only be about twenty or so."

"How many kids?"

Well, there's Livy. You know she's planning on marrying you."

"Very funny."

Brenna shook her head. "You're just like all the rest of your cousins, Brady Randell. No matter what age, the women flock to you."

The only woman Brady wanted was determined to hold him at an arm's length. "I prefer my ladies over the age of consent. Anyway, I'm married to the air force. And I like my women willing, but not long-term."

"I've heard that before," Brenna said. "Even a world-champion bull rider, Dylan 'Dare Devil' Gentry had succumbed to love of the right woman." With a knowing smile, she headed toward the door and called out, "See you later."

Whoa, just because his cousins and brother found marriage agreeable didn't mean the institution was for him. He'd never given much thought about a wife and kids. It had always been the military, his career. He'd known men who'd done it, handled a family and flying. His dad hadn't been one of them.

Georgia Randell had been on her own more often than with her husband during their marriage. Maybe that had been the reason Brady hadn't sought out a long-term relationship. Or was it the fact that he'd just never met a woman who made him want to change his priorities?

Surprisingly, his thoughts turned to Lindsey.

A week later Lindsey had returned from Thanksgiving with her parents. It had been the first time in memory she'd hadn't wanted to be home for a holiday. It was hard to see her mother's sadness. It was also hard to keep her secret from them. She'd managed to get through it and was now more determined than ever to talk with Jack's boys.

Her first call was at the Rocking R to check on Tess's stallion. In truth she hoped she'd run into Brady. She hadn't been able to get him out of her thoughts since she'd dropped him off after their night together. She kept playing it over in her head, the hungry kisses, the way he'd touched her. Brady had distracted her from thinking about everything else.

Lindsey climbed out of her SUV and headed toward the barn, forcing herself not to look toward the cottage. On her trek through the corral, she tried to stay focused on important things like the reason she'd come to San Angelo. The reason she still needed to talk about with the Randells. And she was running out of time. What was more important, Jack was running out of time.

Inside the barn she went toward Whiskey's stall and set down her case. The animal greeted her eagerly.

"Hi, boy," she crooned, thinking about her mother and what she'd been going through.

Gail Randell was strong and independent, and she loved Jack fiercely. For the past eighteen years, they'd been each other's salvation. After her mother's abusive relationship with her first husband finally ended, she'd been left with next to nothing and a ten-year-old daughter to raise.

One day Jack had shown up at the ranch. He'd just been released from prison and needed a job. With little money, her mom hired him. Over time, Jack told them about his past, his sons and all the mistakes he'd made in his lifetime.

It took years, but together they built a thriving horse-breeding business and—in the meantime—fell in love. And now Jack could possibly die. Tears threatened, and Lindsey quickly blinked them away. She wasn't ready to lose him. Not for a long, long time.

"Lindsey."

She swung around to see Brady walking toward her, his booted cast strapped around his lower leg. He still looked good dressed in jeans and his familiar flight jacket. That was when she realized she'd been attracted to him from the first time she laid eyes on the handsome pilot. She'd missed him.

"Oh, Brady. Hi."

He didn't smile back. "Is something wrong?"

She shook her head. "I needed to check Whiskey."

He frowned. "That's right, you've been gone."

"Just over Thanksgiving." She smiled. "My mom made a big fuss with a turkey, dressing and tons of pies. How about you?"

He shrugged. "I spent it with Luke and Tess and a few assorted cousins."

Had he missed her not being around? Probably not.

She glanced away from his stare. "It's nice to have family."

"Haven't decided that yet. I'm not into big crowds."

She knew he was still getting used to the Randells. If she'd learned anything since being here, it was that the Randells could be a little overwhelming. Not that she wouldn't love to be a part of their clan.

"Well, speaking for myself," she began, "I'd never turn down all that turkey and dressing. And, oh, the pies." She sighed. "Pumpkin's my favorite, but I wouldn't say no to pecan or warm apple pie with tons of whipped cream."

Brady had trouble not reacting to Lindsey's enthusiasm, and he wasn't talking about the food. Well, maybe the whipped cream. He grabbed her by the hand and led her the short distance to the tack room.

"Brady, this isn't a good idea," she began as he shut the door behind them.

He looked into her gorgeous eyes, and a thrill shot through him as he drew her into his arms. "Hell, I know that. But I've wanted to do this since that night at your cabin. It's been too damn long." He bent his head and captured her mouth.

Lindsey made him forget everything, but she also made him feel things. Things he didn't have any business feeling, things that went beyond need, desire, gratification. Nothing had prepared him for Lindsey Stafford.

Brady broke off the kiss, willing himself to slow his breathing. "Just a little something to make sure you haven't forgotten about me." He stared into her incredible green eyes and nearly lost it again.

He didn't wait for a response, his mouth closed over hers again. Her soft moan stirred him as his hands went inside her jacket and began to move over her luscious curves. He had about enough brain power left to realize where this was leading. He pulled back and took a breath, seeing her mouth swollen from his kisses. His gaze moved to her blouse, the rise and fall of her breasts.

"Damn!" He backed away. He didn't need someone like Lindsey in his life, but that didn't stop him wanting her.

She blushed. "We seem to get in these situations…" she began.

"Situations!" he groaned. "Situation? Hell, woman, we practically go up in flames whenever we're together."

Lindsey glanced away. "Then it's better if we stay away from each other."

Before Brady could agree wholeheartedly, he heard his name called out. What now? He shot her one last look, then went out the door to find his sister-in-law coming down the aisle.

"Brady. I've been looking for you."

"What's up?"

"I wanted to remind you about the family dinner at Hank's place tonight."

Brady bit back a curse. "Look, Tess, I don't think I can handle—"

She rested her hand on her hips. "Brady, they're having this dinner for you. Come on, we weren't able to all get together at Thanksgiving and this is the best time. We're just family." Her gaze wandered toward the tack room door to see Lindsey walk out. "Oh… Lindsey. Hi. Sorry I wasn't here to meet you."

"That's okay. I was just starting to examine Whiskey."

Tess nodded, but she wasn't fooled over the story. "I'm glad you're here because I wanted to extend an invitation to you for tonight, too."

Lindsey shook her head. "No, no, I'm not intruding on family. But you need to go, Brady."

Brady liked Tess's idea. "Not without you."

Tess smiled. "Well, you two work it out. Just be at Hank's place about six." She disappeared down the aisle.

Once they were alone, Brady turned toward Lindsey. "Look, I'm not into family things. So if you go, some of the focus will be off me."

"And on me," she said. "And there's another problem, Brady, everyone will think we're a couple."

"Of course. It's only natural you'd be attracted to a devastatingly handsome fighter pilot."

She fought a smile. "Oh, really?"

He grinned. "They're going to speculate, anyway. Why not let them?"

He saw the doubt in those eyes. "Brady, you really think that settles it?"

"Oh, Doc, as far as I'm concerned, this is far from being settled."

Brady was a coward. He'd faced danger at 10,000 feet, but meeting the entire Randell clan terrified him. He'd met all the cousins at one time or the other, but never all together.

"Relax, Brady. This isn't a firing squad," Lindsey said, sitting in the passenger seat in his brother's BMW.

"That might be easier than the series of questions I'm going to get tonight."

That had been one of the reasons he'd wanted to bring Lindsey, hoping it would direct attention off him.

"Big tough guy like you can handle it," she said. "Besides, you're good-looking and charming, so the women will love you. You're a fighter pilot, so the men will be envious, and the kids will go crazy to hear your stories."

He couldn't help but grin. "You think I'm good-looking?"

She glared at him. "Like that's something you don't know. But maybe I did go a bit overboard when I used the word *charming*."

He drove under the Circle B Ranch archway. "Sorry, it's too late to take it back."

"The one thing you don't lack is ego," she told him.

He'd known a lot of women, but none like Lindsey. He knew that might not be a good thing. He parked next to the trucks that lined the new barnlike structure. He shut off the engine and turned to her.

"Hey, I know who I am." He thumbed his chest. "A

damn good fighter pilot. Would you want anyone but the best defending your country?"

Her green eyes locked with his. "No. I only want the best."

He gave her his best cocky grin. "You got him, Doc." Brady climbed out of the car to help her. His gaze moved over her. She wore a pair of black slacks and a rust-colored sweater under a black leather jacket. Her hair was pulled up away from her face showing off hoop earrings.

"You look nice tonight."

"Thank you. I should have brought something."

"We brought wine." He pulled the bag out of the backseat. "I'm sure the ladies will like that."

Lindsey took a deep breath and released it. She shouldn't have come. Although technically she was a stepsister and stepcousin. As far as the Randells knew she was the new veterinarian. And there was a possibility that if the Randells discovered her deception, she wouldn't be invited back.

Hank walked toward them, smiling. "Hello, Lindsey."

"Hello, Hank," she said.

He turned to Brady. "And the guest of honor."

"If you keep saying that, I'm going to leave. There was no need for this get-together."

The older man laughed. "You don't know women very well. Come on, you two, let's go and see everyone."

They entered the large structure that had been built a few years back and used as the guest ranch's meeting hall with a cafeteria-style kitchen. In one section, there were linen-covered tables decorated for the party.

The noise level was nearly deafening as several kids ran around chasing each other, having a good time.

Lindsey had already met several of the brothers, but not all the wives.

"Hey, cuz, it's nice you made it." Chance pulled a pretty blonde against his side. "You haven't had the pleasure of meeting my wife, Joy. Joy, this is Brady and Dr. Lindsey Stafford."

"Hello, Joy," Brady said.

"Brady, Lindsey, it's nice to finally meet you both." She pointed to a name tag across her upper chest and then handed them theirs already filled in. "This should simplify things a little."

"I appreciate that," Lindsey said as she saw Brenna Gentry standing with Tess across the room. She smiled and sent a friendly wave toward them.

Lindsey took a breath and released it as she stole a glance at Jack's other sons. She'd gotten a big shock the other day when she learned about Jarred Trager and Wyatt and Dylan Gentry. Lindsey believed with all her heart that Jack deserved to know about them.

Chance's voice interrupted her thoughts. "We'll take a pass on giving all the children's names—"

"That's because you can't name them all," his brother Cade said as he handed Brady a beer.

Chance glared. "No, I just think their parents should handle it. This family can be a little much all at once."

"You think?" he murmured, and took a drink from his longneck bottle.

Hank and Ella stepped into the circle. "Welcome to the family, Brady."

Hank didn't forget her, either. "Welcome, too, Lindsey. Glad you could make it."

"Thank you for inviting me to share in your family dinner."

The older man frowned. "You'll always be welcome here. We have a saying, 'You don't have to be blood to be in this family.'" He nodded. "And our hope is that you'll want to be a permanent part of our community, too. We want you to stay on here."

She wanted that, too, but she couldn't, not until things were settled for her. "Honestly, I have been thinking about it." She couldn't make a decision yet. "Thank you so much for the offer." She saw Tess setting food on the table. "I think I'll go help the women." She walked off before anyone could stop her.

Brady's gaze followed Lindsey. He wondered why she was so evasive about Hank's offer.

Suddenly he saw the group of kids gathering. He had his own problems to worry about.

"Uncle Brady," Livy called as she ran to him.

He couldn't help but smile as the cute five-year-old came up to him along with another group of little girls. "Hi, Uncle Brady."

"Hello, princess." He bent over to her level.

"These are my cousins, Sarah Ann, Cassie and Kristin."

"Hello, ladies. My, aren't you all looking pretty."

His words drew girlish giggles.

Interest grew as more of the younger generation wandered over. The boys. "Who do we have here?"

Livy took over the introductions again. "This is Evan and he's nine years old." She pointed to a tall, lanky boy. "Jeff is fourteen." Another tall teenager. "Brandon is the oldest, and he's nineteen. His brother is James Henry and he's seven. All the rest are with their mommies."

"It's nice to meet you all." Brady held out his hand and shook the boys' hands.

It was Jeff who spoke first. "Are you really a captain in the air force?"

"Yes, sir. I am. I'm also a certified pilot on the F-15 and F-16."

"You got a call sign?" Brandon asked.

"They call me 'Rebel' Randell. But we won't get into the reasons why."

"That's so cool," another boy said.

Then a little girl stepped up. Her name tag read Cassie. "Does your leg hurt?"

He looked down at the boot cast strapped on his lower leg. "Sometimes." He backed up, found a chair and sat down. "But not right now."

Livy moved in closer to Brady as if staking her claim. "Uncle Brady is going to marry me," the five-year-old announced.

"Is that true?" Sarah Ann, belonging to Brenna and Dylan, asked.

He looked up just as Lindsey arrived. Their gazes met, causing his pulse to race. "Yes, she's my best girl. She's going to take care of me when I'm old."

He stood and leaned toward Lindsey and whispered, "At least, it's the best offer I've had so far."

By ten-thirty that night Brady was parking at Lindsey's cabin. She didn't argue when he climbed out and came around to her side. Silently they walked down the slope to her cabin.

"So tonight you're going to let me walk you to the door?"

She stopped. "Not if your leg is bothering you."

"My leg is fine," he assured her.

Lindsey was nervous, more than any other time she'd gone out with a man. And she couldn't deny any longer this had been a date. They showed up at a family function together. And since they hadn't been able to keep their hands off each other, it would be wise to say a quick good-night and lock the door.

Right. She knew that wasn't going to happen, especially after having seen a different side to Brady tonight. How he'd interacted with the cousins and shown a softer side with the kids, patiently answering all their questions. So he wasn't the total tough guy he'd led her to believe.

How was she supposed to distance herself from this man?

After unlocking the door, she turned to face Brady, meeting his heated gaze. It was impossible. Silently she led him inside.

The room was illuminated by the dim light she'd left on. She saw his handsome face, along with the need reflected in his dark eyes.

Lindsey just wanted to drink in the beauty of the man. An inner strength and gentleness was underneath the cocky attitude.

The corner of his mouth twitched, then he lowered his head and brushed his lips across hers. The touch was featherlight, causing her to want more. Ache for more.

Then his mouth found its way to her ear, and she shivered at the sensations he created. She gasped as he tugged on the hoop earring, causing other parts of her body to clench.

"You have to have the sexiest ears," he breathed. His hand moved upward and cupped her face. "But they've got nothing on your mouth." He dipped and took a nibble.

She gasped and made a moaning sound. Oh, how she wanted more, so much more.

He didn't disappoint her as his mouth closed over hers, angling his lips just perfectly to hers. Then his tongue slipped along the seam of her mouth, and she opened for him, welcomed him inside.

She clutched at his shirt, then slipped her arms around his waist, wanting to get closer to him. Brady helped things move on as he slid her coat off her shoulders, letting it drop to the floor, followed quickly by his. Next, it was her sweater that hit the ground, then his shirt disappeared.

He finally released her but never took his gaze from her. "I want you, Lindsey. But whether I stay or go is up to you."

She could turn him away. That would be for the best, but the feelings she felt for this man wouldn't let her deny herself this night. "Please, Brady, stay with me."

Brady gave a slight tug and they walked together into the bedroom. Once beside the large bed, he kissed her again and again. Then he sat down on the mattress and took off one boot and the cast. Lindsey removed her shoes, but when she started to take off her slacks, he stopped her and did it for her.

Standing there in her panties and bra, she enjoyed the hungry look in his eyes.

"You're so beautiful," he whispered and closed his mouth over hers until they both slipped onto the bed. Next came her bra.

She gave a moan as he circled one nipple with his tongue, causing the peak to harden. She arched her body and he opened his lips to take what she offered.

His easy hands moved over her warm skin, touching and stroking. It wasn't long before the rest of their clothes disappeared, and he lifted his body over hers. He paused as their gazes locked. She could see how tightly he was holding on to his self-control.

When it came to Brady Randell, she soon discovered she had no control.

Chapter 7

Lindsey woke with a start. She blinked to clear the fog from her head as the bright sunlight came through the window. She also heard the sound of the shower running. That was when the picture of a naked Brady Randell climbing into her bed and making love to her, again and again, flashed through her mind.

With a groan she flopped back on the pillow, clutching the blanket against her own nakedness. She rolled onto her side and inhaled the man's intoxicating scent, causing her to relive the pleasure he'd given her during their night together. She'd never experienced anything like it. Ever.

And she never would again. Not with this man.

She sat up. Her only alternative to correct this big error in judgment was to tell Brady the truth.

The bathroom door opened and the man in question

came into the room. Oh, my. He was naked except for a towel wrapped around his waist. Beads of water still clung to his broad chest, then found their way down to his washboard-hard stomach.

With the last of her resolve, she forced her attention back to his face. Darn the man, he was grinning.

"Good morning, darlin'," he said as he limped to the bed, leaned down and planted a lingering kiss on her surprised mouth. "Yep, it's definitely starting out to be a good one, too."

"It's a late one." She glanced away. With a death grip on her blanket, Lindsey looked at the clock. Seven-thirty. "Oh, no, I need to be at the clinic by eight-thirty."

His gaze moved over her as a slow cocky smile crossed his tempting lips. "So I can't talk you into calling in late?"

She opened her mouth to answer, but no response came out. Good Lord, she was thinking about it. Was she crazy? "No!" she croaked. "I have scheduled appointments."

He looked disappointed. "Maybe later. Tonight?"

This had gone way too far, and she needed to tell him everything. "Yes, tonight. Now, I've got to get into the shower."

He nodded. "While you're showering, I'll fix breakfast."

He walked to where he'd dropped his jeans last night. She looked away as he slipped on his pants, then fastened his leg brace under the slit pant leg.

He grabbed his shirt and boot and headed for the door. He stopped and looked over his shoulder. "I could bring you coffee while you're in the shower."

She forced a smile. "No, thanks, I can wait."

"Well, holler if you need anything."

"I won't." She continued to sit there. "Now, would you mind?"

Brady wanted to hang around, just to see her blush some more. Lindsey wasn't dealing well with the morning-after routine. Not that he was a pro at this, either, but he wouldn't turn down an invitation to join her in another shower. But he knew that wasn't going to happen, so he wouldn't push it.

"I'll get coffee started."

He heard a murmured "thank you" as he walked out and closed the door. She wanted privacy. Okay, he'd give her that, he thought as he put on his sock and boot. He knew last night that Lindsey Stafford wasn't the type who usually brought men home. He liked that about her. Hell, he just plain liked her. A lot.

He made his way into the small kitchen, opened the coffee canister and scooped the correct amount into the coffeemaker, added water and turned it on.

Why was he still hanging around? That wasn't like him. He never wanted to give a woman the impression that this would lead to anything permanent. Over the years he'd tried relationships, but his career always came first. He couldn't blame women for not wanting to wait around for him.

Brady thought back to his own dad. He knew his parents' marriage wasn't perfect, but they loved each other, and their limited time together had been special to them. He'd always wondered if he'd find someone that he could love that much.

So far, no woman had held his interest beyond the casual stage. He'd decided long ago that a personal life would have to wait until he was a civilian again. He glanced down at his leg with the cast. That might come sooner than he wanted it to.

It had been a long few months since his accident. He glanced toward the bedroom door. Last night he hadn't thought about anything but being with Lindsey. She was different than any woman he'd known in the past. He liked her independence. She was self-assured in her work, and he especially liked how she cared about her patients. No doubt she could handle almost anything.

He took orange juice out of the refrigerator, noticing the shelves were bare. Toast would have to do, for now, but he owed Lindsey some decent food. Maybe he should have her over to his place for a change.

Whoa, he stopped. Was he crazy? His future was so uncertain, he couldn't begin to figure anything else out in his life.

Did he want this to go further? Suddenly he pictured the pretty redhead in bed last night and this morning. Oh, yeah, he wanted to see where this could lead, at least for a little while.

A knock sounded on the cabin door. Brady hesitated but decided that the Randells knew he'd taken Lindsey home last night. Besides, he was a little old to sneak out the back.

He opened the door to find a stranger wearing a sheepskin jacket. A black Stetson sat on his head. He had his back to him. At first he thought it was someone from the construction crew, then the man turned around.

Brady's breath caught as his gaze moved over the man's face, the square jaw and deep-set brown eyes. He had thick, steel-gray hair and a broad forehead, partially covered with a cowboy hat.

Damn, if he wasn't a dead ringer for his dad.

The older man frowned. "I'm sorry, I must have gotten the wrong cabin."

"Well, it all depends on who you're looking for," Brady said. "If it's a Randell, I'm your man, Uncle Jack."

The man's eyes narrowed, then he examined Brady closer. "You're Sam's boy?"

Brady couldn't believe it. Jack Randell had come back. "I'm one of them—Brady. Luke is the one you probably know about." What was he doing here after all these years? "If you're looking for your boys—"

"No! I'm not." He shook his head. "Actually, I'm looking for Lindsey Stafford's cabin."

Okay, he was confused now. Why would his uncle be looking for the vet?

Just then the bedroom door opened and Lindsey came rushing out, pulling on a sweater over her blouse. "I sure could use that coffee," she began. "But that's all I have time for." She finally glanced up and saw the two men at the door. She paled, then managed to say, "Jack. What are you doing here?"

Jack moved past Brady and into the cabin. "Funny, I came to ask you the same question."

Lindsey swallowed and tried to slow her heart rate. It didn't help. She stole a glance at Brady's confused look. She hadn't wanted him to find out this way.

She went to Jack. "I told you I was job hunting."

"Except you purposely left out the part about coming to San Angelo," Jack said. "If it wasn't for your friend, Kelly, I wouldn't have discovered what you're up to." He gave her a stern look. "Lin, we discussed this, and you agreed you'd stay out of it."

She took in his gaunt face. He'd lost weight. "I can't,

Jack." She turned to Brady. "Brady, this is my stepfather, Jack Randell."

"Isn't this a kick? Your stepfather is my uncle. How about that for a coincidence."

Her voice softened. "I was going to tell you, I just couldn't find the right time."

His dark gaze grew hard. "Then I guess Uncle Jack showing up solved your problem." He looked at the older man. "You're legendary in these parts. And after all these years you come back. I'm curious if that's how you're going to greet your sons. You gonna just knock on the door. Surprise, here I am."

Jack shook his head. "I'm not going to disturb their lives. Lin and I are going back to Ft. Worth."

"No, Jack, you can't leave. You're here now, you've got to tell them."

Jack straightened. "Lindsey, I told you I'm not going there."

Brady grabbed his coat off the chair. "I'll let you two fight this out," he said as he headed for the door.

Lindsey went after him. "Brady, please." She grabbed his arm when he reached the porch. "You've got to let me explain."

"Why, so you can make an excuse about why you lied to everyone?"

"No, I didn't lie, everything I told you was true." She blinked at tears, biting back the words her stepfather refused to share with his family.

His eyes flashed. "So he sent you here to scout for sympathy."

That hurt her. "No. He wasn't going to contact his sons at all. This was all my idea." She rubbed the chill from her arms. "When I saw the ad for the veterinarian's position, I told myself I just wanted to meet one of Jack's boys. He'd talked about them for years, and Travis was doing the interview. I couldn't believe how much he looked like Jack. Then when he offered me the job, I found myself taking it."

She looked out at the scene of the incredibly beautiful valley. "Who wouldn't, Brady? I've heard stories about the Randell boys since Jack came to work on our ranch when I was ten years old." She didn't reveal that she'd always wanted to be part of that large family.

Brady jammed his hat on his head. "Then if you think he's so great, go back home with him. Believe me, when the brothers find out, there will be hell to pay."

She stiffened. "Then I'll pay because I'm not leaving here, not until Jack sees his sons." She fought her anger and tears. "And I plan to do everything I can to help him, and I'm not letting him lose—" she hesitated "—this chance to resolve things, not without a fight. So if you're going to run and tell the cousins, fine. I'll be ready for them."

Before she could leave, Brady grabbed her. "Dammit, Lindsey. Do you realize what kind of position you've put me in? I have nothing against Jack, but I owe some loyalty to my cousins. We're business partners."

She nodded, knowing Jack had more at stake. He could lose everything. "I know. And I owe my loyalty to the man I think of as my father. The man who helped raise me, who believed in me when I didn't believe in myself." She folded her arms over her chest. "Jack might have made a lot of mistakes when he was younger, but he's paid a heck of a price. He spent years in prison, lost his boys, his family." She looked Brady in the eye. "Mom and I did, too. I didn't lie about my childhood.

Jack made us a family. Deep down, he's a good man,
Brady. For God's sake, he's a Randell, too."

Brady cursed and paced the porch. "Hell, Lindsey,
you're asking me to be his cheering section. I can't do
it. I don't know how I can help you without causing a
big family upheaval. And I'm not crazy enough to go
against six brothers."

"Six brothers?"

Lindsey and Brady turned around to see Jack right
behind them. "What are you talking about?"

Lindsey sighed and went to Jack. "It was something
I learned just a few weeks ago." She took a breath. "You
have three other sons, Jack. Jarred Trager, and twins
Wyatt and Dylan Gentry. They've come here to live, too."

Jack paled and his eyes closed momentarily. "No
wonder I'm so hated. Dammit, Lindsey, we're leaving."

She shook her head. "No, Jack, you can't. You've got
to see this through."

"Well, I'm out of here." Brady started up the steps to
where his car was parked.

Lindsey went after him. "Brady, wait. What are you
going to do?"

He shook his head. "You tell me, Lindsey. What
should I do? Just pretend I didn't see Jack Randell here?"

"No. But I just want a little time."

"Why? No amount of time will make this situation
better."

"I know that. But I wasn't expecting Jack on my doorstep this morning." She couldn't blame him for feeling
this way, especially after last night. She should have told
him. "I'd already invited you back tonight, and I was
going to tell you then."

"For another seduction so I wouldn't care about any of this deception?"

That hurt more than she wanted to admit to him. "You pursued me. You kept showing up at my door. I didn't set out for anything to happen between us." She could see by his steely look he didn't believe her. "Fine, do whatever you need to do, Brady. But I'm going to do any and everything I can to help Jack."

Lindsey turned around and made her way down the steps, hating that she'd allowed Brady Randell to get close to her. Well, never again. Ignoring Jack, she marched inside the cabin to the phone. She punched the number to the clinic and asked the receptionist to reschedule her morning appointments.

Jack had wandered back inside, too. "Give it up, Lindsey. Get packed and let's go home before anyone gets hurt."

"Stop it, Jack. I'm not letting you off the hook that easily. You're sick. Your sons are here." She released a breath. "You're the one who taught me never to give up, and now you want to. No. Forget it, I won't let you. I'm going to fight, Mom's going to fight, and you're going to fight, too." Tears filled her eyes. "We love you too much to let you go."

His eyes were sad. "You might just have to, Lin."

He came to her and hugged her close. She shut her eyes and allowed herself to feel his strength, his tenderness and the love she'd come to cherish. He'd saved her so many times over the years, she had to save him. She wasn't ready to let him go. No, not yet. She pulled back and wiped the tears away. "At the very least, Jack, you've got to see your sons."

He couldn't seem to say anything to that.

But she knew he wanted that, too. She punched out numbers on the phone.

"Lin, who are you calling?"

"I hope it's the one person who can help us. Hank Barrett."

About twenty minutes later Brady pulled up at the house. He parked the car and left the keys on the seat. He wasn't anxious to talk with Luke or Tess or anyone.

This way he didn't have to explain anything. Damn. The tranquil life he'd known since coming here was about to end. All hell was going to break loose, even if Jack Randell was smart enough to turn around and head for Ft. Worth. Brady knew he'd been here. He knew that Lindsey Stafford was Jack's stepdaughter.

Did Lindsey really come here on her own, or had Jack sent her to test out the waters? To see if his sons would be receptive to their father.

Brady shook his head. "It's none of my business." He didn't want it to be. He hadn't had Randells in his life growing up, but they'd gathered him into the fold even before he'd arrived here. He recalled waking up after surgery to see, not only Luke but Chance and Cade.

Brady thought back to Lindsey. Jack might have acted like a bastard to his sons, but he could see that father and daughter loved each other.

Brady climbed the single step to the porch. He sat down on the railing, recalling how Lindsey had responded to him last night. She'd held nothing back. After just a few weeks, he'd quickly learned she was that way about everything. She was fierce about her animals. He didn't doubt her love and loyalty for her family. For Jack.

"So you finally made it home."

Brady turned to see Luke coming up the path. "I didn't know I needed to check in."

"I'm not your keeper, Brady. I think it's great that you're getting along with Lindsey."

That was an understatement. "It's short-lived. We both know I'm going to be leaving soon."

Luke watched him. "You don't have to sound so anxious to go. We've kind of gotten used to having you around."

"Hell, you've only known me a few months."

"And you're my brother." He stared out at the corral. "Even though you're a pain in the butt sometimes, there's a bond between us. You feel it, too. We're family. We should be able to depend on each other."

That was Brady's problem. For so long he only depended on himself. He wasn't sure he could change—he thought of Lindsey—for anyone.

It took Hank an hour before he could get away to go and see Lindsey. She sounded anxious on the phone. He hoped she wasn't going to tell him she was leaving the valley. Well, he was going to do his darnedest to change her mind.

He parked his truck and climbed out, and that was when he spotted the black Ford crew cab pickup with the gold lettering for Stafford Horse Farm, Ft. Worth, Texas. So Lindsey's parents had come to visit her.

A strange feeling gnawed at his gut as he made his way to the cabin door. Then suddenly the pieces fit together. But before he could knock, the door opened and a large man stepped into view.

Deep-set brown eyes stared back at him, examining him closely. About sixty, with thick gray hair, he was wide-shouldered with an imposing barrel chest. He'd looked a lot older than his years, but Hank still had no trouble recognizing him. He'd seen those features every time he looked at his boys.

"Hello, Jack. I wondered if this day would ever come."

"Yeah, the rotten bastard came back."

"No, I was gonna say, I didn't think you had the… *cojones* to face your past. What changed your mind?"

Jack blinked. "Nothing. I came to get Lindsey. I don't want her exposed to my mess."

So his hunch had been right. "I thought I'd recognized the name when Lindsey mentioned it." He studied the man closely. "I'd heard you settled in the Dallas/Ft. Worth area after your release, and got a job at the Stafford Horse Farm. I take it Lindsey is your stepdaughter."

Lindsey appeared. "And proud of it. Hello, Hank."

She stepped back to allow him inside. Removing his hat, Hank followed Jack to the seating area by the fireplace. He took a seat across from Jack, watching the man. So different from the young, cocky, know-it-all guy who couldn't seem to stay home for his wife and boys. When he did, he ran his daddy's ranch into bankruptcy. Yet worst of all was when he'd been arrested for cattle rustling and was sent off to prison, leaving his three sons alone.

That was decades ago, but some scars never fade, especially for the kids left behind.

Lindsey came in carrying a tray with coffee. She set it on the table. "Thank you, Lindsey." He picked up the steaming mug and took a sip. "Well, Jack. Tell me what this is all about."

Jack exchanged a look with Lindsey, but she spoke first. "Hank, Jack, didn't ever plan to come back here. My mom and I urged him many times, but he wouldn't do it."

"It was for the best," Jack said. "I knew the boys were settled with you, and you gave them a good life. I thank you for that Hank."

Hank nodded. "If that's true, why now?"

"It was because I came here." Lindsey exchanged another look with Jack. "I saw the ad for a vet and that Travis Randell was doing the interview, and I got curious. By the end of it I found I was agreeing to come here. I never meant to deceive anyone, but there wasn't a good time to blurt out who I was."

Jack interrupted. "I want her to return home and forget about this. I don't want any trouble, Hank. The boys are settled." He glanced away. "Lindsey tells me that I have three other sons."

Hank nodded. "Jarred Trager. Do you remember an Audrey Trager?"

Hank had to admit he got satisfaction seeing Jack uncomfortable. "Yes, I do."

"Then there's the twins, Wyatt and Dylan Gentry. Wyatt ended up buying your half of the Rocking R."

Hank could see more recognition and pain flash across Jack's face. "The ranch was in pretty bad shape when Wyatt got it, but it's a showcase now. Dylan showed up a few months later. He'd been badly injured by a bull while on the rodeo circuit."

"Dylan Gentry. He was world champion a few years back," Jack said.

Hank nodded again. "All the boys live around here now, they all married, happily."

Jack nearly jumped from his chair. "Stop. I have no right to know these things. I gave up those rights long ago."

Lindsey could see the pain in her stepfather's eyes.

She wished he'd let her tell Hank about his illness. "Jack, you've always wanted to know how the boys were doing."

He swung around to his daughter. "It's worse knowing. I'm never going to be a part of their lives, or their children's lives." He drew a breath and calmed down. "I need to get back home to your mother."

Her mother? "You didn't tell Mom you came here?"

He shook his head. "I thought I could bring you home before she found out. She'd just worry."

"Jack, she's going to worry, anyway," Lindsey said, then turned to Hank. "The reason I came here was I was hoping his sons could help."

"Lindsey…" Jack sent her a warning look. "We're going home. I'm not going to see the boys."

"They're not boys anymore, Jack," Hank told him. "They're men and can make their own choices."

"Please, Jack," Lindsey pleaded. "You'll regret not talking to them before you leave."

She could see the pain in his face. "I can't mess up their lives again," he said. "I just can't, nothing is worth that."

Lindsey turned to Hank, fighting tears. "Please, make him understand this might be his chance to settle things."

"But it's a chance I'm not taking," Jack argued.

Hank held up his hand to stop them. "I think it's not up to you, Jack. It's your sons' decision."

Chapter 8

By the end of the day, Lindsey was exhausted. After the confrontation with Brady and Jack, the last thing she wanted to do was to take a call at the Rocking R Ranch. But after hearing Tess's concern about her colicky mare, Lindsey got there as soon as she could.

She wasn't ready to see Brady again, so she entered the barn on the corral side. How immature was that? As if she should care, since her job here would be coming to an end shortly. Just as soon as Hank talked to the brothers, Travis would ask her to leave.

She didn't want to think about how much she wanted to stay on. And if she were lucky enough to buy into a practice, this one would be perfect. She loved the area.

But she wouldn't leave Jack, not when he had to start treatment again. She wanted to be there for him and her mother.

Tess met her at the barn door. "Oh, Lindsey, thanks for coming so soon."

"Not a problem. How's Lady doing?"

Before Tess could answer, the horse whinnied. "As you can tell she's not good. She's been taking in a lot of water, and her respiration is rapid. We've had her off her feed all day." They headed out to the corral where Brandon and Luke were walking the animal.

Lindsey saw right away the animal was excited and thrashing as the teenager tried to keep her under control.

With a closer look, Lindsey was pretty sure what the problem was. "I think she's having intestinal spasms. Hear the gut noises?"

Both Luke and Tess nodded. "Yes."

"Spasmodic colic. Bring her into a stall," she told Luke.

Luke followed her orders, and led the mare inside. Once the examination was finished and an ailment was confirmed, Lindsey went to her bag, filled a syringe and injected the mare with an analgesic to relax the intestines. Slowly Lady began to calm.

She sent Brandon to her car for some supplies, mineral oil and lubricated tubing. With the others help, she administered a hearty dose of oil to the animal. Then they waited and let nature take its course. Soon after, the treatment began to take effect.

Nearly two hours later, a smelly and dirty Lindsey walked back to the car. Tess and Luke were still with Lady and Brandon had gone on home. The good thing about her fatigue was she hadn't had time to think about Jack waiting back at the cabin. She also knew he was going to try and convince her to come home with him.

Home. She wanted San Angelo to be her home, but knew that was pretty much impossible now.

Lindsey glanced up and paused, seeing a large figure in the shadows. Brady was leaning against her car. A shiver went through her. Why this man? Why did this man have to cause her to feel, to want, to desire?

He spoke first. "Is Lady all right?"

Lindsey continued toward the back of the SUV. "She is now." She set her case on the ground and opened the hatch. Brady came back and lifted the case to set it inside. "That's quite a fragrance you're wearing, Doc."

She knew she smelled, but the mare was better, and that was all that mattered. "It's one of the hazards of the job. That's what happens when you work around animals. Not a big deal, it'll wash out." She snapped her fingers. "That's right, you jet jockeys go for another kind of horsepower."

She was pushing him, but she didn't care. It was her only defense. She'd needed his support this morning when Jack showed up, and it hurt when he walked out. "Just so you know, I called Hank, and he talked with Jack. They're deciding what do." She slammed the hatch. "So don't worry, you're off the hook, Captain." She started for the driver's side, but he grabbed her arm to stop her.

"All right, so I didn't handle things well this morning." His gaze bore into her. "I'm new at dealing with family situations."

"You didn't handle anything, Brady, you walked away." She'd needed him, too. "After last night…" She hesitated then tried to pull away but he held tight.

"Dammit, Lindsey. It was a shock to find out my uncle is your stepfather."

"Okay, I blew it," she admitted. "But I never dreamed

things would go so far, either. Just believe me when I say I was planning to tell you everything tonight."

He held her hand tighter. "Now that I've had a chance to think about it, I promise to listen to the whole story."

She needed to believe he was on her side, but couldn't yet. "Brady, I can't do this. I'm tired and dirty and I need to get back to the cabin. Jack is waiting."

He straightened. "That's it? You're just walking away?"

She didn't want to, but there wasn't any choice. "I can't worry about anything but Jack right now. He needs to see his sons, Brady. If only to close that door on his past mistakes. It's not going to be easy for any of us. You might have to choose sides." She didn't wait for an answer as she climbed into the car.

She couldn't bear to lose another man she loved.

Lindsey drove back to the cabin, praying for some good news. So far, she'd messed up royally when she only wanted to help.

Her biggest mistake was falling for Captain Brady Randell. No matter how things turned out for her job here, or for Jack, Brady was still going back to the air force. And he wasn't going to worry about the girl he left behind.

Great, she'd finally trusted a man and it was someone who didn't want the same things she did.

After parking behind the cabin, Lindsey walked down the slope. She didn't want Jack to see her worried, so she put on a smile as she walked inside. On the sofa Jack and her mother were in a tight embrace.

"Mom, you're here?"

Gail Stafford Randell pulled out of her husband's arms and stood. She wasn't much taller than her daughter, but her short hair was brown and she had large hazel eyes. At fifty-five, she looked trim in her dark slacks and teal sweater.

"Since I can't believe anything anyone in this family tells me, I decided I'd better come myself."

Lindsey felt tears rush to the surface. "I'm sorry, Mom. I never meant to make such a mess of everything."

"I know you didn't, honey. I'm still upset with Jack, though. He should have told me right away that the leukemia returned." She gave him an irritated look. "But, Lindsey, you should have let me in on your plan. I would have helped you."

Jack came up next to his wife. "And if I'd have faced my responsibilities years ago, we wouldn't be in this mess." His eyes narrowed. "But I'm telling you both right now, I won't coerce my sons. They don't owe me a thing. So they're not to know about my condition. Ever. You both have to promise me that you won't tell them."

Lindsey didn't want to, but she agreed. "What is Hank going to do?"

"He's talking to the boys tonight." He sighed. "So we'll know tomorrow if they decide to meet with me. I have no idea what to say to Chance, Cade and Travis. But even worse is Jarred, Wyatt and Dylan."

"We'll deal with it together." Gail's arm slipped around her husband's waist. The exchange of love Lindsey saw caused her chest to tighten. She couldn't help but envy what they shared.

Jack leaned down and kissed his wife. "That's because I have you, Gail. We'll get through this like we have everything else, as a family."

Her mother nodded. Tears filled her eyes as she rested

her head against her husband's chest. Jack wrapped her in his strong arms.

Lindsey suddenly felt like a fifth wheel. She glanced at her watch. "I need to get out of these smelly clothes and shower. I have another appointment."

"I bet you haven't eaten," her mother said.

Lindsey started for the bedroom. "Don't worry about me, I'll get something while I'm out. I'll probably be gone for hours. So please, you two take the bed."

"Honey, no," her mother said. "We can go to a hotel."

"No, I want you here. I'll just crash on the sofa when and if I get home."

She disappeared into her bedroom, then into the shower. Under the warm spray, she cried for her parents, for the Randells, for the years she'd taken for granted. Mostly she cried for herself, and the family she might lose.

Hank had summoned all six brothers to the house that night, but told Chance, Cade and Travis to come earlier. The four of them sat around the large kitchen table. The pine surface had many scars from the kids who'd eaten here for years. It was also the place where there had been many family discussions, punishments had been handed out and big announcements made. But never once in over twenty years, had he been able to tell his boys that their father had come home. Until tonight.

"I called all the brothers, but I wanted to talk to you three first."

The trio exchanged looks. "Come on, Hank, just tell us," Cade said.

"Okay. Jack is back."

He kept an eye on the three men he'd called his sons

for over the last two decades. Their expressions were controlled, but he could see their underlying anger.

"What the hell does he want?" Cade finally asked. He'd always been the one to anger the fastest.

"Well, from what I learned today, he wants to see you boys," Hank told them. "Jack has been living outside Ft. Worth. He's been remarried for about a dozen years, and he breeds horses with his wife. You might have heard of the Stafford Breeding Farm."

"Wait a minute," Travis began. "Stafford. You can't mean to tell me that Lindsey Stafford is related to Jack?"

Hank nodded. "His stepdaughter. Lindsey told me she's wanted to tell you all who she was from the beginning, but never found the right time."

Travis spoke up. "So, she's trying to cozy up to us so Jack can come back into our lives?"

Hank raised a hand. "I don't think that's it. Lindsey swears she came here because she's always wanted to meet Jack's sons, and she found the opportunity when Travis went looking for Dr. Hillman's replacement."

"Does she think we're just going to welcome him back into the fold?" Chance said and shook his head. "I can't do it, Hank."

Travis and Cade murmured pretty much the same sentiment.

Hank hadn't hoped for much more. "Okay, but you know you're missing a good opportunity here. I mean, you always had questions you needed to ask him. If you refuse to see Jack, there might not be another chance."

Chance frowned. "I don't have much to say to him. When he got out of jail, he called and asked for money, which I gave him to stay out of our lives."

"And he's done that," Hank said. "I don't think he

would be here if it weren't for Lindsey. She's the one who's campaigned for him to come back. She told me she was always curious about you three. Jack always talked about you."

"She should have told us who she was," Travis said.

"Would you have offered her the job?"

Travis folded his arms over his chest. "I'm not sure. Damn, she's a good vet. And everyone only has great things to say about her."

Cade spoke up. "How long would they, if they knew she was Jack's stepdaughter? People have long memories."

"And you boys have turned the name of Randell around to mean something good," Hank said. "There's a few old-timers who won't let go of what happened years ago, but you three have never listened to the talk. You've proven yourselves over and over again. You're your own men. And you're nothing like Jack. I'm so proud of you three, I can't even tell you."

The brothers sat up a little straighter.

"If it's any help," Hank went on, "Jack has turned his life around, too. The Stafford Horse Farm has a reputation as a top breeder in the area. Isn't it nice to know that he's doing well, too? That he's finally taken responsibility."

"I guess I wouldn't mind seeing him," Chance said, and looked at Hank.

The oldest of the three, Chance had been the one who'd tried to shield his brothers. He worked to keep them together, trying to be a man at fourteen. "I think I speak for all of us, that we haven't considered Jack our father for a long time," Chance said. "Not since we sat here that first time and you gave three scared kids a home."

Hank swallowed hard against the sudden emotion.

"Did we ever thank you?" Cade asked.

Hank nodded. "Every day when I watched you three grow into fine young men. A...a father couldn't be more proud."

Later that night a rainstorm moved into the area, dropping the temperature ten degrees. Brady was staying dry inside and fixing some soup. He'd planned his evening with supper and a strenuous workout, hoping to take the edge off his restlessness.

Now, if he could only stop the recurring thoughts of last night and Lindsey. How she'd felt in his arms, all soft and curvy. How her hands moved over his body, her mouth on his skin. He closed his eyes and his gut tightened as a renewed ache coursed through him.

A knock on the door brought him back to reality. He wiped his hand over his face. "You've got to pull it together," he warned himself as he walked across the room. He hoped the late-night caller wasn't his brother, wanting to go over business. He definitely wasn't in the mood.

Brady pulled open the door to tell Luke just that when he found Lindsey on the porch. She looked cold and miserable.

His heart soared. "Well, this is a switch. I'm usually pounding on your door."

She shivered. "My mother is at the cabin with Jack. I think they need to be alone." Those sad green eyes met his, then glanced away. "I didn't have anywhere else to go," she whispered.

He felt another tug inside his chest. "You do now."

In one swift motion he lifted her into his arms and over the threshold into the warm house.

"I know you're angry with me," she began, but he cut her off with a kiss so intense that when it finally ended they were both breathless.

"I'm getting over it." He brushed his mouth across hers again, loving the soft purring sounds she made.

"I didn't come here for this, Brady." She drew a breath. "Last night was a crazy mistake, for both of us. We don't need to repeat it."

"I'll go along with crazy, but what happened between us wasn't a mistake. It was damn incredible."

She pushed away from him. "Don't, Brady, I can't think straight when you say things like that. And I need to keep a clear head." She took another step back. "Along with a favor."

He shrugged. "Ask away."

"Let me hang out here for a while. Maybe sleep on your sofa."

His gaze searched her face. "You want to stay here?"

She nodded. "My mom and Jack need some time alone. I'm kind of the odd man out. I could go to a motel if it's a bother."

Lindsey Stafford definitely bothered him, in so many ways he'd lost count. He raised an eyebrow as the rain pounded against the roof. "How can I send you out in this? You hungry?"

She nodded and followed him into the kitchen. "I could eat."

"It's just tomato soup and grilled cheese."

"Some of my favorites," she said. "Let me help." She went to the hot griddle on the stove. A loaf of bread and cheese already sat on the counter. "How many sandwiches would you like?"

"Two, but you don't have to cook them."

"I think I owe you a little kitchen time."

"If you insist." He went to the refrigerator and took out a jug of milk. He held it up. "This okay?"

Lindsey nodded and placed the buttered bread on the grill. She shouldn't have come here to Brady. She glanced at the handsome jet jockey with the day's growth of beard across his square jaw. He was too sexy for comfort. Those dark, deep-set eyes could pierce right through her resolve. Oh, yeah, she was in trouble. But she still didn't want to go anywhere else.

"Hey, stop thinking about it," Brady said, calling her back from her reverie. "Jack and the Randells will handle things."

"I can't help it," she told him. There was more riding on this visit than just patching up old times. "I never wanted to hurt anyone. They probably hate me now."

Brady came to her. "Stop. I've only known the Randells for a short time. If I've learned anything about them it's that they're fair. You didn't do anything to them. Their beef is with Jack. And from what I've heard they've got good reason." He kissed the end of her nose, then took the spatula from her and flipped the sandwiches. "Now go sit down before you burn the food."

She huffed, unable to stop her smile. "I wasn't burning anything. They taste better with a dark, almost burnt crust."

"No. Golden brown is the only way." He scooped the cheese sandwiches off the grill. She carried the soup bowl then she glanced at the wall to see the calendar with the big red X marked at the tenth of the month.

She nodded to it. "What's that? D-day?"

"It's my next doctor's visit. Dr. Pahl is going to be the one who gives me the okay to shed this cast."

That was just a few days away. She looked across the table at Brady. She'd trusted him enough to share herself with him last night, body and soul. And she quickly discovered she wanted more time. "And if your leg has healed properly, do you go back to flying?"

He took a spoonful of soup. "I wish it was that easy. No, even with my doctor's okay, I still need the okay from a board of review to see if I'm fit to fly fighters again."

"You mean physically fit?"

"And mentally." He took a hearty bite of his sandwich. "No one wants any unstable pilots out there flying military aircraft."

"You aren't unstable." To herself she added, *A little stubborn, cocky and, oh, yeah, arrogant.*

"Thanks for the vote of confidence, but it's standard procedure that has to be followed."

"Well, I'm sure you're going to do fine," she said halfheartedly, knowing it was what Brady wanted, what he loved to do. She suddenly wasn't hungry anymore. "I guess both our lives will be changing soon."

His dark eyes locked with hers. "Why? You going somewhere?"

She shrugged. "This was only temporary. I doubt that I'm going to be staying here much longer." And she had to be back in Ft. Worth to help her mother with Jack.

"Doc, I doubt the Randells are going to send you away. You're too good at your job. Besides, I like the idea of coming back here and seeing you."

God, she was pathetic. She was actually thinking about waiting around for a man who couldn't make her any promises.

"Dream on, fly boy, like I'll be holding my breath for your return," she lied.

Brady pinned her with a long, heated stare. She tried to draw in air, but it was difficult.

"Even as much as I might want to stay, Doc, I have a commitment to the air force."

"And I have a commitment to my career. I need to set up practice. My family is important to me. So I should go back to the Dallas/Ft. Worth area."

He scooted back his chair, reached for her and pulled her toward him.

She put up token resistance. "Brady, this isn't helping the situation." She went to him, anyway, allowing him to sit her on his lap.

He kissed her below the ear. "You know what, Doc?"

She gasped as a shiver went through her, and she wrapped her hands around his neck. "No, what?"

His mouth worked its way along her jaw. "When I look into your big, green eyes, you knock me out, you make me forget everything," he murmured. He raised his head, but his hands continued to move over her body, her bottom, up her back, drawing her in a tight embrace. "And when you're in my arms and I feel your body against mine, you make me forget everything but making love to you."

She tried to ignore the feelings, too. She pulled away and stood. It would be so easy to take the pleasure he offered, use it to help make her forget.

He came up behind her. "Lindsey?"

She turned around and saw the concern on his face. "I'm sorry, Brady. I can't do this." She hesitated. "I should just leave." She tried to get past him, but he reached for her.

"The hell you are. Tell me what's going on."

"Just because I don't want to go to bed with you—"

"Hell, I've been shot down before, but I think there's something else going on here. Talk to me, Doc," he said in a husky voice as he reached for her.

She buried her face in his chest. God, it felt good just to lean on someone.

"It's Jack." She raised her head and looked him in the eye. "He's sick."

"How sick?"

"Very. That's the reason Mom and I tried to get him to come here and see his sons. He refused over and over. So when I saw the ad for the veterinarian…"

"You came here to try and pave the way for Jack," he finished for her.

She nodded. "He's not happy with me right now. And even though I'm here, he still made me swear not to tell Chance, Cade and Travis about it."

"Did he make you swear not to tell me?"

She looked at him. "No, but…"

He tugged her to the sofa and made her sit down beside him. "Come on, Lindsey, maybe I can help."

Brady might not love her, but she found she trusted him. She needed him to get through this. "Jack has leukemia."

He cursed and pulled her to him. It was like the floodgates opened as she began to tell him the four-year story. She shed tears as he held her. She fell asleep with the sound of his words in her ear, "Don't worry, Lindsey. It's going to be all right."

Chapter 9

The next morning, the rain was gone and the sun was shining. Brady ached to move and get the circulation back in his arm. He glanced down at Lindsey. Just as she'd been all night, she was curled up against him.

A strange feeling tightened his chest. She'd been carrying quite a burden around on those small shoulders of hers. And he felt privileged and humbled that she'd trusted him enough to share it with him.

She stirred in her sleep, shifting closer, and her breasts brushed against his chest. He bit down on his lip, feeling his body stir. She was killing him in more ways than one. He wanted Lindsey. He had from the moment he'd opened his eyes and seen her that first day on his porch. Keeping his hands off her during their evening together had been difficult, especially since they'd made love just the night before. He knew what it felt like to touch her, to feel her body react to the pleasure he'd given her.

He also knew that his longing hadn't stopped, his desire hadn't been quenched. He still wanted her more than ever. But right now she needed a friend more than a lover.

He grimaced. Friends with a woman? It had never been his style, but this pretty redhead had changed his mind about a lot of things. She'd pushed her way into his solitary life, making him rethink all other commitments.

Lindsey stirred once again. This time she blinked, then finally opened those incredible green eyes.

"Good morning, Doc."

With a gasp Lindsey sat up as she tried to regain some brain function. She'd spent the night with this man. She glanced down in relief to see they were both dressed and sharing the sofa in Brady's house. Memories flooded back and she remembered it all, especially the things she'd told him.

She brushed her hair away from her face. "I should get back to the cabin." She started to stand, but Brady stopped her.

"What is it about mornings that you're always so fired up to leave?" he asked. "Or are you just running out on me?"

She didn't want to acknowledge the closeness they'd shared last night. It had been far more intimate than anything physical that had taken place between them before. Now she'd shared her heart with this man.

"I just need to check on my parents."

"Okay, go call, but you better tell them you have plans this morning."

She raised an eyebrow. "I do?"

He nodded. Even with his hair mussed and his beard

heavy, he was sexy as all get-out. "It's Wednesday and the clinic is closed this morning," he reminded her. "So how about playing hooky with me?"

She didn't like where this was leading. "Brady, I told you last night—"

"Doc, I'd like nothing better than a repeat of our night together." His voice turned husky. "Making love with you was incredible. But you're not ready."

She found herself blushing. Would she ever be ready for someone like Captain Brady Randell?

A lazy smile appeared on his handsome face. "So get sex off your mind, along with everything else, for a little while anyway. We're going horseback riding."

"You can ride?"

"I've been able to most of my life."

She frowned. "You know what I mean. With your bad leg."

"My leg is fine. I'm sure I can handle Dusty. Come on. I've been cooped up too long. I need to see some sky."

She got up so he could stand, too. "I'll still need to check my messages to see if there are any emergencies." She quickly went through about a half-dozen voice mails. One was from her mom. Lindsey returned the call and relieved her mother's concerns. She also heard about the meeting this morning between Jack and his sons. Once Lindsey hung up, Brady handed her a cup of coffee.

"Here, I think you need this."

"Thanks." She took the mug. "I also need a shower."

"I could use one, too. You go first, and I'll get in a short workout."

She nodded. "I carry a change of clothes in my car."

"I'll get them. You hit the shower." He headed for the door, but she stopped him.

"Brady, thank you for last night. You could have taken advantage of the situation."

He nodded. "Just so you know, Doc, I'm not always going to be a nice guy. Not when I want something. And I want you."

Hank wasn't sure how he was going to handle this meeting with Jack. He'd expected it years ago. Now the boys were adults, he wasn't even needed here, except that Chance asked him to come along.

Although the three sons had turned into six in the past few years, Chance, Cade and Travis were going to talk with Jack first. Jarred, Wyatt and Dylan would be arriving a little later.

Hank and Chance drove from the Circle B, and they were to meet Cade and Travis along the creek. As they got out of the truck, they saw the tall figure of Jack Randell already waiting under the trees.

They made their way down the slope beside Lindsey's cabin where they saw an attractive woman on the porch. He knew she must be Jack's wife and Lindsey's mother, Gail Stafford Randell. Hank nodded in greeting, not wanting to stop and visit at this time.

"Damn," Chance hissed and stopped on the path. "I didn't think it would be this hard."

"It's time to face him," Hank said.

"I know, let's get it over with." Chance nodded at the two riders coming in. "Here come Cade and Travis."

They rode in from the direction of Travis and Josie's house. Hank's chest tightened at the thought of his own daughter, Josie Gutierrez. He hadn't learned about her existence until she came to find him. He'd welcomed her with open arms, then after her marriage to Travis, he'd gifted her with Circle B acreage to build a home. He'd divided the rest of the property between the boys he considered his sons, Chance, Cade and Travis.

They made their way to the edge of the creek, and to Jack. The two Randell men faced each other as if they were gunslingers from the Old West, instead of father and son. There was more silence as Cade and Travis dismounted and stood alongside their older brother. This was how it had been for years. You got one Randell brother, you got them all.

Chance spoke. "Well, we're here. What do you want?"

"Not a thing," Jack assured them, "except to see that y'all are doing okay."

"We're just fine. No thanks to you," Cade said.

Jack's gaze examined them all closely. "Yes, you boys have turned out fine." He took a breath. "I know this is a little late, but I want to apologize for not being around to raise you, and for causing you so many problems. I know it couldn't have been easy after I got sent away."

Hank could see the emotions all the men held in check.

"You're right," Travis said. "It wasn't easy, but as you can see, we survived. So it's a little late to be worrying about us now."

Jack nodded, looking pale under his tan, weathered skin. "Yes, you turned out fine. Thank you, Hank."

Hank nodded. "My pleasure."

Jack slipped off his hat and ran fingers through his hair. "There's one other thing I want to ask. You can be angry with me all you want, but don't take our problems out on Lindsey. She's innocent in all this. She only wanted to meet you all."

"She should have told us who she was," Travis said.

"Maybe, but I'm asking you to not hold that against her. She's a good veterinarian, and that's all that should matter."

Cade spoke up this time. "Or she might be a way for you to worm your way back into our lives."

Jack looked stricken. "If I'd wanted that I wouldn't have waited over twenty years." He put his hat on his head. "When a man gets to a certain age, he realizes he needs to make peace with his past. So I promise you that when I leave here today, it will be for the last time."

Brady had forgotten how good it felt to be in the saddle. The last time he'd ridden had been on his dad's ranch a few years back. He wasn't going to wait that long again.

He was on Dusty, and Lindsey was on Luke's roan gelding, Rebel. They were headed for the valley as the sun warmed up the early December air. Although they had worn jackets, he didn't doubt that they'd have them off before long.

"This was a great idea," Lindsey said.

"I come up with a few." He rested his hand against the saddle horn, giving his horse the lead.

"Your leg feeling okay?"

He grinned. "I told you, it's fine." In fact, he hadn't thought about it once. His concentration had been on Lindsey. She was smiling. He hadn't seen that in a while.

"I thought we'd head for the valley," Brady said. "It wouldn't hurt to check on the herd to see if they're okay."

"Good. It's been a few weeks since I've had the time to go by."

"You've had a few things going on, Doc." They rode side by side as they approached the rise. "Besides, there haven't been any incidents since the mare was shot. Maybe Hank's new security system is doing its job."

They started down toward the creek, looking for the mustangs. Instead, they saw a group of men.

Lindsey pulled up on the reins. "It's Jack. He's with Chance, Cade and Travis." She looked at Brady. "Maybe we should leave."

Brady watched the exchange between the men. His cousins were agitated. "They don't look happy."

"Oh, Brady, Jack's not as well as he's been pretending. And this stress isn't helping."

He reached for her hand and squeezed it. "Then tell his sons about their father's illness."

She shook her head. "Jack would never forgive me."

Brady wanted to shake them all. "Then the least we can do is even the odds. Come on, let's go stand with your father."

They made their way down and dismounted by the trees. Brady escorted Lindsey the rest of the way down to the group.

"Good morning, cousins," Brady said. "Hank, Uncle Jack."

"Lindsey, you shouldn't be here," Jack said.

"Maybe I should, since I'm the one who started all this." She looked at the three brothers. "It was never my intention to cause trouble."

"Jack's right, Lindsey," Cade said. "This doesn't concern you."

"Yes, it does," she corrected him. "Jack has been my father for the past dozen years. I love him." She fought tears. "Okay, he's made mistakes, but we all have."

"Lin, please." Jack went to her. "You don't need to

defend me. We all know what took place all those years ago. I need to own up to it with my boys."

"Dammit, we're not your boys," Chance hissed.

Jack looked stricken. "I know. I gave up that privilege a long time ago."

There was only silence, until they heard the sound of the riders. It was Jarred, Wyatt and Dylan.

"We heard shots fired," Jarred called out.

Hank cursed. "Any ponies hit?"

Wyatt shook his head. "The herd scattered, but I think they're okay."

"Where did the shots come from?"

He pointed toward the west. "Same area as before."

"Well, this is going to stop today." Chance headed toward Lindsey. "You think I can borrow your horse?"

"Of course. I'll go to the cabin."

Chance went to Dusty and mounted up. His brothers did the same.

Brady was going to ride, too, but Hank stopped him. "Let's go in the truck. If the boys can't reach them, we'll be able to head them off."

Jack followed the group up toward the parking lot. "Mind if I go along?"

"I don't see why not," Hank told him.

Gail Stafford was waiting on the porch, but Jack only called to her that he'd be back soon.

"Take care of your mother," Jack said.

When Lindsey started to argue, Brady reached for her. "Look, it'll be better if you stay here. Then I don't have to worry about you, too."

She nodded. "Just watch out for Jack."

"Sure." He leaned down and gave her a quick kiss.

"We'll be back soon." He tipped his hat to Gail, then hurried to Hank's truck.

"You drive, Brady," Hank insisted, then headed for the passenger side while Jack climbed in the back door.

Brady started the engine and headed toward the highway, all the time aware of the danger. "Maybe you should call the sheriff, Hank."

Hank pulled out his cell phone. "A lot of good it'll do us."

"It's a precaution. If anything happens today, we want it on record that we called the authorities."

Jack spoke up from the backseat. "I take it these guys have taken potshots at the ponies before."

"We've had two wounded in the past few months. Thanks to Lindsey, the little buckskin mare recovered."

"That's my girl," Jack said proudly.

Hank continued to fill him in as Brady turned off the highway. Jack climbed out to open the gate, then returned to the truck.

"The lock's been busted," he told them.

Hank's fist hit the dashboard. "I'll get these guys if it's the last thing I do. And I might just tan their hides before I turn them over to the sheriff."

"I might just hold them down for you." Brady drove along the bumpy dirt road, then turned at the fork. After another half mile, he pulled off and parked. They all climbed out, then Hank took two rifles off the rack in the back window of the truck.

"I'm not going in without backup," he said.

Brady called Chance to learn their location, then he silently walked toward the spot where he and Lindsey had found the camp once before. He heard voices, and used a hand signal to alert Hank and Jack that he was going closer.

The thick mesquite bushes were great cover so he could peer at the intruders. Four teenage boys were sitting on the downed logs, drinking.

Brady returned. "There's four of them," he said. "Teenagers. They have two rifles, but it gets worse. They're passing around a fifth of whiskey."

"Somebody raided their daddy's liquor cabinet," Jack said.

"Their parents aren't going to be happy to have to bail them out of jail, either," Hank added. "I'm pressing charges."

Brady wasn't crazy about dealing with drunk kids, especially holding firearms. He pulled out his phone and called the sheriff again, telling him what they'd found.

Closing his phone, he reported, "A deputy is on his way."

"I'm not letting them get away. So it looks like we're on our own," Hank said.

Brady looked at Jack, noticing his rapid breathing and pale complexion. "Are you okay?"

Jack brushed off the concern. "Sure, I'm fine. I'll hang back in case one of them tries to run."

They circled the area, then Hank showed himself first. He cocked his rifle and pointed it. "Okay, boys, the party's over."

The teenagers jumped up, shouting curses. One tall, thin boy boldly stepped forward. "It's only an old man."

"Well this old man is going to make your life miserable." Hank waved the rifle. "Now, move away from the weapons. We don't want anyone to get hurt."

"We don't have to listen to you," the same kid mouthed off.

"Look, I'm the one holding the rifle on you. And you're trespassing on my land, shooting at defenseless animals. Wild mustangs. So I'd suggest you keep your mouth shut. Now, move." He waved the barrel of the rifle to show the direction.

Brady came into view. "I'd do as he says if I were you."

They reluctantly walked away from their whiskey and rifles. "My daddy isn't gonna like what you done," one of the boys said as he swayed on his feet.

"If your daddy's smart, he'll whip your butt for this stunt."

The boy cursed. "Old man, you're gonna be sorry. My daddy is important in this town."

Brady could see one of the smaller kids looking panicky. Then suddenly the boy took off running. "Dammit." He looked at the other kids. "Don't even think about it."

Suddenly they heard the boy cry out. Brady went to see that Jack had tackled the kid. Brady smiled. "Hey, Jack, you need some help?"

"No, I got him."

Brady turned back to the other boys to see if they'd lost their attitudes.

"What are you going to do to us?" the kid asked.

"Nothing. We're turning you over to the sheriff."

Just then Chance came riding in. "Good, you got 'em." He climbed down as Jack brought in the other boy.

Chance took the rope off his saddle and began tying the boys' hands.

Brady gave his rifle to Cade when he arrived, then went to help Jack. The man was leaning against the kid's truck. They tied the teenager's hands with rope from the truck bed. Brady directed him toward Chance, then came back to Jack.

"You don't look so good," he said, seeing the blood drain from Jack's face. "I think we should head back."

"I wouldn't mind that." He pushed himself off the truck, swayed, then collapsed.

Jack Randell was unconscious before he hit the ground.

Chapter 10

An hour later, trying to control her panic, Lindsey and her mother hurried through the hospital doors and upstairs to the third floor. Brady had called about Jack's collapse and instructed her where to come, but she had no idea what condition her stepfather was in.

All the way up the elevator, she couldn't help but blame herself for this mess. If only she hadn't come here....

"Stop trying to second-guess yourself, Lindsey," her mother said. "Jack needed to come back here and see his boys."

"But I could have handled things differently." She bit back the tears. "And if Chance, Cade and Travis knew about Dad's condition, they could help him."

Her mother gripped her hand. "And we both know Jack would never ask them."

The doors opened and they went to the desk to get information. She looked around for Brady.

Not only Brady, but every one of Jack's sons were in the waiting area. Chance, Cade and Travis stood by the window, and talking with Brady were Jarred, Wyatt and Dylan. When Brady saw her, she felt her chest tighten. She needed him. He didn't disappoint her as he came to her.

He hugged her close. It felt so good, she never wanted to leave the safety of his arms. Finally she raised her head. "Where's my dad?"

"He's down the hall. Dr. Hartley is with him." He looked at her mother. "Mrs. Randell, I'm Brady Randell. I'm sorry about your husband. We got him here as soon as possible."

"Thank you." Gail nodded, fighting tears. "He's been really sick. We need to get him back home."

Before Brady could speak, the doctor came out of the room down the hall. Gail Randell went to him, and Lindsey followed her. "Dr. Hartley, I'm Gail Randell, how is my husband?"

The gray-haired specialist frowned. "He's a sick man, Mrs. Randell. Thanks to the information your daughter gave us over the phone, I've been in touch with his oncologist in Ft. Worth." He sighed. "I don't need to tell you Mr. Randell's condition is serious."

Gail shook her head.

"The recurrence of his leukemia and the failure of all aggressive treatments leaves a bone marrow transplant as his only option," the doctor stressed. "He's on the national donor list, so there isn't much else we can do for him."

"Is...is he going to die?" her mother asked.

Dr. Hartley paused, not needing to say the words. Then he glanced at the men in the waiting area. "Unless you can find a relative to be a donor."

Lindsey felt her mother's trembling hand. "Can I see him?"

With his nod, Gail released her daughter, then went with the doctor. Lindsey turned around to find Brady standing behind her. "Thank you for all your help."

"Hell, I didn't do anything. Not yet, anyway." He went down the hall to Jack's room. He caught Dr. Hartley just outside. "Doctor, I'm Jack Randell's nephew. Where do I go to be tested as a donor?"

Lindsey caught up to hear his words. Her chest tightened. Brady hadn't hesitated to give her father this chance for survive. At that moment she couldn't love him more. "Oh, Brady."

"It's okay, Lindsey." He pulled her close. "We're not giving up yet."

"Give up what?" Chance asked as he showed up, followed by his brothers. "What's wrong with Jack?"

With a reassuring glance from Brady, Lindsey announced, "Jack has acute lymphocytic leukemia. He needs a bone marrow transplant."

"I'm getting tested." Brady held Lindsey tighter as he watched his cousins absorb the information.

"So that's what he came back for?" Cade asked.

Brady stiffened. "Will you get rid of the attitude? This isn't the time to drag up the past. Whatever you think about your father, let it go. Jack could be dying."

He glanced at the group of Randell brothers who circled him and Lindsey. "Even with the good, the bad and the ugly, your stepsister loves that man in there." He pointed toward Jack's room. "The same man who made all those mistakes years ago. But I think he's redeemed himself a little because of how hard he's worked and the accomplishments he's made the past twenty years."

Brady started to walk away. "Oh, and the reason Jack came here was to bring his daughter back to Ft. Worth. He didn't want her involved in his mess. But Lindsey convinced him to at least see his sons. All he wanted from you boys was to make peace."

He turned away. "Okay, Doctor, show me where I need to go." He kissed Lindsey, promised to be back, then went off with the doctor. By the time he got to the elevators, he discovered the other Randells had followed him. "What now?"

"Maybe we want to be tested, too," Travis said. "We're probably a better match than you, anyway." His gaze narrowed. "You got a problem with that?"

"None whatsoever." Brady only prayed that someone was a match for Jack.

A few hours later, when Brady got back upstairs, he saw his brother, Luke, and suddenly he felt pretty lucky to have him there.

"Hey, I hear it's been a pretty busy morning."

"Yeah. Lindsey's having a tough time. We're all waiting to see if any of us are a match as a marrow donor."

"I hear you started things off."

Brady shrugged. "I couldn't just stand by and not do anything." He sighed. "I look at Lindsey and can see how much she loves him." He caught his brother's gaze. "The man had to do something right to gain her loyalty."

"Lindsey's pretty special. You care about her, too."

"Yeah, but that doesn't mean it's headed anywhere."

Luke smiled. "Not long ago I thought the same thing about Tess."

* * *

In the waiting room, Lindsey couldn't believe she was sitting with her stepbrothers. They were actually carrying on a conversation, wanting to know about the years with Jack.

"I wasn't exactly a model teenager," she told them.

"That makes me happy," Chance said, "knowing you gave Jack a rough time. I love payback."

"Oh, I did that and more. I ran away more times than I could count." She looked over at Jarred, Wyatt and Dylan. They had stayed in the background most of the day, although they volunteered to be tested as donors along with the other brothers. "About the age of fifteen I realized he wasn't going to give up on me."

"He never would, either."

Lindsey swung around to see her mother had joined them. When the men started to stand, she motioned for them to stay seated.

"How is Jack?" Lindsey asked.

"He's resting comfortably." She blew out a breath. "Jack asked to see Jarred, Wyatt and Dylan." She raised a hand. "But he'll understand if you don't want to see him."

The three glanced at each other. "I guess it's about time we met him," Jarred said as he stood. The others did the same and they all went off to the room.

Gail turned back to the group and sat down in one of the vacant chairs. "I've wanted to meet you all for so long." She put on a smile. "Jack has spoken of you boys nearly every day since we met. When he first came to the ranch, he'd just been released from prison. He needed a job and I needed help with our rundown farm. The only place I had for him to stay was the barn."

She blinked rapidly. "He worked from sunup to sundown, doing needed repairs and working with the four horses that I was able to hang on to.

"When Jack finally began to talk, it all just poured out of him. That's how I learned about you boys. He had pictures, too. Of course, you were all a lot younger then." She scanned the row of large, strapping men. She nodded at Chance. "You're Chance. Your hair is the lightest sandy brown, and your eyes, too." She continued her search. "Cade, you're the tallest. And Travis, you're the baby of the family."

"Not any longer," he said. "Wyatt and Dylan are."

"If you take away nothing else, just know Jack was proud of all of you, although he knew he had nothing to do with it. He was just happy that you had someone like Mr. Barrett to take care of you."

"Yeah, we were lucky," Travis said. "Hank was the father that Jack never could be."

Gail nodded. "Just because he gave you up doesn't mean that you aren't in his heart."

Lindsey glanced around at the men, seeing the raw emotion in their eyes, and the way their throats worked as they swallowed back more feelings than they could admit.

"I can't thank you all enough for offering Jack this chance." She brushed away a tear and smiled. "Even if it doesn't work out, Lindsey and I will never forget what you've done."

The room was silent. Then came sound of footsteps as Dr. Hartley made his way to the group.

"Mrs. Randell. It looks like we have a donor match."

There was a pause, then Cade said, "Don't keep us in suspense, Doctor. Who is it?"

The doctor scanned the three remaining Randell brothers. "It's Chance."

* * *

The following Monday, Brady sat in Dr. Pahl's office, waiting anxiously for the news as the orthopedic surgeon looked over the X rays and MRI again.

"Your fracture has healed nicely," he said. "And there's no permanent damage to the muscle or tendon." The young doctor sat down on the front edge of his desk. "In other words, Captain, I'm releasing you and sending you back to active duty."

Brady had wanted this for months, but now that it was actually happening, it seemed too soon. "That's great news."

The doctor gave a curt nod. "By this time next week you'll be back at your home base in Utah."

Brady wanted to be happy, but he knew he had a way to go before he was able to climb back into the cockpit. "Thank you, Doctor. You'll never know how much this means to me." He stood and shook the doctor's hand.

"You're welcome, Captain. I'll send all your medical records to your commanding officer. Good luck."

Brady walked out of the office, without his cast for the first time in months. A smile broke out as he took off in a near run through the parking lot. He started the car and pulled out into the street to go back to the ranch.

Suddenly it seemed a lifetime ago since he'd been at Hill AFB. It had been. A long four months since he'd been to his apartment just off the base. He'd been deployed overseas for a few weeks when the accident happened and they flew him back to the States.

To San Angelo. To his family. Although they had crowded him sometimes, he'd found he kind of liked being part of the craziness. The family get-togethers. It was the first time he'd spent Thanksgiving with relatives.

Then there was Lindsey. Being with her had been like nothing else he'd experienced with a woman. Yet, since that night in the hospital, he hadn't seen or heard from her. Mostly it was his fault. He knew he'd be leaving soon, and she needed to be with her family. He'd called her a few times, but got her voice mail. He'd never left any messages.

Lindsey had her family here, and she was busy with the vet practice. Now more than ever, their lives were starting to run in different directions.

In a few days she'd return to Ft. Worth for Jack's procedure. Since Chance had agreed to be the marrow donor, they were busy doing the final prep for the surgery. And by then Brady would be on his way to Utah and his squadron.

Brady decided not to push his attentions on Lindsey. He needed his own space, too. All he'd done was think, and it had only been about Lindsey. She'd become more important to him than he'd thought possible. She was the first person he wanted to share his news with. He passed the ranch and headed for the cabin. He didn't know what he was going to say, only that he needed to see her.

Lindsey stacked her suitcases by the door and glanced around the cabin that had been her home for the past few months. A tightness constricted her chest, and she fought tears. She'd come to think of the place as hers. She'd never forget the time she'd spent here with Brady. The night they'd made love. Never before had she given herself so completely to a man, body and soul…and heart.

She closed her eyes, reliving his touch, each caress and each kiss. How she prayed it would never end. During those hours in his arms, she'd fallen in love with him. Then she woke up the next morning knowing she had to let him go. He'd be returning to the air force, and she was headed back home with her parents.

No more delays, either. She opened the door and stepped out onto the porch, but stopped suddenly when she ran into a hard body.

"Oh," she gasped, and looked up. "Brady?"

He smiled, but his hands remained on her waist. "Hi, Doc. Catch you at a bad time?"

She wasn't sure she could answer. It had been four days since she'd seen him. She shook her head. "Do you need something?"

"I just wanted to see you." He kept coming toward her until she backed through the door. "I missed you."

I've missed you, too, she cried silently. "I pretty much stayed at the hospital. Mom needed me."

He played with the hat in his hand. "That's understandable. Is everything going okay with the upcoming marrow transplant?"

She nodded. "Chance is on his way to Ft. Worth." She stole a glance at him. "I never got to thank you for helping us, for being the first to volunteer to be a donor."

He shrugged. "Not a big deal. I knew my cousins would step up."

"Well, I'll never forget it," she told him.

He studied her for a long time. "Are you coming back here after the procedure? I hear there's a permanent position to fill."

It was hard to answer. She wanted to, but not when

Brady would be coming back and forth, too. "Hank and
Dr. Hillman have both talked to me about it." She shook
her head, unable to tell him the real reason, that she
didn't want to run into him. "I don't think it's such a
good idea, especially with my relationship to Jack."

"I doubt the brothers are the type to hold a grudge
against you."

"It's still best I stay close to home. Jack and Mom
need me right now. At least for a few months."

"I'm sure they'll want you to go ahead with your
own career."

"Whether that's true or not, my family will always
come first. I should find a job around Ft. Worth." She
glanced down to notice he was missing his cast. "Oh,
Brady, you went to the doctor?"

He nodded. "He released me this morning. My leg is
healed perfectly. You're the first person I've told."

She didn't want to read anything into his comment.
"When do you go back?"

"I need to report to my base Monday morning."

Her heart ached, but she put on a smile. "That's wonderful news. You can fly again."

He raised an eyebrow. "That's not confirmed yet,
Doc. But I'll know soon. They're reviewing my accident right now."

"You'll get back into the cockpit. I have complete confidence that "Rebel" will be flying once again. You'll
be back to doing what you love."

He hesitated. "I'm not so sure anymore, Doc. A lot of
things have changed in the past few months…since the
accident. Since you." His gaze went to hers in a heated
look. "I came to realize how my career was all I had."

"But you have a brother now and cousins." She smiled. "And a cute little niece who adores you."

He shrugged. "Yeah, and I ran headlong into a beautiful redheaded vet who put me in my place."

She shrugged. "I didn't want you to get bored while your leg was healing. It's a known fact fighter pilots are a cocky lot."

"I've heard more colorful words used to describe me. How did you manage to put up with me?"

It was easy, she whispered to herself. "By humbling you to do my dirty work."

"You have an incredible way with animals. Following you around was fascinating."

"There are easier ways to kill time."

At that he reached for her and pulled her into a tight embrace. "Doc, believe me, killing time was the last thing on my mind. Those nights I spent with you meant something. More than you'll ever know. At least if this is going to end, can't we be honest with each other?"

She didn't want honesty. "Why? What good would it do, Brady? Sorry. I'm a big girl. I've accepted that you're leaving." She was lying big-time.

He nodded. "Dammit, Lindsey. I have a commitment to the air force."

"And I respect you for that."

"Hell, Doc, I wish you didn't. You don't think I want more for us? I want you so bad, I want to kidnap you and steal you away with me." His mouth came down on hers in a bruising kiss, then it gentled as his arms cradled her against him.

His hard body pressed to hers, creating an unbearable need only Brady could fill. She whimpered softly and wrapped her hands around his neck, arching her body into his, wanting to grasp this moment and this feeling forever.

"Brady," she breathed, and pulled back. "We can't keep doing this." She loved him so much it was killing her.

He finally stepped back. His dark eyes narrowed, as his hands cupped her face. "I could get lost in you so easily. Your eyes mesmerize me, your body tempts me. Ah, hell, Doc, you make me forget everything."

"Problem is, Brady, we can't forget our obligations."

His gaze locked with hers. "I wish… I wish we had more time. Wish things could be different."

She stepped back, putting more space between them. "No, Brady. We always knew it could come to this point. You have a military career. You're a Fighting Falcon pilot. You have to be so proud of that. I am."

He nodded. "I'm proud of you, too, Doc. You have a pretty good career started yourself, wherever you decide to practice. But I have to say I wish you were coming back here. I like to think about you with the mustangs. That little buckskin mare wouldn't be here if you hadn't nursed her back."

"And you helped catch the guys who were shooting at them." She paused, her voice grew soft. This was goodbye and they both knew it. "I only wish the best for you, too, Captain." She turned away to catch her breath, then looked back at him. Big mistake. She straightened defensively. "Look, Brady, I have an appointment I have to get to. Then I'll be leaving tomorrow."

He continued to stare at her. "So this is it? We just go our separate ways?"

"There doesn't seem to be any choice."

* * *

The following twenty-four hours seemed endless. Lindsey was gone. Brady was leaving the next day, so he took advantage of the little time he had left. He ignored Luke's request to see the progress of the Golden Meadow project. He trusted his brother's expertise. Instead he took refuge in horseback riding. He'd only had one other opportunity, and that had been with Lindsey. Oh, God, he wished now he could have more time with her.

Brady pulled on Dusty's reins as they arrived at the creek that edged the valley. Maybe he'd come here to remember his time with Lindsey, or maybe it was to say goodbye to what they'd shared here. There was no telling when he'd be back.

His commanding officer had called earlier, telling him of the review board meeting. That they would have the results by the time he returned to the base. That would be 1600 hours on Monday when he was to report to the base.

Then his thoughts turned back to Lindsey. Their last kiss, their bad goodbye. The longing he'd felt since she'd left the valley. She just tore out his heart and walked away. He took a breath. Oh, damn. At this moment, never seeing her again seemed harder than anything. Now he realized how his parents must have felt whenever they were separated. How does a marriage survive when you're apart so much?

He glanced out at the herd of mustangs and saw the buckskin mare Lindsey had treated. She belonged here, working with the ponies, making sure they were healthy and safe.

Everything she loved was here.

When Brady heard his name called out, he turned around and saw his brother riding toward him in the golf cart.

"Hey, you're a hard guy to track down."

"I've been around. Something wrong?"

Luke smiled. "No, I'd say everything is going right. Joy called from Ft. Worth. The bone marrow transplant is scheduled for Tuesday morning. I thought you'd want to know."

Brady closed his eyes momentarily. Lindsey had to be happy, but scared, too. "Thanks."

"I was kind of surprised you didn't go to be with her."

"I don't think she needed me around."

Luke shrugged. "Funny, it didn't seem that way to me. You two seemed pretty tight these past few weeks."

"Things change," Brady said. "Doc decided to return to Ft. Worth, and I have to go back to my squadron."

His older brother frowned. "You're not worried about being cleared to fly again are you?"

"No. It's just a lot of things are different now."

Luke smiled. "A woman always changes things. If it's the right woman, it's all good."

"What if I'm not ready for *that* woman?"

Luke grinned this time. "Are we ever really ready? But take it from me, having Tess in my life makes it worthwhile. You can lose everything and it doesn't matter, not when you know she loves you."

Brady suddenly realized that he wanted Lindsey with him. "How can I ask Lindsey to give up everything she's worked for and follow me around from base to base?"

"I don't know." Luke shrugged. "But I think you need to give her the opportunity to decide."

Brady blew out a breath. "Doesn't seem fair."

Luke patted his brother on the back. "Cousin Chance once told me that Randell men seem to fall hard for their women. And they love forever.

"So ask yourself, brother, do you want Lindsey forever?"

Chapter 11

The next afternoon Lindsey stood in the hospital room watching Jack sleep. He wore a surgical mask over the lower half of his face, to keep him as germ free as possible. It was worth the inconvenience before and after the procedure. The important thing was after the marrow transplant, she knew Jack was going to get better. Tomorrow would be a long day for all of them. Her mother was back at the hotel resting, too.

Lindsey looked out the window at the cold December day. So many times in the last week she'd thanked God for this miracle. Not only for the bone marrow, but the chance Jack had gotten to see his sons again. She doubted the Randell brothers would ever take him back as their father, but they'd all moved on enough from the past to want to help.

She felt the raw emotions surface again and fought

them. She needed to be strong to handle the next few days. But not everything was so easy to put aside or forget. She thought about Brady. He'd probably gone back to Utah by now. Over the past few days, Tess had called several times to keep her informed, but she hadn't heard anything about Brady's review board. Not that Lindsey had asked.

"You're looking awfully worried." Jack's voice broke through her reverie. "Is there something else the doctor's told you?"

"No. Just that you're going to be around a long time." She kept a safe distance. "You should be resting."

"Seems that's all I've been doing," he told her. "Speaking of which, aren't you tired of hanging around my room?"

"Someone has to make sure you behave yourself."

He ran a hand over his gray hair. "I've been too weak to do anything else." He glanced around. "Please, tell me your mother left to get some rest."

"Yes, about an hour ago."

"Then I want you to go, too." He raised a hand when she started to argue. "Please, Lin, you need to get out of here for a while."

She bit down on her lip. "Are you trying to get rid of me."

"Oh, no, darlin'." He held out a hand and she came to him. "I know this has been hard on you and your mother, but it's going to be okay."

"We don't want to lose you."

"You won't. We have our miracle. A second chance." He hugged her close as her tears fell freely. Finally he spoke again. "I have a feeling this might be about something else entirely. Maybe a certain air force captain."

She pulled herself together and stood. "It doesn't matter. He's gone back to the base. I'm not going to run after him, either. Not when he didn't have a problem leaving me."

Jack pulled the surgical mask down to make a point. "He's in the air force, Lin. He doesn't have a choice."

She raised a hand. "I know, I know. The military comes first. I just wanted him to care enough about me to ask if I want to share that part of his life."

"There's no doubt Brady cares for you, Lin, but he has commitments. You've got to give him time to work through them." Jack smiled. "You're a lot like your mother. Believe me, you won't be easy for him to forget."

She wanted to believe him, but Brady was still gone. And she was here…alone.

"You're tired, honey. You need to get some rest, too. You've spent all your time helping me." He gripped her hand. "How can I thank you for bringing me together with my boys? Starting tomorrow, I'm going to take charge of this family again. What can I do to help you?"

She loved him so much. "Just stay around a long, long time."

He grinned. "I'll do my darnedest."

"Good." She smiled.

Suddenly a familiar figure appeared at the glass partition. It was Brady, looking tall and handsome in his air force blue dress uniform, his cap tucked under his arm. His once-shaggy black hair was now cut military short.

Her heart accelerated more as she glanced up at the man's face, and familiar brown eyes stared back at her.

"Hi, Doc," he said from the doorway. "Your mother told me you were visiting your dad." He turned to the bed. "Hello, sir. I hope I'm not disturbing you."

Jack sat straighter in the bed and replaced his mask. "No, of course not. I wish I could invite you in, but there are rules."

Brady smiled. "Not a problem, sir. Wouldn't want to do anything to upset tomorrow's procedure."

"That might not be taking place if you hadn't started things. I'm grateful to you for offering to be a donor."

"I'm glad everything worked out."

Lindsey couldn't believe he'd shown up here. "Brady, I thought you were going back to your base."

He checked his watch. "I am. I just took a detour. My connecting flight leaves in a few hours. But I wanted to see how Jack and you were doing."

She felt herself blush.

Her father spoke. "I'm doing fine, Brady, even better after tomorrow."

"I wish you only the best, sir."

"And I appreciate you coming by," Jack said. "We never got much of a chance to talk. Sam and I were close growing up, but things changed over the years. I believe your father would be happy his sons are back at the Rocking R." He smiled. "I hope if you ever get back to Ft. Worth, you'll stop in and see us. I'll tell you some great stories about your daddy."

Brady nodded. "I'd like that, sir. Right now, I have some things to straighten out with my career." He turned to Lindsey. "And lately things have gotten more complicated."

Lindsey could feel the heat of his gaze, making her uncomfortable. "Dad, I think I will go back to the hotel."

Brady stepped in. "Lindsey, could I talk with you?"

She sighed. "I don't think there's anything to say."

He blocked the doorway. "Please, let me walk you out."

She nodded, then glanced at her stepfather. "Now, you better get some rest, too. Bye, Jack."

Brady said his goodbye, too, and allowed Lindsey out into the corridor, then they walked to the elevators.

Her chest tightened at the thought of talking with him. "What are you really doing here, Brady? We already said everything."

"You think we could find somewhere to talk?" He checked his watch. "Maybe I can walk you to your car. You look dead on your feet."

"Just what every woman wants to hear."

He took a step closer. "I didn't mean it that way. You're a beautiful woman, Lindsey. Missing some sleep could never take that away." He took her by the arm and walked her to the elevator. Silently they rode down to the first floor, then out the front doors and across to the parking structure.

Lindsey walked fast, aching to get this over. Soon they were next to her SUV.

She drew a calming breath. "Why are you really here, Brady?"

"I wanted to make sure you were okay. I couldn't leave things the way they were, Doc. Without letting you know what you mean to me."

Before she could speak, his mouth closed over hers in a tender kiss that only made her want more. More than he could give her.

He pulled back. "I told myself I wouldn't do that." Frowning, he cursed. "But I can't help remembering how you felt in my arms." He paced back and forth. The sound of his shoes echoed in the deserted structure. Then suddenly he stopped in front of her. "I never expected to find someone like you. Someone who made it so damn hard to walk away." He drew a long breath. "And as much as I want to make you promises, Lindsey, I can't right now."

She loved this man, and right now nothing else mattered but that. "I'm not asking you to, Brady."

"You deserve more. I don't want to leave you, but I committed time to the air force. I could be deployed again."

She hated the fact that she understood. Yet she was afraid for him, too. "That's an excuse, Brady. We all have commitments, but that doesn't mean we can't work out some sort of compromise."

He rested his forehead against hers. "I've got some ghosts to face—obligations." He checked his watch. "I have to go. My flight leaves…"

Lindsey nodded. It took every bit of strength inside her to step back. The air force was his life. Flying was his passion. She'd known that from the start.

With tears blurring her vision, she watched him walk out of her life.

Chapter 12

It was more than a week later, just days before Christmas, when Lindsey found herself back in San Angelo. Hank had called and convinced her to stay on as the veterinarian, if only temporarily. Since Brady was gone and she hadn't heard from him, there wasn't any reason she couldn't return to what she loved to do. And with Jack on the mend from his successful transplant, she could leave Ft. Worth.

She walked out onto the porch of the same cabin she'd stayed in before. It was hard to push aside the memories, all the time she and Brady had shared here.

She wanted to forget him, but she loved this man who put duty and love of his country at top priority. She only wanted a small part of his life and for him to let her go with him. Had he been deployed overseas? No matter where he'd gone, there was no denying she loved him.

Lindsey glanced up into the cloudless sky. She hoped he was happy now. She hugged her jacket closer for warmth as she wandered down the path toward the creek. The small herd of mustangs grazed in the golden meadow grass.

She was doing what she loved, too. In a place she'd come to love like a home. Even if she didn't stay on after Dr. Hillman's practice was sold, Hank had invited her to come back periodically and check the ponies.

Hank Barrett hadn't been subtle in trying to convince her to stay permanently. She wanted so much to live here and be around the Randells. To keep that one link between Jack and his sons.

Still she missed Brady, wanted the best for him. "I hope you've banished your ghosts," she whispered into the cool breeze.

"I have, Doc," a familiar voice answered.

She turned around to see Brady on Dusty. He wore his same bomber jacket and cowboy hat. And a silly grin.

She blinked several times, wondering if she'd wanted to see him so badly that she dreamed him up. "Brady? How? You're here?"

He swung his leg over the horse's rump and jumped down. "Surprised?"

"Well, you seem to pop up everywhere." She didn't like this. "Are you home for the holidays?"

"You could say that." He walked toward her. "But mostly I'm here to see you."

"I thought you'd gone back on active duty. Tess said you aced the review board."

"I did. I've even been up in an F-16, and everything went fine. Great, in fact. No more nightmares about the crash. I only dream of you these days."

She refused to get excited. "I'm happy for you."

Brady had been hoping for a friendlier welcome. "I'm glad you came back here, Lindsey. It's where you belong." He moved closer. "I'm selfish, since I like having you around."

She stiffened. "So you think I'm going to be around for your convenience whenever you come home on leave? Well, think again, fly boy. You can just turn around and ride off."

Brady couldn't help but smile. God, he'd missed her. "Never again, Doc. I care too much for you." He tried to reach for her, but she stepped back.

"If you do, then why do you keep coming after me, then leaving me again?" She clenched her fists. "How many times do you expect me to say goodbye to you?"

He sobered. "I'm not saying goodbye, Lindsey. I came by your cabin because I wanted to see you, tell you how I feel."

She bit her lower lip. "We both know how it will turn out," she said, then started up the hill toward the cabin.

Brady tied Dusty's reins to a nearby tree and strode after her. "You aren't even going to hear me out?"

"Why? So you can tell me again how much the military means to you? I know how much, Brady."

"No, Lindsey, you mean more."

She turned around and shouted. "Prove it. Ask me to go with you."

Brady was taken aback by her request. "Okay. Lindsey Stafford, will you go with me?"

She looked shocked, then said, "Yes, Brady. I'll go wherever you go."

He continued up the hill until he stood before her.

"You'd do that, Doc? You'd go off with me without knowing what the future holds?"

She nodded slowly. "We'd be together."

"What if I go as close as Laughlin Air Force in Del Rio." He raised an eyebrow. "Or say we only have to go as far as the Rocking R's foreman's cottage? That's where we'll live until I build us a bigger house."

Her pretty green eyes narrowed suspiciously.

He let out a long breath. "In two and a half months I'm resigning from active duty."

She gasped. "No, Brady, you can't do that. You love to fly. And I'd never ask you to give it up."

Fighting his own emotions, he reached for her and pulled her close. "I know you wouldn't. God, that's one of the reasons I love you so much."

She searched his face. "I love you, too. But I can't let you do this."

He placed a finger over her lips. "Listen to me first. I'm not resigning my commission. If I decide to take a flight instructor job at Laughlin we'd be close by in Del Rio. The other choice is that I go into the air force reserves. I still get to fly." He smiled. "I hope you can put up with me being gone one weekend a month and two weeks in the summer."

She finally smiled. "I want you to be happy, Brady."

"I've discovered I'm happy when I'm with you. So I'm leaning toward going into the reserves."

"Then I'm happy, too…as long as I get you the rest of the time, fly boy."

His hold tightened. "If I get you, too." His head lowered and his mouth captured hers. The kiss was tender yet hungry, letting Lindsey know how much he cared and wanted a life with her.

When he broke off the kiss, Brady stepped back and reached into his inside jacket pocket, finding his hands were shaking. "I'd planned to do this tonight over a candlelight dinner, but I can't wait any longer. I want everything settled between us." He kissed her again. "I've asked you to wait too many times." He pulled out a black velvet box and opened it, showing off the pear-shaped diamond in a platinum setting.

Lindsey gasped as Brady got down on one knee.

"God, Lindsey, I love you so much. You've become my heart, my soul. I want us to build a life together. Have kids and raise them here in this valley." He swallowed hard. "Will you marry me?"

"Oh, Brady. Yes, I'll marry you."

He stood and slipped the ring on her finger, then she went into his arms. He kissed her again and again. "It's all going to be so good for us, Doc. I've talked with the other Randells. They want me to be the pilot for a flight service to bring guests to the valley. And if you still want it, you can tell Dr. Hillman that you want to buy his practice."

"Whoa, Brady. Do you have any idea what a veterinarian clinic and practice cost?"

"No, but I have money saved, plus my half of the sale of the valley land to Hank. And besides, you're a wonderful vet, Doc. And it's what you always wanted."

She smiled and touched his face. "You are what I always wanted. A good man who loves me. And a big family to share everything with."

He grinned. "Be careful what you ask for. We've got more family than we know what to do with."

"Oh, no," Lindsey gasped. "Including your niece,

Livy. How are you going to tell her that you aren't going to marry her?"

He pulled Lindsey against him. "I'll let her down gently. I'll tell her how much I love you, and she'll understand. And I do love you, Doc."

It was true. Lindsey was the only thing he needed in his life. She was his family. Well, maybe a few Randells thrown in the mix wouldn't hurt.

Epilogue

Six months later, spring had come to the valley. Lindsey looked at her parents seated on the cabin porch. They'd rented it during their visit here. The Randells had had to adjust to her parents being around after Lindsey's marriage to Brady. And thanks to the bone marrow from Chance, Jack's leukemia was in remission.

They were all learning that life was fragile.

Jack had been grateful for every day, and for the opportunity to come back to see his sons. Of course, he could never take the place of Hank, but he had never planned to. Lindsey knew Jack had been given a second chance in many things, and he wasn't about to mess it up.

She would never forget her wedding day, having Jack there to give her away, and all the Randells showing up to celebrate their special day.

She'd been Mrs. Brady Randell for only a month, and

never realized how much she could love another person. Now they were trying to adjust to their new life together. For the time being, Brady had declined the instructor's job at Laughlin. He'd chosen to resign from active duty and make a permanent home here in the valley.

He had just finished up his two weeks of reserve duty and only returned home yesterday. Lindsey felt the heat rise to her face, recalling how Brady spent most of the night, showing her how much he'd missed her.

She sighed. Marriage was wonderful.

Today they planned to ride with the Randell cousins and Hank to check the mustangs. He'd heard one of the mares had dropped a foal. She wanted to make sure everything was all right. Besides, she enjoyed riding with Brady. It wasn't an F-16, but he'd told her riding around his own ranch with his wife was thrill enough.

As a wedding gift, Brady had bought them two quarter horse yearlings from Chance's breeding stables. His cousin had named the large black stallion Wild Blue Yonder. For Lindsey, a sweet roan filly named Captain's Doc. They'd gotten a reduced family price with the promise that Chance got their first foal, and a discount on Lindsey's veterinarian services.

Right now Dusty and Lady were tied to the post, waiting for everyone. Brady had to go with Luke to the construction site for some final details for this next weekend. They were expecting a large crowd at the Golden Meadow Estates open house.

She glanced up the hill to see Brady's truck pulling up, and a rush of feelings raced through her. He came down the steps toward the cabin, stopping briefly to say hello to her parents. Then he continued toward her.

Brady's excitement grew as he neared, picked her up in his arms and kissed her soundly. "God, I missed you," he groaned.

"We've only been separated an hour."

He kissed her again. "I'm talking about the last two weeks."

"I thought you made up for that last night…and this morning." She smiled. "And again after breakfast."

"Never enough."

Lindsey stepped back. "Well, you're going to have to postpone showing me your undying love, because right now we're supposed to go round up some mustangs."

He reluctantly released her. "Okay, but remember where I left off."

"Not a problem." She looked up toward the cabin and waved at Jack and her mom.

He gripped her hand. "I'm glad your parents could come for a visit. It's good for the cousins, too."

"Were you surprised when Chance asked them here?"

He shook his head. "No. It's time to heal."

"And I think there's a place for all of us here in the valley." She looked at her husband. "I also think your dad would be happy that you and Luke are back here now."

Brady found he had a lot to be grateful for, starting with the day he woke up in the hospital and found his family…and love.

Up on the hill, Hank sat on his horse, his wife, Ella, next to him on the bay gelding he'd given her on her birthday a few years back.

He rested his arm on the saddle horn and looked down at the valley. A herd of wild ponies were grazing in the serene meadow, unaware that anything was going on. Just as he wanted everything to be. Undisturbed.

"Well, are you happy now?" Ella asked.

He tipped his hat back and grinned. "Yes, I am. It's pretty amazing that I can keep enjoying this place." He glanced toward the cabin and saw Jack and Gail. He never thought he'd see the day that that man would come back here. And Hank couldn't be happier. Chance, Cade and Travis needed this closure to their past. Jarred, Wyatt and Dylan had needed to know their roots, too.

"You've done good, Hank Barrett. Not only did you manage to raise some fine sons, but you've seen to it that these ponies are protected from any harm."

Hank's horse shifted as he looked out over the acres of untouched land. He felt a little selfish to have all this beauty, but it wasn't only for him. "It's just the way it should be. We never should forget our past, and the mustangs were a big part of it."

Several riders began to appear. Chance came from one direction along with Cade and Travis. From the west rode Jarred, Wyatt and Dylan. They met and rode up the rise together. They were a formidable group of men on horseback. Hank glanced back over his shoulder and saw Luke and Tess coming from the direction of the Rocking R. He was touched that they all wanted to help with the mustangs. But he knew his boys loved the ponies.

Something caught his eye, and he turned to the creek to see Brady and Lindsey. "Our family keeps growing."

"With more weddings comes more babies," Ella said excitedly. "I wonder who'll be first among the cousins."

Hank Barrett grinned. "Doesn't matter. I say, bring 'em on. There's plenty of love to go around."

He would teach them about the history of this valley. How family was the most important thing. And how the Randells and the mustangs could live together in harmony in this special valley for many generations to come.

* * * * *

"There's an open bottle of very expensive scotch on the counter, just waiting for someone to enjoy it." She laughed again, softly this time. "And I'd *really* like to hear the story of how Danger Dan turned into a lawman."

Dan grimaced. He hated that stupid nickname Ryan had made up, even if he *had* earned it back then. Especially coming from Mack.

"Is your husband waiting upstairs?" Dan wasn't sure where that question came from, but, to be fair, all Mack had ever talked about was leaving Gallant Lake, having a big wedding and a bigger house. The girl had goals, and from what he'd heard, she'd reached every one of them.

"I don't have a husband anymore." She brushed past him and headed toward the counter. "So are you joining me or not?"

Dan glanced at his watch, not sure how to digest that information. "I'm off duty in fifteen minutes."

Her long hair swung back and forth as she walked ahead of him. So did her hips. *Damn.*

"And you're all about following the rules now? You really have changed, haven't you? Pity. I guess I'm drinking my first glass alone. You'll just have to catch up."

He frowned. Mackenzie had been strong-willed, but never sassy. Never the type to sneak into her father's store alone for an after-hours drink. Not the type to taunt him. Not the type to break the rules.

Looked like he wasn't the only one who'd changed since high school.

Don't miss
Her Homecoming Wish *by Jo McNally,*
available February 2020 wherever
Harlequin® Special Edition books and ebooks are sold.

Harlequin.com

"Don't look at me like that, April."

She raised her gaze to his. "Like what?"

His fingers tightened in her hair and her mouth ran dry.
She swallowed. Moistened her lips.

She wasn't sure if she moved first. Or if it was him.

But then his mouth was on hers and like everything
else about him, she felt engulfed by an inferno. Or maybe
the burning was coming from inside her.

There was no way to know.

No reason to care.

Her hands slid up the granite chest, behind his neck,
where his skin felt even hotter beneath her fingertips, and
slipped through his thick hair, which was not hot, but
instead felt cool and unexpectedly silky.

His arm around her tightened, his hand pressing her
closer while his kiss deepened. Consuming. Exhilarating.

Her head was whirling, sounds roaring.

It was only a kiss.

But she was melting.

She was flying.

And then she realized the sounds weren't just inside her head.

Someone was laying on a horn.

She jerked back, her gaze skittering over Jed's as they both turned to peer through the curtain of white light shining over them.

"Mind getting at least one of these vehicles out of the way?" The shout was male and obviously amused.

"Oh for cryin'—" She exhaled. "That's my uncle Matthew," she told Jed, pushing him away. "And I'm sorry to say, but we are probably never going to live this down."

Don't miss
A Promise to Keep *by Allison Leigh,*
available March 2020 wherever
Harlequin Special Edition books and ebooks are sold.

Harlequin.com

IF YOU ENJOYED THIS BOOK
WE THINK YOU WILL ALSO LOVE

LOVE INSPIRED
INSPIRATIONAL ROMANCE

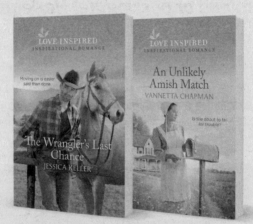

Uplifting stories of faith, forgiveness and hope.

Fall in love with stories where faith helps
guide you through life's challenges, and discover
the promise of a new beginning.

6 NEW BOOKS AVAILABLE EVERY MONTH!

LIXSERIES2020

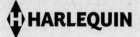
HARLEQUIN

Heartfelt or suspenseful, inspiring or passionate, Harlequin has your happily-ever-after.

With new books published
every month, you are sure to find the
satisfying escape you know you deserve.

SIGN UP FOR THE HARLEQUIN NEWSLETTER
Be the first to hear about great new
reads and exciting offers!

Harlequin.com/newsletters

Love Harlequin romance?

DISCOVER.

Be the first to find out about promotions, news and exclusive content!

Facebook.com/HarlequinBooks

Twitter.com/HarlequinBooks

Instagram.com/HarlequinBooks

Pinterest.com/HarlequinBooks

ReaderService.com

EXPLORE.

Sign up for the Harlequin e-newsletter and download a free book from any series at **TryHarlequin.com**

CONNECT.

Join our Harlequin community to share your thoughts and connect with other romance readers!
Facebook.com/groups/HarlequinConnection

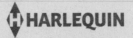